"No, no." Maria's chocolate brown eyes flashed. "I only want to teach him a lesson. He is still my husband, you know, Caterina and Gianni's father. You can't say these things. Listen, I have a plan which will hurt him, but will also benefit us. I want him back, but I want him back on my terms. His business is his real mistress, his favourite game. The only people he respects are those who can beat him at it."

The brothers shook their heads.

"But how can you beat him?" Sergio, the eldest, growled in coarse Neapolitan patois. He shrugged his shoulders as he spoke. "Pyon is a shit, but he's a powerful man. There is only one way to stop him."

"NO!" Maria was desperately regretting flying to her family for support. "No. I will do it my way. The way to beat him is with allies. There is no shortage of them. Pyon has a lot of enemies for a lot of reasons, and, for the moment, his enemies are my friends. Please, you must leave it to me. I can do it."

"Okay," said Sergio. "We'll let you try it your way first. But remember, Maria, it is the whole Gatti family that he has insulted, not only you. So, if you fail, we will have to deal with it."

**Also by the same author,
and available from NEL:**

RAGS
WARRIOR'S SON

About the author

Peter Burden left school when he was sixteen and took various jobs before joining the rag trade. In 1975 he founded Midnight Blue, a chain of shops and a brand of jeans. He has also run a talking book company and has recently opened the second in a chain of furniture shops.

He lives in Herefordshire with his wife and three children, and is currently at work on his fourth novel.

PETER BURDEN

PYON

NEW ENGLISH LIBRARY
Hodder and Stoughton

Copyright © Peter Burden 1991

First published in Great Britain in 1991
by New English Library hardbacks

*New English Library paperback edition
1992*

Printed and bound in Great Britain for
Hodder and Stoughton Paperbacks, a
division of Hodder and Stoughton Ltd,
Mill Road, Dunton Green, Sevenoaks,
Kent TN13 2YA (Editorial Office: 47
Bedford Square, London WC1B 3DP)
by Clays Ltd, St Ives plc. Typeset
by Hewer Text Composition Services,
Edinburgh.

British Library C.I.P.
Burden, Peter
Pyon.
I. Title
823[F]

ISBN 0–450–56796–6

For my mother

Acknowledgments

My thanks to Jerry Wilson, Damian Russell, Harry Chandler and John Bright-Holmes for their help in the researching or the writing of this book.

Ile Vermont

"Christy?" A soft whisper.

The big man's eyelids flicked up and he focused on a light brown face and black eyes an arm's length above him. He closed his eyes again with a smile.

"Do you want to eat? Would you like me to cook dinner?" The girl spoke with a soft French accent which pleased him. She gazed down fondly at the large, well-muscled body. A sheen of sweat gleamed through the tangle of body hair which had once alarmed her so much.

He did not answer at once. He allowed the sound of small waves lapping on fine sand and the flutings and whistlings of the tourerelles and Indian martins to wash over him. He lifted a hand, found her cheek and stroked it.

When he spoke, his voice came from deep in his chest with the cadences and vowels of southern Ireland. It was a voice which he had consciously nurtured more than thirty years before. It was a tool, a weapon, his favourite instrument.

"D'you know," he murmured, "when I was a kid, I always saw angels as tall Anglo-Saxon fellas, blond hair, with wings, of course." He opened his eyes and smiled at the girl. "But I was completely wrong."

He lifted his head and shoulders to kiss the wide brown lips, then swung his legs off the canvas bed on which he had been lying.

"What I'd like is one of your creole fish stews. Be nice to my chef, though. I don't want him feeling hurt and redundant; at least, I don't want him quitting."

"I'll be nice to him." She squeezed his arm with long fingers before turning to stride along the white beach. He watched the breeze flutter the hem of the small square of cotton which was all that covered her from breasts to buttocks.

She turned and called over her shoulder, "It will be

ready in an hour. Don't be late." She gave a little wave and disappeared among the casuarina trees that fringed the beach.

It was a long time since anyone had told him not to be late. For a moment it made him feel like the innocent, kindly thirteen-year-old he had once been. At fifty, he was grateful for that.

He stood up, and walked the thirty or so yards to the shoreline, which curved away behind him on both sides, the outer edge of his new possession, his own small kingdom, the *Ile Vermont*, twelve square miles surrounded by the Indian Ocean. He looked across the pale turquoise lagoon that separated his island from Mauritius, the "mainland", a mile to the west and apparently on the point of being flattened by a big red dropping sun.

Christy Pyon turned to survey his island; the small tree-covered hill that gave it its name, the brilliant lush gardens around the great creole plantation house, just visible over the tops of the hurricane palms, and he felt good.

Pyon usually felt good – because he was a pragmatist: there seemed little point in achieving all that he had and not being happy. Any regrets he might have had were suppressed, or at least relegated to a part of his mind where they would cause no trouble.

He stretched, turned and walked out into the blue-green waves. When he reached deeper water, he plunged in and swam strongly for ten minutes, parallel to the shore, before heading back towards the beach. He walked ashore opposite a gap in the trees where a path from the house emerged. In a simple thatched beach hut, he gathered up a towel and a cotton robe in which he wrapped himself before strolling up the shallow stone steps.

The house lay a quarter of a mile up a slight incline, seventy feet above sea level. The entrance was in the original two-storeyed central part which had been built a hundred and fifty years before with great blocks of volcanic rock and much human sweat.

It had been dilapidated when Pyon bought the island from a half-crazy son of an aristocratic French diplomat who was convinced that none of his wife's offspring was his own, and anxious to leave no tangible assets for them to claim.

Now the old house had become the cross-bar of an "H". The two long new wings sympathetically echoed it, though drawn with a lighter touch. Plants clambered and flowered over the walls and carved timber verandahs. Golden-red cardinal birds and butterflies flitted beneath the eaves, living in confident symbiosis with the building. Among the leaves, the windows were now squares of bright pink, reflecting the just-bedded sun.

As Pyon climbed the last few steps to the front door, it was opened for him by a silent respectful Mauritian Hindu in black trousers and a white jacket. Pyon nodded his thanks and passed into a high, neo-medieval hall. He carried on with the sleek bulk of a battle-cruiser towards the suite of offices that occupied the south wing of the house. A pair of ten-foot-high, panelled rosewood doors gave into a reception area with marbled walls, thick grey carpet and a jungle of indoor palms, which could have been in London, Frankfurt or Manhattan, but which had never received any visitors. All the paraphernalia of state-of-the-art business communications were there: screens, fax machines, printers, a large international time clock and two well-groomed, efficient women – one English, one Eurasian – to receive, decipher and despatch the constant stream of information that arrived by satellite, by undersea cable, by short-wave radio, even by human messenger on this remote, unheard-of island. As an extra precaution when Pyon bought the island, he had telephone cable laid from the mainland and, by the simple but costly expedient of renting a permanently open line, had given it a London 734 number.

The secretaries were used to Pyon appearing in his office in whatever he happened to be wearing at the time. They looked up and smiled. Pyon glanced at the clock. It was Friday, six-thirty here, three-thirty British summer time. He returned the girls' smiles and opened the door to his own office. This was not a large room, not in relation to the decisions taken in it; twenty feet by twenty feet, with the south wall entirely taken up by a window that faced out across the shoulder of the hill, over the canopy of trees to the ocean beyond.

Another wall was taken up by a large Burne-Jones painting and facing this, floor to ceiling, was a wall of books. Set on an Afghan carpet of antique beauty there was a large desk and chair of light unpolished oak which faced the window, and a bulky armchair with a lamp beside it and a drinks cabinet.

Pyon poured himself half a tumblerful of Black Bush Irish whiskey before picking up the receiver of a pre-war, black bakelite telephone. There was no dial on the instrument, which he had taken from his mother's house twenty-five years before.

"Annie?" he boomed into it.

"Yes, Mr Pyon."

"Get me Newberry, and if he's still having lunch, track him down. And scramble it."

"Yes, Mr Pyon."

He put the receiver back and sat in his desk chair. He opened a drawer and pulled out a thick manila folder. He extracted the first sheet of paper and stared at it until the telephone rang thirty seconds later.

"Hello, Pyon." A flat, colourless voice, from which only the rougher cockney edges had been rubbed away. The two words carried deference and truculence.

"How much Chemco have we bought this week?" Pyon asked.

There was a pause. "Just over half a million."

"Is that all?"

Pyon could almost hear Newberry's shrug. "You said take it quietly."

"At least the price hasn't moved. Western General have agreed to sell their five million at $5.20."

"Good God. When did they tell you?"

"Two or three hours ago. And we're holding just over five million now. Thank God Chemco have not made any progress with the AIDS vaccine. Berstein was going to make an announcement this week, but had to cancel it."

"I hadn't heard that."

"Well," said Pyon, "I'm closer to the middle where I am."

"Where are you, by the way?"

"Never you mind. Now just listen to this. The American

4

and British banks have confirmed their support for our bond issue. We can go for it now."

"How far?"

"They're at $4.24 at the moment. Go on buying till we've twenty-one million, or the price goes over $6, whichever comes soonest. That'll give us just under five per cent."

"They might get to six bloody quickly."

"Not now; not till Monday and maybe not then. Buy in London till they close, then in New York, then start in Tokyo and Sydney on Monday morning."

"Not a very original sort of a raid."

"We don't get points for being original, but there's no reason why it shouldn't work. And Berstein's cancelling his announcement will cease to be a mere rumour, it'll be a lead story in the Sunday papers. That'll damp down enthusiasm for a bit."

"Are you sure we're right to go now?" Newberry was doubtful.

"Of course I'm not bloody sure – I'm not God. But the balance of probability and my gut tell me to go now. So, get on with it. And if I were you, I'd get a couple of hundred thousand of 'em for myself."

"Okay, Pyon. It's your neck."

"Right. If we've reached our target by the middle of next week, set up a press conference in New York for the week after. I'll announce our bid and its terms then."

"That's a bit quick, isn't it?"

"Why not? Anyway, I wanted to be in the south of France the following week."

"Christ, you're going a bit soft, aren't you? This is the biggest bid we've ever made. You can't write the timetable yourself, you know."

"Of course I'll come back from France if I have to. In the meantime, just get back to me every hour the markets are open."

"Will do."

The line, six thousand miles of it, went dead.

Pyon replaced the receiver and leaned back in his chair. He dispelled the twinge of doubt brought on by Newberry's manner. In the end, he thought, Ken was the same as most other people. His loyalty came very expensive, but, provided it was paid for, it would not fail. In a code they well understood, Pyon had offered to underwrite any loss that Ken might incur in buying 200,000 Chemco shares. There would be no loss, but to Ken, instinctively cautious, the offer represented a risk-free chance of making £100,000 in three days, before selling them on to Pyon. Good wages by any international standard.

Pyon stood up, walked out of his office and beamed at the two women outside. He rubbed his black hair with the towel that was still draped round his neck and pushed through the rosewood doors into the old part of the house.

Natalie

In stock markets around the world, Christy Pyon's corporate victims and his rivals lived in fear of his boldness and foresight; he was a famous predator. Yet in his relationship with Natalie, it was she who had stalked him.

When she first saw him, she knew nothing about him other than that his blue eyes, when he turned them on to hers, overwhelmed her. They seemed to convey, in a short glance, warmth, humour, admiration, understanding and power.

That had been over six months before and he had been in a restaurant in Port Louis with three other men, Mauritian politicians, government men, opponents of her father. She had come in with her parents and one of her brothers to dine, to celebrate her first job, as a junior teacher at the Convent of Our Lady in Curepipe, in the milder, upland centre of the island. She was nineteen, ingenuous and Catholic, but she was bright, too, and loved to be made to laugh.

The restaurant was almost full. Natalie and her parents were half-a-dozen tables from Pyon's party, but three or four times, Natalie's eyes met his.

In Pyon's first reaction to her, she sensed that there was more than simple lust. She was not unaware that she was more than usually attractive, even by the high standards of the Indian Ocean Islands, but it irked her that men's interest always seemed to focus only on her body. In Pyon's admiration, however, she detected reluctance, evidence of a conscience.

It was she who made the first move, not on that occasion, but two days later when, to her surprise, she saw him at Mass in Curepipe. Tourists were seldom seen in church; it was not for this that people came to Mauritius. He recognised her, of course, and it was a simple matter for her to leave the church alongside him. Outside, in the hot, quiet sunshine, among blossomed-filled trees, she smiled, acknowledging their previous long-distance encounter.

"Hello. Are you on holiday here?" She assumed he was not.

He shook his head. "No. Are you?"

"Of course not," she smiled. "What brings you to church? We don't often see visitors here."

"That's a difficult question. It makes a change to go to Mass in a beautiful building. Where I was born, in England, most of the Catholic churches look like public lavatories with crosses on them." He shrugged. "I go to Mass because I go to Mass. I've been a lucky man; I ought to thank someone, don't you think? What about you? D'you live near here?"

"Yes. I have a little room in the convent."

"I hope you'll excuse my saying so, but you don't look much like a nun."

"Don't you think I look holy enough?"

"I've always found holiness rather deceptive, but I think you're destined to fulfil a less" – he lifted an eyebrow and one side of his mouth – "austere calling."

"Childbearing can be quite hard too, you know."

"So can fatherhood. But we can't stand here discussing all sorts of important issues without knowing each other's names. I'm Christy Pyon."

"I'm Natalie Felix." She held out a hand which Pyon raised to his lips.

"So, Natalie, if you're not a nun, what are you?"

"I'm a teacher." She drew her shoulders back and eyed him severely.

Pyon laughed at her charade. "Would you ever give me a lesson on the history of this island?"

"Of course. I like to tell people about my little country. When would you like me to?"

"Lunchtime, today?"

"All right. My mother is expecting me, but I'll telephone her; she won't mind. Where do you want this lesson?"

"What's the best place in the island to eat lunch on Sunday?"

She named a restaurant which she said was a short walk away.

"Right," he said, "I'll meet you at one at the convent gates, if you tell me where they are."

"Just there." She pointed at a neo-gothic stone building on the other side of the tree-lined road.

Natalie walked down to the gates a quarter of an hour early. She stood back a little, out of sight of the road, but through the shrubs she was just able to see anyone who approached. She had not watched Pyon leave the churchyard that morning and she had no idea how he would arrive now.

He walked. She could hear heavy footsteps in the road before he came into view.

It was hard to guess his age. Mid-forties, probably, thick black hair, upright, sixteen stone and six feet four. His progress along the pavement suggested complete control over his actions and invulnerable optimism; he seemed to push his presence before him like the bow-wave of a ship.

As he reached the gates, her body warmed then cooled and she shivered a little. She walked a few paces down the drive to meet him.

For a moment she was uncharacteristically shy. He saw that. "Hello, Natalie. I hope you won't mind my saying on such brief acquaintance that you look very lovely."

She had changed into a plain, short white cotton dress and had gathered her gleaming black hair into a white bow.

She relaxed. "That's no way to talk to your new teacher."

"I'm sorry, Miss." Pyon looked put down, then grinned. "I'm glad you didn't chicken out. I'll be a tricky pupil."

"That'll be good practice for me. I'm a very new school-mistress. In fact, I've only just started."

"Well, it'll do you good to kick off with a bit of a challenge. However, I promise to pay attention. Now, shall we walk?"

When they sat down in the restaurant, Pyon asked her advice and ordered a simple, delicious meal of white fish, spicy sauce and tropical vegetables.. Only in the matter of wines did he display any flamboyance – the cost of shipping made Dom Perignon and Chablis expensive commodities in Mauritius.

As it happened, Pyon did want to know more about Mauritius: its history, geography and politics, its economy and its gossip. All information was like nourishment to him, the food on which his ideas grew fat.

At that first lunch, Pyon was quite happy to listen, and look at the sparkling young Creole. He did not want to talk about himself.

But getting involved with women had not been part of his purpose in Mauritius. He had invited Natalie to join him because she was quite exceptionally goodlooking, and promised to be good company for lunch; that was all. He had no intention to taking it any further. As the meal progressed, though, he had to fight hard to resist an alarming reaction to her.

Pyon wanted to resist, for he was a self-indulgent man, and one of his indulgences was a part-illusory notion that he did not hurt individuals with whom he came into contact, unless they deserved it. Natalie, he was sure, would have slept with him, and he wanted that very much. But whatever she might think she did not need a man like him in her life. He already had two families and for this girl to get caught up in and destabilise the complex equilibrium of his existence would lead to frustration and unhappiness for all of them.

A couple of days after her lunch with Pyon, Natalie rang a school friend whose brother, Jean, was a keen young official in the Ministry of Home Affairs. Jean was more than happy to have the chance to do something for the lovely Natalie.

When he arrived at the café opposite the market where they had arranged to meet, he was disappointed to discover that she wanted to know about another man, much older and foreign.

"He's called Christy Pyon. I think he's English and he was having dinner with your boss in Port Louis last week."

Jean nodded his solemn brown head. "Yes. He has applied for residence, but he wants special tax concessions. He wants to create a headquarters here for his business."

Natalie flushed with pleasure. "You mean, he wants to live here?"

"As far as I can tell. Mind you, this is all meant to be very hush-hush. For God's sake, don't tell anyone else."

"What is this business he wants to do?"

"If you read the financial pages of any European papers, you would know that. He controls one of the biggest construction, mining and chemicals corporations in the world, Southern Hemisphere Resources."

"That's really strange," Natalie said thoughtfully. "He didn't seem a bit like a tycoon to me."

"Well he is, one of the biggest. He is a very powerful man – and very dangerous, I should think."

"Dangerous? It's not possible," Natalie exclaimed. "He was so kind."

"Not dangerous in a physical way, I suppose, though I don't know; you can't be as successful as he is without treading on people. He is certainly ruthless in business. He buys and sells companies like that woman over there buys and sells mangoes." He nodded at the market opposite, where a crowd seethed around a large fruit stall overseen by a vast, toothlessly smiling old Creole. "And when he sells the parts he doesn't want, sometimes thousands of people lose jobs. In London they used to call it 'asset stripping'. now they call it 'rationalisation'."

"You make him sound horrible, but I know he isn't."

"Do you? Why do you want to know about him, anyway?"

"I had lunch with him last Sunday. He said he wanted a lesson on the history of Mauritius."

"Was that all he wanted?"

"Actually, I think it was. He was charming and made no hints at anything else. And when I suggested another lesson, as a sort of joke, he was quite definite that one was

10

enough and left. But he was very kind and I'd like to see him again."

"That shouldn't be hard. He's just bought the *Ile Vermont*. He wants to rebuild the mansion and make his offices there."

"What an odd thing to do. Surely there are no phones or electricity or anything, and it's at least a mile off shore."

"He's not worried about that. He wants to lay cables out there, and put in satellite receivers and God knows what else, though he says there will only be half-a-dozen staff and a few domestics. He's supposed to be rather eccentric."

"What about a family? Does he have a family?"

"I don't know. Nobody had mentioned a Mrs Pyon, but these tycoons don't usually involve their wives in this sort of thing."

He spoke with the wisdom of a young man who had spent a year in London and a year in Paris studying politics and economics. Natalie was not in a position to refute his generalisations, but she was sure that Pyon was not the monster that Jean implied.

She wanted to know more, but Jean had nothing concrete. he promised, not very sincerely, to let her know if he did learn anything, and told her once again: "He seems to want to keep this place a secret. I would be in a lot of trouble if the Ministry heard I'd been talking."

Natalie promised, and rewarded Jean with a dazzling, hope-provoking smile.

A few days later, Jean obtained an invitation for Natalie to a reception at which Pyon would be present.

Pyon saw her immediately she walked into the old colonial ballroom. She shone among the three hundred or so people there, and Pyon weakened. He broke off the conversation he was having and walked straight across to her.

"I didn't expect to see my teacher here," Pyon greeted Natalie. He noticed Jean, shuffling and grimacing, and held out his hand. "How d'you do. I'm Christy Pyon. Don't I know you from the Ministry?"

Jean nodded and took Pyon's hand. "Jean Marceau. I'm Monsieur Briande's assistant."

"Of course. And you've come with the lovely Natalie. Lucky man. You'll not mind if I grab her for a few minutes? She's been teaching me all about the island and I've a few queries for her."

Jean, thus charmingly but irresistibly dismissed, wandered off into the crowd.

Natalie wondered what Pyon would tell her. "I'm surprised you're still here, Mr Pyon."

Pyon laughed. "Are you? I'll admit that a week in one place is unusual for me, but I'm leaving tomorrow."

Natalie tried to hide her disappointment. "Where for?"

"Europe," he replied vaguely, "then America."

"Will you be coming back to *Maurice*?"

"I think I will. And perhaps then you would be kind enough to continue my education?"

Natalie flashed a smile. "Of course. Will you bring your family next time?"

Pyon's lips tightened a little.

"How did you know I had a family?"

"I don't. I'm guessing. But it would be rather unusual for a man like you not to have a family."

Pyon smiled. "You're right, of course." He continued to gaze at her, still smiling, then appeared to come to a decision. "Now, I'd better let you go, before your boyfriend starts planning his suicide."

"He's not my boyfriend," Natalie protested quickly.

"I know that, angel. I'll see you before too long for my next lesson." He gave a sideways nod of his head, and the crowd parted before him as he made his way back to a group of anxious government functionaries.

Pyon did not sleep on the *Ile Vermont* until the building and all its equipment were functioning. That cables had been laid and several boat-loads of electronic equipment been installed on the island within months was beyond anyone's experience in Mauritius; that, at the same time, the mansion had been rebuilt and extended to three times its original size was a small miracle. When it was ready for Pyon to move in, Natalie said as much.

"It looks as though you're going to be kept up-to-date

with everything that's going on anywhere in the world with all these receivers and direct lines, faxes and computer screens."

He laughed. "We Messiahs have to work the odd miracle to keep up the confidence of the faithful."

The week before he was due to move in, he telephoned Natalie from Italy and asked her if she would be his first dinner-guest.

A shining black Range Rover – a kind of vehicle seldom seen in Mauritius – called at Natalie's parents' bungalow in Quatre Bornes, a few miles from Curepipe. Natalie sensed that this, Pyon's first night on the *Ile Vermont*, would be a significant watershed in her life and she had not wanted to be collected from the convent, because her mother's objections would be easier to cope with than the nuns'.

The grinning black face of Pyon's factotum, André, gleamed from the driver's window of the car as Natalie ran down the short path to the lane where he waited for her. She walked round and let herself into the front passenger door. André turned the car, and bounced back up the road to the main highway.

He tried to engage her in general chat about recent events – sporting and political – on the island, but she had not seen Pyon for a month and she was too preoccupied with her own thoughts to listen properly. Only after an hour's drive up to the north-east of the island, did she start to become aware of where they were. André had turned off the road, between high waving walls of sugar-cane, and the Range Rover bumped down a track to Pyon's newly-built jetty, beside which was now moored a glossy new thirty-foot Riva launch.

André laughed. "Look, the boss got a flashy new ferry. I hope he don't get that stuck on the reef too much."

"Do you drive it, André?"

He nodded with an excited grin.

"Then I don't give it much of a chance."

"Hey, you'll see, Mam'selle Natalie, I a shit-hot driver."

He parked the car, climbed out and strolled round to

open Natalie's door for her. They walked down to the jetty where the launch hung in still, clear water above the white coral sand of the lagoon. André handed her down and leaped in beside her to shatter the silence with the big diesel engines.

Pyon was sitting with a telephone beside him on the west-facing verandah. The spluttering of the Riva reached him across the flat water and he glanced up to see André steer the boat towards the island in a big lazy curve.

He got to his feet with a smile, and dropped down the steps to the beach two at a time. As he reached his own landing stage, André was already swinging the launch alongside it. Natalie looked up at him with a broad grin, and he stretched down his hand to help her up. He pulled and she shot up into his arms like a cork from a bottle. They hugged one another and laughed.

André jumped out and made the launch fast to the jetty.

"You going to need this again tonight, boss?" he asked.

Pyon looked down at Natalie with a question on his face.

She shook her head with a mischievous smile. "I won't need it," she said.

The sun painted a broad, bloody smear across the western sky as it sank behind the spiky basalt peaks that night.

Pyon and Natalie ate on the verandah in the tropical dusk. Pyon's new chef apparently wanted to show off his skills in every aspect of Mauritian vernacular cooking, and produced a breathtaking meal of spicy, Franco-Indian cuisine. Pyon had stocked his wine cellar from France and found some hefty vintages from the *Bôuche du Rhone* that seemed to enhance well the surprising contrasts provided by the gastronomic meeting of east and west. The food and wine were potent stimuli to the heat already generated by the tension between two highly physical people.

The sun had long since retired, and now candles in storm holders guttered in the eddying offshoots of the evening south-east trade wind. The chorus of insects and the frantic flutterings of successful kamikaze bugs did not interfere with their conversation and their tacit understanding of what was to follow.

They talked about each other, and each other's relationships. Pyon wanted to reveal himself to Natalie in a way he had never done to anyone else. He had always been a good listener, which was apt to surprise many people. He was, in an academic way, interested in other people's opinions, but he never normally asked their advice. Now, though, he was in a dilemma and he thought Natalie might be able to help.

"Have I ever talked to you about my son, Julian? I think you might be able to give me some advice."

Natalie shrugged. "I'll try. How old did you say he is? It's only young children I know about – being the eldest of six."

"I'll bet that's a great source of wisdom. I had no brothers or sisters, or a real father, for that matter. But Julian is twenty-eight. The trouble is, he doesn't take after me. Not that there's anything wrong in that – I'm no saint – but he seems actively to resent me."

Natalie looked across into Pyon's frank, blue eyes. "Did you always travel around so much? Did you see him a lot when he was younger?" she asked.

"Regrettably, no. But I was good to him whenever I did. I've always been in a position to provide anything he ever wanted, as long as he could justify it, but he's not shown much gratitude. Now he won't listen to a thing I say."

"And you're not used to that," Natalie added.

"Is my overbearing arrogance so obvious, or have people been telling you about me?"

"I have found out a bit about you," Natalie admitted, "but only from business magazines. The photographs were clear enough, though you looked much younger, like a boy, but I couldn't recognise you from the descriptions."

"Ah well, Jesus himself got a pretty terrible press when he first got going. The old scribes and pharisees put in a lot of influential bad-mouthing because he was upsetting their cartel. That's happened throughout history."

"You didn't think I looked much like a nun and I don't think you look much like a second Messiah. But what about your son?"

15

"I want to help him, but frankly don't know how. He went to a rotten university when he could have got into Oxford, but he thought Oxford was too elitist. By the end of his first year, he knew everything, so he left and tried to be a journalist – a very young, opinionated and ignorant journalist to whom, not surprisingly, editors were reluctant to give space.

"He ended up writing pompous, ill-researched and unreadable articles for a so-called 'alternative' left-wing rag, which folded pretty soon after he joined them. Then he drifted into television. He had some friends who were producing what they called 'investigative' documentaries. They weren't investigating so much as digging for dirt. If their researches revealed that institutions or public figures were actually in the right over some issue or other, they simply didn't air them. They even had a pathetically unsuccessful go at myself. I'm used to people trying to pillory me, but it hurt when my own son was involved.

"Now he says he's got the chance to direct a feature film – about two homosexual steel-workers, a Yemeni and a Yorkshireman, in Sheffield, I ask you – and he's got the gall to come asking me to fund it because no one else will. What am I going to do?"

Natalie waited a moment before answering. She did not understand all the nuances of what he had said, but she sensed he was sad rather than angry about it.

"Would it help your relationship with him?" she asked.

"I don't know. That's why I want your advice."

"Do you want to?"

"I don't think I'm right, but, yes, I want to."

"Then do it," Natalie shrugged. "Of course, it's probably too late to ever win back his affection, and you've obviously been a terrible father. But at least he'll know that you've given him the chance to do something that's important to him when no one else would."

Angry doubt flashed in Pyon's vivid, blue eyes in a way that reminded Natalie of her youngest, eight-year-old brother. She put her hand on his arm. "Sorry. Maybe I shouldn't have said you were a terrible father. I don't really know enough about it."

Pyon nodded his head thoughtfully. "It is better to say

16

what you think. D'you promise you'll always say what you think?"

"I can't help it. I'm not a diplomat."

Pyon laughed. "That's obvious, thank God. I can't stand diplomats, or any other kind of flannelling bullshitter, though that includes about ninety-five per cent of the people I have to deal with." He became serious. "So you think I should give Julian the money for his film? Right, then, I will."

"But really," Natalie protested, "I'm sure you haven't told me enough about it all."

Pyon gave her an impatient smile. "Don't underestimate yourself. You've a natural instinct for identifying the bullseye. If I ever become so egocentric that I have to buy my own newspaper, you'll be my first appointment to the Readers' Problem Page." He gave a great bellow of laughter and leaned over to kiss her; and she knew that he was laughing at his own potential weaknesses.

They had been talking freely, with few inhibitions, for two or three hours. Natalie decided that the time had come for her to take the initiative.

"Christy, I believe you when you say that honesty between people is one of the most valuable gifts they can give each other. So, I want to be honest with you."

Pyon looked back at her and for a moment a curtain seemed to fall across his eyes; suddenly they offered nothing.

Natalie understood. She radiated a smile deep into him. "I want to make love with you now."

The curtain of doubt which had shaded Pyon's eyes lifted, and they shone with relief.

"Amen to that," he muttered huskily.

It was a night of nights. It could have been a month, or a second. It was for both of them the most supreme of conjugations.

This was not breaking and entering; it was mutual colonisation. An harmonious unification of two beings. The sharp pain, and the recurring bliss that followed provided an experience so fulfilling to her that Natalie thought it would last her whole life. And Pyon was beyond coherent thought when finally he drifted into

17

sleep as the sun sparkled on the far side of the hill behind them.

Newberry

In the West End of London, the spring sun shone weakly on the broad plane leaves and the cherry blossom. Kenneth Newberry sat at a large desk in Christy Pyon's office, staring with surly grey eyes through wide sash windows at the building on the other side of the Mayfair street. His face was small and sharp and his hair a lank grey-brown. He wore a slightly iridescent suit, a cream shirt and his golf club tie. He did not seem to match the Wyatt fireplace and the Adam plasterwork of the room.

He had just replaced the receiver at the end of his telephone conversation with Pyon and was trying to swallow the rancour that Pyon's attitude always evoked in him. He had contributed as much as Pyon in the early days, but now he felt no more than a servant who received enormous tips. Pyon was big on bullshit, but he, Newberry, had always done most of the fixing; he was the principal mechanic of their operation. After nearly thirty years, it was time to break loose and be his own man.

Good God, Newberry reflected, the man won't even tell me where he is and I'm his oldest ally. Probably cheating on his Italian slag of a wife somewhere. And this Chemco deal, it's ridiculous; it's too bloody big. He must have lost his marbles. Still, it's a chance to organise a monster wedge before going off to do my own thing.

He picked up the telephone again and asked his secretary to get Lenny Shemilt.

"Hello, Lenny?"

"Yes, Ken." A quiet, Levantine voice.

"He's going for it, buying five per cent then bidding for the rest with a fucking great bond issue. I can't see him pulling it off but our price and Chemco's are going to be on a roller-coaster for the next few months."

"Fine. Keep me posted, but don't phone from there in future."

"Oh, yeah, right. Sorry."

The Persian Lebanese had put the phone down, and Newberry prickled with embarrassment. Still, there was no doubt that Shemilt would do what he said he would; there was too much money to be made.

Invitation to Cannes

Natalie found it very satisfying to cook for Pyon. It seemed the only material thing she could give him. He ate her meals with the extra relish provided by the affection with which she had prepared them.

That evening, as they ate her Mauritian *bouillabaisse* on the verandah, he asked her for the first time to come away with him.

"That film I funded for Julian. It's been made already. They did it in six months. It must be better than I thought, they're showing it at the Cannes Festival. It's in a couple of weeks, when your school's on holiday. Would you come with me to see it?"

The invitation took Natalie by surprise. Not answering, she stood and walked to the rail of the verandah where she leaned and listened to the night sounds from the gardens and the lagoon. She stayed silent for a while, and so, patiently, did Pyon.

She turned and shook her head. "No, Christy. It would change everything. I've told you, I truly don't want to know about your other life or to be involved in it. I'm happy with the part of you I have."

"But surely you won't be for ever?"

Natalie's eyes sparked. "Please, Christy, don't judge me by other women you know."

"I'm sorry." Pyon was contrite. "You're right; you're not the same."

Natalie walked back to the table, sat opposite him and

19

smiled over the fresh frangipani flowers in a bowl between them.

"You've never told me about your family, only about Julian, and I haven't asked because I don't want to know. Maybe that's selfish, but they have nothing to do with what there is between us. I know what kind of man you are, and that there are a lot of sides to you. I feel I know the best side, that's why I'm happy with that. I love that part of you which you share with me. I don't know that I'd love all the other parts. I don't care about your money; I want nothing from you that you could buy with it. I'm happy being a schoolmistress. I love teaching my children, watching them grow up and learn. That's a real joy, and it's the children who give it. I wouldn't give up that joy for anyone, and I don't expect you to give up the things that please you. It seems to me that business is a huge game which you love to play. I know nothing about it, and I don't want to learn, any more than I want to learn about cricket, but I have no right to keep you from it." She shrugged. "So, let's stay as we are."

A long deep sigh resonated in Pyon's chest. "I thought you'd say no, and I understand. But you must understand that I've reached a point where I want to share more with you; to subject you, if you like, to some of the brash realities of my life. Though I am a self-sufficient man, I'm still just a man."

There was a bleakness in his eyes that Natalie had not seen before.

"Christy," she said, "I don't want to disappoint you. Just let me think about it first, though."

It said much for Pyon's influence – though Natalie did not know this – that he was given a suite at the Carlton in Cannes and a Rolls-Royce to meet them from Nice airport with just two days' notice before the beginning of the film festival.

Natalie had finally succumbed. She felt that Pyon wanted her not for mere decoration but for support, and that, although he was not admitting it, he felt unable to deal fairly with Julian on his own. She was not certain she could help, but she wanted to try.

She was effervescent with excitement about her first visit to Europe. Pyon joined in her enthusiasm, and blithely answered the torrent of questions with which she bombarded him. He disguised from her the apprehension he felt as each minute brought them ten miles closer to Cannes.

Pyon was running a risk which he had not even considered in fifteen years; he was taking a beautiful woman to a function, the very existence of which relied on a seething mass of hungry media folk, not to mention the paparazzi.

He had not only refused to allow himself to be photographed for more than fifteen years; during that time he had not once given an interview. He had been savaged by the press once too often, and had learned that they could never be anything but destructive for a man like him. He was naturally gregarious, indeed he frequently relied on his physical presence to get his way, and he was not a recluse by choice. Now he was walking into the lion's den.

In deciding to come to Cannes, he was allowing two elements in his life to overcome his dislike of such public events. He wanted to support his son, whom he saw slipping away from him, and he wanted to enjoy his new experience of the movie industry with Natalie. And, with a gambler's perverse sense of danger, he wanted to see if he could get away with it.

He had developed a sixth sense and an elaborate pattern of behaviour to avoid contact with the press, and besides, since his face had not been publicly displayed for so long, he usually went unrecognised. At this critical moment in his largest ever takeover bid, his being spotted with Natalie was potentially disastrous. But he did not tell Natalie, and the very irresponsibility of what he was doing gave a tingling edge to the whole trip.

Anyway, he told himself in self-justification, it's the stars and starlets that the paparazzi will be pursuing.

They reached the Carlton unmolested, and were afforded the privacy which this establishment was accustomed to supply.

Natalie was overwhelmed with the glamour of it all: the great crush of people, beautiful and not so beautiful, on the

21

pavements; the famous names above the shops; the grand
hotels along the Croisette. She drank it all in like a small
child at her first funfair.

She looked down from the window of the salon of their
suite, sipping champagne and asking Pyon questions. But
she came back into the room when, within an hour of their
arriving, Julian joined them.

At first sight, Julian appeared to have little genetic connection with his father – only the same intense blue eyes. He
was tall, though not as tall as Pyon, and lanky. His styleless,
mid-brown hair hung around good but gaunt features. Without stopping to consider why, Natalie immediately felt sorry
for him. She had been right. His biggest problem was being
Pyon's son. This was one of the reasons for Pyon bringing
her to Cannes.

It was a French film which attracted the biggest audience
at the festival. It was the most tipped for the *Palme d'Or*,
and everyone wanted to be sure of having seen it. When the
showing was over, Pyon and Natalie were caught inextricably
in the scrum of people leaving. Pyon cursed; it was exactly
what he had wanted to avoid.

As they burst into the lobby of the theatre, he lowered his
head and put an arm around Natalie to keep her by his side.
He gave her a quick smile of encouragement and apology.
She squeezed his arm, grateful for his concern.

At that moment, the crowd in front parted to skirt round a
gathering of apparently oblivious stars. In front of this group
the photographers jostled each other, clicking and whirring,
shouting to get their victims' attention.

One of them spotted Natalie. A girl like that had to be
someone. He subjected her, and her unrecognised escort,
to a volley of flashes. Pyon glanced up at him in fury,
considered trying to grab his camera, but opted instead to
spin Natalie round and hustle her back into the crowd which
was still spilling from the auditorium.

The French photographer had not noticed the anger. He
merely made a mental note to find out who the girl was,
before turning his attention back to more obvious targets.

It was a few days before he was able to identify the dusky

subject of the half-dozen frames on a roll he had developed. And that was by the sheer chance of being outside the Carlton waiting for that year's hot star to emerge. A hundred francs to the doorman yielded only the name of the man.

At first, this did not mean anything to the photographer, but mentioning it later to one of the older English gossip writers, he realized that he had a paparazzo's scoop. He swore his companion to a mutually beneficial secrecy and they set about marketing their very expensive morsel, while Christy Pyon cursed his weakness in lowering his normally impenetrable guard. It was such a small event on the face of it, but it could complicate the already delicate balance of his relationships; worse, it could also do devastating damage to the mighty deal he had launched.

Maria

"Signora Pyon?"

Maria, Christy Pyon's second wife, glanced up and shaded her eyes from the strong morning sun. She saw her Sardinian housemaid standing in the French windows of the white, rough-rendered house.

"*Si?*"

"Giuliano has brought the papers from Porto Cervo. Do you want them out here?"

Maria dismissed the maid with a nod and stretched. She blinked and sat up on the day-bed where she had been dozing. She leaned across to the table beside her and refilled her coffee cup from a large pot. She drank from it slowly and looked down from her terrace, over the tops of scrubby Mediterranean pines to the long curve of sand and pale turquoise sea beyond. The ferocious wind of the night before had blown itself out and left the air still and unusually quiet.

God, it's dull here, she thought. She should really be in Rome during May. That's where everyone would be.

She stood up, and her silk dressing-gown fell open. She

glanced down with gratitude at her 35-year-old body: her large, still self-supporting breasts; tanned, sleek hips and a stomach that had, despite two children but with hours of weekly exercise, remained firm. She put her hand to her pubic mound and caressed the thick black silky curls.

Where the hell was Pyon?

She hadn't seen him for three weeks. His normal absences had become longer and more frequent over the last year. He was very busy, of course. There was something about one or other of his companies in the papers almost every day. How strange that other women should be envious about this, when all it meant was that she was even more neglected than usual.

She heard the chauffeur coming with the papers. Slowly she wrapped the robe around her and tied the sash.

"Leave them on the table," she said and the surly young Sardinian wordlessly dropped them there and left.

The silence that followed was broken by the ringing of a telephone. Maria heard the maid answer it before walking out on to the terrace.

"Signora, it's Caterina."

Maria groaned to herself. Almost every morning the girl, just thirteen, telephoned from her convent in England to say that she was homesick.

"Tell her that I've gone shopping and that I'll ring her back tonight."

"Signora, she's crying very much."

"Oh, all right," Maria said, annoyed by the accusation in her maid's eye. "I'll speak to her."

She walked into the house and settled herself on a chaise longue in the wide, airy drawing-room before picking up the receiver.

"Hello, *carissima*."

"Oh, Mama. I'm so unhappy."

"Yes, dear. I know, but you'll soon get used to it."

"No. I'm not just homesick. It's Papa – in the papers. It's awful."

"Well, Caterina, your father's a big businessman and a lot of people are envious of his success, so they write unkind, untrue things about him."

More deep sobbing reached Maria down the line. She glanced at her fingernails, wondering what to do for lunch.

"But there's a photograph," her daughter finally said, "of Papa with a beautiful woman who's only twenty, and his arm is round her, and it says that he's in love with her."

Maria became instantly rigid, her face grey. Her brain seemed to seize up. She could not speak.

"Mama, Mama? Are you still there?"

"Yes," Maria managed to say faintly, then, with an effort, "Don't worry about it, darling. It's just stories being spread by his business rivals." She gritted her teeth. "Of course he's not in love with this woman."

"But Mama, he's smiling at her and she's smiling. It's awful and all the other girls have seen it and they're really sorry for me and Mother Agnes has said I must pray for him."

"Caterina," Maria said sharply, "you just tell everyone that it's a story put about by other, jealous people. The woman is probably someone he's just met and you know how your father is always charming and polite. I expect he was trying to cheer her up about something. Now, darling, don't worry. I'll ask Papa to ring you, all right?"

"Oh no! Don't, please. I don't want to talk to him."

"All right, all right. I'll ring you later and I'll talk to Mother Agnes. Now I must go. Cheer up, there's no need to worry. *Ciao*."

The sobbing started again. "Goodbye, Mama. Please ring me soon."

Maria put the receiver down and lay back, quaking with shock and jealous fury.

No wonder she hardly saw him now.

As long as she had known Pyon, or at least since the first hurricane of physical greed for each other had died down, he had been polite and considerate to her, even though – she knew, everyone knew – he continued to see his ex-wife in England. He had to, he said, for his children's sake. She could tolerate that. But now, he seemed scarcely to notice her when he came to Amalfi or Sardinia.

It must be true.

She slid off the chaise longue and walked back to the terrace to see if the Italian papers had printed anything about this new element in the continuing, gripping tale of the life of Christy Pyon.

She scoured the papers and found only a brief report on the financial pages of Pyon's problems in his bid for the giant American pharmaceutical corporation, Chemco.

She relaxed a little. If there were the remotest grounds for the story which the English paper had published, the Italians would surely have run it – probably even without any grounds.

But at the bottom of the stack of papers was a tabloid, colour gossip magazine, a weekly which prided itself on late exclusives. It was bought by millions of Italians, many of whom were reluctant to admit it.

At first she did not take in the badly printed photograph on the front page. It was very grainy, obviously blown up from a long shot. After gazing at it for a moment, the horror of it hit Maria. It was definitely Pyon. There was no doubt, from his demeanour and the smile on the face of the dark-skinned beauty beside him, that she was going to be humiliated.

The blood of twenty generations of hard, unforgiving Neapolitans seethed through her. She hurled the magazine across the terrace and strode up and down, grinding her teeth, planning a pre-emptive strike against the man with whom she had been obsessed for fifteen years and whom she had never been able to contain.

Twenty minutes later she telephoned her brother Sergio, and booked a plane to Naples.

Maeve

In England, deep in the rolling Marcher country of Herefordshire, a woman was contemplating with misgiving a photograph on the Nigel Dempster page of the *Daily Mail*.

Maeve Pyon was approaching seventy, straight-backed and handsome still, with a warm complexion and clear blue eyes. She sat with the paper on the table beside her breakfast. She lifted her gaze from the photo to the patchwork of golden rape, pink apple-blossom, russet earth, green pasture and ancient woodland that draped the hills and valleys she could see from her breakfast table. The twin tumps of Canon Pyon Hill and Butthouse Knap provided a view which had calmed her and given her security ever since, fifty years ago, she arrived at the medieval, stone manor house of which she was mistress.

When, those fifty years before, she had first stepped through the back door of the house, to take up her duties as house-maid, she had been a terrified, ingenuous peasant girl, unsure which of the two big brothers from her neighbouring village back home in Wicklow was responsible for the act which had caused her to run away, her heart filled with shame and her womb with a baby begun just eight weeks since.

But she was not so ingenuous as not to realise very quickly that Jack Pyon, her new employer, had been at least infatuated, if not actually in love with her from the moment he set eyes on her. She was the very model of an innocent, vulnerable, blue-eyed colleen. And Jack Pyon was a weak, peevish man who, at the age of forty, had never successfully wooed or won a woman. He was consumed with bitter frustration: at his incompetence in managing the fifteen hundred Herefordshire acres he had inherited; at his lack of friends and a confidante since his mother had died; and at his inability to fulfil his sexual urges other than by infrequent, mortifying trips to brothels in the seedier parts of London or Birmingham.

When he first saw Maeve O'Donnell, he could tell from her wide nervous eyes that here, at last, was a woman over whom he had some power. For one thing, he was her employer, and she was obviously desperate for the job because, with characteristic meanness, he had asked the agency for the cheapest girl they could send him.

On her first night in the house, he could not resist his

urge to tiptoe the creaking boards of corridors and stairs to her bedroom door. Only the sound of her sobbing prevented him from going in and taking what he had already decided was his by right. It was not out of any sense of compassion that he did not enter, merely out of the wish to avoid getting involved in someone else's misery.

The next day, Jack Pyon was so eager to look at his new prize that he did not leave the house. The girl had gone about her tasks, trying to demonstrate her willingness and competence, to ensure the temporary security that the job gave her. He had interpreted this as a wish to impress him personally; the girl was, he thought, obviously in awe of him and admired him.

That night, nothing could have stopped him making the journey up the back stairs to her attic room.

She had lain silent and motionless as he shed his nightshirt and clambered in beside her on the iron-framed bed. She shivered with resigned disgust as he lifted her nightdress and plunged himself into her for a few brief moments before collapsing into shuddering, groaning limpness.

The baby was still small in her, and he had not been aware of the slight swelling in her stomach. He had not hurt her; indeed, the whole event was over almost before she was aware it had begun. When, half an hour later, he slipped wordlessly from her bed to go back to his room, it was only the natural course of her pregnancy that brought on physical nausea and vomiting.

When he arrived again in her room the following night, she accepted him impassively. The only demand on her that he appeared to make was that she should be a receptacle for him. He seemed unconcerned that she should derive any enjoyment from the act.

And so it went on for several weeks. Maeve gradually realised that she had developed a considerable power over her employer. It became clear to her that he lived for these nightly encounters. Her confidence grew, and with her confidence, an idea.

She started to be as agreeable as she could to him, smiling over her shoulder at him as she cleaned out the fire-grates or dusted the heavy-framed portraits in the drawing-room. When they met in corridors or bedrooms, she let him maul her with fumbling, jerky hands and accepted his thin, greedy kisses on her own warm lips.

The guilt that this deception caused her was far outweighed by the wish to provide a secure home for the child within her. She had told no one in Ireland when she ran away, nor had she allowed anyone a hint of her reason for going. If this child were to be born with a legitimate father, at least her family would be spared the shame in public that she had suffered in private. Although Jack Pyon possessed no personal qualities that attracted her, he seemed to her to be the answer to a prayer.

One night when he arrived at her bedroom, she was sitting up in bed, with the single naked bulb still lit. She had brushed her long, black hair to her shoulders, applied a little rouge to her cheeks and her hands were crossed on her lap.

Jack Pyon was stunned by her serene beauty and the soft steady gaze that met him.

"I'm sorry, sir," she said with firmness in her soft Wicklow voice, "you can't tonight; I don't feel too well. You're going to be a father."

It was Jack Pyon's unwillingness to consider cause and effect, or to look at any long-term consequences that made him such a bad farmer. Similarly, the possibility of a pregnancy had scarcely crossed his mind. For a moment he was dumb-struck.

Then, as he gazed at her, he relaxed. A self-satisfied smile broke across his face. He walked over to the bed and bestowed a kiss on her that could almost have been affectionate.

"That's fine," he said. "Let's just hope it's a boy." He sat on the end of the bed and continued to look at her warmly until his peevishness returned. "I suppose that means I won't be able to sleep with you until it's born."

"Oh, no. I've just got to get over the early sickness."

"When did it happen; I mean, when was it conceived?"

"Right when I first came, it must have been."

Abruptly, Jack Pyon got to his feet. "We must celebrate," he said, and left the room. On his way down to the cellar, where several cases of old champagne had lain unopened since his father's death, he felt, for the first time, the equal of his neighbouring farmers and landowners. He was going to be a man with a family, and a wife who, despite her obviously humble origins, was ten times more beautiful than any of theirs, and no doubt she would give birth to a fine-looking son. Anyway, no one would know her background; it was not like marrying a girl from the village or the stockman's daughter.

He opened a dusty wooden case and took out a bottle of twenty-year-old Krug. On his way back up, he collected two glasses from a cabinet in the drawing-room and carried them all up to the poky bedroom on the second floor.

As he inexpertly uncorked the bottle, and vinous froth dribbled on to the bed, he announced, "Well, as I'm the father of your baby, you can call me Jack, and, of course, you must become Mrs Pyon."

Maeve contrived to look taken aback. "But I can't," she protested.

Jack Pyon shrugged. "You haven't any choice. You can't have a bastard. You certainly wouldn't be able to stay here if you did."

Maeve squeezed a few bleak tears. "But, sir, I can't marry you. I'm just the maid."

"Oh, I've already thought about that. It doesn't matter; you're not English, and anyway, plenty of men have married chorus-girls and things with pretty doubtful backgrounds and it usually works out all right."

"But I'm a Catholic. I can only be married in a Catholic church."

Jack Pyon thought a moment. He was, nominally, Church of England, but it meant nothing to him. He could not have cared less about the religious aspects of the ceremony.

"That's all right. I don't mind. I think there's a smart Catholic church in Birmingham – the Oratory. We'll have a very quiet wedding there. We only need a couple of witnesses. I'll arrange it tomorrow."

"But the child will have to be Catholic too," she said, as if she knew this would be an insuperable obstacle.

"Fine, fine. Why not? The vicar here's a bloody fool anyway."

"But," she said, "I'm not sure that I love you."

This was a gamble, but she wanted to preclude any possible notion he might develop that she had planned this marriage, not he.

"You will. I'm not such a bad fellow – just don't talk much or socialise. Anyway, as I said, you haven't got much choice."

In the drawing-rooms of the neighbouring farms and estates, around the stock-pens in Hereford market, and in the bars of the small city, the matter of Jack Pyon's marriage did crop up, between discussions about the likelihood of war and Mr Chamberlain's futile efforts at diplomacy with Adolf Hitler. Jack Pyon had been right in guessing that Maeve's beauty would neutralize most disapproval.

"Lucky little bugger," the farmers growled grudgingly to one another.

"I've no doubt that there'll be a baby rather too soon," the mistresses of the big houses agreed.

Jack Pyon and his doings, though, were not customarily a source of interest. And, on the September day on which a big healthy boy was born in the manor house – several months too soon, by most people's reckoning – Britain declared war on Germany, and other, bigger matters preoccupied the land.

Maeve insisted on calling the black-haired child Christy and he was baptized by one of the Benedictine monks in the abbey on the outskirts of Hereford.

The call to arms and the armament factories meant that only an aged housekeeper remained at the manor, and Maeve's duties as lady of the house did not much differ from her duties as maid.

But despite her husband's boorish ineptness, she was happy. It was a miracle to her that within a year of leaving Ireland in disgrace, she had become the respectably married mother of a fine little son, living in the relative comfort of a venerable old house surrounded by its own productive acres.

31

She soon found, too, that by experience and instinct she knew more about land and animal husbandry than Jack Pyon. It seemed that he was only too glad to leave decisions to her. He had been relieved that his age exempted him from call up, and derived considerable satisfaction from bossing the local tradesmen as an officer in the Home Guard.

The child was a pleasure to rear. He slept and ate well, was seldom ill and was quick to learn. Maeve taught him to read and write before Jack sent him off to a private school. During the holidays he divided his time between reading, curled up in a large chair in the small library, and scouting around the estate, picking off game at first with a catapult and later with a four-ten which his proud father bought him.

After the War, life in England did not return to normal and, everyone surmised, never would. Standards of living on the big estates had declined, it seemed, irreversibly. Nevertheless, a competent farmer could still make a good living, and Maeve was very competent. Jack Pyon was happy to spend his time shooting over his and his neighbours' land in the winters, and fishing on his own beat, high up the Wye towards Builth Wells, in the summer. He developed more of a taste for whisky and became, though quite unaware of it, even more disagreeable than he had been as a younger man.

He was puzzled and a little disappointed that though his sexual drive was as strong – and as unsatiating – as ever, Maeve had not become pregnant again. His wife knew that the fault lay with him, but kept that knowledge to herself, and was relieved as each passing year proved her right.

To compensate, Jack Pyon was very pleased with his son, who was growing into a tall, handsome boy and who displayed none of his father's personal characteristics.

Young Christy, for his part, took little notice of Jack Pyon. He was polite and superficially respectful to him because his mother asked him to be, but he felt no filial affection for him; he found his mawkish displays of paternal pride embarrassing, he had nothing in common with him, and he never sought his company.

Christy, meanwhile, enjoyed his school, not so much for the education as for the opportunity to pit his wits and his strength against the other boys. In the subjects and games that interested him he excelled, and in those that did not he made no effort at all.

Despite his father's relative wealth, at least in terms of assets, Christy Pyon was given the minimum pocket money, and this took the edge off his influence over the other boys in the school. He knew that it was futile to ask his father for more and resented the idea of asking his mother. Instead, he took to spending his school holidays shooting and netting rabbits by the score and selling them through a sympathetic farmer, who also disposed of the pelts of the foxes he trapped in the woods. He soon found that with a little self-denial and a lot of hard work, he could return to school at the beginning of the term with a lot of money in his pocket. This gave him an additional, gratifying confidence and put him in an insuperable position.

When Christy was twelve, his father went to spend a few days fishing on the Wye, which was swelled by late spring rain. They were told afterwards that he must have had a great deal to drink with his lunch. The ghillie said that he had suggested that it would be better not to fish with the river in such a spate, but had been dismissed with a curse, to watch the fisherman lurch out across the white water to the quieter, deeper pool where the salmon should have been resting up.

Jack Pyon had slipped, disappeared beneath the water and, by the time the ghillie reached him, had gasped his lungs full of water.

Christy and his mother wore black. The vicar tried to think of something nice to say. The gathered locals looked solemn and mouthed the traditional condolences. But no one really cared, no one was going to miss Jack Pyon.

Christy was appalled and shamed by his own lack of grief, but nothing that he could say to himself evoked any sense of bereavement. He was not an unkind boy and though his father had held little interest for him, he wanted to feel that Jack Pyon's life had provided at least a little inspiration for him. Fervently, he prayed at Mass for his father's soul and for forgiveness for not feeling more sadness.

His mother did not let him see that she was struggling with similar problems. She treated her husband's grave with a calm piety whose source was more a sense of Christian duty than any sense of loss. Her principal private emotion was relief. She assuaged her guilt to some extent by persuading herself that, in the thirteen years she had known him, she had at least given Jack Pyon a little happiness which no one else had been prepared to give.

A few weeks after the funeral, Maeve quietly told Christy that Jack Pyon had not been his natural father. The boy's first reaction was also relief, but in his case because it excused his lack of interest in Jack Pyon. And then he was curious.

But Maeve said, "Christy, I'll never tell you who your father is. He doesn't know and you'll never know. It would only cause unhappiness and disrupt other people's lives. But you will meet your grandmother at last. Now that Jack is dead, I can ask her to stay. I never wanted to before. She would never have understood why I married him."

Christy loved the sixty-year-old Irishwoman from the first moment he met her. She was the widow of a struggling smallholder and had the wisdom, patience and humour that came from facing up squarely to the task of raising thirteen children in rural penury.

His grandmother asked Christy if he would like to come and stay in her cottage on the western slopes of the Wicklow mountains. He happily agreed, and in the summer holiday before his first term at public school, he went by train and ferry to be met in Rosslare by a large, red-faced and almost incomprehensible uncle.

Christy felt an immediate affinity with his Irish relations and tried to understand why his mother had kept him from them for so long. When he came back to England to his new Benedictine school, he felt as if he had a completely new identity. He enjoyed this; he relished the sensation of being an outsider on the inside. He felt free to choose which aspects of his two cultures he should adopt and soon developed a reputation for being a formidable eccentric.

The gentle monks did their best with this elusive boy, but

realised that he would learn thoroughly only what he wanted to, and ignore what he did not.

He had learned not to abuse his strength and influence among the other boys and only got into trouble for periodic, unauthorised visits to Hereford races and the illegal bookmaker in the narrow street at the back of the city hall.

His visits to Ireland became a regular feature in his life, giving him an enthusiasm for steeplechasing and gambling, and a definite Irish lilt to his newly-broken voice.

Maeve blossomed. She was still in her mid-thirties and in complete possession of the house and its land. Typically, Jack Pyon had died intestate. Distant relations had made specious claims on Jack's estate, but Maeve had calmly and sweetly repelled them. There was, after all, a perfectly eligible heir. Despite the compromise and dishonesty she had been forced to use as a young woman, she was not hard, but she was very tough. She evoked the respect of the neighbouring farmers who could only admire the astuteness with which she ran her affairs. Slowly, she had been accepted among the normally reticent, Anglo-Celtic Herefordians.

Christy, though, was too much for them. His confidence and cleverness, his assumed Irishness did not appeal to them. They could not deny that he shot well, rode well and was a first-class rugger player – outwardly an impressive young man. But they could not trust him.

The boy was indifferent to this. He was protected against pressure from his peers by the cloak of dual nationality. He extracted from his position as the heir to a large, profitable farm only those aspects which appealed to him. He had become good at providing himself with an income by bold, judicious gambling at the races and by using an instinctive eye for a horse. His opinion of what made a good hunter and his ability to bargain down to the lowest threshold had made him steady and increasing profits since his mid-teens. He became a regular sight at horse sales for miles around, often cadging a lift home for himself and any new purchase he had made. He made his own decisions about everything he did and was influenced by nobody except his mother.

She perceived in him a growing restlessness and ambitiousness that she knew would be hard to contain. She made it clear to him that she intended to carry on running the farm for the foreseeable future, and as the end of his schooldays drew near, she encouraged him to think about an alternative career to farming, at least for a few years.

It was obvious that the uneven quality of his performance at sixth-form subjects would not lead on to university. The monks sadly told Maeve that they felt they had failed to help Christy achieve anything like his true potential. But she understood and assured them that they could have done nothing more with him than they had.

Two months before his eighteenth birthday, Christy left school with a few O-levels and one A-level in English to his name.

This had no bearing on his plans. He had no intention of settling down to be his mother's assistant on the farm. He was quite happy for her to go on running it for as long as she liked.

Before he committed himself to agricultural ties in a remote, sleepy English county, he wanted to see a lot more of the world.

Christy in London

When Christy Pyon arrived in London, shortly after leaving school, he brought with him the addresses of one or two school friends in the shabby but genteel surroundings of South Kensington.

He also had a name and address in Kilburn, a district of north-west London where the recent waves of fortune-seeking Irishmen had settled. A week after booking into a clean, pretty guest house, overlooking the Regent's Canal in Little Venice, he ventured up the broad avenues of Maida Vale towards the less inviting prospect of Kilburn.

A few hungry mongrels skulked between rusting pre-war cars which lined the run-down street. The trees which had been optimistically planted by a late-Victorian developer stood at irregular intervals now along the cracked and pitted pavement. They looked forlorn and abused in their scruffy autumn clothing.

There were grassless little patches of littered garden in front of the long terrace of five-storey houses. Chunks of Dutch-looking ornamentation were falling away from the gables and window mullions of the grimy red-brick buildings.

In a ground-floor bed-sitting-room, a man in baggy gaberdine trousers and an old army singlet heard the sound of firm footfalls outside in the Sunday morning quiet. He propped himself up on the bed where he lay and shook his head a couple of times to clear the effects of last night's stout. The footsteps stopped outside his window, then clicked up the worn stone steps to the front door. After an interval during which the visitor must have been examining the confusion of names by the doorbells, there was a loud clattering on the broken bell in the front bed-sitter. The occupant scowled and heaved himself off the bed to the window. He twitched aside the tablecloth that was pinned up to serve as a curtain and inspected his unwelcome intruder.

Brian Nolan did not immediately recognise the tall young man who stood on the top step, glancing around impatiently, but the handsome features and bright blue eyes seemed familiar. His visitor was unmistakably Irish and, therefore, unlikely to be from any bothersome official body. Though still slightly mistrustful of the expensive-looking coat and broad-brimmed fedora that the man wore, Nolan tugged on a dirty checked lumberjack shirt and padded barefoot out into the hall. He opened the front door twelve inches and focused his bleary eyes on a beaming face.

"Well?" he asked with more aggression than he felt.

"Brian, is it? Brian Nolan?" the young man asked.

"It is. And who are you?"

The young man extended a hand.

"I'm your cousin, Christy, for God's sake. I've been out to stay with our grandmother in Wicklow. I met you there. Have you forgotten?"

With a reciprocal grin, Nolan opened the door wider to invite his cousin in.

"B'Jaysus, but you were a little fella the last time I saw you. What's happened to you since? You look as though you just won the Irish Sweeps Derby." He stopped, recollecting that this was his rich relation, the half-English son of his Auntie Maeve.

Christy Pyon stepped through the shabby door and followed his cousin into a room full of discarded clothing and unfinished meals of fish and chips.

Christy ignored the squalor.

"I didn't win the Irish Sweeps, but I'd a twenty-to-one winner at Ally Pally yesterday."

Brian Nolan was impressed. "Did you, by God?" He shook his head. "I wish to hell I had."

"I heard a whisper," Christy explained.

"That's what you need. If you hear another, would you ever let your cousin know, for God's sake."

"Sure I will. I hope you don't mind me coming round to see you. I've been living down at Little Venice for a week and I thought I should look up a few of my relations, and I thought, Sunday morning, I might catch you."

"Quite right. Just hang on a moment, and I'll get meself dressed and we'll go and have a couple of pints. There's not a lot to offer you here, I'm afraid."

Christy sat in a rickety chair while Nolan ran a blunt razor over his chin and swapped his singlet for a clean white shirt that he miraculously found in a drawer. Before they left, Nolan said tentatively, "I'm not really in funds this mornin', and though the landlord of the pub's a fine sort of a Wexford man, he'll not advance a lot of credit."

"You don't have to worry about that," Christy said expansively. "The drinks are on me."

They walked a few hundred yards up to Kilburn High Road and into a saloon the size of a barn. The doors had only just been opened and it was almost deserted. The air was still thick with the stale smell of the previous night's spillage and the consumption of several thousand cheap cigarettes.

Christy ordered them a pint each of stout and they stood at the bar to drink it.

"Well, Brian, what are you doing here in London?" Christy asked.

"I'm on the buildings, like everyone else round here."

"Why is everyone on the buildings?"

Nolan shrugged. "You know how it is. You like to work with your own kind. The money's not great but there's usually work."

"Who do you work for, then?"

"Sort of an agency. There's a sharp little fella called Newberry that a lot of us work for. Well, we don't exactly work for him, but he finds us the work and pays us by the hour. If there's no work, he pays what he calls a retainer, which isn't much."

"How much does he charge his customers for your time, then?"

Nolan shrugged. "Jesus, I wouldn't know."

"But it might be twice as much as you're getting."

"It might or it might not, but it suits me."

"Are there a lot of you working for this fella?"

"Sure, hundreds. Irish, Poles, Blacks, all sorts."

"Did you ever try to get a bigger wage out of this man Newberry?"

Nolan shook his head. "There's no point in rocking the boat. If you complain, he just gives you no more work."

"Not if you all complained at once. How many of you are Irish?"

"Sixty or seventy, I should think."

"All builders?"

"Sure. Brickies, chippies, hoddies and such."

Christy looked at him speculatively for a moment. "Would you have another drink?" he asked.

Nolan nodded, and glanced down the long bar to where two other men, similar to himself, had propped themselves.

"Are they friends of yours?" Christy asked.

"Sure."

Christy turned to them. "Would you join me for a drink?" he called.

They grinned their acceptance and moved up the bar to Christy and his cousin. Brian Nolan introduced them.

"Christy thinks we should ask for more money."

They shook their heads.

"We've tried once, but it's tricky, y'know. We're not contributing a lot to Her Majesty's coffers," one said.

"Sure, Newberry's got us by the balls."

"That's where you're wrong. I'll bet he needs you as much as you need him. Only you must act together."

"He won't have no union bullshit."

"You don't have to be in a union to wield a bit of influence. Now, how about telling me all about it, and maybe I could be your representative, and twist his arm a little."

The three men appraised him. He was young, but looked as though he had plenty of money, and he had undeniable presence.

Brian Nolan said thoughtfully, "The young fella had a twenty-to-one winner yesterday, with a bit of information, wasn't it?"

Christy nodded.

The builders acknowledged the value of sources of such practical information. To find and nurture them showed experience beyond this boy's years.

"Tell us how you'd go about representin' us, then."

On the buildings

At twenty-five, Ken Newberry had all the self-confidence that a hard upbringing in the East End of London could give. He was not a big man, but he had always been sharper than his peers. Where they used muscle, he used guile and it had not taken him long to work out how he could profit from their muscle.

He had built up a pool of unskilled and semi-skilled building workers and had managed to acquire contracts to supply his labourers to the larger construction companies as and when they needed them. For the days his men were working, he received at least twice what he was paying them. On the few days they were not working he paid them a pittance of a retainer. Names, addresses and taxes were largely ignored, but the system gave some kind of security to disorientated, desperate immigrants.

Of the 240 men currently on his payroll, sixty were from the Irish ghetto in Kilburn. They were the most willing and, until now, the least demanding of his workforce.

Confronting Ken Newberry in his flashy office was a well-dressed youth of eighteen. This young man, who had introduced himself with the curious-sounding name of Christy Pyon, was a lot heftier than Newberry and – disconcertingly – at least as sharp as he. What was more, he purported to represent Newberry's Irish labourers.

The Cockney entrepreneur was puzzled by the young man's voice. It lay somewhere between upper-class English and an Irish brogue. The complete confidence with which he used it was making Newberry uneasy.

"You're paying my fellas even less than the Greeks and the Blacks," Christy Pyon was telling him. "You're making a 150 per cent mark-up on their wage. That is going to stop."

"'Ere, 'oo d'you fink you are? Some Paddy trade-unionist? Those geezers are 'appy with what they're gettin'. What d'you wanna go upsettin' 'em for? Let me tell you, mush, 'ooever you are, I've got a lot of big blokes workin' for me, and there's other things besides 'ods they like chuckin' about – especially if they're on overtime."

Christy Pyon crossed his legs and leaned back in an uncomfortable, "contemporary" chair opposite Newberry. He smiled and his bright blue eyes glinted beneath dark brows.

"You're a sharp, eager little fella, aren't you? But you're not very sophisticated. And making money – big money – is a sophisticated business. I'll not ask you again what you're going to do about the terms and conditions of the men I represent, because I can see that you're too dumb to realise that you have to do anything." Pyon slowly uncrossed his legs, stood, put his hands on Newberry's desk and leaned across it. "My men are no longer working for you. From now on, they're employed by me." From his inside breast pocket, he took a business card and put it on the desk. "There's my address. If you ever want a job, I could probably find room for you in my organisation."

He straightened himself, smiled with a sideways nod of his head and left Newberry's office for the taxi he had asked to wait in the street outside.

Newberry watched him go with astonishment. He was used to settling business differences with a lot of swearing and a bit of violence. But this big, soft-spoken man was obviously sure of the loyalty of the Irishmen, traditionally the most useful in a brawl. Newberry realised that he was up against a new type of adversary.

A little research had shown Christy Pyon how much money Newberry was making. And he was confident that he could do the same and better, especially with the natural support of his fellow Irishmen.

It was only a matter of shortening the margins, by upping wages and lowering charges, to take the business away from Newberry's operation. Then he would offer a better service, be more selective about the men he took on, until such time as he was strong enough to expand and start making proper money.

He financed the operation by asking the construction companies, in return for substantially lower rates, to pay him by the day, while persuading the workforce that while they were to get higher wages, they would have them a week in arrears. To persuade them, he used the simple expedient of telling them the truth, explaining why it was necessary. The Irishmen listened; he spoke their language, drank Guinness and Paddys and seemed to know a lot about the horses. Some of them – those that still went – even saw him at Mass; they trusted him.

Within weeks not only the Irish but most of Newberry's workforce whom Pyon thought usable had come across for the bigger wages. Pyon widened the geographical area of his operation, using empty vegetable lorries returning from Covent Garden, or any other transport he could find to deliver men to the sites. He drummed up business from dozens of new customers, until he reached a point where he seldom had to pay a man his retainer for doing nothing.

He had taken a gamble, using no one's money but his own, and it was beginning to pay off. After six months of struggling and juggling his bank balance, working sixteen hours a day to arrange the most efficient use of his labour force, Pyon knew that he was succeeding.

He was more certain of this when, one sunny Monday morning, he watched Ken Newberry walk through the gates of his yard in Kilburn and pick his way across the clutter of vans and tools to a Nissen hut that was now Pyon's office.

The corrugated "sausage-roll" hut had been partitioned to provide a reception area where Pyon's indefatigable secretary greeted visitors as if they were arriving for an audience with an ambassador.

Newberry could not stop himself responding to this formality. Even in these surroundings, Pyon managed to create an atmosphere of energy and power. And the loyalty displayed by the people around him did not escape Newberry. The idea of hitching his star to this man – at least for a while – was beginning to make real sense.

Pyon rose from his chair behind a large oak table which he had found abandoned on one of the sites where his men were working. He walked round to welcome the small cockney. Newberry tried not to shrink before Pyon's gaze.

"Morning, Ken. I was hoping you might drop round one of these days. No hard feelings any more?"

It was three months since they had communicated.

"No." Ken waved his hand dismissively. "Water under the bridge. Know what I mean?"

"Of course I do. I'm sure you've had other fish to fry."

"S'matter of fact, I 'ave. I've got a couple of building contracts that you'll never get near."

Pyon raised an eyebrow, prepared to write this off as an idle boast.

"Yeah, Council job. They only give out these sort of jobs to their own, you know, those of us who knows the score."

"You mean you've bought the job?"

"That's right."

Pyon pondered the plausibility of this. He had certainly never been able to get close to any Council work in the East End of London, where there were still a lot of bomb sites to fill, and where a special kind of relationship was important in securing contracts.

He shrugged. "Well, I'll only buy the jobs off you if there's any margin left."

"Don't you worry about that, mush. There's plenty of margin left. That's the point of the deal. And I'm not trying to sell 'em."

"But you can't do them yourself. You've no workforce to speak of."

"Nah," Newberry agreed. "But you have. And I think you might be interested in talking about what you could call a joint venture."

Pyon laughed. "You mean, in return for your aiming them at me, you want a job?"

"No, Christy. When you see the size of 'em, I think you'll see why I'm talkin' about a partnership."

Besides calling on his cousin in Kilburn, Pyon had also followed up contacts at some more respectable addresses in Kensington. He was welcomed because he was a goodlooking young man with a lot of charm and it did not take him long to push through this first wave of contacts to find other young men who enjoyed the same pace of life and provocative dialogue as he did, as well as girls and gambling. And he had the energy to put in a frantic, demanding day's work before enjoying himself into the early hours of most mornings.

But all the time he was cautious with the money his business was beginning to make. His social pleasures were either free or funded by his gambling. He had found others, partial kindred spirits, who were close to the centre of the racing world and who were happy to pass on information that took much of the risk from betting on horses.

One gloomy Saturday morning he woke with his heart pounding. The quality of information he had received the previous night made him as certain as it was ever possible to be that all the jockeys in that day's novice hurdle at Newbury had planned a result to their own private advantage. He called on the willing services of twenty of his workforce to help him out. Each of them was despatched to individual bookmakers, right across London, each with instructions to place a bet of £100 pounds to win, at the prevailing price of sixteen-to-one, just before the off.

For the first time in his life, he felt nervous as he sat in his office listening to the race on an old bakelite wireless on top of a filing cabinet on the far side of the room. It was his biggest gamble to date, and even though he knew the result was pre-ordained, the chosen horse could still fall and cost him two thousand pounds.

It was a two-mile race. Ken Newberry walked into the office when the horses were two furlongs from home.

Newberry switched off the wireless.

"Look, Christy, what the hell's going on? Why aren't Barney and his blokes working?"

Pyon leaped to his feet and crossed the room to turn the wireless back on. Newberry stood in his way.

"Christy, come on. What's going on? What are you up to?"

"Get the fuck out of the way. I was listening to a race carrying a lot of my money." Pyon reached past him and turned on the radio just in time to hear the announcer give the name of the horse who had come third.

"For God's sake, Ken, what'd you do that for? Now I don't know if my bloody animal won or not."

"Never mind your bloody punting. Why aren't those geezers working?"

"It's Saturday, Ken."

"Yeah, but they always work Saturday morning."

"Well, not this morning. They were doing a little job for me."

"Placin' your bets, I suppose. But we've got a business to run."

Pyon grasped Newberry by the narrow lapels of his heavily slubbed wool jacket. "Don't you ever tell me what to do. And don't you forget who invited you in. The lads have a right to Saturdays off if they want. I've had twenty of 'em all over town, fifty slobs apiece if the horse came in. And now, for Christ sake, I've got to find out if we won."

Pyon had lifted Newberry on to his tiptoes. He let him drop back on his heels and stormed out of the hut. Two red-faced, stout men were running into the yard.

"Well?" Pyon yelled.

"He did it, Guv'nor! Didn't you hear? He fockin' did it!"

Within the hour, all Pyon's runners had returned with the winnings – £32,000. Each of the twenty men took their £50, and the drinks at the cavernous pub in Kilburn were all on Pyon that night. Ken Newberry, deflated, came with them, and grudgingly acknowledged Pyon's win.

Pyon, big-hearted, put an arm around his shoulder. "D'you see, it was worth it? These fellas will be loyal fellas for a long time to come. Worth losing half a day's work for that, don't you think?"

"Sure, but s'posin' the nag hadn't won?"

Pyon's bright, young eyes shone with unassailable confidence. "But he did, Ken, or I wouldn't have backed him, would I?"

As a result of the novice race at Newbury, Pyon bought a small house in a picturesque mews off the Brompton Road and gradually became a familiar sight around Knightsbridge and Chelsea.

Despite their mothers' misgivings, debutantes were keen to secure him for their parties, and after just two years in London, he was already something of a personality.

In the meantime, his business expanded. Off the back of the Council jobs that Ken Newberry had brought in, Pyon started his own small building company, largely involved in converting dilapidated West Kensington houses into flats, but also able to tender for small commercial contracts. He was not in a position to compete with most of his clients, who were the major companies, and he was careful to avoid that kind of conflict of interest while the labour supply business was still his main activity. But that would not be the case for ever.

Since Ken Newberry had joined Pyon, he had become a very useful lieutenant. Pyon had recognised his uses at their first confrontation in Newberry's office. And Newberry had reluctantly realised that Pyon had the confidence and charisma to open doors he could never open himself. They were not friends in any social sense, but they knew they

needed each other. At the same time, Newberry had prag-
matically accepted his position as second fiddle. They made
a formidable team.

Liz

At the same time as Maria Pyon was boarding a private jet
in Sardinia, and Maeve Pyon was pondering her son's career
from her Herefordshire manor house, another woman was
staring at the photograph in the *Daily Mail*.

She was sitting on a sofa in the traditionally decorated
first-floor drawing-room of a large Mayfair house. The faint
noise of London's morning traffic reached her down the quiet,
private mews in which the house stood. From the back of the
house she could hear the plaintive sound of Andean pan-pipes
and a Colombian harp on a record-player, signalling that
Laura was awake. She contemplated with trepidation Laura's
reaction to this new development in the bizarre life of a
father of whom she deeply disapproved, and whom she
deeply loved.

In the quiet house, Elizabeth Pyon remained seated and
gazed at the photo of her ex-husband; her ex-husband who
still treated her like his wife when he saw her, and whom
it seemed impossible to replace. She was waiting for their
daughter to finish showering and dressing, and dreading the
inevitable phone-call from their son, Julian. God knows, she
thought, it was Julian's fault that Christy had been at such a
public event as the Cannes Film Festival, but, she supposed,
she could hardly blame Julian for the beautiful Mauritian girl
on Pyon's arm. Nor for the one-sided smile which she had
first seen thirty years before.

Liz had first spoken to Christy Pyon at a summer ball
at a gloomy Victorian mansion in Northamptonshire. The
grandson of the industrialist who had built it had been bullied
by his wife into tearing himself away from his racehorses, his

estate and his shoot to host the ball. His two daughters, like
a pair of affable spaniels, had been well-schooled and were
now ready to go out and retrieve what they could. Most of
the young men whom they had met that season, and who
had been invited to the ball were proving to be unwilling
quarry.

Christy Pyon, though, felt sorry for them. He knew them
both from the race-courses which they frequented with their
father. They had even once or twice given him useful tips.
They were only too glad of his attention, and it had not
escaped Pyon's notice that if one spent a bit of time with the
less attractive girls, the more attractive ones were inclined to
muster, just to show off their advantage.

Elizabeth Wolesley had also observed this, but she could
not bring herself to attract his attention too obviously.

She was having a tolerable time of it, but the whole
archaic ritual of the Season was beginning to pall on her.
The only thing that lifted this event was the presence of
Christy Pyon.

She had not really met Christy. She had been on the fringe
of conversations where he was the centre, and had been
attracted by his unconventionality, and the racy reputation
that preceded him. Already, most of the mothers had tried
to have him expunged from the list of suitable young men
to entertain, but their wilful daughters had for the most part
prevailed.

She was determined that evening, if she could, to be noticed
by him.

She was lucky, and ready to make use of a well-tested
ploy when the chance was offered. She was returning from
the cloakroom, on her own, stumbling on high heels along a
corridor of woven hessian matting towards the main marquee,
when she saw him, also alone, walking straight towards her.
It took very little to decide to allow her shawl to slip from
her shoulders, just before he reached her.

Christy saw the garment fall and dived for it with exaggerated gallantry. He swept it up and wrapped it round her
with an almost imperceptible squeeze of her shoulders.

"I'm glad it wasn't just a handkerchief you dropped."

She looked into his smiling eyes, and knew that he knew

she had done it deliberately. But he was smiling, not laughing at her.

"Thanks," she said, and, with a burst of confidence, "You're Christy Pyon, aren't you?"

"I certainly am. And you're Liz Wolesley."

"Good Lord! How did you know?"

"I asked, of course. You don't think I happened to be out here by chance, do you?"

Liz could scarcely believe that this dashing figure had actively sought her out, and abruptly, her confidence left her. She could think of nothing to say.

"Come on," Christy said, "I'll take you back to the party." In a parody of an old-fashioned gesture, he offered her his arm and led her back to the glittering swirl of the marquee.

Pyon's ability to carry off such gallantry with flamboyance was one of his attractions for many of the girls; that and his apparent indifference to the impression he made on any of them.

Liz, at nineteen, was no different in her reaction. Like the other girls who had done this Season with her, she had thought she knew as much as there was to know about men. In fact, she had really only been exposed to those from a very narrow seam of society: young Guards officers; rich undergraduates, still up at Oxford; conventional sons of landowners, trying to justify their inheritance by spending a few years at Cirencester Agricultural College.

Although Christy Pyon was the same age as these, he seemed to Elizabeth to be on an altogether higher plane. He knew more, was more commanding and the brightness of his eyes was much more confidently erotic.

Sitting with her at a table, after her daring attempt to rock'n'roll in an ankle-length dress of silk moire, he fixed these eyes on her and talked about her, always flirting and flattering her with his special charm.

They danced once more – a smoochy shuffle – and Liz felt his warm, bristly cheek against her, but he made no attempt to make more serious physical overtures. And afterwards, to her disappointment, he made no effort to arrange to see her again.

But as the summer wore on, she met him on several more occasions, and their conversation would continue where it had left off the previous time. Between these encounters, awkward soldiers would mumble down the phone to ask her to dinner and the sons of earls would bark invitations to country balls, but all she wanted to hear was Christy Pyon's soft, deep voice. He did not ring, though, or turn up on the doorstep of her father's house in Mulberry Walk, Chelsea. She knew she was pretty, but she began to think she was just too innocent and naive for Christy Pyon – and she longed to show him that she was not.

Since first seeing her, Pyon had marked Liz Wolesley for himself. She was beautiful in a classic, Anglo-Saxon way, but she had the enthusiasm and the sense of humour of a Celt. He was captivated by her naivety and her openness; it was so complementary to his own more worldly outlook. He made up his mind that he wanted her, but he was reluctant to frighten her by overwhelming her. He was sure they would have plenty of opportunities to meet without his having to specifically arrange it; at cocktail parties, dances, Royal Ascot and nightclubs.

Each time he saw her, he was more sure of his own feelings, but he was still not completely confident that she reciprocated, and he wanted no chance of a rebuff. Without seeking it, he learned a bit about her. At school she had had academic ambitions which her father, the holder of an early nineteenth-century barony, had not encouraged; she had a large number of eager, pursuing admirers, none of whom were alleged to have achieved the ultimate conquest of her.

Pyon was not concerned about her nobility or her virginity. He was too aware of the more fundamental and valuable qualities of his mother to rate such things highly. Elizabeth Wolesley sensed this and felt confident that she was right to have fallen in love with him.

Several months after Pyon had first met Elizabeth, he was asked to a private view of an exhibition of surrealist paintings by a young Greek artist. He had already bought a few cheap works by unknowns and, though not an obvious buyer, he was the sort of energetic, striking young man that people liked to have at their gallery parties.

The unexpected sight of Elizabeth Wolesley, youthfully elegant and quite at home among the half-smart, half-bohemian throng, was all he needed finally to decide to take the initiative.

He grabbed a glass of warm champagne from a table by the entrance and politely pushed his way through to her.

"Hello," he said simply, smiling at her with his intense blue eyes.

She could not avoid showing her pleasure at seeing him.

"I'm going to ask you something which you are not allowed to refuse," he went on, and was about to specify his demand when she broke in.

"It's okay. I'll have dinner with you," she laughed. "And about time too."

They left quite soon, only interested in being with each other now. Pyon drove them in his Jaguar to a small old-fashioned French restaurant in Dean Street, Soho. Over a red-checked tablecloth, guttering candle and bottles of Burgundy, they talked in the way they had both been wanting to since they had first met.

Elizabeth told Pyon about her new job.

"You know I told you I wanted to go into journalism, well, I'm a full-time scribbler now," she said with pride. "Of course, it's not exactly hard-nosed Fleet Street stuff – just fashion and gossip for *Queen* magazine."

"It's a start," said Pyon, pleased by her enthusiasm. "Where's it going to go from there?"

"Writing leaders for *The Times*, I expect."

"I don't think I'd like to go to bed with a *Times* leader writer."

"Oh. All right then, I'll tell them I won't do it." She smiled back at him, her mind made up.

Pyon could barely control himself. Their main course had not yet arrived, but he wanted to leap up and take Elizabeth home right then.

But she laughed and said, "I think we'd better have dinner first." And they did not need to talk about it again.

Pyon wanted to tell her about his plans, not to impress

her, but because he had never felt able to tell anyone else about them.

"I feel," he said without conceit, "that I have a certain ability to influence people and their lives which I should not abuse."

"I don't really see you as a Winston Churchill or a Harold Macmillan," Elizabeth remarked. "And anyway, why should you want to influence people?"

"That I couldn't say for sure. Maybe it's genetic, or something in my childhood, but I just feel that I need to influence people. It's not vanity. It's more like a vocation. There seem to me to be several ways of fulfilling this calling. For instance, it could be done on a one-to-one basis, but I'm not talking about that; to be frank, I don't think I'm very interested in individuals. Of course, I'm interested in you, and my mother, and my relations in Ireland. But I can't seem to whip up much enthusiasm for individuals I don't know – I'd be a lousy doctor or priest."

"That sounds awfully selfish."

"Maybe it is," he shrugged, "but I'm trying to be honest. I hate bullshit. But I am interested in people in general, people *en masse*, as it were, who need direction."

"So you want to be a politician, and tell people what they ought to be doing?"

Pyon shook his head. "No, I don't. I want to show them the options, help them make up their minds, and point out the ways of achieving their objectives."

"But you're only twenty. What makes you think that *you* know the options and which are right and how to realise them?"

"I don't – yet. Not all of them, but I think that I will."

"It all sounds rather arrogant to me, but you seem to know heaps more than most of the young twits I meet."

"Well, that's something. But I don't want to be a politician. There are several ways in which you can influence large numbers of fellow citizens, if you're that way inclined. Politics is one, but there are also the arts, entertainment and business."

"The arts and entertainment I'll accept, especially with

television becoming so important, but how can you do it through business?"

"There are thousands of ways. For a start, the products you make and sell, or, in my case, the structures I build. And then again, if you're running a business that provides a pay packet for several thousand people, you have a very direct influence on a lot of lives. Also, if you achieve that level of success, people are bound to believe that you know something they don't. If I were to become an employer on that scale, the deployment of my resources could have a major impact, even in a nation of fifty million. And it could be absolutely critical in some small African country."

"But Christy," Elizabeth was looking at him bemused, "do you mean all this? Are you really that ambitious? You don't seem sort of . . . serious enough."

He laughed. "I'm serious about it, all right, but that doesn't mean I don't enjoy a bit of fun, and you and I, we're going to have a lot of fun together."

That night, it was fun. It was tenderness; it was mutual, sublime enjoyment. Christy was gentle, thoughtful, eager for her always to remember that first time with happiness and elation.

For Pyon, it was the fulfilment of an aim from which nothing could have kept him. His dynamism and ambition were nourished and grew on the achieving of it. His confidence, already considerable, seemed to reach out and touch the people he dealt with every day. And having been asked aboard, Elizabeth was happy to ride with him.

Marriage

Lord and Lady Barnstaple, Elizabeth's parents, however, were less happy. On the face of it, there was not much in Christy Pyon to which they could seriously object. Paternally, at least, he came from a worthy old family. And although his mother's origins were obscurely humble, her looks and the respect with which, they were told, she was regarded by her Herefordian neighbours tended to discount that.

Christy would inherit the small estate, and while his involvement in the building industry seemed rather disreputable, he was clearly able to look after his finances.

But there was something vaguely alarming about the young man's manner which was exaggerated by his Irish lilt and his way with words. He was polite, certainly – all their friends thought him charming and good company. Somehow, though, he seemed to be laughing at them. He was too much in control of himself for his twenty years. And he was altogether too un-English. Added to that, he was a Catholic. Although the Barnstaples had several quite eminent Catholic acquaintances, and the daughters of some of their friends had married Catholics, they maintained a nineteenth-century Tory mistrust of popery.

They had met Christy Pyon several times. Once he had spent a weekend at Nethercombe, the Barnstaple family home in Somerset. He had shot superbly and earned grudging respect from Lord Barnstaple in spite of declaring that he had first taught himself to shoot by hunting rabbits and foxes for pocket-money.

But when Pyon, with his tongue not entirely in his cheek, invited Elizabeth's father to have lunch with him, Lord Barnstaple arrived at their rendezvous in the Turf Club feeling helpless against the inevitable course of events.

"Remember," Elizabeth had said, "he hates foreign food." And Pyon had booked a table at Simpson's in the Strand.

The two men, having greeted each other warily, managed to keep up a reasonably lively, general conversation until, when they had eaten most of their roast beef, Pyon decided to bring their meeting round to its point.

"The reason I asked you to lunch, Lord Barnstaple," he said, "apart from the pleasure of hearing your views on current affairs, was that I wanted you to be the first to know that Liz and I are planning to get married."

Lord Barnstaple did not speak at once. He concentrated on a thick slice of bloody meat, before gazing around and observing, it seemed, to the room in general, "It's odd how throughout history women have been attracted to shits."

Pyon had been expecting some reaction of this kind, and smiled. He did not say anything, but refilled their glasses from a bottle of Château Latour.

Lord Barnstaple looked embarrassed. "I'm sorry. That must have sounded rather rude. I was thinking about men like Byron."

"Byron was a clever, goodlooking fella. I don't mind being compared to him," Pyon said lightly.

"No, really. I'm sorry. I must admit that I foresaw this conversation, but I'm afraid I've rather got off on the wrong foot."

"As poor old Byron must have done quite frequently," Pyon remarked.

"Quite." Lord Barnstaple tried to laugh. "What I wanted to say was that a lot of marriages between two young, attractive people often go wrong very quickly."

"If a marriage is going to go wrong, it seems to me that it's better it should do so quickly. But I have no intention of letting ours go wrong. I have no doubts at all about it, nor has Liz."

"I don't believe she has," Lord Barnstaple reluctantly agreed. "But you're both so young. How can you be so sure? I don't know much about your business, but you're obviously ambitious, and in my experience, ambitious types need constant change."

"Lord Barnstaple, I don't know what I can say to reassure you. I can only give you my most solemn word that I will never, ever, let your daughter down."

Barnstaple sighed and gave a resigned smile. "The days of a father being able to coerce his daughter in the matter of marriage are well past. So, though I am doubtful – I'm sorry to be so personal – Marjorie and I will do our best to be optimistic about it. I know Marjorie will enjoy arranging a wedding at Nethercombe.

"Curiously enough," he went on, "it will be the first time for about fifty years. Most of my aunts and great-aunts ran away to marry."

The marriage between Mr Christy Pyon and the Honourable Elizabeth Wolesley was well attended and well reported in gossip columns and glossy magazines. Pyon was portrayed as a glamorous playboy, better known for a couple of spectacular gambling coups than for the hard work and steady nerves that had created an already noteworthy young company.

In a way, this image suited Pyon. It tended to wrong-foot people with whom he might be negotiating for the first time; they underestimated his fierce competitiveness and direct, uncluttered approach to business.

At the time of his wedding, he was not really rich. His rapid expansion into the construction industry and some speculative, as yet unrealised land purchases meant that the banks had first call on most of his assets. However, he had bought – very cheaply in a rag-bag sale of dilapidated houses and bomb sites – a fine, big and very run-down Georgian house in the still unfashionable area of west Chelsea. By using his own builders for odd periods when they were uncommitted elsewhere, he slowly and economically restored the house to an enviable showpiece.

Liz, working as a part-time journalist from home and already expecting their first child, threw herself with natural flair into the project, pleasing Pyon with her enthusiasm and decisiveness.

When the house was finished a year after their marriage, it contained one floor devoted to children's rooms and nurseries, whose first occupant was due any time now.

Julian Pyon was born without problems in the autumn of 1960. His father was hugely proud of him. So were both his grandmothers. An air of tranquil domesticity descended on the house and the new family, and provided a secure background for Pyon's frantic commercial activity.

"Never buy a horse, unless . . ."

Unlike most ambitious men Christy Pyon was prepared to be patient. While he was quite ready to double-or-quit for a few hundred pounds playing backgammon, or place the occasional large bet on a near certainty, he was guarded about the extent to which he wanted to take risks in business.

He had started the business teetering on a knife-edge between his clients' payments and his workers' wages, but profits had been carefully protected, and assets had been bought on the basis he had learned several years before from the West Country horse-dealers: "Never buy a horse unless you are certain you can sell it the next day for at least what you gave for it."

In buying building sites for development, he was quite prepared to take a quick profit if a good one was offered, so he could finance his long-term projects with less reliance on the banks. He was always realistic about the limits to what could be done with his current resources.

He also knew that to achieve the really spectacular growth he wanted, he would eventually need the muscle and financial flexibility of a publicly quoted company. He gave himself four years to reach that stage.

Christy Pyon's personality continued to dominate his relationship with Ken Newberry, despite Newberry's seven years' seniority. Pyon had a way of dealing with his men that let them accept him as friend and boss. If he was on a site at the end of a day, he would often take a group of them to the nearest pub for a drink, and drop one or two of them home if they were on his way.

And, though Ken Newberry was sharp and could usually spot the flaws in a deal, he lacked Pyon's creativity. It was Pyon who saw the opportunities and new ways to exploit them. And he was never happier than when confronted with a problem.

He listened to what his builders had to say and often acted on their practical advice, which he found was usually more useful than his building surveyors'. Normally he would take a foreman and one or two of his more experienced men with him when first going to look at a job.

One morning, in the spring of 1962, Pyon drove two of his most trusted Irishmen to see a site in Bristol. He had recently bought a convertible Jaguar XK150, and was taking it out for its first long run. He removed the roof and crammed one of the bulky men into the tiny space behind the front seats.

He drove out of London on the Great West Road, and, once they were past Reading and the traffic had thinned, he opened up the throttle along the wide Bath road between Newbury and Marlborough. The builders sat ashen-faced and silent as they watched the speedometer needle hover between 120 mph and 130 mph, and the Jaguar passed all other traffic as if it were stationary.

Pyon glanced at the faces of his passengers and laughed at their distress. "Don't worry, lads, I'll look after you," he shouted above the roar of the engine and the howling wind.

The men did not speak until Pyon drew up outside the building site in the centre of Bristol. They clambered out and headed straight for a pub on the opposite side of the road.

"We'll need a drink, Christy, before we look at any bloody site," one of them shouted over his shoulder.

Pyon parked and followed them in, and found them leaning on the bar trying to regain their equilibrium.

"I'll join you," he said, and laughed as he drank a pint of Guinness with them. "I suppose you've never been faster than a donkey-cart before."

After a couple of drinks, the builders announced that they were ready to look at the job, and the three of them crossed back over the road to inspect the pit in the ground that was to become a large shop and five floors of offices.

After an hour or so of looking at plans and practical matters like access and water supply, they were ready to go.

"Right," said Pyon, "let's see if we can get back faster than we came."

"No, Christy. Me and Barney, we're not getting back in that fockin' car."

"What d'you mean? How are you going to get home to London?" Pyon laughed.

"We'll go in the train."

"Okay, if you don't want a bit of excitement."

"We don't want a bit of death."

"You'd be as safe with me as you would be in the train, but it's up to you. Get in and I'll drop you at the station."

"Thanks, Christy, but we'll walk."

Pyon looked at their set faces. "Don't you trust me, then?"

"It's not you, it's the car we don't trust."

Pyon laughed again. "All right then. I'll see you in the morning."

He leapt into his car without opening the door, and roared off towards the London road.

When he reached his office, Ken Newberry was waiting for him.

"What you done with the two paddies then?"

"They didn't like my new car, and refused to get back in when we'd finished."

"I don't bloody blame 'em. Anyway, never mind them, I've got a little problem for you. We've been offered twenty grand for that horrible site by London Bridge."

"What's the problem? Let's take it," said Pyon.

"He wants to pay half in cash."

"So? It only stands us in at ten thousand on the books. We tell the revenue we just wanted to get out and get our money back. We'll split the ten thousand cash between us."

"Yeah, sure. That's not the problem. I want to use my five grand to pay for my new house. But I'll have to show where I got it from."

"No problem at all," said Pyon. "We can get it into your account as clean as a whistle, and free of all tax."

"How?"

"When we've got the cash, I'll show you."

Three days later, Pyon and Newberry walked into London's newest and grandest casino, established in a fine early nineteenth-century building, just off Berkeley Square. The place was crammed.

"For Christ's sake, Pyon. What are we doing here? I don't

want to piss it all away." Newberry felt awkward in a dinner jacket and in an atmosphere of sophistication outside his experience.

"Don't worry. We're not going to lose anything. Well, maybe just a little. Now, go and put yourself near the end of that roulette table." He indicated the busiest and noisiest table in the room. "Bung the croupier fifty quid and ask for five-pound chips. Then just bet one at a time, anywhere you like. I'd play the evens shots; that way you'll be seen to be having a few wins. When I come and stand beside you, don't forget, you don't know me. Then just do as I've told you, okay?"

Newberry nodded doubtfully.

"I'll see you in a moment, then," Pyon said, and walked to the cashier behind his brass bars. He thrust £5,000 through the gap. "A thousand in twenties, the rest in fifties, please."

"Certainly, sir. Good luck." He pushed the piles of chips back to Pyon, who smiled with a wink, and put most of them into his pockets.

He squeezed in beside Newberry in time to see him triumphantly scoop a pile of chips off the number thirty-six which had just come up. Pyon gave his partner a quick smile of congratulation, and scattered a few chips on to the bottom end of the table. After a while, he separated out a stack of £1,000-worth of the heavy plastic tokens and pushed them a few inches towards Newberry's stack.

The croupier span again and the little silver ball jumped and jerked its way towards its destination. All eyes were on the wheel. Newberry surreptitiously slid Pyon's chips towards his own. He remained at the table for one more spin, and lost. He picked up the two piles of chips without anyone taking any notice, and wandered off to another table.

A little later, Pyon was beside him again, and the procedure was repeated. Within an hour, Pyon had transferred £5,000 to Newberry.

Beneath the shouts of a group of excited winning punters, Pyon said quickly, "Tell the cashier you want to cash them now, and that you want a cheque. Then leave and I'll see you in half an hour at the Black Sheep."

Newberry nodded, and made his way over to the brass cage.

Pyon carried on playing where he was, and to his surprise won £230 in three spins. He cashed his chips with the cashier, who commiserated.

"Not so good tonight then, sir."

"I'm afraid not, but there's always Ascot tomorrow," Pyon said with a show of boldness.

Ten minutes later, he found Ken Newberry sitting in their rendezvous – a dingy basement drinking-club – with a bottle of champagne in a bucket beside him.

"Thanks, Christy. That couldn't have gone better. I've got a cheque for five-and-a-half grand in my pocket, and no tax to pay. It's funny, isn't it, I've never even had a quid on a dog before, I always thought it was a mug's game."

"It is, Ken, and don't you forget it. Personally, I only like to bet on certainties. Still, I made a few hundred tonight. It just shows, when you don't particularly care, Lady Luck often smiles sweetest."

"I'll drink to her," said Ken, hurling the contents of a champagne glass down his throat, and the two of them spent the rest of the night between the drinking clubs of Shepherd Market. They arrived at their office next morning unshaven and still in evening dress. The two men who had been with Pyon to Bristol laughed at their condition.

"Maybe we should have come with you," one of them said. "You look as though you've done some kind of damage."

It was rare for Pyon to stay out all night, and Liz would tolerantly accept his excuse that these things were sometimes necessary for business. But generally, he liked to keep his business life and his social life in separate compartments. There was a constant stream of visitors to the Chelsea house, and to Herefordshire at weekends. Pyon had taken over one of the farmhouses on the edge of his mother's estate. He liked to go back there but he did not want his mother to feel he was putting any pressure on her.

Most of these visitors had no connection with Pyon's business. His friends' occupations or standing were irrelevant to Pyon. What mattered was that they could make him laugh, and that they held strong, well-defended opinions. In the country, some shot, some fished, some never left the house, and in London they ranged from hardened gamblers to sophisticated Jesuits.

LWPC flotation

Three years after the birth of Julian, a daughter, Laura, was born and Pyon enjoyed the completely new sensation of being father to a girl. The happiness in the household seemed set to last.

By this time Pyon was ready to invite one of the smaller merchant banks to undertake the public flotation of his group of companies.

The umbrella holding group which he had formed was called London and West Property and Construction Ltd. It consisted of twelve individual companies, including the original labour supply company which still functioned, but of which the major clients were now his other companies, and two building firms in London, one involved in medium-scale commercial building, the other in suburban house building. There was a building company in Bristol, heavily engaged in the continuing reconstruction of that city, and another in Swindon. Pyon foresaw that the drastic cuts to Britain's railway network made by Dr Beeching would lead to severe cutbacks in that West Country town's principal industry. It seemed likely to him that political pressures would demand investment in newer industries to mop up the surplus labour.

As well as these active building operations, there were a number of property development companies. One of these simply traded property, two others owned sites in London and in the West Country, and the remaining four were owned fifty per cent by Pyon's company with various partner organisations – development companies without their own building divisions who had gone into business with Pyon to provide that advantage.

The group had been built swiftly, and a lot of its projects were at the planning stage. It presented a portfolio with a wide span of potential profit.

The whole mood of the mid-sixties in Britain was optimistic and expansionist. The new Labour government, in order to finance the fulfilment of their manifesto pledges, had a deliberately loose-handed control on the money supply.

The time looked right for flotation, and Pyon took the then unusual step of appointing a public relations company to maximise its impact.

The PR people decided to concentrate their campaign around Pyon as a personality. The track records of the main companies in the group spoke well enough for themselves; what they were selling was the vast potential, and the ability of the dynamic young Christy Pyon to realise it.

While Pyon had a reputation as a bit of a gambler, a glamorous high-roller with a lovely wife, a grand house in Chelsea and a few racehorses, there was no dirt to hide. He was too young to have closets containing skeletons. Hard-nosed investment managers, generally unconcerned by such considerations, examined the figures and liked them, but even they were not uninfluenced by the photographs of the handsome young optimist.

London and West Property and Construction – LWPC – was to issue twenty million ten-shilling shares, of which eight million would be offered to the public. Ken Newberry was to receive a million shares as a result of an option deal Pyon had done with him five years before, and the partners in the half-owned development companies agreed to be bought out for a little under a million shares in the new public holding company.

Pyon would retain the balance and overall control.

The shares were offered at fifteen shillings, and the issue was comfortably over-subscribed. When they hit the open market, they traded at more than a pound.

The flotation coincided with Pyon's twenty-sixth birthday and he held a dual celebration at a recently-opened nightclub in Berkeley Square. He and Liz were snapped by press photographers leaving together at three in the morning, with their arms around each other and laughing. The caption in the evening paper next day read: "Christy Pyon celebrates his £10 million birthday present." Editors knew that the public liked the freewheeling, exuberant young entrepreneur, who seemed to symbolise a re-awakened British confidence.

The public and many professional investors may have approved of Pyon, but for an entrenched section of the City and the establishment he was altogether too young, too ebullient for their taste. He played too hard, worked too hard and was too forthright. And in spite of his apparently English background, they did not trust his flamboyant Irishness.

In certain county halls he had not endeared himself by refusing to subscribe to any of the practices which surrounded planning and public building matters.

When he tendered for a contract to build a hospital or a school he made sure that the public knew the details and figures. This made it a lot harder for the committees to take covert decisions which might have favoured other vested interests. When he met obstacles, he supplied welcome ammunition to the opposition party, whichever that may have been, in the county councils.

So it was with quiet satisfaction that those who disapproved of Pyon read the newspaper headlines only six weeks after the public flotation of his company.

"PLAYBOY PYON IN MAJOR TAX FIDDLE," yelled the popular press. "LWPC under investigation for PAYE irregularities," announced the serious papers.

Pyon had done nothing more than to continue Ken Newberry's original, and perfectly legal, practice of treating the men in his workforce as self-employed. These men represented 80 per cent of the labour on all his building sites. They were responsible for paying their own taxes, and very few of them did.

The headlines caused an instant, severe tumble in LWPC's share price. Commentators who, a few weeks before, had been lauding Pyon's energy and enterprise were now castigating him for dishonourable, unpatriotic practices.

Swiftly, fuelled by rival interests and envy, there was

a transformation of Pyon's reputation from acceptable freewheeler to reprehensible buccaneer.

Pyon defended himself in an outspoken television interview in which he pointed out that he had merely made use of a loophole in the tax laws and that every business in the country made use of loopholes if they were aware of their existence and knew how to. He claimed that he was the victim of hypocritical envy and that if parliament changed what, he conceded, was an unsatisfactory law, he would of course comply with it.

But the damage was done.

Pyon was branded in public as a rogue and pirate and he knew that the English, having been offered a hero who had then been transformed into a villain, would be reluctant to forgive him.

Pyon's only close connection in the British establishment was his father-in-law, Lord Barnstaple who, to Pyon's surprise, stayed loyal. Most of his friends remained loyal too, though there was a marked decrease in the number of invitations dropping through the letterbox of his Chelsea house.

Liz made no pretence of understanding the details of her husband's business, but she trusted him and refused to be affected by the adverse press comment that rumbled on for several months. She loved Pyon unreservedly and had complete faith in him. She knew that he would never allow his family to suffer and considered herself unusually lucky. She did not resent the increasing amount of time that Pyon spent in his office, or in the gaming clubs where he relaxed. She had always accepted that she could never monopolise him or expect him to be permanently tied to home, especially during this crisis.

But, as the crisis passed, Pyon seemed to become even more preoccupied with his business.

Aggregates

The inquiry into LWPC's payroll practices ended somewhat flatly with a recommendation that the law be changed. Institutional investors had quietly bought as many of LWPC's

shares as they could when the price bottomed out at 7/3. They
watched smugly as over the next year it crept back up to its
previous high, and beyond.

But the isolation that Pyon felt as a result of his public
castigation did not diminish; it bred within him greater
self-sufficiency and more courage. It did not surprise him
that more and more propositions were coming his way. Most
were building and property projects, and a few were of only
tangential connection with his core business. It was some of
these that fascinated him most.

At the time of the public flotation, he had made Ken
Newberry chief executive of the building division, while
he himself became executive group chairman. Newberry
was a committed workaholic and thrived on the diverse
administrative problems, leaving Pyon free to do what he
had always liked most since his schoolboy, horse-coping
days, which was buying and selling – the doing of deals.

Though the principles were the same, he was now engaged
in a more sophisticated form of trading. He found it ceaselessly
fascinating to examine other companies, private and public,
where useful assets had been overlooked and undervalued.
Initially what he sought were businesses with developable
property and land, irrespective of their main trading activity:
a meat wholesaler with a warehouse by Liverpool Street
Station; a small shoemaker with a factory in the centre
of Northampton; a chain of cinemas on the south coast –
companies whose profits bore no relation to the potential
value of their assets.

In buying these companies Pyon used all his charm and
persuasiveness. He did not want to rob the owners, but
he only bought bargains. More often than not, he simply
re-sited the business in a more suitable, less valuable location,
and after tidying up its operation, sold it on as a going
concern. He aimed, usually successfully, to end up with a
new development site as his profit on the deal.

His first major diversion outside property was in the
unglamorous field of aggregates. LWPC was a large consumer
of sand and gravel. From the earliest days, Ken Newberry
had always bought keenly from the smaller extraction companies. He mentioned to Pyon that one of them in the

Thames Valley near Staines was coming to the end of its deposits.

The owners of the gravel pit were a family who had originally been horse-traders, supplying animals to the bargees who plied the river until the end of the nineteenth century. They had acquired a hundred acres of thin-soiled riverside pasture to graze their stock. When the horse-trading dried up, they discovered that what lay beneath the soil was far more lucrative than anything they had ever kept above it. They thought they had struck gold and for the next two generations they had led a profligate, thriftless existence, behaving as if their seam would never run out.

The last of the line was on his third wife and twenty-third racehorse when he became conscious of the future. His hundred acres were nearly exhausted and all that was left was a series of murky, litter-filled ponds, boggy round the edges and reviled as a local eyesore. Pyon's offer of £50,000 seemed like a miracle, and he accepted it quickly, before Pyon changed his mind.

LWPC began to recoup their purchase price with council waste-disposal contracts. They bought land and made applications to extract gravel further west, in the plain between the Thames and the Kennet. After a fight and the early use of specialist planning barristers, they were granted permission. Once the last ton of aggregate had been taken from the Staines site, the uncomplicated and serviceable equipment was transported west along the Thames Valley.

Pyon's long-term aim in Staines had been to provide himself with a land bank for residential house-building in what he perceived to be an increasingly convenient suburb. But in doing the deal, he developed a taste for the various profitable activities that purchasing low grade land in river flood-plains could lead to.

His public reputation, never recovered from the battering it had received over the PAYE enquiry, did not help in his pursuit of permits to extract. He encountered vicious and increasing opprobrium as objectors became more concerned about the environment, and more articulate in fighting their case.

But he never flinched from appearing as a principal witness

at hearings and public inquiries, and he became adept at presenting a rational point of view. More often than not, he won.

"You will never achieve protection of landscape without specific legislation," he told one hostile meeting. "No voluntary codes or loose guide-lines are going to stop companies extracting gravel. In this case, it might just as well be ours, which views the pits as potentially useful or valuable land. We will infill, landscape and make whatever good use your planning authorities at the time will permit us to. And it's you who elect these bodies."

Stop-Go

When the International Monetary Fund tightened the screws on the money supply in Britain in the late 1960s Pyon ran his companies on a short rein. Nevertheless, he was planning to broaden his horizons so that he was ready for the next boom which the cyclical nature of financial markets told him was inevitable.

One medium-sized mineral company that he bought had several subsidiary mining operations in Africa. This had been its attraction for him. While sterling was tight, he found it invigorating and challenging to raise loans in other currencies. He also used his still youthful but powerful personality and his horse-trading guile on African politicians who were responsible for granting mineral extraction licences: aluminium, manganese and rock phosphate from West Africa; nobium, zirconium, tungsten and tin from the east side of the continent. He found that he enjoyed international wheeling and dealing, where financial bureaucracy was less restrictive, and developed a strong taste for trading in commodities where market forces were paramount.

By the end of the 1960s, half of LWPC's profits were being made in Africa, from its partial ownership of six mining companies in four countries.

After Edward Heath's unexpected victory, when a new Tory government came into power, the brakes were recklessly taken off the economy and Britain was awash with money.

Pyon was concerned about the underlying problems in the country and reckoned that the boom would be short-lived. But he was well prepared to take advantage and, along with companies like Cavenham, Slater Walker and Barclay Securities, he launched LWPC into an unprecedented frenzy of acquisition, earning himself – sometimes justly, sometimes not – a reputation as an asset-stripper. He countered this charge with the argument that he was simply making each of the companies more productive, and encouraging a more efficient use of the shareholders' capital.

Pyon picked up several outstanding bargains in England: a major construction company with existing civil engineering contracts in the Middle East and Sri Lanka, a small quarry, a grossly over-stretched and mismanaged property company and an ailing film studio. But it was in Europe and America that he expended most of his effort.

While Pyon was the head of LWPC, and the architect of its ten-fold expansion in three years, Ken Newberry was its chief engineer. It was normal now for Pyon to open negotiations in principle and then hand over to Newberry to thrash out the minutiae. Sometimes he would come back into the discussion, when Newberry indicated that there was an opening, and completely re-negotiate the terms to great advantage. He and Newberry would play a soft and hard double act, with Pyon, the acknowledged boss, taking the hard line. It worked well, and Newberry prospered as much as he could ever have expected in his role as fall-guy and chief of staff to Pyon. It made him very rich, but it did not make him happy.

The sense of weakness he had felt when he first lost to Pyon was becoming a nagging resentment. And this was greatly aggravated by Pyon's actions when the market collapsed in 1974.

The two partners were in Newberry's office in a building recently bought by LWPC from an early victim of the property crash. It was one of a fine Georgian terrace of houses in a quiet Mayfair street. Liz had arranged the low-key, tasteful decoration of the place. Pyon had wanted an air of solidity and reliability about the place, with a dash of excitement provided by some of the more spectacular pictures he had bought.

Newberry still did not feel comfortable in it. That afternoon, without allowing Pyon to see it, he was positively squirming.

"Ken, what have you been doing? You must have lost your marbles. For God's sake, man, I thought you knew why I insisted on selling everything but the best last year. You agreed that it was the thing to do. Look at us now. No borrowings at all and twenty-five million in cash with the arse fallen out of the property market and the FT index at one-fifty. We're in a fabulous position, just as we planned."

Newberry winced. "I did think you sold off some of the companies too soon and too cheap."

"But I didn't, did I?" Pyon paused, and turned the full glare of his blue eyes on to his partner. "You didn't? You didn't buy some of them yourself?"

"No, no, of course not." Newberry tried not to whine. "Only that site in Bournemouth. After all, you wanted to let it go for not much more than we gave for it."

"And a bloody sight more than we'd get for it today. And you borrowed the lot, I suppose?"

Pyon walked across the sparsely furnished room and stared out of the window. He had two courses of action. The realistic or the vain. He could either dump Newberry now, or he could bail him out and evoke his loyal gratitude. He turned back to face the man who had shared most of his setbacks and successes over the last fifteen years.

"Okay, Ken. You say you're overgeared. Is that just a euphemism for skint?"

"Of course I'm not skint."

"Don't bullshit me!" Pyon bellowed. "Tell me the fucking truth, or I can't help you. God knows you owe it to me – getting involved in your own wheeler-dealing."

"You do deals in your own right," Newberry protested.

"Sure, but only after I've offered you the chance to come in. That was always your choice." Pyon paused and forced himself to be calm. He gazed into the back of Newberry's eyes. "Now tell me the whole story."

That month, Pyon bought back in the forty-five per cent of LWPC which he did not own, including all of Ken Newberry's shares. For these he paid double the current market price, and Newberry was able to redeem his financial position. In return, Newberry had to accept that while he was still chief executive to Pyon's chairman, he was now an employee, and no longer a shareholder.

Pyon, on the other hand, had the satisfaction of knowing that he had controlled his own greed where others – and there were many thousands besides Newberry – had not. He arranged for LWPC to become the property of various Liechtenstein *Anstalten*, Netherlands Antilles Holding companies, and Panamanian corporations which were owned by a number of discretionary trusts of which he and his family were the exclusive – and usually untraceable – beneficiaries.

A whole new career in the global market lay before him. He was ready for it. It was a long way from the Hay-on-Wye horse market, but in its essentials it was the same.

A complex international empire

In 1974 Pyon was thirty-five and flush with the success of a series of coups that his timely decision to go liquid in Britain had enabled him to pull off.

He was enjoying his ascendancy in the international business world, which meant that he now spent most of his time travelling. He was reluctant to stop. He had grown out of the habit of going home. When he did stay in his London house, it was seldom for more than a week at a time.

During those visits, he was an affectionate and considerate husband. But Liz knew that, in truth, she had lost him. They did not talk as they had in the early days about Pyon's ambitions – he seemed already to have achieved most of them. Though, when Liz asked him when he was going to deploy his influence to the good of his fellow citizens, he became testy: "I will, I will in time. I haven't reached the state of equilibrium that's necessary for that sort of thing, and it's very hard to stop the momentum, there's so much further to fall now. It's like being a lumberjack rolling a log on a river of shit."

He and Liz still made love, but for Pyon it was an affectionate, rather than passionate activity. As he was still – increasingly, it seemed – a passionate man, he had discreetly found outlets for his surplus sexual energy. He did not want to hurt Liz. He made certain that the other women he slept with were a long way from home and respected his wish for discretion. Rumours filtered back to England, but nothing substantive; no newspaper reports or photographs, and Liz felt that she could do no more than shrug off the rumours and welcome him when he came home.

She was, in any case, largely occupied with her children, fourteen and eleven now, and a burgeoning interest in breeding horses.

Pyon had started buying racehorses ten years before; jumpers at first, then, when he thought he was ready to compete successfully, flat-horses. He had willingly passed on a pair of good mares to Liz when she had asked if she could breed from them, and from this tenuous start she had made some small success and was becoming a respected producer of bloodstock. She had chosen the stallions to whom she sent her mares with great care. She did not ignore the "fashionableness" of a stallion, which was what prompted buyers to take notice of a yearling at the sales, but she did not allow it to be paramount. In her first year, she had produced a colt who had been top lot on his day at the October sales at Newmarket. And in her second year, she had had a filly accepted for the prestigious High Flyer sale in September. Pyon was effusive about her success and boasted about it in a way he never boasted about his own achievements.

Cleverly, and quite openly, Liz had suggested that Pyon combine his love of his Irish roots with her interest in horse-breeding by buying a suitable estate in Ireland.

She found a splendid, neglected early Georgian mansion with three thousand acres south-west of the Wicklow mountains in County Carlow, and he agreed to buy it. The local Irish, in the main, welcomed him as a prodigal son. They were glad to see a man who was ostensibly one of them in the massive, run-down Anglo-Irish house.

Liz had no trouble in finding keen and generally competent staff to do up the house and work on her stud. She soon settled into a comfortable routine of travelling between London and Wicklow, not entirely unhappily resigned to the part-time condition of her marriage. She still considered herself fortunate that at least her husband was kind and compliant when she saw him, and had not exposed her to any humiliation.

Laura loved her father with demonstrative enthusiasm, but Julian, one year into his Benedictine school in Yorkshire, was showing worrying signs of resentment towards him. Liz pointed this out to Pyon, who looked guilty but said, "Fathers aren't essential. Mine gave me nothing."

"Maybe he had nothing to give, but you have. Julian can see that and he wants more of you."

"Okay, Liz. I'll try to do more for him."

But he had not – beyond taking him on occasional trips to Europe, where Julian had been sent off to look at the sights with a secretary, and then sat in the six-seater jet on the way home, listening to his father dictating letters or booming down the telephone. And when his father had patted him on the head, saying, "I love you, boy," Julian had not believed him.

Pyon considered that a boy should find his own feet, establish his own interests in the way that he had done. He was careful not to indulge his son, or bring him up with everything handed to him on a plate.

Pyon was anyway so occupied with running what was now a complicated and diverse commercial empire that he simply did not find time for domestic matters. He trusted Liz's competence, listened to her, provided her with whatever she needed and felt that he was being fair.

Monaco

It was Maria Gatti's father who had introduced her to Christy. Pyon and Gian-Battista Gatti had a mutual friend and banker, a German-Swiss, who had invited them to dinner at his villa in Monaco.

Gatti brought Maria, who was then a blooming and confident nineteen-year-old. Since she had grown into a beautiful, quick-witted young woman, he loved to show her off and watch men's reactions as she fascinated and rebuffed them.

Maria had picked up twenty new dresses in Rome on her way to Monaco, she spoke French and English, and she had met most of the more flamboyant characters who inhabited the shores of the Mediterranean from St Tropez to Positano.

She had always loved to spend her summers on her father's elegant old yacht *Speranza*, which each year cruised slowly up the coast from Naples. Since she had been a small girl, she had been used to teasing her father's male guests, whether billionaire industrialists, film directors, couturiers, movie stars or gigolos.

Gian-Battista would look at her proudly and say, "Nobody's going to take you for a ride, are they? It's going to need quite a man to deal with you; I wonder if such a man exists."

He realised that such a man did exist within minutes of introducing his daughter to Christy Pyon. When Pyon found himself beside Gatti's daughter at dinner in Monaco, his sense of fairness deserted him. This tall, ripe Italian girl presented a new and irresistible challenge.

"Now, I wonder what prompted our host to place a temptation like you next to me?" he asked her.

"Don't you like temptation?"

"It's the resisting of it I'm not partial to."

"Are you a weak man, then?"

Pyon smiled. "Oh, yes."

"Well, I'm not really a temptation; I'm not offering you anything."

"You're not? Thank God for that. When I was a boy, the priests used to tell us to avoid 'Occasions of Sin'."

"I don't think I'd like to be thought of as that. Besides, this whole town is an occasion of sin, as you call it."

"Nothing could be further from my thoughts," Pyon said as his eyes pulled away her clothing and caressed her warm body.

She was, he observed, so deliciously confident, so perceptive and provocative. Her long, rich brown hair fell on tanned shoulders. A silk dress of ochre and deep turquoise clung to large soft breasts that shook slightly with her husky laugh. Deep, chocolate-coloured eyes showed her excitement at his understated, but unequivocal intentions.

Pyon could not deny these intentions any more than he could stop the erection swelling uncomfortably in his Sea Island cotton underwear.

Abruptly, he turned to the banker's wife on his other side and brought her into a new conversation with Maria. They discussed pictures, yachts, the pollution of the Mediterranean and the over-exploitation of its coastlines. And during these conversations, Maria and Pyon kept up a separate, explicit dialogue with their eyes.

When dinner was over, and Gian-Battista Gatti summoned his daughter to leave with him, Pyon made no suggestion that he should meet her again.

Gian-Battista said, "You must have dinner with us on board *Speranza*. I shall be selling her soon when my new boat is ready."

Pyon nodded. "I'd like to." But no specific date was fixed.

For the next few days, Pyon grappled with deeply self-serving municipal officials over the proposed building of a shopping and sports centre on the outskirts of Nice. Often, and uncharacteristically, his mind wandered from the project to the tantalising challenge of Maria Gatti.

This lack of control over his mental activity worried him a little, but excited him a lot. He could not dispel recurring visions of himself and the soft, husky woman coupling with continuous, infinite variation; he knew that eventually he would have to, however unpredictable the consequences.

He spoke to Dieter, the Swiss banker, about it as they sat out on his terrace intently discussing a flotation to finance a marina Pyon hoped to build in Florida.

"Boy, I want to fuck that girl!"

"I beg your pardon?"

"I want to fuck Gatti's lovely daughter. I'm sure everyone else in Monaco does too. They won't – but I will."

"Good heavens, Christy. I have never heard you talk like that before. I thought you and Liz were very happy." The

Swiss man's staunch Calvinism showed. "And you're still a Catholic, aren't you?"

"Yes, of course I am. But being a Catholic doesn't mean you don't sometimes want to screw women who aren't your wife."

"You may want to, but that doesn't mean you should. It's so disruptive."

"You're right of course, Dieter, but I've never felt such an urge."

The banker shook his head with disapproval. "You may still be a young man, but you're in an important, almost public position. I'm a banker, not a priest, yet I must tell you to be very careful not to do anything to offend the people you do business with."

"Good God, man! People I do business with are concerned about their profits, not my morals."

"You would be surprised by how much that isn't so, usually for reasons of hypocrisy or envy."

Speranza

Three days later *Speranza* was still lying in the harbour at Monaco. She was moored broadside to the quay, too long to lie stern on, and her twin funnels towered over the sleek, angular white motor yachts at either end of her. She was an old-fashioned vessel, built on the grand scale of the inter-war years, with much visible teak and brass.

It was half-past eight on a fine Cote d'Azur spring morning. Pyon was standing on the harbour wall, looking down on *Speranza*'s decks. He had hoped he might see Maria, but there were only a few members of the white-clad crew about. He was disappointed, though not particularly surprised, not to see her; but he continued to gaze at *Speranza*, and as he gazed, his admiration for the elegant vessel grew.

Although he had known Gatti for a while, he had not seen the boat before. As the sun glinted off the brass foghorns and the token rigging – and the red, blue and white Panamanian flag fluttered on the stern – the old boat had a substantial, comfortable air; a man could enjoy weeks at a time of complete independence on a vessel like that.

Abruptly, Pyon turned and strode along the harbour wall to the stone steps which led down to the quay. He descended two at a time and walked briskly to *Speranza*'s gangplank.

"Ahoy," he hailed one of the crew who hovered above. "Is Signor Gatti aboard?"

"*Si, signor.*"

"Tell him that Christy Pyon would like to come up."

The sailor disappeared. A few moments later, Gian-Battista Gatti emerged from an upper saloon door. There was an embarrassed smile on his swarthy, wrinkled face.

"Christy, my friend, how nice to see you. Come on board," he called down.

When Pyon reached the top of the gangplank, Gatti greeted him with a double handshake. "I'm sorry," he said, "I should have invited you before."

"That's why I invited myself," Pyon laughed. "I'd never seen *Speranza*, and I tell you something, I'm very impressed."

Gatti led the way into the for'ard saloon, whose large windows overlooked the harbour, the palm-lined, meticulously tidy streets and the golden-pink Grimaldi Palace on top of its cliff.

"Coffee?" the Italian asked.

Pyon nodded. "Please."

A crewman was despatched.

Pyon walked across to see the view. "Have you sold the old girl yet?"

"This boat, you mean?"

"Yes."

Pyon heard a smile in Gatti's voice. "Not yet."

"What d'you want for her?"

"Not much. She's old and not very fashionable. The Arabs all want things that look like space-rockets."

"So, how much?" Pyon turned to look at him.

"Two million dollars."

"I'll give you a million for her," Pyon said lightly.

"A million and three-quarters."

"A million and a quarter," Pyon offered more firmly.

"A million and a half," Gatti proposed with a finality that Pyon recognised.

"Done," he said, and held out his hand to Gatti who accepted it with a hard shake.

"But remember," Gatti said, "my daughter does not come with her."

Maria did not appear in the yacht while Pyon was there that morning, nor over the next two days during which he and Gatti finalised their deal. Pyon agreed that *Speranza* would not be handed over to him for another three months, until Gatti's new boat was due to be delivered to Naples from Hamburg.

Pyon bit back his urge to ask after Maria, restricting himself at their final meeting to saying, "Give my regards to your lovely daughter," which Gatti acknowledged with a surly nod.

Pyon had done all that he usefully could on the Nice project. Officials and politicians had been spoken to and, where necessary, offered rewards disguised as consultancy fees. Insofar as public opinion was a factor, Pyon had dealt with it by nursing the local newspapers, and talking of major advertising, when the time came. He left Monaco for East Africa where he was engaged in tricky negotiations with two governments. He had recently bought an interest in a group of South African mining companies and this was causing difficulties with some of his operations in other parts of the continent.

After this, Pyon returned to London, where he updated Ken Newberry on the various actions he had taken. He watched one of his fillies fail to win the One Thousand Guineas, and flew to Ireland to divide his time between fruitless attempts to extract salmon from the Slaney and negotiating over the phone for the purchase of the land in the Florida Keys where he planned to build the marina.

Three months after he had agreed to buy *Speranza*, he arrived in Naples, looking forward to a few weeks on the yacht which he was now due to pick up. The old master of the boat had elected to stay with it, to Gatti's annoyance, and an otherwise entirely new crew had been assembled.

It was June and hot, and with considerable relief, Pyon stood on the bridge as *Speranza* headed out into the breezes of the Tyrrhenian Sea. He planned to cruise via Sardinia and Corsica to the Cote d'Azur, where Liz and their two children were staying in a house outside Grasse.

As *Speranza* pulled out of the Bay of Naples, leaving Vesuvius floating in a murky haze, Pyon went below for a detailed inspection of his new, waterborne domain.

When he told Liz about the yacht, she had been excited about the idea of redecorating the interior of such a grand old boat, but when he mentioned his plan to treat it as a mobile office, she had misgivings. Knowing Pyon's capacity for impatience in new, untested circumstances, she suggested he make the first trip without her to get used to the running of the vessel. When he had arrived in Naples, he had announced provocatively that he wanted to be skipper when he was on board.

Now they were under way, Pyon told the disgruntled master he was going to have a look around the boat on his own. His tour of inspection was thorough. It was an hour or so before he reached the last of the guest cabins. As he opened the door he was aware of a woman's scent. It was vaguely familiar. Almost unconsciously, he was trying to place it, when he saw a body lying face down on a massive bed.

He drew in his breath with a quick heave of his chest. He had recognised at once the long black hair and curving haunches.

She lifted her head and propped her chin on her hands to look sideways at him, rubbing her eyes.

"Goodness, are we moving? Where are we?" she said sleepily.

"An hour out of Naples."

"Oh no! I must have fallen asleep. I just wanted a last look at the old *Speranza*."

Pyon assumed a look of concern. "I'd better turn her about and head back then, hadn't I?"

Maria Gatti rolled over and moved herself up the bed so that she leaned against the headboard. She smoothed her dress down to her knees and shook her head. "No. My father would be too angry."

"Not as angry as he's going to be if we don't turn back."

Maria smiled. "True, but who cares?"

Pyon took a few steps towards the bed and stood over her, looking down. His eyes sparkled. "If you were my daughter, I'd be very angry."

"If I were your daughter, you wouldn't be looking at me like that."

Pyon picked up the telephone beside the bed and keyed the number for the bridge.

"This is Pyon. I'm going to be tied up for a couple of hours. Just stick on the same heading until I tell you to change."

He walked to the cabin door and closed it.

When he turned around, Maria had not moved. Her wide lips were slightly parted; the lids were lowered over her liquid eyes.

"Only a couple of hours?" she said in her quiet, husky voice.

A large, happy smile spread across Pyon's face. "You look like some luscious fruit, waiting to be plucked," he said.

"So," Maria invited, "pluck me."

Divorce

Lord Barnstaple strode up the front steps of his daughter's Chelsea house. The front door opened before he reached the top, and Liz flung herself into her father's arms. Her tear-filled eyes did not register the curious stares of passers-by on the damp, autumn morning.

Lord Barnstaple patted his daughter's back. "Come on, Liz. We'd better go inside."

She nodded and turned to lead him in. She showed him

to a small study at the back of the house. "I'll just get some coffee," she sniffed, and went to the kitchen.

When she returned and poured them both a cup, they sat opposite one another on small sofas either side of an unlit fire. Her father spoke gently. "All right, tell me what's happened."

"Oh, Pa, I should have told you and Mummy before, but I've been hoping it was going to be all right." She took a gulp from a large French coffee cup. "It all started last June when Christy first picked up the boat from Naples to bring it to France. You can't imagine how humiliating it all was. When I heard *Speranza* had arrived at the marina in La Napoule, I drove down from the villa with Julian and Laura, so excited about seeing the boat and Christy. We parked and asked where she was moored, then walked right round the marina to the far side. Christy had phoned to tell us to be there at midday, but we hadn't wanted to wait. It was only half-past ten and he obviously wasn't expecting us." Liz gulped. "He was on the deck, in full view of everyone – I can still hardly believe it – saying goodbye to this Italian girl."

Her voice faltered as she remembered the scene. "He had his arms right around her and was kissing her like a lion having his lunch. Julian saw them first; he just said, 'I don't think Dad's expecting us. I'm going back to the car,' and he went. When I realised what was happening, I simply couldn't move."

She looked at her father, glowering opposite her. Before he could speak she quickly went on, "I don't want to paint too black a picture of Christy's behaviour. Frankly, I'd suspected for ages that there have been girlfriends, but I'd never been confronted with any evidence. I think he's always been very discreet. I've got used to seeing him for odd weekends, or a few days at a time here or in Wicklow. I've been able to live with that. And, let's face it, he looks after me very well financially. But it's been hard for Julian and this seems to be the last straw as far as he's concerned."

"Is it the last straw as far as you're concerned, too?" her father asked.

"Wrong metaphor," Liz replied, "it's only the first and it's a lot more than a straw. This was the first time I'd seen him angry, presumably because he was guilty; he'd been very careless and caught red-handed, and that's what really worried me. Normally he'd never have run the risk of being found out."

"What did you do, when you saw him on the boat?"

"I just stayed rooted to the spot until the girl had walked down the gangplank, waved goodbye and climbed into the back of Christy's car which was waiting there. I didn't want to look as she drove past, but I couldn't help it. Of course, she didn't know who we were and didn't take any notice. But I got a good look at her, she's a stunning girl, in a tarty, Latin sort of way.

"By that time Julian had disappeared, so Laura and I walked the last fifty yards to the yacht and climbed the gangplank. Christy had gone back in, so I shouted, 'Ahoy, Cap'n Pyon,' trying to sound normal, not very successfully though, because when he appeared through a door, even under that deep tan of his, he paled. All the blood drained from his face, he looked sort of *eau de nil* and very guilty."

"By God, so he should," Lord Barnstaple half-whispered.

"No, Daddy, please don't get angry."

"What d'you mean, 'Don't get angry'? When he first told me you were getting married he gave me his most solemn word that he would never let you down. And I accepted his word in good faith."

"He hates to go back on his word. It's an article of his faith in himself that he never makes statements that he doesn't intend to stand by. Whatever happens, he'll convince himself that he's behaved honourably."

"However he chooses to put it, he's already let you down. What did he say when he saw you?"

"He said hello, quite calmly, and then he asked if I had seen his guest leaving. I said yes, and he was quiet for a moment. Then he said, 'I'm sorry if you're upset. I can't say I'm sorry for what happened between me and Maria, because that would be a lie. You've just got to believe that I didn't plan it. The girl is Gatti's daughter and she deliberately stowed away before I left Naples – she's a very beautiful and single-minded individual, and I succumbed.' He shrugged and said, 'What else can I say?' Well of course there was a lot else he could have said, but he looked so genuinely remorseful, that I just said, 'Let's talk about it later.' Laura was standing behind me still. I'd forgotten she was there. I was worried how she would react, but curiously, she wasn't taking it too badly. After this confrontation, Christy reverted to type and was full of enthusiasm for the boat and insisted on showing us all round it. He went and got Julian himself, but I don't think he managed to mend any bridges. He suggested we move on to the boat and cruise down to Portofino in a few days. Without saying anything, we sort of agreed not to mention the Maria incident, and things felt almost normal, though of course I couldn't get the picture of him and the girl out of my head.

"So, in spite of everything, the trip was fun. I convinced myself that Christy was regretting the whole affair, and things would be more or less as before. You might think that's pretty wet of me, to take it lying down like that, but even when Christy's not around, he is so omnipresent that it's hard to imagine life without him. Anyway, the crew were charming – I think they felt rather sorry for me, which was embarrassing – and by the time we reached Portofino, I was reasonably relaxed. I thought to myself he's probably been doing this for years. Why should I let my catching him once change anything? And I think I could have lived with that. But now . . ." Liz hunched her back and leaned forward on the sofa and her shoulders heaved as she began to sob.

Her father came over and sat beside her. He put his arm around her and squeezed. "Liz, my poor little Liz. What's happened now?"

Liz sat up, wiped her eyes and blew her nose. "He appeared here yesterday evening, without any warning – and he usually lets me know a few days before he's coming to London. He said he couldn't stay because he was on his way to New York. Then he said he had something difficult to tell me. He found it difficult all right. He's carried on seeing Maria – quite often, he said – and she's pregnant. There's absolutely no question of an abortion – what did I think he should do?"

Liz leaned back on the sofa and gazed at the pattern on the curtain pelmets. "What the hell am I supposed to think, or do, or say?"

"What do your instincts tell you?" Lord Barnstaple asked.

"My immediate reaction was to go out and slaughter this bloody girl and beat Christy's brains in till he promised not to stray again. Not very practical or civilised solutions." She shrugged. "I want me and the children to be happy. I suppose one part of me wants Pyon to be happy too. I know damned well he wants to marry Maria and for the foreseeable future, he won't be happy until he has – nor will we. It seems to me to be a question of opting for whichever course is going to create the least misery in the long run."

"Are you saying you're prepared to divorce him?"

"Yes, I suppose I am."

"But Christy's always made a thing of being a Catholic, and presumably this Italian girl is too."

"Christy does wear his Catholicism rather openly, but that isn't simply a posture of eccentric defiance, because it's such an unlikely thing for him to be. Having said that, this is a problem for him; he's always said that there's no point in making promises if you haven't got the guts to see them through. That's why he's put the ball in my court – he wants me to be the one to break the promise."

"But that's ludicrous, dishonest clap-trap," Lord Barnstaple blustered.

"It isn't entirely. I think that if I say I won't, then he won't. It's grossly unfair, really, but he doesn't mean it like that."

Her father shook his head. "You're being far too kind. The man has behaved like a complete shit. He deserves no sympathy from you."

"Maybe you're right, but I don't feel so. At least he's been straight about it and tried to stick to his own, peculiar code of ethics. Curiously, I don't think he loves me any less than he has done for the last ten years. He doesn't want to lose me at all, but he must be infatuated with this girl. I'm sure it's 90 per cent physical and he wouldn't be the first man who enjoyed a change, would he?"

She turned to look at her father's mild display of guilt.

"Yes, but," he spluttered, "getting a teenage girl pregnant, for goodness' sake. That's just bloody irresponsible."

"But, Dad, what is the point of being vindictive? Sure I

feel hurt, but not rejected. He wants to go on seeing me and the children. In fact, very little will change in practical terms. In spite of what you and everyone else may think, Christy is a very warm-hearted man. He's sometimes insensitive because he doesn't think like other people. He needs people in general, I suppose, but he's never dependent on any one individual."

Liz stood up from the sofa, to strengthen her decision. "I'm not saying I like the situation; it's miserable as hell at the moment, but in the end I can cope. I will divorce him and I don't want to hear recriminations from you or Mummy. It's not inconceivable that he may change his mind, or come back later. And if he does, I'll have him back."

Her father was angry and puzzled. "That seems the most extraordinary reaction. The man has let you down completely. He has humiliated you in front of your children. What are all your friends going to say?"

"I couldn't care less what anyone says. I just want you to try to understand my decision. If you can't, it's too bad. I only ask that you are extra kind to Julian. I know he's rather tricky. Christy's never had the patience to be any help, so he won't suffer any more than he already has, but he needs all the confidence anyone is prepared to give him if he's to make the most of himself."

"Of course, he must come and spend some time at Nethercombe. And so must you and Laura. Why not come and spend a couple of weeks now? Everything seems very gloomy in London anyway. This new Wilson government is making an even bigger balls-up than Heath's. Anyone with gumption seems to be leaving England like rats from a sinking ship."

"Including us," said Liz. "We're moving to Ireland."

"What! Selling up here?"

Liz nodded. "It's been the plan for some time. Actually, in the circumstances, I'm very glad. A change of scene will help me to cope with everything. Christy is buying a large house in Mayfair, which he wants me and the family to use, but I've a lot to do in Carlow, and this house reminds me of the first four or five years of our marriage when we were really very happy."

"Well, I think you're being very brave. I know you too well

to argue with you – and divorcing Christy is obviously the best thing to do. Just make sure you get the right settlement."

"That's already taken care of. The children and I have been beneficiaries of various trusts for some time, and I personally own a sizeable lump of shares in LWPC. As far as I am concerned, there's no question of Christy being unfair about money."

"I hope you're right."

"And please remember what I said, I want no recriminations against him. He may have behaved like a small selfish boy, but he is not an evil man."

Qualities of a wife

Christy Pyon married Maria Gatti in a civil ceremony in Naples. Relations of neither family were present, and at the small service of blessing that Gian-Battista Gatti had arranged in Amalfi, only Maria's tearful mother and sisters were in attendance.

Gian-Battista had tackled Pyon on the question of a Vatican annulment, but Pyon had rejected the idea as bogus. "I've no grounds; there are children. I'll just have to live with my sins."

"And so, unfortunately, will my daughter," Gatti had growled.

The pregnancy which had precipitated the events ended with a miscarriage in the fifth month.

Maria was relieved, but Pyon was bitterly disappointed; he felt that nature had tricked him. He was, though, concerned for Maria and uneasy about her equanimity. She laughed at this. "With the amount of fertiliser you produce, it shouldn't take long for another to appear."

Secretly, though, Maria put herself on the Pill. She wanted to enjoy a few more years unfettered by children. She was mistress now of the historic mansion Pyon had bought for them on the cliffs above Positano, and was making the most of her freedom. Pyon's new obsession with privacy was rather tiresome, but she loved to see the envious faces of the girls in the town and the clients in the Roman couturiers.

Sometimes, always discreetly, she travelled with Pyon, to New York, Nice, Kenya, but never to London or Ireland.

She knew that he visited his first wife and children every few weeks. When she challenged him over this, he did not raise his voice or give any obvious physical display of anger, but his eyes hardened and drove through her in a way that overwhelmed any ideas of rebellion. "Never," he said, "interfere, or try to come between myself and my children or their mother."

For the most part, the first year of their marriage was a continuous feast of physical sensations. Pyon thrived on it and pushed to the back of his mind the fact that Maria had not become pregnant again. But his doubts about her intentions grew until he decided to confront her with them. They were lying after making love in the big bed of *Speranza*'s master stateroom. It was the first night they had spent together for two weeks and Pyon had released an explosion of pent-up energy into her.

"If that doesn't make you pregnant, I don't know what the hell will. Do you?"

The strength of Pyon's personality compelled her to tell the truth, even though she knew this would anger him.

But his outward reactions were calm. He demanded that she hand over the pills – all of them – which he ceremoniously flushed down the lavatory.

Maria was not ashamed of her deception, but she realised it had altered Pyon's view of her. This time when she became pregnant, she fervently hoped that nothing would go wrong, and took every precaution that an expectant mother could.

She was rewarded more by Pyon's pleasure than by Caterina, the baby daughter who was born. Despite the arrival of a starchy English nanny and a Sicilian nursery maid, she found motherhood a debilitating tie. Her own mother, thrilled by the birth, was appalled by her lack of maternal feelings and reproached her for it; so, more obliquely, did Pyon.

Through this birth and the birth two years later of their son, Gianni, Pyon became aware of the fact that those aspects of Maria's personality which had originally attracted him were not the qualities of a satisfactory wife. He had married Maria because he thought he loved her, not because he wanted to impress his friends; that Maria had the ability to appear always dramatically striking was a poor trade-off against her lack of wifely attributes.

But he had made the commitment and he would stand by it. Gian-Battista Gatti was aware of the souring of relations between his daughter and Pyon, but he did not blame his son-in-law. Indeed, he demonstrated his regard for him by sometimes giving him precedence over his own sons at family gatherings. Pyon guessed that this was, as much as anything else, a ploy to keep the young Gattis on their toes, but it only increased the resentment of him they already harboured.

Entering the US market

During the depression of the second half of the 1970s, Pyon had avoided expanding in Britain, which he considered the hardest hit of the Western economies. His reputation, sullied by the tax scandal after his company's public flotation, had never recovered. Newspaper columnists and satirical magazines had for several years kept up a steady stream of flak at the slightest pretext. When he left his first wife for an Italian teenager, whom nobody had been able to see, he had been portrayed as an over-sexed, overbearing monster. With perverse inevitability, the more efficient he became at avoiding the press, the more obsessed they were with writing any story or innuendo, however skimpy the grounds. But they were invariably balked in their attempts to illustrate their articles with photographs.

On occasions, Pyon had been tempted to sue. But seeing

the experience of other, higher-profile entrepreneurs, he realised that proving a libel inaccurate was not always effective in protecting a reputation.

He tended now to leave the running of his British companies to Ken Newberry. Newberry had, on the face of it, come to terms with his eclipse by Pyon at the time of the stock market crash. He knew he had been lucky to crawl out from under more or less intact, but the experience had left him a great deal more cautious. He was happy to let Pyon take the major decisions, and the risks, while he concentrated on the efficient turning of the cogs of the diverse empire.

Newberry had married a South London bookmaker's daughter who harboured social ambitions. He bought a large and ugly Victorian house in what he referred to as Royal Berkshire and severed most of his connections in the East End. He joined exclusive golf clubs that were patronised by successful comedians and television personalities and sent his children to smart private schools. When he and Pyon met socially, usually once a month, he bored him with tales of his burgeoning status and Pyon knew that, provided Newberry had enough money to satisfy his wife's ideas of social standing in Sunningdale, he would cause no problems.

In the meantime, Pyon had entered the US market in a big way.

He had sought allies among the major Massachusetts Catholic families. His forthright Irishness earned him friends and a respect he was unused to in England. When he needed back-up for large-scale takeovers, he had no difficulty finding it.

He targetted for predation old, moribund companies in mining or smoke-stack industries, always looking for hidden, undervalued real estate. He continuously refined his formula for imposing slick, uncompromising management, but he combined this with enough charm not to hurt too many people's pride. His policy was to avoid job losses whenever it was possible, and he always approached the union bosses in secret before making a serious move. If he sensed that opposition was going to make the effort not worth the prize, he backed off without any public show of defeat.

During the 1980s, his skills as a corporate predator became

legendary and in most American eyes, he was regarded as a hero of free enterprise, not the pariah he had been portrayed as in Britain.

One of his first moves had been to identify the most able of the financial public relations operators in New York. Bob MacFarlane, a Scottish emigré who understood Pyon's mistrust of the press in Britain, rose to the challenge. Pyon paid an enormous retainer to have a call on MacFarlane's time whenever he needed it. And the constant barrage of positive copy with which the press was bombarded showed early dividends. Not a statement was issued or press conference presided over by MacFarlane without the negative nuances being identified and sifted out, and the favourable aspects of Pyon's plans – more jobs, environmental improvements, contributions to local charities – irresistibly presented. Thus, despite Pyon's unwillingness to show himself directly, legends about the mystery Irishman abounded, and generally struck a favourable note with the American public.

Nevertheless, as conditions in England changed under Margaret Thatcher, he was tempted back. Many opportunities were emerging, and the Big Bang in the City of London was going to make it the best international base from which to carry on his business. It was anyway nearly twenty years since he had first attracted unfriendly publicity, and attitudes had changed. He was convinced too that, such was his international standing, he was immune to any serious effects from a hostile domestic media. In this, his main concern was that his mother, still fit and running an efficient farm in Herefordshire, should not be hurt.

Maeve Pyon was not hurt. She was proud of Christy, and accepted the acrimony directed at her son as an insignificant side-effect of success. She was sad about his divorce from Liz and marriage to Maria, whose motives she did not trust. She issued frequent summonses to Liz and the children to visit her in Herefordshire. These were willingly obeyed. Liz had grown close to the tough old Irishwoman, so obviously the source of many of the strengths which she admired in Pyon.

Since the divorce, Maeve's initial anger towards her son had been mollified by the fact that he still spent a lot of time with Liz and the children. Privately, she nursed a hope that he might go back to her.

Any temptation she had ever had to identify Christy's father had long passed. She knew that her son recognised, indeed celebrated his Irishness without reservation, while she herself, in sympathy with her surroundings, had become more English. She had not wanted to meet Maria, but she was disappointed never to have seen her two half-Italian grandchildren.

She made sure, though, that she saw as much as she could of Julian and Laura.

Laura

Laura Pyon had inherited much of her father's Irishness. Outwardly, she was a tall, more striking version of her grandmother, Maeve. She was dark-haired, blue-eyed and vigorously unconventional. When she left school – a convent in Berkshire – she went to study art in London at Hornsey and dabbled in prevailing movements from peace to punk.

On the whole, outside her art, her concerns were sociological rather than political. And she tended to view these matters impersonally. She was unaware of the bogusness of not applying quite the same principles to her own life. She neither approved nor disapproved of her father's activities and reputation; her love for him was straightforward and unchallengeable. She was quite unafraid of him and forthright and logical in her criticism of him. At the time of Pyon's visit to Cannes with Natalie, she was the only member of his English family to have met her Italian counterparts.

This had come about when, touring around the art hot-spots of Italy in the mid-1980s, she had detoured to Amalfi and knocked on the door of the elegant white mansion on the edge of the cliffs.

She had announced herself as Laura Pyon and had been shown in by an astonished maid who scuttled off with trepidation, evidently to summon Maria who appeared a few moments later.

Maria's tight lips and icily guarded gaze were not welcoming. She immediately recognised Pyon in the girl, and felt threatened. Laura was barely ten years younger than she was and patently in control of herself.

"You're my husband's English daughter, aren't you?"

Laura nodded as she studied the woman she had seen once, briefly, ten years before in the back of a car at La Napoule. She did not recognise her; Maria did not look old, but her face had changed with the loss of youthful spontaneity.

"Why have you come?" Maria asked. "Did your father know you were coming?"

"No. He didn't. Is he here?"

Maria shook her head. "He's not here much. You must know what he's like." She shrugged. "He's maybe in America, or on the boat in Antigua. He's coming next week for Gianni's first communion."

Laura smiled at her father's bizarre code of priorities.

"I'd like to see him. I'm going to stay with a friend in Positano; you won't mind if I come to the first communion, will you?" She went on before Maria could answer, "Actually, I've been looking forward to meeting my brother and sister."

"Half-brother, half-sister," corrected Maria. "They are not here." She offered no more and started stonily at her step-daughter.

Laura was not fazed. She guessed from Maria's attitude that the children were not far away. "Oh well, I'll call round another time. And don't forget to tell Pa that I'm coming to Gianni's communion. I expect there's a lunch afterwards, isn't there?"

Maria nodded with a tight mouth.

"Great," smiled Laura, "I'll look forward to that. I'd better be going now. I'll drop in to see Caterina and Gianni soon."

She turned and walked out of the front door which had not been closed behind her since Maria had reluctantly beckoned her through it. She walked with swinging steps down the long drive, between fragrant shrubs and swaying flowers towards an elaborate wrought-iron gate. The old gate-keeper, who had let her in without demur, bared his toothless gums in recognition of her obvious relationship to his revered master and opened the gates for her.

She had parked her rented Fiat a few hundred yards down the hill and strolled thoughtfully alongside the high white walls of her father's garden.

She had forgiven Pyon – indeed never condemned him – for Maria. She had always felt indulgent towards him and, in spite of her mother's hurt, treated his affair and marriage to Maria as she might the aberration of a likeable boy who had not yet grown up. Meeting Maria had confirmed that attitude.

Maria was clearly a stupid bitch. Cunning, no doubt, and street-wise, but without an abstract idea in her head. Her father could not possibly love, or ever have loved her in the way he had her own mother.

Yet such was the strength of Pyon's character that Laura did not feel he had ever really left them. She had seen him as much since the divorce ten years ago as she had before. As she had grown older and more articulate, her regular contact with him had become richer and more rewarding. He had always been adamant, though, that he did not discuss Maria or his Italian family. Laura judged that he felt, if not shame, at least an awareness of a mistake which he was reluctant to acknowledge.

"Remorse is a fruitless emotion," he had once said when she had probed him. "I don't live an 'If Only' life, and I'm glad you don't either."

For several years, Laura had wanted to meet Maria, to see for herself. She had known that her relief would be in inverse proportion to Maria's insensitivity.

With a sense of optimism, and sympathy towards her father, she drove the craggy coastal road to Positano where a boyfriend – a fierce young revolutionary – was staying with his rich Milanese parents. Laura was enjoying the paradox of Lorenzo fervently spouting socialist ideas as they ate lavish meals between bouts of love-making on board his parents' unequivocally capitalist yacht.

Laura did not return to her father's cliff-top *palazzo* until the first communion celebration. She parked near the church and saw Pyon outside the open doors, beaming and shaking hands with an unlikely mingling of the Gatti family and a cosmopolitan group of friends who happened to be in the area at the time. Laura was unsure whether her father saw this event as a significantly religious one, or an excuse for a party.

Besides Gianni and his supporters, there were several other families whose offspring were also to take part in communion for the first time at this Mass. The fathers, more likely than not on one of their two or three visits each year to the church, were dressed in their best suits, while their first communicant daughters behaved like mini-brides in mini-wedding dresses.

Pyon, happening to glance up as Laura approached, gave her a broad smile of welcome. He walked towards her to greet her with a kiss on her cheek and a large arm around her shoulder.

"It's a real treat to see you, darlin'. Maria said you were coming." He made a slight, apologetic gesture with his face and hands. "Be kind to her, won't you. She's a bit put out, meeting one of you after all this time."

"It seemed to me that Maria is quite good at looking after herself, but of course I'll be kind; you know me."

"Well . . . yes," he said doubtfully, "I do. Anyway, how are you?"

"Fine. Pleased to see you. Overcome by curiosity."

"I heard that you wanted to meet the kids. As a matter of fact, when your mother told me that you were on the loose in Italy, I was sure you'd find your way here. You were always too damn curious. Still, I suppose no harm will come of it."

"Don't worry, Pa. But is there any chance we can spend a bit of time together, for one of our lovely long discussions?"

"Discussions? More like verbal fisticuffs. Yes, of course I'll have time. We'll have lunch tomorrow, just you and I. Where are you staying?"

"On a yacht in Positano. It belongs to the parents of a friend."

"A boyfriend?"

"Sort of."

"I see. Do you want to bring him to lunch?"

"Certainly not. You'd hate him."

"Me? Hate? I hate no one. D'you love him?"

"God knows. I enjoy being with him, but not all the time."

Pyon looked at her with involuntary jealous speculation. "You tell me all about it tomorrow."

Laura laughed. "No way. It's my turn to keep secrets."

Pyon affected a look of hurt which was half genuine. "Ah well, you'll come up to lunch at the house after Mass, now, won't you?"

"I'd love to."

"Okay." He waved towards the church where the last of the congregation were filing in. "Come and sit up at the front with me."

Laura shook her head. "I'll just lurk quietly at the back."

Pyon grunted. "Do as you like. You're probably right."

He turned and walked between the massive carved doors towards a pew in the front row. Laura slipped into an empty space at the back. She knelt, briefly, out of habit, and pondered her father's unabashed duality.

Watching the ceremony unfold before her, feeling apart but with a familiarity instilled by ten years of daily Mass as a schoolgirl, she experienced no obvious emotion stronger than nostalgia. But her father – taller than the men of Maria's family, but dark like them – tanned and Italian-suited, assumed a posture of solemn but knowing piety oddly similar to his male in-laws'. Such was his presence, though, that it seemed to be he rather than the priest who was the master of ceremonies.

She could only admire him for the spontaneity of his command of events. There was nothing contrived or dishonest about it; he was answerable to no one – except, Laura thought, his mother, his first wife and her children. Laura was aware of the reflected strength this bestowed on her. But, beyond that, she did love him. She rejoiced in the rare occasions that he displayed uncertainty, and therefore humanity. And she had frequently confirmed her love by the simple test of imagining her reaction to his death.

Afterwards, at a lunch for over forty people, Laura kept her promise to her father and restrained her inclination to condemn. She found herself anyway drawn to her two nervous and confused siblings. In contrast to their parents, they seemed shy and thoughtful with constantly wide eyes. The girl, Caterina, was nine. Her mother had obviously not told her how pretty a child she was, nor given her any other confidence in herself. She and Gianni both spoke good English without precocity. Laura placed herself next to the boy at lunch to talk to him in her erratic Italian.

"Are you really my sister?" he asked. "You're more like my mother."

Laura resisted the urge to refute this. "Didn't you know about me before?" she asked.

"Yes, a bit. Papa's talked about you. He said that when Caterina and I go to school in England we would meet you."

"You're coming to school in England, then?"

"I think so. That's why we learn English now."

"Your English is much better than my Italian."

"Shall we talk it?" he asked eagerly.

"Later. I must practise." She did not want the boy to be inhibited in any way. She did feel more like a mother – or, at least, an aunt – to him than a sister. She had already observed that Maria's maternal instincts were well under control, and knew that her father's contact with his children, though warm, was sporadic.

When lunch was over she spoke to other people in the party who, when they realised who she was, did not disguise their surprise at seeing her there. From time to time she glanced across the crowd towards Pyon to see if he was showing any signs of unease. He appeared not to be. Laura relaxed too and enjoyed this hitherto unknown side of her father's life. But the Gatti clan remained aloof.

She looked for Caterina, and beckoned her away from a group of her Italian uncles. She asked her if she was looking forward to coming to England, and reassured her with the promise that she would come and visit her when she arrived at her convent in two years' time, the same convent, it transpired, to which Laura herself had been. The girl was grateful for Laura's attention and became more talkative. Laura encouraged her and probed gently into the kind of life her father led with his Italian family. They chatted easily for twenty minutes before they were interrupted. Maria placed herself between them and scowled suspiciously at Laura.

"Caterina has been telling me how she's looking forward to coming to England," Laura said conversationally.

"Has she? I think it's a crazy idea; she's too nervous. I don't know why your father insists, she's not a secure child."

"Maybe a change of background would help her, then," Laura suggested. "She certainly won't feel threatened at the convent."

"She doesn't feel threatened here. She has a lovely home; everything she could want. Her father is very indulgent, except with his time."

"He wasn't very indulgent towards me either," Laura shrugged. "I wonder why he spends so little time here?" She looked around and over the tops of the small palms towards the silver-blue sea. "It's such a wonderful setting, but he seems to be in England or Ireland more than here."

Caterina was shuffling uneasily beside her mother, who glanced down at her.

"Go and talk to the other children." Maria dismissed her and the girl wandered off with a quick, doubtful smile at Laura.

Maria turned her back to her step-daughter. "Listen to me. You shouldn't have come here. I don't want you seeing my children. Your father didn't want you to come here, ever. You know that, don't you?"

Outwardly, Laura remained calm. "Yes, I know that; but not because he didn't want to see me. I imagine he guessed what I'd think of you, and that probably embarrassed him. Now I've met you and seen you with your children, I can see why." She gave a quick cold smile and walked away, out on to the terrace where her father was sitting – holding court with a group of admirers.

For a few moments, Maria was paralysed with anger. Then, with flaming eyes, she stormed out behind Laura.

Laura had just joined her father, and was about to say 'Goodbye' to him, when her step-mother reached them.

There was a pronounced quiver in Maria's deep voice. "How dare you insult me like that," she shouted. "Get out of my house, you slut."

Pyon glanced furiously at the faces of the two women. He clutched the arms of his chair in a supreme effort to control himself. He closed his eyes for a moment. When he opened them, he forced a patient smile across his face and held up his hands with a calming gesture.

"For heaven's sake," he said with deceptive mildness. "What have you two been arguing about?"

"This young bitch – I don't care if she's your daughter – had the gall to insult me in my own house."

"She is my daughter, and this house is also mine," Pyon said.

"Your house? You're never here to call it yours. As for your daughter, you must ask her to leave."

"I'm going anyway," Laura said airily.

"And don't ever come here again," Maria spat.

"I'll decide that," Pyon growled.

Laura leaned down to give him a farewell kiss. "I'm sorry she's in such a state, Pa," she whispered in English. "I promise I didn't say anything particularly rude."

"I don't believe you, and I did warn you," he sighed. "I'll meet you tomorrow at the San Pietro, at one."

Laura straightened and nodded. "Bye, Pa." She waved at Caterina and, ignoring Maria and the stares of the now silent crowd of guests, she walked to her car.

With complete composure, she got into her car and drove away calmly. Only when she was out of sight of the house and the people around it, did she let go.

Her shoulders heaved with the release of tension and tears welled in her eyes. She had gone to the party determined not to provoke a scene. She was ashamed and angry at her weakness, she had also seen the anger and frustration behind her father's overtly calm handling of Maria.

This gave Laura hope. It suggested that Maria had become an irrelevance in Pyon's life, and that, sooner or later, his lack of interest would overcome his urge to display righteousness and lead either to a reconciliation with Laura's own mother – whom, she was sure, he still loved and respected – or, more alarmingly, to another, more significant relationship.

When they met the next day, Pyon's affectionate greeting carried no hint of accusation or censure over the row with Maria.

"I would have been astonished," he said, "if you two had not had a go at each other. I'm not blaming you because, frankly, I know damn well how provocative Maria can be. But would you agree with me that it won't be beneficial for you to meet her again?"

Laura nodded and smiled. "For someone who always gets his way by bullying, you've a surprising line in soft soap."

"Some people won't be bullied." He smiled with one side of his mouth. "Even this old block, off which you are an undoubted chip, can recognise that!"

"But I really am very sorry. I didn't want to rise and I promise I didn't say anything too terrible. I don't suppose you want to talk about it though, do you?"

"Not really. I think you understand."

She nodded.

Pyon went on, with a change of tone, "So, have you been enjoying Italy?"

"Oh yes. I've always liked it. It's been great to spend a few months here. My Italian's improved so I've been able to communicate much more with the more interesting people I meet. And knowing the language has made it easier to understand the art."

"So what do you understand about Italian art?"

"Mostly that its beauty disguises the deeply embedded chauvinism of its creators. Certainly that seems to me to be true of most periods. And I think modern Italian art has more to do with style and design than with art."

Pyon raised an eyebrow. "My goodness, there's a sweeping condemnation!"

"Well, yes. But I might as well have a definable view for others to try and knock down."

"Sure. A strongly held view is a lot more constructive than no view at all. When I first started to admire and buy Pre-Raphaelites, some art folk were forever looking down their noses, as if I were some sentimental peasant. But they've been as good as any investment I've ever made, and I love them."

"And if you love them, that's because you are a sentimental peasant! And the fact that the market for Pre-Raphaelites has boomed doesn't make them any less soppy and irrelevant than they were twenty years ago."

"Compared with what was being produced twenty years ago, they'll be relevant for longer. Sixties artists were just digging frantically for the ultimate banality. They were scraping the barrel to find where the bottom was and they found it in the Campbell's soup tin. I'm all for design in packaging, but not all over my drawing-room."

"Experiments are necessary in art," Laura said.

"Of course. But not, in the main, successful."

Laura looked at him with affection. "You do really like your pictures, don't you. It must be very confusing to people, when you're nailing them to the floor of your office over some deal, to see you surrounded by a load of facile religious tear-jerkers."

"If I were in the habit of nailing people to the floor, as you put it, I wouldn't do it in front of my pictures."

They bantered gently, knowing each other well, differing from each other mainly in the priorities of their differing sexes. Without anything being directly said, Pyon acknowledged Laura's view that Maria had been a gross mistake, and that his only allegiance to her was over the children. Laura made one direct reference.

"When Caterina and Gianni come to England, I think it would be good for them to see something of Julian and me, even Mummy. I can't see them fitting into the Gatti brotherhood."

Pyon nodded his agreement. "But they're not weapons, d'you understand?"

Deliberately moving away from the topic, he tried to lead Laura into some revelations about her relationships, but she would not be drawn.

"I promise," she said, "that when I have problems, I'll come and ask your advice, which I probably won't take. But everything's under control at the moment."

They had been together three hours when Pyon announced regretfully that he had to go. He was flying back to London.

As he opened her car door for her, Laura asked, "Will you see Mummy?"

"I will."

"Give her lots of love, won't you?"

"Of course I will, darlin'. Goodbye, you little devil, and God bless you."

Laura laughed and blew him a kiss as she drove away.

Laura saw her father every few months over the next four years. Their relationship remained close and forthright. But that lunch in Amalfi remained fixed in her mind as their warmest encounter.

She knew that her father was becoming increasingly frustrated by the emptiness of his marriage to Maria. At the same time, Pyon's stature as nothing less than a world-class tycoon had given him the total confidence which allows for periods of complete and relaxed detachment. Without losing any incisiveness, he could afford to be more circumspect and philosophical. Nevertheless, Laura observed, when he turned his mind to business, there had been no lessening of the tension and dynamism that surrounded him.

"Pa," she had asked him when the two of them were dining alone as they often did, "you've already got more money than any individual could possibly need; why do you bother about making more?"

Pyon shrugged. "Habit." He extracted a large Upmann cigar from the corner of his mouth and waved it around. "Like nicotine. My physiology is used to large intakes of adrenalin and I'd feel deprived if it were cut off." Still smiling, he went on, "I could also say with some sincerity that I hate to see badly-run companies with underused assets. We've become quite flabby here in England, and in the States. Our complacency could lead to complete industrial annihilation by the Japs or, God help us, the Koreans. People like me have a real role to play in ensuring the future of Western liberal capitalism."

"Oh yeah?" interrupted Laura with agitated cynicism. "Then why don't the Western media hail you as a saviour of our way of life – for all it's worth?"

"A long time ago, they tried to kick me when I was down, and they missed; they couldn't touch me. But the press, above all, like to bear a grudge. If they've given a dog a bad name, they're reluctant to turn around and say they were wrong. And for years I've operated very successfully by keeping out of their way. My lack of interest in personal publicity is confusing and frustrating to them. But don't undervalue the freedom offered by our system of regulated greed. There are losers, sure, but there are an awful lot more winners than in a totalitarian regime, be it fascist or communist."

"If winning is related entirely to personal wealth."

"It mostly is, darlin', and there's a positive side to that. I'll give you an example; famine in the Horn of Africa has been a fact of life for centuries, but it's only now, with unprecedented prosperity in the West, that fellas like Bob Geldof can persuade people to send tens of millions of pounds to ease those famines. The impoverished folk of Ethiopia are not in a position to help battered London wives, or Washington junkies, even if they had time to care about them, because they're too damn poor and too busy trying to stay alive. For those of us who are not actually saints, charity has always been a leisure pursuit."

"That's a specious argument, and you know it. As a percentage of the gross income of Western nations, the amounts we send are negligible."

"I dare say the recipients are glad of it, though. My point is that it is only prosperity that allows ordinary people to be charitable."

"Anyway, I don't believe that saving democratic capitalism is a very important motive in your wheeling and dealing."

"You could be surprised. But I admit to another motive. Some people like to play golf, or watch birds or dig their gardens or play chess; I like doing business, and I like winning." He shrugged. "Is that so reprehensible?"

"Not if no one suffers, but if you win, what about the losers?"

"Most games produce winners and losers. If the losers don't like losing, they shouldn't play."

"What about innocent bystanders – people whose jobs are on the line when you take over a company?"

"My record can answer that. I've created ten times more jobs than I've ever destroyed. And where jobs have been lost, it was already inevitable before I came on the scene. I might only be guilty of having hastened the process, in the long-term interest of a company's health and future ability to provide jobs."

"That sounds like the Tory justification for closing everything down. The only trouble is that it didn't work in England."

"Politics are operated with an even more deplorable set of rules than business, and usually by amateurs. I can't answer for them. But I have achieved a lot of fulfilment. I'm not an arbitrageur – a fella who uses stock exchanges like casinos – I'm a long-term investor."

"None of this has much to do with happiness, though, has it?" said Laura.

"I'll answer that," her father replied, "when you can give me a satisfactory definition of happiness."

Film Festival

Laura had lunch with her brother Julian shortly before he left for Cannes for the showing of his film. She had to tell him that she could not come to France. She had arranged to go to Brazil with a friend – a lover – and she did not want to back out. Julian was hurt, but understood.

"At least," Laura said, "Pa's going. That's a major victory."

"Frankly, I'd rather he didn't," Julian said.

They were in *L'Escargot* in Soho, a restaurant associated

with creative activities and the making of money from them. Laura was indifferent to the lunchers around them, but Julian was critical.

"Most of these publishing people, whether they admit it or not, measure an author's creative ability in book sales," he observed, half eavesdropping on an adjacent table.

"Is there any other exact measure? One man's Archer is another man's Amis – Martin, that is; or one woman's Iris Murdoch is another's Jackie Collins. You could have a comparative cliché count, I suppose, or points for rare words or arcane imagery. But in the end literary judgments are subjective. So he who is most sought after could be said to be the most effective communicator, which is a writer's function."

"You know that's balls," Julian said. "Still, at least it can't be very fulfilling churning out pulp; not much satisfaction or happiness to be derived from that – just money."

"Father once challenged me to supply a satisfactory definition of happiness. I still haven't been able to."

"Were you talking to him about happiness?"

"Yes."

"His?"

"No, just in general. I was trying to bring it round to him, when he shoved me off at a semantic tangent."

"Do you think he's happy?"

"I told you, I can't decide what the word means."

"All right, but before you were unsure of the meaning, would you have said he was happy?"

"I'm sorry to disappoint you, but on the whole, yes, in as much as he's at ease with himself as far as most aspects of his life are concerned."

"I don't see how that's possible. Most of his actions run directly counter to the principles of the religion he purports to uphold. His first marriage ended in disaster, and his second has been festering for years, if not from the word go. And however considerate he may appear to be to Mum when he's here or in Ireland, she's never really got over their divorce. It's all bullshit, their so-called civilised divorce. And he's been a totally useless father to me."

"Not *totally* useless. You couldn't have made your film without him."

"Not him; his money."

"For God's sake, Julian, he made his money available. You couldn't get it anywhere else; at least acknowledge that."

"Why are you on his side?"

"I'm not on any side. I'm just stating the obvious. Whatever his other shortcomings as a father, he made your film possible for no other reason than that he is your father."

"He was trying to buy my affection. He didn't think the picture would ever be finished, let alone successful."

"Maybe, but he did feel that you should have the chance to prove yourself, or not. And the fact that he's coming to Cannes suggests to me that he's proud of your success. God knows, he hates media events like that."

Julian agreed grudgingly. "I suppose so. But then he'll take credit for having backed it."

"Well, he did, so why shouldn't he?"

"It's really bizarre the way you're so defensive of him."

"I wasn't being defensive, just accurate."

"But you do get on well with him, don't you? He seems to take more notice of you than anyone else."

"Not much. If he ever does, it's because I'm female, and he recognises that I inherited some of his more obnoxious characteristics. But he doesn't take much notice of my opinions. I've been telling him for years he should chuck Maria, but he won't."

"Have you seen her since that row in Amalfi?"

"No."

"I'm glad I've never met the silly cow. What's she like now, do you suppose?"

"I haven't a clue, though she didn't strike me as someone who was going to improve with age; just the opposite."

"Why the hell does he stay with her? Why did he marry her?"

"Oh, I can see why he married her. She's still very sexy. She's one of those women whose whole life is devoted to being desirable to men, and she's a strong character in a dumb sort of way. But I'm probably the worst person to describe her to you."

"I should have thought that a thick, sexy bimbo would suit

Dad. He's not interested in ideas or intellectual debate. He never listens to anyone else."

"You're quite wrong. He will listen to a well-argued point of view. He may not appear to be listening because he always seems to have half a dozen things on his mind at once. But I'm always amazed by how much he's taken in. He gave me a very detailed description of your film script. He's as aware as you of the multiple prejudices faced by a gay, working-class Arab in a northern industrial town. He's less sympathetic, that's all."

"What do you mean, 'That's all'? If he'd understood the script, he'd have been sympathetic."

"No, he wouldn't. There are several points of view about the situation it presents. Yours is neither the only, nor, necessarily, the right one. If the film works, it will be because it presents these options. I wish I'd seen it, then I would have a more valid opinion."

Julian scowled. "You're right; you have inherited some of his more obnoxious characteristics. *He* always thinks he's being rational and plausible. Thank God you haven't inherited his politics."

"He doesn't have any politics, beyond pragmatism. I think he's something of a frustrated philosopher. If he has an obvious weakness, it's trying to come to terms with the conflict between his actions and his attitudes."

"It seems to have been a fairly unequal struggle so far."

"But he rather thrives on the struggle."

"You're much too charitable," Julian said testily. "Either a man has some kind of moral or ethical or humanitarian principles which guide his actions, or he hasn't. You can't divorce the two."

"You'll see what I mean one day." Laura shrugged. "Anyway, when you see him in Cannes, try to deal with him by using calm logic, not the kind of ranting sloganeering you always seem to resort to with him. Calling him names won't convince him of anything."

"I haven't any intention of calling him names or ranting. But I'm not going to grovel with gratitude either."

"No, he wouldn't like that; he wouldn't believe it." Laura spoke sharply. Then, like a chameleon, her manner changed to one of affection. "Anyway, let's not argue. Just try and have the best time you can. Even if you don't win a thing, at least you've been accepted to show in Cannes. Where are you going to stay, by the way?"

"Father, of course, is intending to push someone else out of a suite at the Carlton, but I'm renting a little house up beyond Grasse."

"Won't it be a hassle, driving down every day?"

"I dare say, but I don't want to be holed up with all the movie hustlers."

"But Julian, you're one of them, so long as you're there and wanting people to buy your film." She saw him about to object, and went on quickly, "All right, I know you're not really one of them. And I'm sure your film will do brilliantly, whether you hustle it or not."

Ken Newberry padded across the deep, shag-pile pink carpet of his bedroom and drew back the curtains. It was a clear May morning, and the sun beamed through the tops of the beech trees and Wellingtonias that clustered around his much gabled, tile-hung mansion. He smiled with pleased anticipation of a morning on the golf course. He was booked to play a round with the senior partner of LWPC's principal lawyers. It was the first time this important man had accepted Ken's invitation. As always when Pyon was away, he enjoyed the sensation of being in charge, and his own man.

His walked to the door of the room, opened it and called to his fifteen-year-old daughter.

"Samantha, be a good girl and bring the papers up here, will you?"

There was a reluctant moan from a room down the corridor. "Oh, all right, Dad."

"And a cup of tea for your Mum."

Ken climbed back into the enormous bed he shared with his wife, Debbie, who was still asleep. He picked up the telephone and dialled the number of his Mayfair office. His secretary was already at her desk and he began to give her instructions for the day.

His daughter pushed open the door with her foot and shook her long blonde hair from her face to see where she was going. The curtain of hair fell back immediately and she shuffled across the room, placed the tea beside her waking mother and dumped a pile of newspapers on her father's lap where he sat up in bed, still talking to his secretary. As he talked, he idly picked up the *Daily Mail* from the top of the stack and leafed through it. When he reached the middle, he stopped in mid-word and his jaw dropped. He stared in silence at the photograph, and a smile began to spread over his face. "Good God," he whispered to himself.

"Hello? Hello? Mr Newberry, are you there?" his secretary squeaked down the telephone line.

"What? Oh yes, Sue. Sorry, something's come up. I'll ring you later."

He put the phone down slowly, still transfixed by the picture of his long-time colleague and chairman, Christy Pyon, smiling down at a stunning dark-skinned girl around whom his protective arm was wrapped.

He turned to his wife and prodded her in the ribs.

"Here, look at this, Debbie. The silly bugger's gone and dropped himself in it. There'll be hell to pay when the wives see that, and right in the middle of the Chemco takeover!"

It was after nine on a fine evening over the Cote d'Azur. The sun had left a hint of its earlier presence in the warm air. Now a full moon painted a long silver-white streak across the placid Mediterranean beyond the craggy coast.

All but one of the tables in the restaurant of the *Château de la Chèvre d'Or* were occupied. The less sophisticated of the crowd of diners could not help themselves gazing out of the uncovered windows to the coast, sparkling thirteen hundred feet below. Strings of lights were draped along the shoreline and scattered pin-pricks twinkled through the trees on the dark hump of Cap Ferrat. From that height, the movement of cars was discernible, but appeared to belong to some fantasy micro-world. The very altitude of the place gave its clients a sense of superior aloofness.

Most of the people in the room had some connection with the film festival which had ended the day before, twenty-five miles away in Cannes. Many were either famous or beautiful; some were both. Those who were neither were rich.

Congratulations and condolences were tactfully proffered, and condemnation of absent parties delivered. Wh'le sleek bodies were being finely fed, plump egos were even more assiduously nourished. The air was filled with self-important, highly opinionated voices criticising or justifying – American, English, German, Italian and French were blended with a dash of Slavic and Eastern tongues. Cool notes of scent at thousands of pounds a gallon cut across the smell of hot, extravagantly presented seafood.

Even this inward-looking gathering noticed the entrance of Christy Pyon.

The arrival of this legendary but elusive mogul in the movie industry, albeit only as the financier of a low-budget "art" film, had already caused a stir. And this had been whipped into a major topic by the almost unprecedented appearance of the photograph of him which a number of European papers had published. People had forgotten what a big, striking man he was. The mystique which had surrounded him for over a decade had led them to think he was a great deal older than the photograph showed.

That the film had successfully captured awards for its screenplay and its music score seemed like a case of beginner's luck. And of course those in the business told each other the picture would not take any money where it mattered – in America.

But it was not just an interest in prevailing gossip that caused eyes to turn as Pyon shepherded his two guests towards the last empty table by the window; it was the unmistakable aura of a real tycoon amongst a gathering of apprentices. And the girl with him was as beautiful and self-possessed as any in the room.

People who did not already know, guessed that the tall, thin younger man with lank blond hair and a baggy cotton suit was Julian Pyon, director of *Michael and Mustapha*. Those who had not read the gossip-columns wondered which of the two men was with the girl.

Natalie had been excited and fascinated by the festival. She had seen a dozen films and had eagerly compared her views with those of any number of vociferous pundits. She had constantly questioned Pyon on the merits of the films she had seen with him. In some cases, indifferent acting or pretentious direction had confused her, leaving her with the impression that there were nuances she had missed or misinterpreted. She had a clear and straightforward understanding of people and their needs, a supply of universally applicable common sense and sympathy. Her perspective of the films was uncluttered by knowledge of current trends or awe of reputations.

Pyon did not weary of discussing these things with her, but frequently he was too slow in his response to satisfy her. Then she sought Julian's views and was impressed by his quick and thorough assessment of what he had seen, views delivered with such confidence that at first they convinced her. But she became aware that he formed his judgments on much narrower criteria than she. His prejudices baffled her and seemed contradictory.

Besides this, she could not avoid noticing his hostility towards his father, which was in contrast to the slightly awkward but tolerant affection with which Pyon attempted to deal with him. At the same time, this very tolerance of Pyon's suggested some weakness or guilt about his son. It was the first time Natalie had ever seen him not entirely in control.

Pyon, Natalie and Julian sat down at their table to a volatile cocktail of emotions. In the chauffeur-driven car on the way from Cannes there had been a tacit agreement that congratulations would prevail and criticism be suspended.

Pyon justly credited Julian with finding – or at least being the first to notice and champion – the original script, and with having chosen a composer with the old-fashioned versatility and experience to knit together the series of short, oddly connected cuts that characterised his direction.

Julian had noticed Natalie's puzzled reaction to the aggression which clouded conversation with his father. Anxious not to alienate her, he decided to try and follow the advice Laura had given him in London. Blandly he asked, "Dad, what was your genuine reaction to *Michael and Mustapha* – I mean the characters themselves?"

"I was sorry for them, of course. You shouldn't assume, as I think you do, that I'd condemn them out of hand."

"I wasn't assuming that, but I can't imagine you being sympathetic to them."

"I was sorry for them, but you're right, I was not sympathetic to them."

"D'you mean you pitied them?" Julian's voice was rising.

"Yes. Because they made no effort to overcome the difficulties and prejudices that faced them. We all face prejudice to a greater or lesser extent – you less than most, as it happens. I had to deal with being Irish in an Anglo-Saxon world." He lifted a hand to cut off his son's retaliation. "No, let me finish. Your characters were entirely passive. Homosexuality is a state of mind, not a physiological disorder. In my experience, it is possible to exercise control over one's state of mind, should one so wish; so, many of the problems and frustrations caused by homosexuality could be avoided. You will probably call this reprehensible suppression, but the most ordinary of men are, I suspect, capable of the most bizarre sexual fantasies and urges, but 99 per cent of them control them, and relegate them to the primeval areas of their mind where they belong. This is not suppression, merely a recognition of the difference between men and beasts."

"You're entirely wrong!" Julian blustered. "Homosexuality is a congenital condition. Why should people born with it be denied any sexuality?"

"If that is true, for the same reason that congenitally blind people are denied sight. But I believe it's a state of mind, therefore controllable. Anyway, sex is not an absolutely fundamental requirement for a full and happy life."

"How the hell would you know that?" Julian countered triumphantly.

Christy's instinct was to snap angrily, dismissively, but his son would consider that a sign of defeat. "All right, but it's not only through our own experiences that we understand human nature. It is possible, though I suspect you can't, to observe in others strengths and gifts that we do not ourselves possess."

"That's rich. You've gone through life, taking what you want from whom you want, breaking all the rules of your religion, and quite aware that you're doing it, but you sit there and tell me how easy it is to be self-denying and saintly. If it's so bloody easy, why aren't you?"

"I'm not a saint, I've never suggested I was. But I've not hurt many people in my life, and I've given work to tens of thousands."

"You make it sound as though you've found people jobs out of some altruistic urge, not to produce a profit for yourself."

"I think we're all agreed that it is better for people to work than not. I can't see that you need to argue about the motives that produce this – the effect is what matters."

Julian gave a bellow of laughter, and a few more eyes swivelled towards their table. "Your logic is totally self-serving. And how can you say that you haven't hurt people? What about my mother? What about your other wife?"

Natalie put a hand on his arm. "Don't do this now, Julian, please." The bitterness in Julian's attack alarmed her.

"It's okay, angel." Pyon said, still calm, and turned to his son. "I admit to being a restless man. But you've no idea how hard I tried to avoid a divorce from your mother. I still love her, of course. She knows that, and she's no less happy than a lot of other women, and a bloody sight more comfortable than most."

Natalie broke in, "Don't talk about it now, either of you. I've loved coming here to France, it's been a completely new experience for me, seeing the films and all the actors and everything, but now I'm sure I shouldn't have come. I told you, Christy, I didn't want to be a part of this side of your life. There is too much tension and dangerous energy around you; you can't help it, you're just that sort of man." She turned her dark brown eyes on Julian. "But Julian, I think you're unfair not to see that your father is a thoughtful man. He may have made mistakes – but not malicious ones, and you must understand the importance of that."

Julian looked on her pleading face, disposed to listen to her. She seemed in control of her attitude to his father while genuinely loving him. Her ingenuousness and simple beauty made aggression towards her impossible.

"Natalie," he said, failing to convey the sense of reasonableness that he wanted to, "I know that you believe what you're saying, but I've known him a lot longer than you."

Pyon looked at Julian with useless anger, detesting his smugness. What had caused it? It could not only be the paternal neglect from which Elizabeth had always claimed he suffered – Laura showed none of the same symptoms. Nevertheless, Pyon felt resentful that this obnoxious young man should make him feel so guilty.

For a moment, inside him, boiled a rage which came close to overwhelming him. He grabbed a large glass of water and gulped it. His hand tightened dangerously round the stem of the glass, but he put it down on the table. He made a calming gesture with both hands.

"Come on now, J. You and I, we always disagree. Let's call a truce. Your movie's won a couple of prizes, and I'm proud of you for that." He placed a large hand on Julian's forearm. "We've had a great time here, and I've enjoyed some of the people and wading through all the bullshit. I tell you what, I'll be happy to look at any other film projects you come up with."

"That's good of you, Dad, but I expect there'll be quite a few backers for my next one."

"But you mustn't forget that it was your father who had faith in you this time," Natalie urged him, and with tact, and patient sensibility, she managed to preserve the peace for the rest of dinner.

Afterwards, they were driven back to the Carlton in Cannes. Pyon suggested they have a last drink in his suite before the driver took Julian back out to Grasse. As soon as they walked in, the telephone rang, and with relief, Pyon went through to take the call in the smallest of the three rooms, which he had made his temporary office.

When it was clear he would not be returning for a while, Julian looked at Natalie with a smile. "Let's have this drink then," he said, and, already fairly drunk, he ordered a bottle of the most expensive champagne in the building. When it arrived, he led Natalie out on to a balcony, where they sat overlooking the crowds still milling on the *Croisette*. They talked about Julian's film and others which they had seen.

Julian misinterpreted Natalie's natural warmth as physical

113

interest in him. He began to imagine himself his father's rival. But a reluctance, born of past rejections, stopped him short of testing her interest with any overt moves. Instead, he steered the conversation around to Pyon, and tried to probe her relationship with his father.

"I can't talk about that with you," she said, "it's not possible to discuss these things with the son of a lover. And anyway, you don't like him, do you?"

"Can you blame me? When I was young, I hardly saw him, and when I did, he criticised everything I did and every decision I made. He tried to belittle me because he resented the fact that I wasn't like him; not in God's image, he probably thought. Thank God I'm not like him. Fortunately, I'm perfectly confident of my own abilities and he can't destroy that confidence whatever he does. Even tonight, he wanted to take something away from the success I've had with *Michaël and Mustapha*."

"I don't think so. He was just making an honest criticism which you had asked for. Would you prefer him to say it was all wonderful just because you're his son?"

"That's not the point." Julian shook his head. "He can't accept that I may be capable of achieving anything outstanding. For years he's been telling me how mediocre my efforts are. He's an egotistical bastard." He gazed at her, challenging her to defend Pyon.

"He is not," she replied patiently. "Other people with big egos are much more self-destructive then he is. He's a perceptive man. He understands people much more than you think. That's one of the reasons for his success. I've seen him with people who work for him. He never bullies them, he persuades them and inspires them. He gives praise when they've earned it, but he always tells them if they're doing something the wrong way."

"You're not kidding. That's all he ever tells me. He doesn't give a toss about anyone else's feelings, though he may disguise that with his alleged charm if, like you, they've got something he wants that he can't buy."

"I think, Julian, you know nothing about your father's feelings."

Julian guffawed. "He hasn't got any." He rose to his feet

with a lurch and leaned on the balcony. "Look, I'm going to go now, before he gets back. But let's meet again soon, anywhere you like." He attempted a confident sexy smile.

Natalie gave a startled shake of her head. "Don't be ridiculous. You don't think . . ." Her voiced faded away with the realisation of the effect of her words.

Julian stared at her, aware of the rejection. "If you haven't seen through the old bastard yet, you will. Then let me know." He walked unsteadily through the French windows into the *salon*. "Sod him. He'll have to be taught that he can't get away with shitting all over everyone forever."

"Even if that's true, I don't think you're the person to teach him." Natalie stood up and walked towards him. She put her hand on his arm to conciliate. "I don't want to be unkind, but you're too close to him to see him properly. His personality is part of yours, whether you like it or not. Try to be more fair about him."

Julian snorted. "The last thing he needs from me is charity. Anyway, tell him I've gone. He can get in touch with me in London if he wants to."

He turned and walked across the room and left with a noisy slamming of the large panelled door.

Amalfi

When Maria had first announced that she was going to marry Pyon, the whole Gatti family had been furious. That he was flamboyant and, at thirty-six, already richer than her father were in Pyon's favour. So was his Catholicism. Against that, he was married, and he didn't come from Southern Italy – even a prospective husband from Piedmont would have been unacceptably foreign to the Gattis.

Maria was still nineteen then, independent and very wilful. To defy her family's sacrosanct breeding traditions had been in itself an irresistible challenge. In any case, she was besotted with the big dazzling-eyed handsome man and would have done anything he asked.

She had been, she recalled, more than willing to go along with Pyon's wish for extreme discretion. With great ingenuity he had selected increasingly bizarre trysting places, and managed to avoid the intrusion of the press. But word of the affair seeped out, and Pyon's name began to be seen on the gossip pages once more. But no photographs. His avoidance of publicity now seemed to become an obsession with him, second only to the expansion of his commercial empire.

As far as Maria knew, not a single photograph of him had been taken, or at least published, since before he had met her – until now, at Cannes. That Pyon had been prepared to risk going to that sort of event showed a significant change in his priorities.

It was too near home. It was too near her.

And that, above all, was what was worrying her as she gazed with horror at the dark, vindictive faces of her three brothers, Sergio, Luigi and Franco. She wanted her husband to suffer; he had viciously insulted her by appearing in public with a half-black teenager. She was hurt, and she wanted her own back. But not like this.

"No, no." Her chocolate brown eyes flashed. "I only want to teach him a lesson. He is still my husband, you know, Caterina and Gianni's father. You can't say these things. Listen, I have a plan which will hurt him, but will also benefit us. I want him back, but I want him back on my terms. His business is his real mistress, his favourite game. The only people he respects are those who can beat him at it."

The brothers shook their heads.

"But how can you beat him?" Sergio, the eldest, growled in coarse Neapolitan patois. He shrugged his shoulders as he spoke. "Pyon is a shit, but he's a powerful man. There is only one way to stop him."

"NO!" Maria was desperately regretting flying to her family for support. "No. I will do it my way. The way to beat him is with allies. There is no shortage of them. Pyon has a lot of enemies for a lot of reasons, and, for the moment, his enemies are my friends. Please, you must leave it to me. I can do it."

The brothers were silent. Franco, twenty-nine and the Young Turk of the family, rose slowly from the chair in which he had been slouching and walked over to put his face a few inches in front of Maria's. "Maria, you're too soft, too much of a woman. This is a problem for men to deal with. We can understand other men, what they think, what they feel, what they will do."

"You're not a bit like Christy. You could never understand him like I do," Maria retorted. "I promise you I can do it." She looked at the three of them, pleading.

"Okay," said Sergio. "Sit down, Franco. We'll let her try it her way first. But remember, Maria, it is the whole Gatti family that he has insulted, not only you. So, if you fail, we will have to deal with it."

Maria Pyon slumped in a seat on an Alitalia 747 bound for London. She tried to pull her fragmented thoughts together and gain some control over her emotions. Her plan was only sketchy so far; she knew that she had to have help from people who would be unsympathetic towards her, if not her aim. She could only hope that they had strong enough reasons of their own to want to respond. Going to her brothers had put events out of her control. She had to succeed, if only to stop the matter ending up in their hands.

She had thought, up until then, that her family had come to terms with her marriage to Christy Pyon. Certainly her father, two years before on his death-bed at home in Naples, had taken Pyon's hand and mumbled, "God bless you, and take care of my precious daughter."

But old Gian-Battista Gatti had been a big man like Pyon, an independent, powerful and charming buccaneer who had built up his fleet of fifteen ships – 750,000 tons of it – from a single, decrepit Capri ferry-boat.

Not one of her brothers, who now ran the shipping company, was half the man their father had been. They had grown up in a luxury that contrasted sharply with the poverty of their Neapolitan cousins. They had come to think of themselves as special, overlooking the fact that it was only their father's money that set them apart. They were rich, truculent, small-minded men, who did not have the capacity to forgive or to reconsider the validity of their entrenched attitudes.

The brothers had a constant fear of Pyon. They were convinced that he had pursued and married their sister to get his hands on Linea Gatti, the family firm.

Maria knew that this consideration had never entered Pyon's head. His personality was too big, too generous even, for that kind of behaviour. And the chances were that this very characteristic would shield her own deviousness from his view.

Chemco

When Christy Pyon flew in from Nice, a car was waiting as his Cessna landed at Heathrow. Pyon strode from the plane to the Mercedes limousine. A secretary and a male assistant ran behind him to keep up.

They all climbed into the back of the car, and as soon as the chauffeur had closed the doors, Pyon picked up the telephone.

"What's Tenbury-Hamilton's number?" he barked at the woman on the seat opposite him.

Surprised by his unusual curtness, Pyon's travelling secretary keyed her lap-top computer and told him the number, adding, "Would you like me to get him for you, Mr Pyon?"

Pyon shook his head and stabbed the telephone with his forefinger.

The number rang, and was answered.

"Anglo-American."

"Get me Tenbury-Hamilton," Pyon boomed.

"Who is calling, please?"

"This is Christy Pyon."

"One moment, Mr Pyon."

As he waited to be put through, Pyon again found himself struggling to overcome the anger that rumbled through his body. He was like a volcano about to erupt. He was alarmed by the reappearance of a physical ire which he thought he had exorcised years ago. The frustration of his week with Julian had re-lit the flames, and the telephone call he had taken the night before in Cannes had fanned them.

He knew well the destructive power of his anger and the incurable wounds it could inflict. But from his scalp to the tips of his toes, the chemicals which this anger had released into his blood disrupted the functions of his internal organs. They had done so with intermittent intensity since the previous night. He had tried to hide this from Natalie – had succeeded in dissipating his fury for a short while in making love to her. But in the early morning, they surged back through his body, and he had no choice but to return to London to deal with the cause of his anger.

He had told Natalie that he was going, and why. He was capable of regretting the precipitateness of their parting. She said she understood, and he believed her. Since kissing her goodbye where she still lay in bed, he had not thought of her.

It was now four weeks since he had launched his audacious and, some said, ridiculous bid to take over one of the world's largest chemical conglomerates.

Chemco was as important as Dupont, Dow or ICI. It was one of the oldest pharmaceutical corporations in the US – as American as baseball, bubblegum and Billy the Kid. It was a core stockholding in Middle America's private portfolios. Its early history lay in the patent medicines which had become part of American folk-lore.

Several small towns in the mid-west owed their existence to Chemco, and its influence now seeped into many areas of American life. One of its more recent acquisitions had been a Texan agricultural bank. The operators of this small bank had made it a particularly attractive proposition. They were slipping through the back door into nationwide activity. While American law forbade any bank operating in more than one state, the catastrophes that had occurred through the mismanagement of hundreds of so-called "thrifts" – Savings and Loans banks – had prompted state and federal authorities to turn a blind eye when an institution from another state was prepared to come in, take them over and sort out the mess.

Blocks of Chemco shares were owned by most American institutions of any size, and by over twenty million individual Americans. To the chagrin of many of these, it had now emerged that the largest single shareholder, with 5 per cent, was Southern Hemisphere Resources.

Southern Hemisphere, known throughout the financial world now as SHR, was an international public company controlled by Christy Pyon. It had been set up ten years before as Pyon's principal vehicle for acquisition. It was in effect a hugely diverse holding company that also traded in the shares of other companies. Its core strength lay in significant holdings in many of Pyon's private companies, with interests in chemicals, mining, civil engineering, property, hotels and leisure on all the world's continents.

SHR's 5 per cent stake in Chemco had been paid for in cash, over $110 million of it, much of which had been provided by a consortium of a dozen American and European banks. The same banks had pledged to support a gargantuan bond issue with which SHR would fund the purchase of the other 95 per cent.

Michael Tenbury-Hamilton was executive chairman of Anglo-American Commercial Trust, a British bank which was the senior partner in the consortium. It was Tenbury-Hamilton who had phoned Pyon in Cannes the evening before.

Pyon, grasping his car phone in a hot hand, had to wait over a minute before he was put through to the banker. During that minute, he felt his temperature rise still further. He clasped the telephone in a white-knuckled grip and flexed the muscles in his face. His two employees looked on, alarmed, not daring to speak.

"Good morning, Christy." The banker's voice was calm, mildly affable and completely in control.

"I'm on my way round to see you," Pyon rasped. "I'll be there in forty-five minutes."

"I'm afraid I won't be here. I have to be at the Bank of England, a meeting of the Court."

"I don't care if you've a date to kiss the Chancellor's backside – this can't wait."

"It'll have to, Christy. I can see you at four this afternoon. I'll say goodbye until then."

With a click, the line was dead.

Pyon stared in fury at the instrument in his hand. He smashed it back on to its cradle, glanced at the worried faces opposite him and glared out of the window. He struggled to bring his thoughts under control.

However severe the provocation, he must not, could not allow himself unpredictable emotional reactions.

These bankers, he reasoned to himself, were not against him; they were simply for themselves. Heavy pressure had been exerted for several weeks, especially on the American banks, to withdraw their support. From their point of view, the equation no longer favoured Pyon.

He tried to reject the notion that the English bankers were going to take this opportunity to demonstrate their disapproval of him. That sort of thing had ceased to be a factor in financial decision-making a dozen or more years ago. Their actions now would be determined only by expediency. They had a lot to gain by supporting Pyon in his quest for Chemco, though not as much as Pyon. But Tenbury-Hamilton's condescending voice continued to ring inside Pyon's head.

God, how he hated the smugness of Anglo-Saxon prats like Tenbury-Hamilton, men who had never taken a risk in their lives, who had travelled on orderly tramlines from school to Oxbridge to a job in the city; slaves to the establishment who treated outsiders with mean-minded contempt, yet were happy to act as financial gofers to the people they excluded. Maybe they were smart enough to realise that it was their very exclusion of people like him that created fanatically driven entrepreneurs who, in taking the risks, became valuable clients.

Pyon had now regained control of his anger. He had been dealing with this sort of situation for years. Nevertheless, this was by far the biggest yet; and there was even greater reason not to be affected by any perceived personal affront. Ultimately, the bankers' desire for profits could be manipulated by his own wealth and power. They were only in it for the money.

The bankers in America had been candid with Pyon from the very start of this deal, even, indeed, during the course of earlier deals. They were going to have public relations difficulties in supporting any alien bid for Chemco. That was why Pyon had raised a substantial proportion of the necessary funds in Europe.

Pyon concluded that, as far as the American banks were concerned, his only chance was to redress the balance of reward.

As Pyon's car glided over the Hammersmith flyover and descended into the tail-back of mid-morning traffic entering central London, he picked up the intercom and told his driver to go to Southern Hemisphere's offices in Mayfair.

With a hint of apology, he spoke to his long-suffering PA. "Jonathan, would you ever pour me a good drop of Black Bush. I need to get a nasty taste out of my mouth."

The quietly-suited young man smiled with the release of tension and delved into the drinks cabinet.

Pyon turned to his secretary. "I'm seeing Tenbury-Hamilton at four. Get hold of Newberry and ask him to be there, and I'll want you there as well."

The woman nodded. As she picked up the phone, she gave a quick smile to her colleague who was pouring Pyon's drink. Pyon saw the exchange, and the reassurance which his outwardly restored calm had provided.

The West End offices of Southern Hemisphere Resources backed on to the mews in which, a few years before, Pyon had bought a house for the use of his English family. It did not connect directly through – Liz had insisted – but it was only a short walk from door to door.

When he arrived at his office, Pyon found Ken Newberry waiting for him.

"Morning, Ken."

Newberry acknowledged the greeting with a nod.

Pyon went on, "We've a pile of work to do. First, I want all American press-cuttings on the deal. Also, extract from our files a list of all share-holders in Chemco holding 1 per cent or more. Check with our friendly New York broker to see if there have been any dodgy-looking purchases. I want a CV and appraisal of every individual we deal with in the English banks; I want to find the hungriest and most vulnerable, preferably one with a bit of flair. And I want to set up a meeting this evening with Leo Jackson, Lenny Shemilt, Adnan al Souf and Morry Weintraub."

"Are you planning a Middle East peace conference?"

"You know those fellas are too busy making money to worry about politics."

"Yeah. Have we got problems, then?"

"Nothing serious. Just a necessary change of tactics. The American banks are getting twitchy."

"I'm not surprised. When I was in the States last week, our bid was the major news story. There's a poxy little town in the middle of nowhere, Minnesota, entirely dependent on the Chemco paint plant. The mayor was going on as if monsters from outer space were going to take them over. He's appealed to the President to invoke some clause in the constitution. They're all bloody paranoid, since the Japs bought the Rockefeller Center and all that."

"What the hell are Bob MacFarlane and his PR people doing?" Pyon shook his head. "It shouldn't be so hard to convince the locals that we have no intention of closing everything down."

"They won't listen, not after you shut down the Lafayette Tyre Company."

"I shut that with the complete agreement of the unions. Everyone knows that. It was losing half a million dollars a week."

"These people aren't talking logic; they're talking visible jobs, and re-election."

"For Christ's sake, I know that. We'll probably have to find someone else to handle the PR. But now, get together all the information I want, and I'll see you later, before we go to Tenbury-Hamilton's."

"Okay, Pyon." Newberry produced a compliant smile.

Pyon saw through to the resentment, and noted it. But he displayed nothing. He left the room thoughtfully, gave a wordless, one-sided smile to the woman in the outer office and descended the fine cantilevered staircase which curved down to the marble-floored hallway. A commissionaire saluted as he opened the front door.

It was a fine May morning. Starlings squabbled and sparrows chirruped noisily in the new-leafed plane trees that lined the street. The tourists ambling along the broad pavements exuded a relaxed, unhurried air, which exacerbated Pyon's sense of isolation as he strode round to the house which he regarded as his London home.

He knew Liz was in London; he had been speaking to her on the phone the day before about Julian's success. He was confident she would still be in; she was not an early starter.

Now, he admitted to himself, he wanted her support.

He let himself in through the neo-Tudor front door and closed it behind him.

"Liz?" His voice boomed through the hall and up the stairs.

A small dark maid trotted in from the back of the house. "Mrs Pyon not in," she said.

"Where is she? When is she back?"

"She don't say," the maid mumbled uneasily.

"Oh Christ!" Pyon was alarmed by the disappointment he felt. Then, more calmly, he said, "Bring some coffee to the study, please." He climbed the broad stairs and took a long corridor to a small library, beyond the drawing-room, overlooking the garden at the back of the house.

He sat on a chair behind a large Victorian mahogany desk on which he placed his feet before picking up the telephone. He was dialling his office, twenty yards away, when he heard someone come through the open door.

"Just put it on that table by the window," he said without looking up.

"Hello, Christy."

Pyon's head jerked up.

"Liz!" He put down the phone and swung his feet off

the desk. He crossed the room to greet his ex-wife with an enthusiastic embrace. "That daft-looking maid said you were out." He bent to kiss her mouth, but she turned her head away.

"I'm sorry, Christy. I told her I didn't want to see you."

"Good God! Why ever not?" Pyon looked at her with exaggerated hurt. "What's the problem? You look very tired."

"So do you, Christy. Why didn't you tell me that you were coming? You didn't mention it on the phone yesterday."

"I didn't intend to come, but," he gave a carefree shake of his head, "a crisis calls."

"Poor old Christy; when doesn't it?"

"Agh, this one's a bit of a monster."

"To do with business?"

"Yes, of course. You must know the trouble I've been having with Chemco."

"The Sunday papers said that if you sold your shares in Chemco now you'd make a profit of twenty million. That sounds a tolerable sort of crisis to me. No," Liz walked away from him, towards the window, "I thought you might be having problems because of this girl from Mauritius."

"Ah . . ." Pyon moved to stand beside his ex-wife; together they looked down on a man, bearded and bare-torsoed, mowing the flawless dark-green lawn in the garden. "You'd heard about that, then?"

"Didn't you know it had been in all the tabloids here?"

"You've got to believe how sorry I am that a thing like that should get in the papers – God knows, I've managed to avoid them for years. As a matter of fact, I didn't know it had for sure. I was spotted but, I thought, not recognised." He heaved his shoulders in resignation, and self-knowledge. "My own people were too shit-scared to tell me, and I never read the rags myself. Does it worry you?"

"For God's sake, Christy, of course it does; and I simply don't believe you didn't know." She sighed. "It's like losing you all over again. I had finally got used to the idea of Maria, but what upsets me about this story is that you were careless enough to allow it to happen, and the girl looks rather nice, which wasn't something one could say about Maria."

"God, I'm sorry, Liz. I'm a terrible man; I take you so for granted. You're quite right, though, Natalie is a nice girl, and she's led a sheltered life. I thought she'd enjoy Cannes, that's all."

"And did she?"

"She did, very much. She's a bright girl, very perceptive. But look, it's nothing for you to worry about. It doesn't change anything between us, you must know that."

Liz looked at him for a moment, forlorn, but a little defiant. "I wish I understood just what there is between us."

"Ah Liz, come on. You're the most important woman in the world to me. You know that. That's why I'm here now. You're the only person I can talk to or ask for support."

"When did you ever need support, Christy?"

"Now. Right now. I told you, I've a crisis on my hands so I came here to see you."

"All the way from your office round the corner?"

"Come on, that's not fair."

He had put an arm around her waist and was about to attempt another kiss, when the maid appeared with the coffee he had asked for.

"Take it to the drawing-room, with another cup for Mrs Pyon," Christy told her. He turned back to Liz. "Okay? Can we talk there? D'you have time?"

Liz nodded and they walked, he with his arm still around her waist, along the corridor to the large, light room, hung with floral curtains and some of the best of Pyon's Pre-Raphaelite pictures.

Liz sat down and leaned back on one of the big cream linen sofas. Pyon stood in front of the empty fireplace.

"So," Liz asked, "what brings on this rare and urgent need for my support?"

"Would you prefer that I needed your support the whole time? I don't often ask your help."

"All right. What's the trouble?"

"Chemco, like I said. This will be the deal of my life. It puts me right in the top ten. Everything about it is perfect; a vast, great, underused, undervalued flabby organisation. There are over three hundred separate companies, almost every one of them with undeveloped potential. But it's so big that no one

126

has yet dared to take it on. And even now, when Chemco is screaming for a White Knight, like some great fat maiden who's kidded herself she's about to be raped, no Sir Galahad has appeared. Of course the locals, the politicians and the papers have rallied round to defend a corporation that's been a regular gravy train. They're running a vitriolic campaign against myself, suggesting that every employee is going to be put out of a job. They're grabbing at straws, anti-trust laws and my fitness to own a bank. They know they've no case, but it'll take fifty lawyers a year or more to prove it, by which time, they hope, I'll have gone away. They're also blackmailing the American banks into withdrawing their support for me. And this afternoon, the pompous prats in the London banks are going to use this as an excuse to do the same."

"Why should the English banks want an excuse?"

"You know they've never liked me in the City. You remember how they behaved when I first floated LWPC."

"For goodness sake, Christy, that was twenty-five years ago. Most of the people around then must be dead by now."

"Of course they're not. The senior men now were impressionable office-boys then. You can never entirely shake off the prejudice of the City of London. Look at poor old Bob Maxwell."

"Poor old Bob Maxwell indeed! Why are you still so sensitive? Maybe these bankers simply think you'd be better off taking your profit now, rather than waiting years for lawyers to thrash out the legality of your bid."

Pyon looked down at her and slowly shook his head. "You know me better than that, Liz. I'm not going to give in now. I can't miss this one. There'll never be another chance like it."

"But Christy, surely it's not the end of the world if you don't get it. You'll have made a colossal amount of money which you don't need. Why not just relax and put it down to circumstances beyond your control?"

"That is the point, really, not the money. You might as well ask a mountaineer: why bother with Everest when you've already done Mont Blanc?"

"Oh Christy," Liz sighed with resilient affection, "I know what you're saying. I'm just suggesting you alter your perspective. You're as manic as you were thirty years ago, only then it was some tumbled-down warehouse in the back end of Bradford. I wish I could say something helpful now."

"You can. Let me tell you all about it and why it matters. I need you, and only you, really, to understand my motives. God knows, it would be hard to make them look good on a press release, but I would like you to know, even, dare I suggest it, applaud my reasons. It is not a simple question of vanity; I don't care personally that few people will be pleased when I pull it off, but I do want you to be."

"I will be, Christy, but do you really think it's possible?"

Pyon smiled. "It'll be a hell of a fight, and not entirely clean, but I'll do it."

"I dare say you will, and I'll back you. But in return, will you promise me something? While you're engaged in the battle, could you try not to neglect Laura and Julian – especially J?"

"Good God, I've just spent a week with Julian. He's no excuse to consider himself short of paternal consideration. I'll overlook the fact that he's not shown much gratitude for the money I put into his film, nor for the time I've taken over it."

"If Julian is difficult, and I admit he is, it's mainly because you're his father."

"I know that, but a bigger helping of Irish genes would have helped."

"Like Laura?"

"Well, yes. How is she, by the way? Did she go to Brazil?"

"Eventually, last weekend." Liz sighed. "It's odd – but obvious I suppose – I find it very difficult to keep the peace with Laura. I guess it's a question of genes and sex."

Pyon laughed. "Sex, genes and hormones – the cause of all the world's problems. But don't worry about Laura. She's full of ideals and desires which she can't reconcile but in the end she'll settle down and be either a fully committed idealist or a fully-uncommitted pragmatist. The function of child-bearing usually favours pragmatism."

"Is that what you'd prefer?"

"Not necessarily."

Liz looked at him thoughtfully and poured them some more coffee. "I think you're still as confused as she is."

"Sure I am. Wouldn't it be as dull as hell to know all the answers? A good working knowledge of human weakness is the only wisdom I possess."

"Nonsense. You're just a bully with a huge ego and a lot of charm."

"Now there's a word. You must tell me what it means some time."

Pyon leaned down and gave his ex-wife a tender kiss which she accepted. "Talking to you has done me a power of good, as always. You're the best woman in the world and I don't deserve you."

"No, you don't, but will you tell me how long you'll be staying this time?"

"A few days for sure. There's a bunch of fellas coming round to see me here tonight, but don't worry about dinner, it'll be too late for that."

Pyon walked towards the door and gave Liz a quick last smile before descending to the hall and out into the cobbled mews. Yet even as he left the house, his muscles tightened, and thoughts of his ex-wife, wife and lover, and his four children became secondary and were overridden.

Five minutes later he was back in his office.

Off the record

"I think, don't you, that it would be prudent if this meeting were rather informal – quite off the record?" Michael Tenbury-Hamilton smiled smoothly across his desk at Christy Pyon.

Pyon smiled back. "You don't say?"

He had realised as soon as he saw Tenbury-Hamilton that he had been too concerned about the banker's tribal considerations and had underestimated his desire for profit. He turned to the secretary, poised to take notes by his side. "Thank you, Avril, you can go. But wait in the building. You too, Ken."

Newberry smiled cannily. He wanted the banker to know that he knew what was going to be said. "Yeah. Of course." He left the large panelled office, opening the door for Pyon's secretary with exaggerated jauntiness.

The door closed behind them.

"I've often wondered why Newberry's still with you," Tenbury-Hamilton remarked.

"You mean because he's rather common? Not sufficiently soigné to be sitting in offices like these?"

"Not just that, no. It's the resentment that's caused by those characteristics."

"It's true that Ken has a chip on both shoulders, and one of them relates directly to me. But that's what makes him worth hanging on to. He's valuable because he's sharp, greedy and aware of his limitations. I didn't go into business because I wanted regular luncheon companions. Nor did I come here to discuss Newberry."

The banker shrugged. "He's an integral part of your business, at the moment, and that makes him part of ours. I don't trust him."

"Would you really trust him more if he'd been to Eton or was a member of the Carlton?"

"Not necessarily, but I'd know what I was dealing with. I must insist that he is not given details of the conversation we are about to have."

"For God's sake, man, d'you think I just got off the boat? I have been in this situation quite a few times before, you may recall, and you've done very nicely out of it. I don't need any lectures in acquisition tactics."

"No, of course you don't." Tenbury-Hamilton stood up and walked over to a fine inlaid Georgian cabinet. "Would you like a drink – Black Bush, isn't it?"

"Sure, then let's get on with it."

A Waterford decanter issued four loud glugs. The banker walked round and handed a heavy glass to Pyon.

"There's not a lot to say, really. The Americans are going

to have to renege on their commitment to support your bond issue. There's been too much political pressure applied, and a lot of heavyweight lobbying. It's hard to guess what that will do to the SHR price, or, for that matter, to the price of Chemco. This AIDS vaccine has been disappointingly slow in making its appearance since they first announced it. We don't know, any more than you, whether it's your raid, or expectations for the vaccine, that has pushed the price up in the last four weeks. Despite Berstein's repeated delay in issuing some kind of progress report, everyone's convinced themselves that Chemco are going to come up with something. If anything, the potential is more exciting than the actuality, because when they *do* introduce the stuff, it's going to be with the Federal Drug Administration for a hell of a time before it can go on the market, even if they really push it through. So the information you fed to the papers when you started buying heavily didn't particularly help, did it?"

"Who knows? I still bought well, in any case. Even now the shares are at least two bucks below the broken up asset value, without the AIDS drug."

"In your opinion," the banker inserted.

"And who has a more valid one? Not you fellas sitting on your butts in Cheapside."

"There are other factors. This frothy market isn't going to last for ever. And I think investors are going to become a little chary of junk bonds of even the most respectable provenance." The banker raised a hand to his left eyebrow and stroked its wayward tufts with his forefinger. "Tell me, will those attending your little gathering tonight be prepared to back your evaluation?"

Even Pyon was shaken by this evidence of ubiquitous intelligence gathering. "Good God almighty, you'll be getting tip-offs from my own mother next. You know the answer to that question."

"Yes, I do. It only remains for me to say that our services are at their disposal – a few removes away, of course – and to wish you the best of luck. We will continue to support you here, for the time being, though that's bound to depend on your clearing bank remaining happy to lead the bond issue, and finding partners for it besides us."

"Of course. But I'm delighted to hear you're continuing to support us in principle. You're more intelligent than you look, Mr Tenbury-Hamilton."

"And so are you, Mr Pyon."

Pyon laughed and drained his glass. "Right. If my chums need your help, they'll contact you through Zurich, will they not?"

"I think that's best."

"And I hope this place is more secure than my bloody office."

Tenbury-Hamilton smiled, and held out a small, white hand. "One last thing. Might I suggest that you re-establish the admirably low public profile you normally maintain? The American public, like our own, is apt to be swayed by trivial and irrelevant misdemeanours."

Pyon grunted and released the other's hand from his firm grasp. "Fucking hacks."

"Quite," he heard the banker say as he turned to leave.

In the grand Victorian lobby of the bank, Pyon found Newberry and his secretary waiting for him.

"Avril, you'll have to take a cab back. Mr Newberry and I've to talk in the car," he told them.

The middle-aged woman who had worked for Pyon for twenty years nodded and walked out on to the busy pavement. Pyon and Newberry made their way through the building to a courtyard where Pyon's Mercedes waited.

Inside the car, Newberry asked, "How'd it go?"

"No problem. Tenbury-Hamilton says he doesn't trust you. Can you tell me why he's wrong?"

"He's a bloody snob. And he's a fool. The reason you can trust me is very simple: I'll make more money that way."

"That's the sort of honest answer I like. I wouldn't want to be relying on intangible qualities such as personal loyalty."

"You know me better than that, Christy, after thirty years."

Pyon turned to look at him. "I wonder if I do?" he said quietly. "Still, let's not ponder these things now. Have you found a friend among our bankers?"

"Yeah. As it happens, I think I have. A greedy little whizz-kid at Anglo-American – one of Tenbury-Hamilton's bright young 'opefuls."

"Master Fielder, by any chance?"

"Yes."

"He's a bright young fella. They're grooming him for the top." Pyon nodded to himself. "But I think he lacks patience."

"He also bought a hundred thousand Chemco, the week before we went for it."

"Did he, b'Jaysus? The naughty boy. But he can't be too bright if we found out."

"Ah, well. He had a terrible bit of bad luck there. He happened to do his deal through the Virgin Islands, and he used our man, Delgado, to do it." Newberry shrugged. "Delgado owes us too many favours to risk letting a thing like that slip through. Our young Jeremy had done everything right, otherwise. Street names and all that."

Pyon smiled at the irony of the coincidence. Not such a coincidence, though there were not that many lawyers in the BVIs. Still, it was the sort of bad luck which could hardly expect a young man to guard against.

"He sounds the sort of fella we need. Have you fixed a meeting?"

"Yeah. Six, at our office."

"Change it to my house."

"Right. Anyone else?"

"No. Just me and him. I'd like to impress on him the privacy of our discussion."

"If that's what you want. The other four are coming there at ten."

"Eagerly?"

"They didn't say."

"Hmm," Pyon murmured. He became silent for a few moments, then said, "From now on you'd better keep away from the front line of this one, just to keep Tenbury-Hamilton happy."

133

Newberry shrugged, and the two men scarcely spoke until they had reached the Southern Hemisphere offices in South Audley Street.

Jeremy Fielder parked his black Porsche in the mews, climbed out and locked it. Unconsciously, preparing himself for a face to face meeting with the legendary Christy Pyon, he shot his cuffs and straightened his Givenchy tie.

Fielder was a stocky man of thirty-one. He stood five foot eight, with a thick neck and the legs of a prop-forward. His hair was short, dark and wiry, beginning to thin on the crown. As he walked quickly across the uneven cobble-stones, his heavy, slightly coarse features twitched and his brown eyes glinted.

He tugged the cast-iron bellpull and a little maid opened the door to him.

"Jeremy Fielder for Mr Pyon," he announced.

The maid held the door wide for him and silently indicated the stairs. Fielder climbed the broad steps, taking in the big dramatic Victorian paintings, interspersed with a few earlier, and equally valuable, pictures of horses. At the top of the stairs he glanced along the corridor and made for the only open door. This gave into a large drawing-room. There was no one there, but he walked in. He made an effort to control a slight trembling of his limbs as he absorbed all the signs of quiet, prodigious opulence, and sensed the personality of its begetter. After five minutes or so, he checked the time on his Cartier watch, and his confidence faltered.

Maybe there was some mistake. Maybe that yobbo henchman of Pyon's was setting him up for something. Maybe – he stiffened – they had discovered his heavily camouflaged act of insider dealing.

Fielder began to feel as he had done twenty years before, waiting in the headmaster's study of his prep school, expecting to be beaten for cheating or dirty play on the rugger field.

He heard the soft thump of footsteps approach the room and his pulse quickened.

When Pyon entered, the young man flushed, and fumbled his fists from his pockets to extend a warm hand towards the famous tycoon.

Pyon took the hand with a short nod. "Evening, Jeremy. Good of you to spare the time."

"Not at all, Mr Pyon. It's a pleasure."

"Pleasure is not the object of the exercise."

"No, no. Of course not."

Pyon put the young man at his ease with a quick upturn of the side of his mouth. "Will you have a drink?"

"Just a Perrier or something, thanks."

Pyon nodded at a drinks cabinet at the side of the room. "Over there, and pour me a Black Bush while you're at it."

When Fielder, regretting his choice, had clattered a few bottles and glasses, and handed a very full tumbler of Irish whiskey to his host, Pyon said, "Okay, sit down. You and the bank you work for have been very close to Southern Hemisphere's bid for Chemco. And we've been pleased with your performance so far. I gather from Ken Newberry that you personally have been working on it full time. Now, I want you to tell me all you know about the progress of our bid."

The banker sat on one of the two beige sofas. Pyon remained standing in the middle of the room.

Fielder gathered his thoughts. After a moment he began confidently, as if delivering a lecture. "Chemco is a diverse, multi-national corporation. Its base is in pharmaceuticals and it's predominantly active in the US, with a number of related holdings throughout the world. Its equity consists of 427 million shares in ordinary stock, currently trading at between $5.95 and $6.05 on exchanges in the States, London, Europe and the Far East. At present the principal shareholder is Southern Hemisphere Resources, which owns about 22 million, bought at between $4 and $6, probably at an average of $5.20 – a total cost of about $110 million." He glanced at Pyon for confirmation.

"About that," Pyon nodded.

"The funding for this purchase has been provided by American and European banks; about $30 million from the States, $70 million in Europe, and $10 million from SHR's own cash resources. The money has been borrowed at prime rate, with the shares as security."

Fielder glanced at Pyon, confident that he was on firm

ground so far. He was about to resume, when Pyon spoke with a quiet growl.

"Tell me about the arbitrageurs and speculators."

Fielder nodded. "There has been substantial profit-taking since SHR started buying seriously in April. Most of the big arbitrageurs have been in and out."

"What about speculators who moved before we did?"

Fielder blinked. "I don't think there were any. The market in Chemco had been pretty sluggish, and no one knew that you were on the prowl. There hadn't been a murmur about it."

"Despite the fact that we were already holding five million?"

"Well, you built that up quietly, and I think that was construed as normal trading, rather than stake-building. After all, SHR has been in and out of a lot of shares on the same scale without going for them."

"So, you don't think anyone got wind of it before we went for it?"

Fielder shook his head. "Not as far as I'm aware."

"I wonder. For instance, there was a little two-bit British Virgin Islands investment company bought a hundred thousand at just under four bucks the day before we started. One of our New York brokers bought the parcel last week at just under six bucks."

Fielder's face paled. He looked down at his stocky thighs and fingered the creases of his navy blue trousers. "I suppose with a corporation that size, with such a wide shareholding, there are always going to be the odd punters who get lucky without particularly expecting it." He looked up and added hurriedly, as if it had just occurred to him, "Maybe they were gambling on the AIDS vaccine announcement."

"Maybe, but the price as it stood then had already taken account of that. Maybe they knew something that Joe Public didn't. What the hell, we'll not bother about some little fella making a quick two hundred grand at our expense. But we'll have to be sure that no bigger punters get to know of any other moves we're planning. From now on, I'll be calling all the shots – personally – and I'll be aware of who knows." He glanced at Fielder's glass. "You look as though you need something a little stronger in your glass. Help yourself."

Fielder was grateful for the opportunity to recover his composure. He stood up and walked quickly to the drinks cabinet, where he poured himself a large vodka and tonic. He returned to the sofa and sat back in it with as much apparent ease as he could convey.

"All right," Pyon continued, "what is your understanding of the current position of our bid?"

"Well, like all reverse takeovers, we've a struggle on our hands. Southern Hemisphere, owning just under 5 per cent of Chemco outright, are offering $4 and one SHR share per Chemco share for the other 95 per cent. SHR's price is fluctuating around $4 at the moment, making a total offer price of $8. On the face of it, a good offer, some analysts say far too good. However, there is almost unanimous resistance to the offer from the other shareholders as well as a number of technical obstacles." Fielder paused to take a drink and glanced at the Irishman for a reaction.

"Okay," said Pyon. "Now, which of the problems we face is the trickiest?"

"That's hard to say at this stage. The smallest technical problem could be one of the most intractable: the fact that one of Chemco's wholly owned subsidiaries, the Agricultural Bank of Texas, operates in twenty separate states through all the Savings and Loans Banks it has acquired over the last couple of years. Each of those states, as well as the Fed, has to accept SHR as a suitable operator. It seems to me that in ruling on this, patriotism could get the better of logic."

"I've no doubt it will, but in the end, our case is unbeatable. We shall be demonstrably strong enough to deal with the liabilities involved. It may cost a lot in time and lawyers, but we will win. I don't see this as a real problem, merely a delaying tactic to encourage us to fold up our tents and steal away with the consolation prize of a fat profit, like Jimmy Goldsmith and Goodyear. Pinpoint for me our greatest actual problem."

"As I see it, there are two that are inextricably linked. It's in the nature of a company like SHR that the share price is volatile, and reflects prevailing confidence in the management, which, frankly, means you. There isn't an analyst in London who could truthfully say that he can

137

make even a good guess at its net asset value at any given moment. Results over the last four years have been stunning, and your decision to go highly liquid in the summer of 1987 has obviously given the share a lustre. But a substantial part of Southern Hemisphere's more permanent holdings are in private subsidiaries which are part-owned by you. Whatever profits they make can be made available or not to the parent company quite arbitrarily, for all practical purposes. So I think SHR's price is very vulnerable, and this leads on to the other problem. We will fund the cash element of our bid with a major bond issue, and we need our shareholders' consent for the paper element.

"We have to issue 405 million new shares, and we have to raise $1.6 billion. The big question is, what will the prospect of a bond issue of that size do to our price? If it drops much below $4, we're going to look distinctly dodgy, and the issue could flop badly. On top of that, our share and cash offer for Chemco will obviously become a lot less generous and even the more pragmatic American institutions who support our bid tacitly at the moment will reject it."

As he was speaking, Fielder slowly crouched further forward on the sofa. Now he stopped talking, and leaned back in the deep cushions, with his hands behind his head. His voice became husky with the knowledge that he was approaching dangerous ground. "My view is that, for the bid to work, Southern Hemisphere's price must be maintained at almost any cost."

"At any cost, you think?" Pyon asked.

"What that cost should be is a matter of the true value of Chemco, and simple arithmetic."

Pyon looked down at the the young man, who was relaxed and confident now, pleased with his presentation.

"You mean a straight, no-holds-barred share support operation? But that would mean breaking the rules," Pyon said quietly.

"Ethics are all very well, but very expensive, it seems to me."

"There are watchdogs, too," Pyon reminded him.

"Blind and toothless for the most part." Fielder was confident again. Pyon, as he had anticipated, had not balked at the suggestion. "And anyway, what if our share price is propped up for a bit? Who suffers?"

"Joe Public, the integrity of the market."

"Joe Public goes to the dog races. He knows that every other race is, as they say, predetermined, but he still goes and has a punt. As for the integrity of the market," Fielder shrugged. "There can be no real integrity in a jungle, just rules that the authorities are seen to enforce occasionally."

"Not so occasionally now, m'boy. You're obviously still young enough to want a bit of danger in your life, as well as a lot of money. So I'll do you a favour, I'll provide a bit of danger and a lot of money. Would you like that?"

Fielder pushed himself forward on the sofa and stood up. Pyon stood six or seven inches taller and the young banker walked a few yards down the large room before he turned to face him. "A lot of money, Mr Pyon? Can you specify?"

"Enough to make you very happy, well, maybe not happy, but very pleased with yourself for a year or two, before your aspirations expand."

"I'm not sure what you're asking me to do, though I've a good idea, and I would need to know what was in it for me before I started taking risks with my career."

Pyon gave him a big, warm smile, and chuckled. "I'm afraid you've already taken at least one large and rather regrettable risk, for a mere $200,000. But I won't be passing the details to the DTI, not yet awhile anyway, maybe never. So, when I say enough, you'll just have to trust my judgement, won't you?"

Ireland and horses

Fielder left the house with a few drops of sweat trickling from his short wiry sideboards. Pyon knew that a blend of blackmail and greed had secured a reliable ally for him. And he had to have someone in one of the banks who knew what was going on. It was quite possible, of course, that others there might suspect what was being done, but as long as they could not be implicated, they were not going to rock the boat. Tenbury-Hamilton would approve, so long as any dubious activity was kept at arm's length from Anglo-American.

Pyon anyway had no misgivings about organising a share support operation. If it was done right, it would be hard to detect, and impossible to prove. The news from New York had been better this evening, too. Chemco's price had moved twenty cents so far that day, which suggested that people were tending to take his bid more seriously. Pyon, unlike Tenbury-Hamilton, was sure that the tantalisingly jerky progress of the AIDS vaccine had had little effect on the price.

Feeling more ebullient about his chances than he had for a few days, he stood in the hall and boomed, "Liz? Where are you?"

After a moment or two she appeared at the top of the stairs. "What are you shouting about, Christy?"

"I'm sorry. I was not shouting, merely calling. Would you like a bite to eat at that new caviar emporium in Bruton Place? We've time before my later guests arrive."

"Yes, I'd like that. Just let me change, then we could walk. It's a lovely evening."

They strolled, arm in arm, like a recently married couple. Pyon enjoyed walking, and felt no loss of dignity; the recent photo in the papers had been so grainy as not to provoke instant recognition.

For an hour or two, he was prepared to put his plans to one side, and turn his mind to domestic issues.

They were greeted with discreet charm by the old-Etonian manager of the restaurant, and sat at the bar to drink a bottle of Krug with him. Among the other early diners there were a well-known racehorse trainer with a couple of his owners, one of whom had recently bought a colt from Liz. They joined them for a while before being shown to a table in a corner of the quiet room. After they had ordered they continued to talk about horses. They had several moderately successful animals in training, including their filly who had come third in the One Thousand Guineas. Pyon promised Liz he would be at Epsom to see the horse run in the Oaks.

Liz became animated as she talked about her mares in Ireland; this was territory where she was confident. Pyon enjoyed their horses, but he did not have Liz's depth of knowledge. He was proud of her commitment and success, and the fact that the Clonegall stud was a self-supporting, indeed, fairly profitable operation. So conversations about bloodstock, like discussions about their children, tended to be held on equal terms. She chided her ex-husband for not having visited the stud in County Carlow for so long. "Really, Christy, people are beginning to feel rejected."

"I'll be over soon, I promise."

"Well, you should, you always seem more relaxed when you're there."

Pyon agreed. "There is an absence of pressure out there. But then, I like pressure."

"But you're much nicer when you're without it."

"You'd get bored to hell with having me around all the time. And I'd only start trying to run things. You wouldn't like that, would you?"

Liz smiled. "No, but it would be nice to have a little more of you, and since you waded in and sort of set yourself up as tribal chieftain, the O'Donnells expect to see more of you. I'm sure you'd enjoy it more than hobnobbing with your Neapolitan in-laws."

Liz saw the wistfulness which passed quickly across his face before he smiled and said, "If I didn't know you better, I might suspect you of trying to entice me away from my wife."

"No, I'm not." She paused, "But I was wondering if your Mauritian friend had."

"For God's sake, Liz, I told you, she's just a bright goodlooking girl I happened to meet. There's nothing serious to it."

They were unobtrusively served with deep purple bortsch and thick cream and a carafe of vodka in a block of ice, then buckwheat blinis, filled with small succulent orbs of beluga caviar which dissolved in their mouths. Liz turned the conversation back to the safe ground of horses. But, towards the end of dinner, she surprised Pyon, looking at him with candid affection, saying, "The horses and the locals aren't the only reasons I'd like you to come to Ireland; I miss you, believe it or not."

Looking at her still-beautiful features, Pyon's pleasure overcame his discomfort. "I promise I'll come more. I told you earlier, right now, I need your support."

"You haven't told me yet what went on at your meeting with Anglo-American."

Calm thoughts of Ireland and horses ebbed from Pyon's consciousness, to be replaced by the more normal alertness of a stalking beast.

"They're still on my side."

"I told you they would be. Why do you still feel that everyone's got it in for you? It's ridiculous after all this time."

"Those people are not going to do me any favours, but the chance of making a few million puts that in perspective for them."

"Do they do anyone favours? Surely, that's not their *raison d'être*?"

"Their *raison d'être* is protecting the status quo; keeping the control within their establishment."

"You've made a great deal more money than most of them."

"Than all of them, but it's the power and influence that they need. That's how they justify their existence, they don't possess the talent to create a deal, but they have the right family connections to put them in a position to decide the fate of those who have not."

"I don't understand what you're complaining about."

"I'm complaining that these wankers are in a position to influence my deals. They've done nothing to earn it."

"And these people who are coming to see you later, are they outsiders, like you?"

"Sure they are, but they're very wealthy, and they've also managed to get the better of the old-Etonian mafia. That's why they'll help me. The bankers won't stop them, because there's money to be made – but they could."

"Our little party"

As Pyon opened the door to their house for Liz, the telephone was ringing. Pyon's chauffeur, Hanks, who doubled as man-servant, appeared from the back of the house. The call was for Pyon.

"Who is it?"

"I'm afraid the gentleman didn't say, sir, but he sounds like an American."

"Okay, I'll take it in the library." He turned to Liz. "This may take a while. If these fellas turn up, will you look after them for me?"

"Fine. Do I know any of them?"

"I don't think so, but they're all fairly civilised."

Pyon bounded up the stairs, and Liz followed more slowly. When she reached the top, the front doorbell, a large bronze object, clanked noisily. Hanks returned from his den to open it to a balding man of medium height, wearing large horn-rimmed glasses and a loud checked suit.

"Hello, Hanks," said the new arrival and, as he caught sight of Liz descending the stairs, "Liz! What a treat. I didn't expect to see you. Where's the big bog-trotter?"

Liz smiled. "Hello, Leo. He's on the phone. Come and have a drink. You're the first of several." She led Leo Jackson into the drawing-room, followed by Hanks.

"Can I get you a drink, madam, sir?" Hanks asked. Liz said no, and Leo Jackson said, "I'm on a diet; champagne for me."

Hanks left the room, and the bubbling entrepreneur, famous for his parties and his taste for young, silly models, took both Liz's hands in his, and kissed her warmly on the lips. "You look fresh as a daisy. The Irish climate must suit you."

"And you look as bald and as lecherous as ever," Liz replied.

Jackson grinned. "You'd better believe it. Do you know who else is turning up tonight?"

"No, I don't. Christy said I wouldn't know any of you."

"Typical. Your husband – sorry, ex-husband – is such an arrogant bugger he probably hasn't ever noticed whom you know and don't know. I can't think why you still put up with him, specially after the pasting the papers have given him."

Liz shrugged. "We have a sort of understanding."

He grunted. "You're much too good for him. What you need is a thoughtful romantic like me. Ah, the eagles gather." He had heard the doorbell ringing again.

"If you disapprove of him so strongly, why do business with him?"

"Business is business. Nobody can sniff out a bargain quite like Pyon. It's his Paddy horse-coper's blood." He glanced across to the door where two more men were being shown in, and gave an unsurprised nod of recognition. "I see Pyon's called a reunion of old campaigners." He turned to Liz. "Do you need an introduction to this pair of crooks?"

Liz nodded.

Jackson announced, "Mrs Christy Pyon, mark one; Lenny Shemilt, Morry Weintraub."

Both men came across to shake Liz's hand. They looked unexceptional, serious and grey-suited. In their mid-fifties, they gave the impression that the making of money was a serious, exclusive activity, to which all other aspects of their lives were incidental.

Liz took each warm fleshy palm in turn and was amused at their impatience at having to make small talk to her while they waited for Pyon.

Hanks had returned to the room with a bottle of champagne, which he started to open. He approached the two financiers. "Champagne, sir, sir?"

Both men shook their heads.

"Water," said Shemilt.

"Coffee," said the other.

Shemilt, a Jewish Iranian from the Lebanon with interests from Hong Kong to Rio, carpets to gold, turned to Leo Jackson. "Is there anyone else coming?"

Jackson shrugged. "I don't know. I should have thought there was enough muscle here to deal with most situations, but I don't know what Pyon has in mind."

Weintraub appeared not to be pleased to see Jackson. "I hope not. If I'd known this was a team game, I wouldn't have come. The more involved, the more chance of a whisper getting out. Has Pyon checked to see if this place is being watched?"

Hanks, handing a glass of water to Shemilt, cleared his throat to announce an interruption. "We have a man at the end of the mews, sir, to monitor any unexpected arrivals. And you might be interested to know that we are also expecting

Mr al Souf. He sent a messenger to say that he would be a little late."

The three men registered surprise and excitement. Even by their standards, Adnan al Souf was very rich indeed. He was from a powerful Egyptian trading dynasty, with strong Saudi connections, counted his assets in billions, and only involved himself in megadeals.

Liz too was surprised, and pleased. Al Souf had bought several yearlings from her. He had a great affection for horses, and was an experienced judge of youngstock. While he employed agents to hone down lists of prospective purchases, he usually found time to make the final decisions himself. He had visited the Clonegall stud the previous autumn, and had behaved with impressive and, as far as Liz could see, genuine courtesy.

He was an attractive man and unexpectedly thoughtful. On occasions, Liz had considered going along with the invitation that lurked, just perceptibly, beneath his polite and unpresumptuous charm. But Pyon's presence, even in his physical absence, had drawn her up.

She had not known that Pyon knew al Souf, and she was intrigued to see how the two would behave towards one another. Neither man could count meekness among his virtues, nor did Pyon readily acknowledge another man's dominant position. But Liz was sure that, whatever Pyon's wealth, Adnan al Souf's was much greater.

Pyon returned to the drawing-room, "Good evenin', gentlemen." His greeting was thick with Irish bonhomie. He glanced at each of the three in turn. "I'm sorry to have kept you waiting. I've just been getting the quiet word from New York. Two of Chemco's biggest shareholders are leaning in our direction though Southern Hemisphere's price is going to be critical. That's why you're here. But we've one more member of the party to arrive. I'm expecting Adnan al Souf." He was surprised there was not more of a reaction from his guests.

Hanks explained. "I'd already told the gentlemen. Mr al Souf sent a message to say he'd be late."

Pyon threw him an irritated glance. "Did he, b'Jaysus? Well, he'd better not be too late or he'll miss the party.

Well, while we're waiting, let's have a drink." Looking at Weintraub and Shemilt, he said, "Have a drop of the hard stuff, get into the party spirit."

"Is this a party?" Weintraub remarked drily.

"You could say that. A double party, really: a support party and a concert party."

"I think," said Liz, "that I'll leave you to it, if you'll excuse me." She had decided that, in the circumstances, it would probably be easier for Pyon if he remained unaware of her familiarity with al Souf.

"Okay, Liz," Pyon said and continued to cajole his restless guests into relaxing.

Liz left the room, and descended to the hall. When she reached the bottom of the stairs, the bell clanked once more. She walked across to the front door and opened it herself.

Three men stood on the wide doorstep. The swarthily handsome face of the man in the middle showed both surprise and pleasure. "Good evening, Liz. I didn't expect you to be here tonight, especially not opening the door to your ex-husband's guests."

Liz returned the greeting and ushered the Arab and his entourage inside. "I was in the hall when the bell rang. I'd just left the gathering upstairs. Would you do something for me, Adnan? I'd rather you didn't mention to Christy that you and I have met. He probably knows you've bought horses from me, but I've never told him about your visits to Clonegall."

"I'm flattered that you should want to keep that a secret from him." Al Souf gave a conspiratorial smile. "And I didn't come here to talk about horses or wives with him."

Liz nodded her thanks. "Let me show you up to the drawing-room where they are. Would your men like to stay in the servants' sitting-room?"

"They'll come with me, thank you."

Pyon greeted al Souf effusively, and introduced him to the other three. The Arab declined a drink, and Hanks left the room.

"Right, I'll not waste any time. I'm sure you all know the state of Southern Hemisphere's bid for Chemco. I

imagine you all agree with my logic in wanting to go for
it. There is a mountain of underused assets to play with,
though I only intend a partial break-up. I know that you,
Adnan, are interested in the Texas bank, and I don't think
you'll have any long-term difficulties getting past the state
regulators."

"There will be no difficulty," the Arab agreed.

"And I am giving you my guarantee that when I control
Chemco, you can have the bank. We'll have to have a
separate discussion about terms, but obviously, I won't be
unreasonable."

"Obviously," al Souf agreed again.

"Right then. The position is that I have five per cent of
Chemco. There's probably at least another fifteen per cent
on my side. Now I could just carry on buying more, but
beyond a certain point that's not possible. First of all, then,
I need your help in acquiring as much Chemco stock as you
can, for which I will guarantee you a fifty-cent premium on
each share. There are still over 400 million shares out there,
so there's a bit of scope."

Weintraub interrupted. "If your offer is accepted while
we're still holding Chemco stock, it could be more profitable
to accept the terms offered like any other stockholder."

"That isn't the deal I'm proposing, though," Pyon said.
"I'm offering guarantees where the position is still wide open.
You build up a stake, support my bid, and when it's accepted,
you sell your stock to Southern Hemisphere at fifty cents over
your buying price, whatever the prevailing market price. If
my offer is not accepted and finally fails, and Chemco's price
drops right back, I still pay you fifty cents profit. The reason,
if it isn't obvious, is that while I'm geared up for my bond
issue, I don't want to go borrowing for straight speculative
share-buying. And anyway, you gentlemen will probably be
able to buy a few blocks that won't be sold to me. Sure,
there'll be a lot of non-sellers, which brings me to the next,
more important of your functions. To make my share/cash
package irresistible, I need to spruce up SHR's apparent
solidity and its price, perhaps by a couple of dollars. That
will mean some heavy buying, at arm's length from m'self.
Legally, we can't be seen to buy back the shares that you buy,

so in the event that SHR's price drops back after a successful bid, which it probably will for a while, I'll guarantee you a profit on them by means of consultancy fees and so on. You'll have to nominate suitable vehicles for that." Pyon looked at the three of them in turn. He shrugged his shoulders with a big one-sided grin. "That's it, really. Nothing to it but a great fat profit and an American bank for Adnan."

"It's totally illegal," said Weintraub.

"Only if we're caught, and that'll only happen if one of us pops round to the DTI to spill the beans. I don't think that's likely, do you?"

"But who else would know?"

"Just one fella in Anglo-American whom I have by the balls, and Ken Newberry. And of course Adnan's men here, but they don't talk, do they?"

Al Souf shook his head.

"Is Newberry safe?" Lenny Shemilt asked.

"Now, Lenny, you know Ken. What do you think?"

"That depends how much he's making out of the deal."

"He's planning to retire after. His wife wants to move to Gloucestershire and be a member of the County, so he has to become a country gentleman. Don't worry about him."

"It sounds simple enough. You'll still be getting Chemco cheap. I might want to hang on to my Southern shares, but you wouldn't mind that," Leo Jackson said. "How much of your stock is there in the market?"

"About fifty million," Pyon replied.

Shemilt nodded. "It sounds all right to me. I'll go for it, but I'll want something in writing."

"Maybe you would, but you shouldn't, and you're not getting anything. You know damned well you don't need it," said Pyon.

"I don't know," said Shemilt. "Who's your man at Anglo-American?"

"Jeremy Fielder."

"He's a bit junior isn't he?"

"He's smart, and he's been handling this bid from the start. He knows exactly what's going on. He'll find a few parcels for you."

"Jeremy's a bright boy," Leo Jackson approved, "and nice

and greedy. I don't know where he gets it from. His parents are lovely people."

"Well, he'll be your contact point. I won't want you phoning me. Let him know your intentions by tomorrow at the latest, and I'll have a separate meet with each of you to agree terms." He turned to the Arab, who had remained silent during the others' questioning. "Adnan, you could come to Ireland. It would be quite normal for you to be visiting our stud, and anyway, you might see something there that catches your eye."

Leo Jackson laughed. "What did I tell you, always a horse-coper."

Al Souf nodded. "I will cancel my visit to Chantilly and come to Ireland instead."

"Leo, Lenny and Morry I can see in Paris, okay?" Pyon looked at them. They all agreed.

"Right then, is anyone going to join Leo and me for a drink to the success of our little party?" Pyon pushed a button by the fireplace to summon Hanks.

The two Jews nodded reluctantly and the Egyptian said, "By all means, if we have finished our discussion, but I should like to leave a little before these other gentlemen, if you don't mind."

"Don't want to be seen keeping bad company, eh?" said Jackson. "Don't blame you, not with Lenny and Morry. We'll let you get clear of Berkeley Square before we go."

"I think we should all leave separately," Weintraub said.

"Quite right," said Pyon as Hanks appeared with a fresh bottle of champagne. "Now, here's to a lovely party!"

Filumena

Julian Pyon was more flattered than he cared to admit by Enzo Fratinelli's invitation to dinner. The Italian film director had defied the passage of time and changing fashions to remain the most admired director among successive waves of emergent, younger movie-makers.

His films were characterised by an apparently unique impressionism. His use of minimal dialogue, soft-focused camera work and inspired locations had never palled. The hours he spent in quiet but forceful discussion with his actors, cameraman, designers and composers led to the creation of flawless films which had sustained him at the peak of his profession.

While making films he was utterly and fanatically single-minded, but between pictures he was affably, even uproariously sociable. He was discreetly rich, but his centrist socialist credentials were untarnished. When he felt like it, he could be an enthusiastic giver of parties, and these events were famous.

But Julian, still high on the success of his film in Cannes, drove to Enzo's rented house in Holland Park, feeling that he was doing the seventy-year-old Italian a favour. Previously Julian's public stance had been that awards were fatuous and gave a transient, disproportionate importance to any work of art. Recently he had managed to suppress this rather austere view, and was prepared to enjoy being flavour of the month.

He turned off Holland Park Avenue in his low-key, top-of-the-range Citroën and hooted at a guitar-toting busker who was ambling across the road. A month ago he would have merely waved the man across with a friendly smile.

When he was shown into the drawing-room where the dozen other guests were already drinking and laughing, Julian's ego quickly deflated. He immediately felt the least important among the eclectic gathering of well-known faces which took polite but not great interest in his arrival. But Fratinelli greeted him warmly enough and introduced him with a quick reference to his recent success, adding, without emphasis, "Such a pity not to get the Best Director, too."

Julian found himself on the edge of an amicable discussion between a Trade and Industry minister and his Opposition shadow. In view of their host's occupation, the subject was the British film industry.

The minister, relaxed and off the record, was happily conceding to his opposite number's position. "Of course our film industry is grossly under-subsidised. The artistic and economic arguments in favour of tax-concessions at least are incontrovertible, but the PM is totally uninterested. She thinks that the cinema has no other function than to entertain the masses and it should be subject to market forces like any third-rate television sit-com. If we can't make movies that put bums on seats as effectively as the Americans, too bad."

"Still, Norman, she won't last forever," said the socialist MP. He turned to Julian, also, apparently, happy to make concessions in private. "And a period of governmental Philistinism can actually have quite an invigorating effect on the arts – so long as it's not too long a period." He laughed. "Artists have less to challenge and become flabby and complacent under benign governments."

Julian had had no experience of politicians in private. He thought the lack of animosity they showed towards each other suggested remarkable insincerity in their public stances. Naively, he said to the minister, "But if you feel the arguments are so strongly in favour of subsidy, why don't you say so in public?"

The two politicians laughed; the question was not worth answering.

"How did you fund *Michael and Mustapha*?" the Tory asked.

"It was very cheap to make," Julian said guardedly.

"Yes, but was it done with British money?"

"Well, yes, mainly."

"And what sort of return will your backers see on their investment?"

"That's hard to say. Obviously the film's going to do well here and in Europe. We've got an American distribution deal, and of course Channel Four came up front with a bit to get the British television rights."

"But does your success in Cannes mean the film will make money?"

"I should think so. It must."

"Maybe the PM's right, then, leaving it to market forces. Presumably the industry considers your film an artistic success, and you say it will be a financial success as well."

"Yes, but financial success shouldn't be a factor. If the film should be made, it should be made."

"It hardly seems worth the bother and expense of making films that nobody's going to look at."

"Now you're beginning to sound more like your public self," Julian crowed.

"Merely arguing a corner. Anyway, you must have been persuasive in raising the funds for your film. Investors naturally want a reasonable chance of a return, and, on the face of it, I don't suppose your project looked like much of a potential box-office hit. What sort of people provide money for that sort of film?"

"Well, as there is no public funding for experimental films like mine, that posed a big problem and I had to take a course of action which went against all my better instincts."

The Labour politician raised his eyebrows with a grin. "Ah, what it is to have a rich father."

Julian reddened. "I had to get the money from somewhere."

"Listen, don't be embarrassed," said the socialist. "You made the film – evidently a very good film. It just annoys me that there are probably dozens of good films unmade due to a lack of rich fathers. This is the main thrust of my argument."

"That there's a lack of rich fathers?" The minister laughed. "That's rather inconsistent with your pip-squeaking policy."

The other politician acknowledged the cheap thrust with a grin, and the conversation moved on to more general political gossip.

For a while, Julian contributed his views, but they were treated as those of an ingenuous outsider. He was looking for a dignified point of exit when he felt a light touch on his arm, accompanied by a waft of musky scent.

"You're Julian Pyon, the film director?" A warm, liquid voice with a Latin lilt.

Julian turned. He saw a pair of brown-black eyes in a tanned face.

"I'm Filumena. I'm a friend of Enzo. I told him I wanted to meet you." Her lips framed the words with overt sensuality.

Julian took in the undisguised shape of her body, the silkiness of her skin, the invitation in her eyes. He attempted a roguish smile. "And though I didn't know it before, I wanted to meet you."

A slight anxiety disappeared from the woman's face. The smile on her beautiful lips grew bigger.

"I really loved *Michael and Mustapha*. I thought it was a brilliant movie. So sensitive."

Julian flushed and said a little doubtfully, "You sound Italian. Are you?"

She nodded.

"And you found that you could identify with a Yemeni and a Yorkshireman in those circumstances?"

"Sure. I really cried for them. They were so sad as Romeo and Juliet, even if they would have been two boys."

Julian grappled with her confusing syntax. "Good. I was trying to deal with universal emotions that supersede racial or sexual characteristics."

"But you're not the same as the two boys, no?"

"God, no," Julian said hastily, then, "I mean, no, but I understand their predicament."

"You have done that very well. And you got the prize – it's fantastic!"

"Well, it was the screenplay that won the prize, and I was chuffed about that."

"I love men with talent," Filumena said.

Julian gathered that she included him in this category. He had seldom been confronted with such blatant advances and he was wondering how to make the most of this opportunity when she said, "I have to see Enzo. I really want to talk to you later, after dinner."

Julian watched her swing her hips across the room, attracting appreciative glances from the other men, and he tingled with thoughts of what he could do with that voluptuous body. She looked as though she was made for love-making; not very bright, but obviously appreciative of life's fundamental values – her reaction to his film showed that. He guessed she was in her mid-thirties. Clusters of tiny wrinkles around her mouth and eyes gave her the look of an experienced woman who knew what she liked and how to respond.

Buoyed up by this promise of future pleasures, Julian relaxed and almost blossomed at dinner between the wives of the two politicians. Both women were highly political, more consistently partisan than their husbands had appeared to Julian, and were unable to indulge in the light-hearted badinage of the men who were opponents by profession.

The Tory wife, though, did not approve of the homosexual urges of Mustapha and Michael. "Less than a hundred years ago, buggery was looked on by the public with as much abhorrence as paedophilia is now. If we extend this liberalisation of attitudes further, in another hundred years' time child-molesting will be presented as a legitimate expression of a person's sexual rights."

"That's absurd," Julian exclaimed, but he bit back his indignation and his dislike of this sort of intellectual parlour-game.

"I see," remarked the Labour MP's wife, "that you take your arguing very seriously. I used to; I still want to, but the awful thing is that it just does become an exercise when it's your job."

"Yes. I saw that in your respective husbands," Julian conceded with regret.

Julian's eye was caught by Filumena, at the other end of the table, and he carried on his discussions with one or other of the women with a spurious light-hearted cynicism.

When dinner was over, the party moved back to the drawing-room and split into three or four groups. Filumena pointedly placed herself beside Julian.

"Did you have good arguments with the two women? They were fancying you like hell."

This had not occurred to Julian, but he gladly accepted the observation. As he spoke, one of the wives was moving across the room towards him. Filumena saw this, and whispered hurriedly, "It would be nice to talk some more with you, another place, no? I get your telephone number from Enzo and give you a call."

"Why don't we go on somewhere tonight?" he suggested quickly.

She shook her head. "No, that's not possible. I call you."

"I hope I'm not breaking anything up," the minister's wife said as she turned to Filumena. "Hello, we didn't really meet before dinner. I'm Tessa Trowbridge."

"This is Filumena, a friend of Enzo's from Italy," Julian said with badly concealed annoyance at the intrusion. But Filumena responded to the other woman's enthusiasm for Italy, particularly the part of Umbria which she and her husband visited each spring. Julian was not in a mood to discuss international trivia and excused himself to join the small group around Fratinelli. Here the conversation about the cinema was hampered by the scanty knowledge of most of the participants, and Julian fretted for an opportunity to talk to Fratinelli on his own. He joined in, but embarrassed himself by making smart-arse remarks to show his inside knowledge and winced inwardly at the Italian's tiny signs of disapproval.

Later, as the party broke up, he received a warm kiss and a promise to be in touch from Filumena, and he left with frustration tempered by the prospect of imminent intimacy with her.

When all Enzo Fratinelli's other guests had left, Filumena remained for a few minutes.

"Well," her host asked in their own language, "did you achieve whatever nefarious purpose you had in mind for the young director?"

The woman nodded with a satisfied smile. "He's a serious boy, isn't he?"

"That's why his little film worked; because he really believed in the cause he was championing. He will find success makes it harder for him to identify with underdogs, and I doubt that he has the talent to compensate for that."

"I don't think he trusts success. He's one of life's natural underdogs. Not surprising, really, with a father like his."

"But you can't choose fathers in the way you can husbands." He looked at her speculatively, as if trying to justify his continuing friendship with her. "You've never really *liked* men, have you, even when you were a flirtatious little twelve-year-old. I hope you don't do anything that will make you look foolish. Good night, Filumena."

County Carlow

In County Carlow, Eire, two men strolled slowly across the deep green meadow that lay by the confluence of the quick little Derry River and the deceptively sedate Slaney. Behind them, over the spreading tops of an avenue of great beeches, the lower, heather-covered foothills of the Wicklow Mountains were sparsely dotted with sheep and white, single-storey dwellings. In front of them, where the meadow was neatly railed, a dozen glossy-coated thoroughbred mares grazed the rich grass.

Tom Brophy carried a leather head collar and a short rope. His brother, Mike, had come to keep Tom company. They were both over seventy, and both had worked at the Clonegall Stud for thirty years. Their duties were not arduous now, but Elizabeth Pyon, and more particularly Maeve, had insisted that they stay when the stud was bought by Christy Pyon for his wife fifteen years before.

They were still healthy, handsome men who held their tall bodies erect, and whose blue eyes still shone clear in their red-brown faces. Their thick, dark hair was testimony to the lack of high ambitions or stresses in their uncomplicated, unmarried lives. They admired Christy Pyon, but they did not envy him. They liked him but they would have liked him more were it not for the sadness they sometimes saw in Elizabeth's eyes.

As they walked towards a bay mare, full almost to bursting point with a late foal, they were talking of their employers.

"They're comin' this afternoon, in a helicopter, Mrs Nolan said, with the Egyptian fella."

"Al Souf?"

"That's the man. He did well, did he not, with the Sadlers Wells colt. He'll want to see his full-brother."

"I should t'ink so. But I wonder how Christy and the missus are gettin' on – after that t'ing in the paper."

"For sure. It's not fair on Lizzy. She's been more forgivin' than he deserves. But he'll not want to hurt her. He's a bit of a playboy, like, but he's not a bad man."

They had reached the mare, and Tom coaxed her to him. He gently stroked her chin and rubbed his nose against her soft muzzle, before slipping on the head collar.

"Come on, darlin'. It's off to have your baby and a bit of love-makin' with a very handsome fella."

"Who's she to go to?" asked Michael.

"Sure and I don't know, but he'll be handsome. Maybe Ninisky this year. Mrs Pyon doesn't want to send them out of Ireland if she can avoid it."

He led the mare back towards the paddock gate. The two men carried on talking about the animals in the stud as they walked slowly up the broad-verged avenue of beeches, passed the front of the classical, granite-built eighteenth-century house to the stable-block beyond.

As they reached the gate in the high walls of the yard, they heard the sound of a twin-engined helicopter approaching over the low tree-covered hill to the east of the house. Tom speedily installed the mare in a stable he had already prepared, and the two brothers walked round to a paddock behind the house where a closely mown circle of grass served as a helipad.

They had never ceased to be fascinated by the helicopters that came and went from Clonegall House. They stood well outside the grass ring and watched as Liz, followed by al Souf and Pyon, stepped down the short ramp and ducked needlessly to get clear of the slowly rotating blades.

Liz smiled and walked straight over to them. "Hello, Tom. Hello, Mike. Everything been all right while I've been away?"

"No trouble at all, Mrs Pyon," Tom said. "We've just brought Ballerina up. She'll foal within the week. She's lookin' happy."

Pyon joined them and put his arm affably around Mike's shoulder. "Well now! How've y'been? Keepin' off the hard stuff, I hope."

"Just Guinness now, Mr Pyon, like Dr McClusky said. That way me liver'll last another twenty years."

"I hope so, Mike, I hope so. Now we've to look after Mr al Souf. He'll be wanting to see round the yard in a while, so tell Brigid and the others to have it looking really pristine, not a straw out of place."

"I will, sir."

"Good man." He turned to Liz and al Souf, who had joined them and were admiring the green fields that swept down to the riverside. "Adnan, the housekeeper will tell your two fellas where you're sleeping. Would you have a quick sharpener before going up?"

The Egyptian nodded. "Then I should like to see this Sadlers Wells colt again."

"You'll like him," said Liz. "He's come on tremendously since you saw him as a foal. He's almost certainly my best yearling. He should do very well in the High Flyer sale at Newmarket next September."

Al Souf smiled. "If I let you send him."

"It'll cost you a great deal to stop me," Liz replied.

"You're beginning to sound quite Irish, Mrs Pyon."

Liz laughed. "I've probably caught that from Christy."

Pyon, Liz and al Souf began walking round to the front of the house, followed by al Souf's attendants and watched by the Brophy brothers.

"D'you t'ink the Arab fancies her?" Mike asked.

"Sure he does. And I'll bet he doesn't like to be denied."

"That'll keep Christy on his toes."

Later, the party dispersed to their rooms to change for dinner.

The day before, from London, Liz had been able to organise an impromptu gathering including an Irish minister of state, an Anglo-Irish earl from the neighbouring estate, and a leading stud owner from Tipperary, all accompanied by their wives.

"Pretty good, for a scratch party," Pyon acknowledged as he watched his ex-wife discard the clothes in which she had flown from London. "You're a very competent woman, y'know. And you seem to have the measure of al Souf. I

dare say you'll get a good price out of him for your colt."
He started to undress too.

"What's all the flattery for, Christy? Are you feeling guilty?" Liz asked.

"No, why should I? As a matter of fact, watching you strip has made me feel a little horny." He removed his underpants to reveal confirmation.

"A little?" Liz laughed, but shook her head. "Not now, Christy. You don't deserve it."

"Oh, come on now. Seeing the way that Arab's lusting after you makes me realise how right he is."

Pyon walked over behind her, put his arms around her naked waist, and let his hands slip over her stomach to her thighs, then between her legs.

"For God's sake, Christy, I'm not some twenty-year-old nymphette that you can turn on at the push of a button. You'll need a lot longer than we've got, if I'm to get anything out of it. So you'll just have to beat down your urges for now." She drew herself away, not angrily, but firmly.

Pyon relinquished his hold with good humour. "You've still got the body of a nymphette, even though you're nearly half a century old."

"You can still remember what a young body looks like, can you, to make a good comparison?" Liz said with light sarcasm.

"Sure I've got a good memory." He wrapped a towel round his waist and walked towards the bathroom. "I'll just have a cold shower, now. And I hope al Souf does too, if he's to sit next to you at dinner."

Dinner was a well-balanced affair, in both guests and cuisine. Liz had a good cook and a lot of experience. With the earl and al Souf on either side, she was able to keep the Arab under control without offending him. She was anyway pleased by his attention. He was charming and clever, and his flirtation was impressively subtle. Even Pyon, glancing down the table from time to time, saw nothing specific to excite his jealousy.

When the women left, in the old-fashioned way that still seemed appropriate to the great house, the minister went to the lavatory, and Pyon took Liz's place.

"You've missed an impressive display of bargaining up at this end of the table," remarked the earl. "Worthy of the hardest copers at the Galway sales."

"Did you buy the colt, then, Adnan?" Pyon asked.

"That depends on you," al Souf replied.

Pyon was on his guard. "It's nothing to do with me. Liz handles all the horses. It's her business."

"But she's your wife."

"As a matter of fact, as you well know, she's not, officially. Regrettably, we're allowed just the one in this part of the world."

"You seem to have overcome the restriction very adeptly," the earl said with an envious smile.

"Up to a point. But here, as I am trying to impress on Adnan, she rules the roost. If you want to buy a horse, you've to buy it from her."

The Arab made no comment. The minister reappeared, sat beside him and engaged him in a conversation about Middle East politics, while Pyon and his neighbour talked local sporting gossip; the earl with the curiously deferential condescension that former great Anglo-Irish landowners adopt with Irishmen who are now much richer and more influential than themselves.

After the port had circulated a couple of times, the men went through to join the women for coffee. The Irish politician told a few shocking stories about his colleagues, and shortly afterwards, he, the earl and the Irish breeder left with their wives.

Al Souf turned to Liz. "Would you consider me very rude if I asked for some time alone with Christy? I must leave early tomorrow."

"As long as you don't think you can squeeze him down on the price of that colt."

"No. That is not my intention."

"I'll leave you in peace, then. Good night."

"Good night, Mrs Pyon. It was a most enjoyable evening."

"Good night, darlin', I'll see you in a while." Pyon gave her a wink and watched her leave the room.

The two men settled into deep armchairs, on either side

of a table on which stood the port and their glasses. Pyon helped himself, and pushed the decanter towards al Souf, who declined.

"You are very lucky, Christy, that she puts up with you."

"Oh, come on now. She's well looked after."

"I imagine, though, that she wasn't too pleased with the publicity you received over the girl in Cannes. And nor were the people involved in the Chemco bid."

"There was nothing to that story. It's only that they've not had anything on me for so long that they blew it up out of all proportion."

"All the more reason for you to be careful. You're very vulnerable at the moment. With such a highly-geared bid, the slightest doubt in people's minds about your ability to manage your affairs will affect people's perceptions. And surely, with the Americans so hostile, you cannot risk it. You'll have to keep your private life under control. It's bad enough already that you run two ménages, without overt infidelity to both women."

"You don't have the odd girlfriend, I suppose," Pyon snapped. "The hypocrisy is astonishing."

"People don't expect me to lead a conventional Western life. They would probably think it rather surprising if I didn't have a somewhat colourful love-life. But you, you must be very careful."

"For God's sake, Adnan, I wasn't born yesterday. I wasn't too happy about the publicity me'self. And my sex-life is really my own business."

"If you need my help to do this deal, it's mine too. And you do need me. I want the bank, certainly, but not as much as you want Chemco. I can bring about that deal for you, with or without the help of the other three members of your little party. And I can spoil it for you."

"I am aware of that, Adnan. But I am not so desperate to get Chemco that I'll be backed into a position where the numbers just don't add up. And you could not launch the bid yourself, because in the public's eyes you're too damned mysterious, and a bloody sight more of a risky propostion than me'self."

"Financially, I don't intend to push you much beyond the terms you have already proposed. Frankly, I am not convinced that the numbers even add up now, unless you have some very inflated idea of the worth of the bank."

"The bank with all its subsidiaries is worth $750 million," Pyon said.

"I will agree to buy it for $600."

"For God's sake, man. We're not talking about some four-legged beast. The worth of the bank is clearly demonstrable. It has assets and profits that are open to the deepest scrutiny. There are accepted formulae for capitalising these."

"Evidently I am using a different formula from yourself."

"You can use whatever formula you like, but I'm tellin' you, it's going to cost you $750 million."

"If it were yours to sell."

"I think we've covered that ground," Pyon said.

Al Souf stood up and walked across the large Afghan carpet that covered the centre of the room, then his heels clicked on the polished oak floorboards. He stopped in front of a large Victorian portrait of a humourless old man in side-whiskers and a frock coat.

"This must be one of Liz's ancestors," al Souf remarked.

"He's not. He came with the house. He lived here for seventy years, so we thought we'd let him stay. Liz isn't as keen on ancestor-worship as most English, and the only ancestors I can be sure of were peasant farmers up in the Wicklows. They never got round to having their portraits painted."

Al Souf walked to another wall to look at a Rossetti painting of Arthurian chivalry. "You are a romantic, aren't you, Christy? I am not, I'm afraid. So here's my offer. I'll pay SHR $650 million for the bank, and you'll throw in the Sadlers Wells colt. I am not interested in your guarantees against losses on the Chemco shares I buy. I will support your bid because I want the bank. For the same reason, nor do I want your consultancy fees to cover losses on SHR shares. And I hope you can control the actions of the other members of your party."

"Don't worry about them. Past successes and future possibilities will keep them in line." Pyon smiled his confidence.

"And as to your offer, I've told you, the colt's not mine to give you, and anyway, it's a bagatelle beside the deal we're talking about."

"Nevertheless, that is what I want. You'll simply have to buy the colt yourself. You have a tradition, don't you, among horse dealers of the seller repaying a little of the purchase price as 'luck money'? Let's consider the colt as my luck money on the purchase of the bank."

Pyon looked at him steadily for a moment, then said; "Make it $675 million."

"And the colt, now, even if you don't acquire Chemco and cannot sell me the bank."

Pyon quickly weighed up the odds with a gambler's instinct. "Done," he said, and extended a hand towards the Egyptian.

"Shouldn't you first have spat on it?" al Souf said, as they confirmed the deal with a firm shake.

"I have managed to rid me'self of some of my old peasant habits," said Pyon, pleased. It was a good bargain.

Al Souf left the following day in Pyon's helicopter.

Pyon and Liz waved from the helipad, each with feelings of gratitude towards the suavely inscrutable Egyptian. As the aircraft disappeared over the top of the trees, they turned to walk to the house. Pyon considered starting negotiations over the colt with Liz, but decided to leave it for a while. There was no rush; al Souf would not seriously expect delivery before next October or November.

After just a day, it was clear that al Souf had already moved into Southern Hemisphere. Major buying was reported, and the financial commentators threw themselves into a guessing game about the identity of the buyer and his reasons.

"How's it going?" Liz asked Pyon as they lunched together on a broad terrace on the west side of the house. "You seem nice and relaxed, in spite of these constant calls from London."

"There's no point being anything else. It's looking good, but it's going to be a long haul. There are an awful lot of Chemco shareholders to convert, and the State banking authorities are going to drag their feet over al Souf until they can see which way public opinion is swinging. The whole deal could take a year or more."

Liz laughed. "You'd better spend a lot of it here. I'm sure you'd be going madder in London."

"I'm going to have to be on the move quite a bit, darlin', I'll have to spend time in the States, I've got to allocate more money to PR over there, though God knows I've spent millions on it already. They're more concerned with images than track records – a whole generation whose brains have been scrambled by advertising. It must be the only nation in the world where elections are won by advertising agencies."

"That sounds fair enough. The prospective government who picks the right agency is showing its practical ability to pick the right experts and advisors."

Pyon laughed. "That's a very un-English realism. Still, maybe you're right. I'll just have to hope I've picked the right horse on Madison Avenue, and give him his head. But look, I'll try and come over here a bit, and rest my weary limbs in the bosom of Old Mother Ireland between battles." He leaned over and gave Liz a light kiss, as if she were Old Mother Ireland herself. "Now, are we to go to the races on Saturday? What did Henry say about Medusa this morning? I hope she's well. I've a good size wager on."

Medusa was their Oaks entry. After her respectable show-ing in the Guineas and one win since, she was half way down the betting, but fancied by a number of the professional observers. She was trained by a man who looked and behaved more like a film star than a racehorse trainer.

"She's working well, apparently; but you know what Henry's like; he believes in nice surprises rather than nasty shocks."

"So, do we have a chance?"

"It'll be worth going."

"Okay, then. I'll stay in London on Saturday night, then I've a meeting in Paris early Monday. I've a bit of preparation to do, so I'll leave Sunday morning."

Liz shrugged. "Fine. Why are you giving me such unac-customed notice of your movements, though?"

"Come on, now, Liz. I always try to let you know what I'm doing."

"Frankly, most of the time I'd rather not know. And if you're going to have anything more to do with dusky teenagers, try not to let the papers know either."

"I wish you wouldn't keep referring to that. I told you it was nothing."

"That's not what Julian said."

"Well, he'd no business to discuss what he knows nothing about. He can be an arrogant tit."

"He's arrogant because he's unsure of himself. I think it's wonderful that his film's done so well, even though I must admit I didn't enjoy it much. He's obviously got talent, but the way you've bullied him all his life, it's not surprising he's a bit touchy."

"Julian's my son, too, you know. I'd great hopes for him, but he's made it bloody hard. I helped him with his film, I've offered to do the same again and more, but he thinks he can do without me now. I can't alter my whole personality to accommodate Julian."

"Don't get so excitable, Christy. You are a difficult man. Most people are terrified of you, and yes, you do have to adapt to your children. They are not yours to command. They are entirely separate beings whose love and respect has to be earned. I've had difficulties with Laura, but I don't blame only her."

"All right, all right. I'll try a little harder with him. Why not ask him to dinner in London on Saturday night?" Pyon suggested.

"If we're at Epsom, my parents will expect to join us, so you'd better not start arguing with him in front of them."

"I give you my word. I am capable of controlling my actions. I just hope he is."

The Oaks

The Oaks was run on a fine day, with a light breeze taking the edge off the sun's heat on Epsom Downs. There was, as usual, a large contingent of City people, some of whom, recognising Pyon, were intrigued to see him in such light spirits. But consistent with his aversion to publicity, he spent most of the time in a private box and refused to be interviewed about Medusa's prospects before the race. But he did suggest that Liz should be.

The filly was slowly rising in the betting as the good-to-firm going was thought to suit her. Liz gave a carefully guarded opinion of their horse's chances to the television audience and rejoined Pyon and her parents in their box.

Lord and Lady Barnstaple, in their seventies now, had reluctantly grown used to their daughter's odd arrangement with her ex-husband and, despite his shortcomings, were on good though not entirely relaxed terms with Pyon himself. Lord Barnstaple had always had a loyal if quietly-expressed admiration for Pyon's guts and determination. He was aware of the opposition he still faced from City institutions, and the resilience with which he dealt with them. He was still glad to accept an invitation from his daughter and her ex-husband.

Liz, looking fresh and ten years younger than her age in turquoise and yellow silk and a small raffia hat, accepted congratulations from the group in the box for her first television appearance.

"I'm sure Christy would have done it better," she said genuinely.

"Quite apart from his dislike of public appearance," her father said, "if he'd talk the horse down, the punters would have assumed he was bluffing, and piled on to it, and if he'd talked it up, they'd have believed him, with the same result. But your performance doesn't seem to have made a lot of difference, yet."

"Have you not made your bet then, Alaric?" Pyon asked.

"I've had her each way at sixteen-to-one since before the Guineas."

"As usual, you've forgotten to tell me until it's too late. I don't think much of nine-to-two now. I did ask you about buying Southern Hemisphere a few months ago, when they were three-seventy something, and you said wait a little. I saw in the papers this morning they're at four eighty-three."

"Stop probing," laughed Pyon. "I don't know why the hell they've gone up, but it suits me fine. Maybe there's a few people out there who don't agree with the financial scribblers about my valuation of Chemco."

"I don't doubt you've got a few supporters, Christy," Lord Barnstaple said with a smile, "but do let me know what's happening. My tiny investments aren't going to rock the boat one way or the other."

"I thought you old fellas only liked to bet on certainties."

"We do. So I'll give Medusa a miss."

In a tight fast finish, Medusa came third, and Pyon's bet showed a decent though not spectacular return. The result was enough to put his party in a good mood as they took the helicopter back to Battersea. They drove from there to Mayfair, and went to their rooms to change before gathering for dinner. Pyon emerged from his dressing-room to hear the front door being opened to Julian. He went down to greet his son.

He put an arm around Julian's shoulder. "Hello, J. It's good to see you. How are you?"

Julian was surprised and relieved at this unaccustomed warmth. "I'm fine, Dad. I hear your horse did well."

"Not bad, not bad. Has there been much development in your film-making plans?"

"An American studio's approached me to do a picture."

"Have they, b'Jaysus? That's terrific. And how's our film doing?"

"*Michael and Mustapha*, do you mean?"

"Yes, our film."

"Okay. It's doing well in France and Scandinavia."

"They like all that stuff about poofs, do they? What about the States?"

"Some great reviews, and it's on a few screens in New York and San Francisco."

"Well, you'd not expect it to be shit hot in the Bible Belt, would you?" Pyon said.

"It's not doing that well in Ireland, either."

"No, it wouldn't. Are we making money yet?"

"With Channel Four's contribution, and advances from distributors, we're into profit now. I think it'll run for quite a while, and there'll probably be a good long-term video market for it, so, you'll make a bit of money out of it."

"And so will you," Pyon added. "What's the story on this American film, then?"

They started to walk up the stairs, and Julian hesitated before answering. "I'm not sure I should talk about it until it's a bit firmer. It's a very good screenplay from an Updike novel. Outside the mainstream of normal Hollywood projects."

"Sounds a bit iffy."

"In an industry where every shiny-suited grease-ball thinks he knows exactly what the public wants, and gets it wrong nine times out of ten, not being in the mainstream can be a commercial advantage."

"Is it being financed by the studio?"

"No, not entirely," Julian replied guardedly.

"Well, let me know if I can help, won't you?"

"Thanks, Dad. I will."

They were in the drawing-room now. Pyon pulled a bottle of champagne from an ice-bucket, poured a couple of glasses and handed one to his son.

"Let's drink to our chums, Michael and Mustapha. May they make us a packet with their beastly habits," he laughed.

"That was not the point of making the film." Julian began to look annoyed.

"Just jokin', Julian. You shouldn't rise. I respect your sympathies, and I know you're not one of them, thank God."

Julian took the clumsily offered olive branch. "No. My sexual aspirations seem to be depressingly normal. These days I don't even seem to mind if a woman doesn't have a brain, as long as she performs with skill and enthusiasm."

"Skill and enthusiasm, eh? Who are you bothering at the moment then?"

"I'm working on a project, you might say. A luscious middle-aged Italian woman I met through Enzo Fratinelli."

"Who's that?" Pyon asked, curious.

"She's called Filumena di Francesci."

Pyon shook his head. "Never heard of her. She can't have much of a past. You've not got the hots for the lovely Natalie, then?"

"I'd rather you didn't talk to me about your affairs, Dad. Natalie's an intelligent and beautiful girl, but you've obviously bulldozed her into your way of thinking. And by the way, I hope you're being thoughtful towards Mum. She was very upset when she heard about her. So was Granny."

"You mean my mother?"

Julian nodded. "I spent a few days in Herefordshire last week and went to see her."

"How was she?" Pyon asked, displaying some guilt.

"You should see her yourself. She says you haven't since Christmas."

"But she can always come and see me, for God's sake. She only has to ring, and I can send the chopper."

"Dad, she's seventy. And you know how proud she is."

"You're right. I'll give her a ring, and go and see her. She should go to Ireland more. They love to see her there."

"I think she finds it rather awkward, being the dowager in the big house, when all her family live in three-roomed cottages."

"Maybe. I take your point. Here come your smart grand-parents now. I've promised your mother we'd both be on best behaviour, okay?"

Julian smiled. "Okay."

Lord and Lady Barnstaple came into the room together.

"Evening, Marjorie, Alaric. What'll you have to drink?" Pyon greeted them.

They spent a while on a further post-mortem of the day's race and were soon joined by Liz. When they went in to dinner, the conversation ranged uncontentiously around horses, the prime minister, farming, and, out of regard for Julian, film-making.

Afterwards, Lady Barnstaple spoke quietly to her daughter. "Christy seems to be a lot more considerate towards you these days," she said. "Maybe that ghastly publicity over the girl in Cannes has done him some good."

"I don't know. You can never tell with him. He still has a lot of charm. The trouble is, when he's using it, he believes in it."

"I'm glad you're not being shrewish about it. That wouldn't achieve anything."

In the drawing-room Lord Barnstaple finished his brandy and announced that he was going to bed. Pyon turned to Julian. "Shall we stroll round to Berkeley Square, and give some of Medusa's winnings to Messrs Aspinall's?"

"Why not?" Julian said, and the two of them set off on foot still in a state of comfortable truce. When they reached the steps of the casino where, years before, Pyon had helped Ken Newberry to launder his money, Pyon said, "Let's have a drink downstairs first."

Julian agreed, and they descended beneath the black canopy to Annabel's.

Inside, they sat at a table in a corner of the room drinking Black Bush, becoming slightly drunk. Julian was aware of the potential danger of this. With an effort, he kept clear of arguments. As they talked, Julian's eyes ranged idly around the room. Suddenly, he jerked himself forward in his chair.

"Good God!" He had seen Filumena.

"What the hell is it?" his father asked.

"Nothing," Julian said hurriedly. "Just someone I hadn't expected to see here."

"A woman?" Pyon asked, looking with interest at any women he could see on the dance floor.

"Yes."

"Well, don't keep her to yourself, ask her over."

"No. As a matter of fact, I think I've had enough of this place."

There was an abrupt change in Pyon's manner.

"Yes, you're right. Let's get the hell out of here. I've an early start tomorrow."

Julian was puzzled by this sudden change in mood, but had decided it would probably be better not to see Filumena in these circumstances, and he certainly didn't want to introduce her to his father. He followed Pyon round the edge of the room to the exit, and hurried to keep up with him as they walked back to the house. When they arrived there, Pyon, with an evident effort to remain affable, asked, "Will you have a nightcap before you go?"

"No thanks. But can I contact you about this film when you get back to London?"

"Sure, sure," his father replied absently. "Any help you want, J."

They bid each other good night on the doorstep, and Pyon watched his son walk up the mews to his car.

At eight o'clock on Sunday morning, Mayfair was peaceful, sunny and almost deserted. Most of the few people to be seen on the silent streets were, like Pyon, heading for early mass at the Jesuit church in Farm Street.

Inside the Victorian gothic building Pyon found his mind wandering from what was happening on the altar. He did not try to keep Natalie out of his thoughts, and when from time to time Liz, Maria or his children forced their way in, he brushed them aside with the conviction that he had treated them all dutifully and generously.

It was Natalie, he thought, who could derive the most benefit from what he had to offer, and she gave him so much back. She made him feel like the fresh, untainted boy he had once been. The vague sense of guilt this cast over his activities of the past thirty years seemed a small price to pay.

Life was going to be tricky for a while, he knew, but he would concentrate on sorting it out when the Chemco deal was done. Then, having reached the climax of his career, he would have time to put his life in order, and the lives of those around him.

He did not want to hurt Liz, but one thing was for sure, Maria would have to go. He had never, he justified himself, been married to her anyway, in the eyes of the Church.

Pyon had breakfast with Liz and her parents.

"Nice church?" Liz asked.

"Yes, fine," Pyon replied.

"Not much it can do for a recidivist like you, I shouldn't have thought," Lord Barnstaple remarked.

"The Lord loves a sinner," Pyon laughed.

"Maybe, but he must love a saint rather more."

"Ah, well. I'll settle for what he'll give me."

"I must say, I'll never understand you Catholics," said Lady Barnstaple.

"To be fair to most of them," Liz said, "Christy is not typical."

Pyon swigged down the rest of his coffee and stood up. "Right, I'm off to Paris, then Italy. I'll be back in a week or so. Will you be here or in Ireland, Liz?"

"I'm going back to Country Carlow tomorrow."

"I'll ring you, then. I'll have to go and see my mother."

"What's brought on this attack of filial duty?" Liz asked.

"I've always been a dutiful son, as well as a dutiful husband, ex-husband and father."

"That depends on your idea of duty," his wife said.

"We'll not go into that now." Pyon leaned down and kissed Liz. "Don't disturb yourselves. Goodbye, Marjorie. Goodbye, Alaric."

He left the room and walked out to his Mercedes, which was purring quietly. Hanks leaped out from the driver's seat and opened the back door for him.

Pyon picked up the Sunday paper that lay on the seat beside him. A small spiteful item on the first page made obscure comparisons between the performance of his filly, and the performance of his company. He flung the paper down with a curse, and talked idly to Hanks while his mind raced between the girl and the deal which were his current obsessions.

Paris

Natalie Felix thanked the maid who had unpacked her cases and looked around in awe at the size and furnishings of the room on the top floor of the Hotel Meurice. She went over to one of the full-length windows to look out at Paris: the elegant jumble of buildings on the left bank across the Tuileries Gardens and the Seine; the Tour de Montparnasse and the Eiffel Tower beneath a blue sky patterned with stripes of high clouds. Directly below, traffic scurried along the Rue de Rivoli, and Sunday morning walkers were strolling between the cafés.

For almost as long as she could remember, she had heard, read and dreamed of Paris. Cannes had been a revelation, but it had nothing of the romance and beauty of this legendary city where the reality surpassed her previous image of the place.

Being away from the convent in term time, if only for a few days, had caused her intense guilt and a sense of disloyalty to the children. She hoped fervently that seeing Paris and being with Pyon would justify this. She sensed the blood of the city rushing through its great, concupiscent body as her own blood warmed with the thought that soon Pyon would be with her.

It was only a matter of weeks since Pyon had kissed her goodbye in Cannes before racing back to London. She had hated to see him go in such a state, and had felt the tension and anger in his touch, and in his love-making. She wanted to console him, and knew that she could. She understood instinctively the complex of conflicting urges that directed him, but she also understood that she would be treading in private, vulnerable areas, dangerous volatile ground that would yield no obvious rewards.

She turned and wandered through into the adjoining sitting-room. An elaborate jade and ormulu clock told her that Pyon would not arrive for another hour. Apart from walking from the taxi to the steps of the hotel, her feet had not touched Parisian ground. She went back into the bedroom, flung a printed cotton bag over her shoulder and went out to the landing to wait impatiently for a lift to take her down.

Outside, the warm sun lit the streets more obliquely than she was used to at this time of day, accentuating the foreignness of the place, in spite of the sound of her native tongue all around. She strolled happily down the colonnade of the Rue de Rivoli towards the Place de la Concorde, gazing into the windows of the shops, and enjoying the spontaneous smiles of the men who walked by.

With a light step, absorbing all the sights and the atmosphere, she crossed the Place de la Concorde to the broad, tree-lined margins of the Avenue des Champs Elysées. As she approached the Rond Point, she saw a café on the other side of the Avenue Matignon, and walked across to sit at one of the tables beside the pavement. She ordered a coffee from a gracefully arrogant waiter and settled down to watch the steady stream of traffic and promenaders.

She noticed a small, scruffy man shambling in her direction. He saw her looking, and gave her a wide toothless leer. He looked harmless, so she gave him a friendly smile, and he quickened his hunched shuffle towards her.

As he neared her, she tried not to show her revulsion at his greasy, pock-marked and black-headed skin, and the grimy old suit that had not been cleaned for years. His eyes showed that he had seen her reaction but the improbable smile remained.

" 'Ello, darling. D'you want to see my pet?"

Natalie recoiled. She shivered with horror. It was as if the sun and the chirruping sparrows had suddenly died. She gazed speechless as the man fumbled in the pockets of his baggy trousers.

Abruptly, with a loud cackle, he pulled out a large, life-like stuffed rat and waggled it under her nose.

Natalie shrieked and nearly fell backwards off her chair. People at nearby tables and the waiters leaning in the doorway hooted with laughter – they had seen it before.

Natalie turned angrily to the waiter who was approaching her with her coffee. "Why are you laughing? He really scared me."

The smooth young man shrugged. "It doesn't bite." He raised an eyebrow at the tramp who ambled away with a triumphant grin.

Natalie felt slightly foolish. She took a couple of gulps from the small cup of thick black coffee and tried to recapture the mood she had been enjoying. The sunlight, the laughing children and cooing pigeons slowly returned to focus, and she began to see the funny side of the incident. She said hello to a small girl who wandered close to her table, and was answered with a dazzling smile.

She was relaxed, but a little lonely when a bulky Frenchman, bulging in a shiny suit, appeared by her side and sat in a chair next to her.

"Hello, Coco. Can I get you a drink?"

"No. No thanks," Natalie replied quickly, "I'm going in a moment."

"Don't be so nervous, baby. I'm not going to pull a rat from my trousers. That old bugger scared the shit out of you, didn't he?" The fat man chortled. "That's how he gets his kicks. It's cheaper than a blow-job in the Bois."

Natalie did not answer. She thought about getting up and leaving, but she had not paid for her coffee.

The Frenchman went on, "Where are you from? You're not black enough and you speak French too well to be an African."

"L'Ile Maurice," Natalie answered reluctantly.

"It's obvious that you haven't been in Paris long. Have you got any friends here?"

Natalie shook her head. "I've never been before." She looked around, trying to think of a way to escape the man's repulsive attentions. Among the cars driving past, she saw a long, silver Cadillac turn off the Rond Point and glide slowly by.

"I could give you a very good job," the fat man was saying. "Plenty of money; nothing dirty – just using your charming smile."

Natalie turned to him and shook her head vigorously. "I don't want a job. I'm on holiday."

"From Maurice? I don't believe you."

Without realising why, from the corner of her eye, Natalie noticed that the silver Cadillac had stopped and was now reversing against the traffic back towards her.

My God, she thought in alarm, these must be his colleagues; they're going to snatch me and drag me into the car.

Her heart thumped wildly, she felt the terror of a cornered hind. In desperation, she leaped to her feet and started to run towards the inside of the café, crashing into tables and customers in her panic. She heard the fat man shout, "Hey, where are you going?" and she reached the entrance where the waiters stood.

"Save me!" she implored them.

"Sure. From what?"

She could not speak. It was like a horrible dream – a dream from which she was abruptly awakened by a booming voice.

175

"Natalie? What the hell's going on?"

She whirled around to see Pyon weaving his way between the open-air tables towards her. There was a look of concern on his face.

"Didn't you want to see me?"

He reached her, and she collapsed against him with tears of relief.

Reassured, Pyon wrapped her in his arms to comfort her. "What happened, angel? What's the trouble?"

"Oh, Christy. I was being very stupid. That fat man sat down and said he wanted to give me a job, and when the big car came back towards us, I thought they were going to grab me."

Pyon roared with laughter. "In broad daylight? Outside a café full of people on a Sunday morning? We're not in the back end of Marseilles, you know. But I can see you're upset, and I'll have a word with the fella who was pestering you."

The fat man was standing by the table where Natalie had left him, open-mouthed between a uniformed chauffeur and another dark-suited, thick-set man. Big drops of sweat had broken out on the folds of his face.

Pyon led Natalie slowly back through the crowded silent tables towards the car whose motor still purred quietly, and opened the rear door for her to climb in. When he had seen her settled in the deep plush seat, he turned and made his way without haste towards the quivering Frenchman. Pyon stopped and stood a foot in front of him. He looked him up and down and slowly shook his head with disdain.

"You're a big fat sweaty slob, aren't you?" Pyon said in English.

The man gazed back at him in terror and said nothing. He understood the tenor, if not the words of Pyon's remark.

"I'm going to give you two useful pieces of advice and a short lesson. First, lay off the fatty substances or your horrible little heart'll pack up on you. Second, check out a girl's connections before you start to proposition her. D'you understand?"

The man nodded wildly; he understood enough.

"Good," said Pyon mildly, "and here's the lesson."

Before the fat man could blink, Pyon drew back his clenched fist a short way beside his waist, then powered it like a sledgehammer into the man's bulging midriff.

There was loud, anguished grunt as the Frenchman collapsed into a gasping heap between Pyon's two men. Pyon stepped over the heap, and the three of them walked quietly to the car. Pyon climbed in through the back door which was still open, and the others got into the front. The driver put the engine into gear and pulled away from the curb to join the steady flow of traffic.

Only Natalie glanced back, to see the fallen man slowly stir, studiously ignored by everyone around him. She turned to Pyon. "Oh, Christy, you will get into trouble."

Pyon laughed. "Maybe, but I doubt it, and it'd be worth it. The fella's not seriously hurt, and I guess it's an occupational hazard in his line of work. I'm only glad I saw you when I did. And by the way, it's wonderful to see you again; I've missed you."

He leaned over and kissed her lightly on the lips while he put an arm around her shoulder.

"I've missed you too. I've never been so glad to see anyone as you just now. It's a miracle you were passing."

"Not really. It's the back way through to the Rue de Rivoli without going all round Concorde. And you were sitting right by the pavement. Any man driving through Paris is looking out for pretty girls, I was bound to see you."

"I expect you saw lots of much prettier girls, they are all so beautifully dressed and sophisticated."

"Only the ones you notice. And I didn't spot any lovelier than you. What were you doing?"

Natalie shrugged. "Just feeling Paris. I had no idea it would be so magical. That fat man spoilt it a bit, and before him a horrible old man came and showed me a rat."

"Showed you a rat?"

"He pulled a dead rat from his pocket and put it under my nose. I screamed and then I felt really stupid." She laughed.

"You've been having a few adventures, haven't you? You've been to the hotel already?"

"Of course. It's a lovely room, with a wonderful view."

"Well, here we are. We'll go on up, and you can enjoy the view and some champagne while I sort out a few problems. We've a table at an excellent establishment off the Place de la Madeleine and then you can decide where we're to go."

Pyon and Natalie ate *foie gras* and *loup*. They drank Chablis and talked as if they had not seen each other for a year.

"What is it about you?" he asked. "You must be a witch. You know me better than my own mother."

"Not a witch – your guardian angel, like you said once."

"An angel, that's for sure. And have you been looking after your pupils well, too?"

"No. Don't ask that. I still feel guilty about leaving them. I only came because I wanted to see you. You seemed so worried when you left Cannes."

"Not worried, just angry. I thought people were letting me down."

"Is that so unusual? In business, surely people are only loyal to themselves?"

"Of course they are. But sometimes, you hope they're going to keep their promises, if only out of expediency. Anyway, it wasn't as bad as I thought. My little deal is making progress, and I'll make you a promise, when I've pulled this one off, I want to take you round the world, and open your eyes a little."

"My eyes are open. Just because I've never been anywhere doesn't mean that I don't know anything."

"Of course it doesn't, darlin'. You're one of the wisest people I know. You've shown me sides to life that I'd forgotten about since I was a kid. I've had some of the best moments of m'life with you in Mauritius."

"But I'm worried now about what will happen. What about Maria, and your first wife? You've seen her, in London?"

"Yes, I did, and went to Ireland with her. To tell you the honest truth, I don't know what the hell to do about Liz. I still love her, you know. Not the way I love you, of course, more like a sister. But she's hoping I've had enough of Maria and might go back to her." Pyon gave a sad shrug. "She was hurt bad enough the first time."

"But Christy," Natalie said with gentle censure, "why did

you go on seeing her? It's not fair to her. She must still think that she's your wife in some ways. Why don't you want to let her go?"

"Hell, I don't know. The admission of failure, maybe; plain ordinary selfishness. Like I say, I love her in a way, and I'd miss her. And she knows a lot about me. She doesn't have your instincts, but she has a lot of experience of me. And she's been loyal, so damn loyal."

"It's a mess, Christy." Natalie's eyes shone angrily. "It's strange that a man who seems to be so in control of his affairs should make such a muddle of his life. I told you, just a few months ago, that I didn't want to be involved in that part of your life, and I still don't, but after I went home from Cannes, I realised that I wanted to be with you, even with the bad side. But Christy, I don't want to be part of making life miserable for Liz, or for anyone else in your family. You must decide. If you can't give her up, you must go back to her and forget me. You must tell her the truth, whatever the truth is."

Pyon leaned forward, with his left elbow on the table, resting his chin in his large palm. He made a face like an upset child, and with his other hand refilled both their glasses from the cold bottle of Barsac which they drank with a simple *tarte tatin*.

"That's tellin' me, isn't it? It's a sight to see your black eyes flash like lightning in a storm. I know you're too good for me, Liz is too good for me. I don't deserve either of you, I'm a rotter, I know it, but I try to give back, you know. I put a lot of energy into other people's lives. Thousands of people depend on me."

"Those are people who work for you. If they weren't working for you, it would be someone else. That's got nothing to do with the people close to you. Look at your son, Julian – he's a clever man, and he has talent, but because he's so messed up about you, it's all used the wrong way."

"He won a prize, for God's sake, with his first film – a film which he couldn't have made without me."

"He wants more than your money – he wants your respect."

"I showed my respect, didn't I? Three million quid's worth."

"I think you know what I mean."

"But he's so goddamn difficult. Mind you, we were getting on a bit better this week. I was out with him last night." Pyon stopped abruptly, reminded of the scene in Annabel's.

"Oh Christ," he said, "don't let's talk about it now. I hear what you say. I'll sort it out. Trust me."

Natalie stretched her hand across to stroke Pyon's cheek with the back of her finger. "Don't look so frustrated. You've just got to decide what you want, and think of other people as people, not possessions. I'll be your lover but never one of your possessions."

"I'll settle for that," he said quietly, and squeezed the small brown hand that rested on his cheek.

After lunch, when the afternoon was well advanced, they left the restaurant. Pyon dismissed the waiting chauffeur, and he walked arm-in-arm with Natalie along the quiet Sunday backstreets off the Rue du Faubourg St Honoré. They walked and walked, talking, looking at the people, in the shop windows, into elegant little private courtyards. As the sun began to slant across l'Etoile, they carried on down the wide margins of the Avenue Foch and on into the Bois where families threw frisbees and chased each other, laughing and shouting. A small, plastic rugger ball landed in front of Pyon. He leaned down, gathered it up and punted it energetically towards a group of appreciative boys who had been passing it to one another.

Natalie smiled. "What a sportsman – boxing and rugby on the same day."

"I'd forgotten about the boxing. It seems like days ago. I hope you weren't too upset by the fisticuffs. It's not a thing I often do."

"As long as the fat toad wasn't badly hurt, I don't mind. He deserved it, and maybe it'll stop him pestering other girls."

"I doubt it will. He might just check 'em out a bit more thoroughly before he starts making offers."

"It was wonderful having you come to my rescue like that."

"We must do it more often."

They laughed, and turned together to walk back to the Meurice, through the respectable elegance of the *seizième*, the skate-boarding crowds at Trocadero and the Place de la Concorde.

Later, after an evening in which Pyon seemed to have relegated all his problems to another world, they lay in a great carved bed in a state of happy synergy. When Natalie fell asleep, she was thinking that she could and would cope with the problems that came from being with a man like Pyon, that she had no choice, and that she did not want a choice.

She even managed to smile when he told her the next morning that three men had come from London to see him, and that his driver would take her anywhere she wanted to go.

"But I don't want to see all these places for the first time without you. How long will you be with these horrible businessmen?"

"They are a pretty horrible lot, but I'll have to get them lunch before they go back. Then you'll have me to yourself for the next three days, I promise."

An unlikely trio

Leo Jackson, Morry Weintraub and Lenny Shemilt had little in common but the desire to make money. Possibly this desire was a result of other less obvious common characteristics, but on the face of it they made an unlikely trio.

Leo Jackson had known Christy Pyon for years. He had first done small property deals with him in the early sixties. In most of their transactions, both had made money, and an easy relationship had grown up between them. But Pyon had gone on to be much bigger. And in pursuing a deliberate policy of non-publicity, the myths had propagated around him and given an added attraction to doing business with him.

Jackson took the opposite view. He was a deliberately

flamboyant character. He believed that a very public display of wealth was good advertising, and attracted deals. He was not an ill-natured man, though, and he did not resent Pyon's greater success. He was, anyway, wealthy, controlling assets worth over fifty million. But he did resent what he considered Pyon's unfair treatment of Liz.

Over the years he had developed an attachment to Liz that was unlike any of his usual, transient infatuations. In the thirty-odd years he had known her, he had never more than kissed Liz on the cheek. But her calm, classic beauty had never ceased to please him. She had never made him feel, as the well-bred wives of some of his other business associates did, that he was an upstart of ineradicable social inferiority. She had a good sense of humour and always laughed with him about his escapades. They were both interested in bloodstock, and Jackson admired her for the knowledge and enthusiasm with which she went about breeding her horses.

Liz had become a sort of icon to Leo Jackson, and it was this as much as the smell of a good deal which had drawn him into the Southern Hemisphere/Chemco deal.

Morry Weintraub, on the other hand, was an apparently passionless individual, a quiet, unmarried loner who refused even to be drawn into the normal family loyalties of his culture. His only interest outside the making of money was opera. He disapproved of many of Pyon's attitudes and activities, but he had known him for a long time, and knew that he was a man who kept his word. Weintraub made his business decisions on unemotional, fiscal grounds, and would not turn down the chance of a reasonable and certain profit.

The third of the group, Lenny Shemilt, was incapable of taking a direct line towards anything. If he was shown a clear-cut path to a profit, he looked for a more devious route, even if it eventually would yield half the sum. It was an obsession of his that, unless he made moves that others did not know about, he could not gain the advantage that led to a private bonus. He did not understand what made Pyon succeed. But he had watched the Irishman's growth with some awe, and had made contact with him, as was his way, via the back door, and Ken Newberry.

Several good share trades had resulted, but Pyon had always known of his involvement, and had openly congratulated him on his astuteness.

The Chemco bid was the big one, though, and he was right on the inside track. Pyon had actually invited him there. The size of the bid and his special contacts provided him with an unprecedented opportunity.

The trio had arrived separately the night before, and booked into the Intercontinental, just around the corner from the Meurice. They met over breakfast, and attempted to chat inconsequentially, until they adjourned, as planned, to Leo Jackson's suite.

Pyon knocked on the door on which a "Do Not Disturb" sign had been hung, and Jackson opened it to him with an effusive welcome.

"Morning, Christy. You look well. I won't ask what you've been up to, or down on for that matter."

"You've the mind of a randy teenager, Leo. I am capable of spending a night on my own, you know. Morning, gentlemen." He nodded towards Weintraub and Shemilt. "I'm sorry to drag you to Paris, but none of you are known here, and afterwards, we're going out to have lunch and look at some horses in Chantilly, which is the purpose of your visit, if you're ever asked."

The three men nodded. Jackson said, "Right. Coffee, anyone?"

They sat down in armchairs, Pyon remained standing. He looked at each of them in turn. "I take it you've already started buying – Chemco and Southern."

None of them answered.

"Well, someone has, and I don't mind if you've started. But you've got to stay with me, or it could go very wrong. Is that clear? We can't have any private parties." His eyes rested on Shemilt. "You know that I'll stand by my guarantees. If you don't accept that, you should leave now."

No one moved.

"Good. I'm glad you trust me. Al Souf is in as well, you'll not be surprised to learn, and he has agreed to pay $675 million for Chemco's banking interests."

"How can you be sure he won't renege?" asked Weintraub.

"Because he's getting it at a hundred million dollar discount, and he knows it. Like all of you, he realises that if we all stick to the very simple plan, we'll all make a lot of money. Any wavering or deviation will jeopardise the deal."

Pyon strolled across to the window and looked down at the traffic in the Rue Castiglione: the businessmen walking briskly to and from their offices, and women setting off on shopping expeditions to the Faubourg St Honoré. He turned back to his three co-conspirators.

"Now, the purpose of this meeting is simply to confirm the deal I outlined in London. I'll not see you in a group, or even individually, other than by chance, which should be avoided, for a year or two after today. Your contact, in emergency, is Fielder at Anglo-American, but try not to use that too much. He will let you know when we are ready to buy your Chemco shares. When SHR has gained control of Chemco, you must sell your SHR shares back into the market, and invoice us through a third party organisation for the following services. Leo, to Chemco for consultation in the bid, using a New York cover. Lenny, also from New York for Public Relations services to SHR; and Morry, from a Bahamian company for legal advice to SHR in respect of the bid. These will represent the losses you have incurred, and there very likely will be losses because Southern's price is bound to drop back when the deal is done. If you want to hang on to them, you're running a risk. You'd do better to sell, and be seen to buy back in later. I can always advise you of a suitable moment to do that."

Pyon walked to the sideboard where the coffee stood, poured himself a fresh cup and added a dash of cognac to it.

"You're all happy, then?" he asked.

"Sounds all right," said Jackson lightly to cover the excitement he felt.

"I can't see any problems," Shemilt acknowledged.

"I don't know," said Weintraub. "Too many people are involved, Pyon. It only takes one person to point the finger afterwards, and we'll all be in big trouble."

"Those who know – and there are only you three, al Souf,

me, Newberry and Fielder – all stand to do very well out of it. Why should anyone point fingers?"

"I don't know. Someone might talk out of turn to a girl or something." He glanced at Jackson.

"For God's sake," Jackson said, "I've managed so far to keep a few secrets from young ladies. You haven't got anything to worry about on that score, chum."

"Now listen, Morry," said Pyon, "you're in. I know you wouldn't be here if you hadn't already decided, so stop winding people up. No one's going to blow any whistles. The thing's very tidy. There's no chance of getting caught, just so long as you do what I've told you. So, let's have a drink to it, then I'll meet you in the Tipperary bar in Chantilly about midday, and we'll talk about horses. There's a French trainer meeting us for lunch, and he thinks you're interested, so try and ask a few intelligent questions."

"But what's the point of that?" asked Weintraub.

"I told you, just in case we've been seen, or anyone has connected us, we've got to have had a reason for being in France together. You're the only one of us who's never had a horse, so it's time you bought a leg or two. It'll make a change from watching big-breasted sopranos."

"I don't gamble," Weintraub said sourly.

"Well, just act the bloody part, okay?"

Weintraub shrugged, and accepted a glass of Krug that Pyon had thrust towards him.

"Now get that down you, stop being an old woman and think of all the money you're going to make."

Actors' Production Company

While Natalie Felix ate a lonely lunch in the Meurice, waiting fretfully for Pyon to return, a woman of head-turning attraction entered a restaurant in St James's, London. Her cool, bold strides did not hint at the uncertainty she felt.

Julian had sounded quite normal when he had telephoned

that morning; a little breathless, but nothing in his voice suggested that he had heard anything against her. She had seen Julian with his father, leaving Annabel's, and had been in a state of nervous apprehension ever since.

Julian was waiting at the table he had booked. He guessed that Filumena would be more comfortable here than in one of his more normal Soho lunching haunts, and he had taken an unusual amount of trouble with his appearance. He'd had his hair cut that morning, and had bought a shirt from one of the new men's shops near Conran. With his long frame draped over a tubular steel chair, he presented a lean, bonily handsome figure.

When he caught sight of his guest walking in, he rose to his feet, and beckoned her over with a quick flush to his pale face. She looked outrageously desirable. The eyes of almost every man in the room followed her passage towards Julian, and the head waiter wished he had placed him on a more prominent table.

She accepted Julian's light kiss on her lips with a squeeze of her hand on his waist.

"Hello, Filumena. Glad you could make it."

As they both sat, she laughed. "Of course I make it. Why did you take so long to ring me?"

"I don't know. I thought you'd be busy."

"I have been busy. Did APC in Los Angeles ring you?" Filumena asked.

"Yes. How did you know about that?"

"I suggest it. I know the boss, Johnny Capra, since I was a little girl. He was a friend of my father. I rang him and said that you are the brightest young European director, and he should have you do a movie for him."

"Good God. He didn't mention you." Julian could not help feeling disappointed that it was not purely through his own efforts that this new project had arisen. "He must think a lot of your judgement. He said he hadn't actually seen *Michael and Mustapha*, but the script has arrived and the writer's done a good job on Updike's novel. I was surprised at APC being interested in it. Of course, they used to make a lot of good pictures in the early fifties and late forties when they were first formed. They were a sort of actors' co-operative then, trying to break the hold that the big studios had over stars and distribution. As a matter of fact, I thought they had gone completely down the drain, and had been taken over as a front for the Mafia." Julian abruptly stopped speaking. He reddened, and glanced at Filumena to see her reaction.

She smiled at his discomfort. "It's okay. People always think that any Italian American with money must have Mafia connections. It's not true. Johnny has struggled hard to get where he is. But you know he has a television station, too, in Australia? Well, they would not accept him if they thought he was with Cosa Nostra."

"No, you're right. He sounded fairly genuine on the phone, at least by Hollywood standards. Anyway, I hope it comes to something. He seemed a bit doubtful about funding for the picture, though."

"I did say to him that your father had put in the money for your first film, and that he might again."

Julian grabbed the bottle of San Pellegrino water in front of him, and sloshed some into a glass in an attempt to cover his anger at her, at his father, and at the studio boss who evidently only saw him as a way to his father's money.

"Why the hell did you do that?" he asked. "Didn't you think that they might want me on my own merits?"

"Don't be so simple," she answered calmly. "Of course he wants you on your own merits; he doesn't want to put up any time or money for a film which is not going to be successful. But these days there must always be extra things you can bring." She shrugged. "If you can bring talent *and* money, that's a bonus. Every movie is so big a risk, the studios like to spread it a little, that's all. It's how the movie business works. It's how life works."

"That's exactly what I object to. I've spent the last few years trying to expose the greed behind every aspect of life in the West, and now, to make a picture with a Hollywood studio, which is what you have to do if you want your work to be widely seen, I have to be part of this wheeler-dealing. Anyway, there's no question of my asking my father. I did consider it, and he probably would cough up; he's trying to make up for being such a bastard to me all his life. Of course it's too late for that, but I wasn't averse to the idea of using him, like he's used other people all his life."

"Is he such a terrible man?" Filumena asked innocently.

"I nearly introduced you to him the other day but I decided against it. I was with him in Annabel's, Saturday night, and I saw you. Who were you with?"

"An old family friend – very old." She made a face. "But why were you there with your father?"

"I said I'd come with him to gamble at Aspinall's, but he changed his mind, thank God. I was trying to get on good terms with him, in case I needed help with this film. But I'm damned if I want to now. It sounds as though APC only want me as a source of funds."

"I tell you not to be so stupid. If you want to make movies, you have to make compromises. You haven't told me why your father is so terrible."

"Do you know anything about him?"

She looked vague. "A little. You sometimes read about him in the papers, but he likes to be secret, doesn't he?"

"Up to a point, as they say. I think it's a carefully contrived way of making people more interested in him."

"Is he still married to your mother?"

"No, he's officially married to some Italian slag-pot – has been for fifteen years. He's got a couple of kids by her, but I don't suppose he sees much of them either. I've never met any of them, thank God, and I hope I never do. I was with him in Cannes, and he had a Mauritian girl with him, half his age, and he was behaving like a teenager; it was sick-making."

Filumena did not say anything for a moment. Her eyes flashed with a strange anger, and Julian was impressed by this evidence of her sympathy for his position.

"He sounds, like you say, a real bastard. You should take his money from him, use him. It would be a lesson to him. You're not going to hurt him by being proud; he'll just think you're a fool. Extract all you can from him, and make sure he doesn't see a profit on it. There could be a lot of possibilities with APC, you know, because Johnny has some difficulties at the moment. But I want you to tell me what your father has done to your mother. Why does she still see him? Why is she a wife to him when he is here?"

"She's a good loyal woman, she's still in love with him, I suspect, at least with the image she had of him as a young man. He must have been quite a contrast to the other men she'd have known, though it must have worn a bit thin after thirty years. But she still defends him. I think she's hoping that maybe he'll leave Maria, the Italian, and come back, but I'm afraid she's wrong. If he leaves Maria, he'll go off with Natalie, the Mauritian girl."

"She sounds like a good woman, your mother. I'd like to meet her."

"What for?" Julian was surprised.

"Because I'm interested in you, Julian." She smiled and put her hand across the table to caress his where it clutched his glass of mineral water. "You don't have to tell her that we are lovers, because we aren't, yet."

Julian smiled back. "But we will be soon. We can go back to my house after lunch."

"Don't be so quick." She gazed at him with her dark eyes. "I think, maybe, I'm a bit old for you."

"No you aren't, for God's sake. I bet you've got none of the hang-ups of a 25-year-old English girl."

"I do still have an appetite. Can we order some lunch, please?"

Over lunch, Julian was surprised by how much Filumena understood of the *double-entendres* with which he tended to spatter his conversation. As he drank, so did she. He became bolder in his flirtation, and so did she. There was an inconvenient but pleasing activity in his crotch as he watched her mouth and breasts.

And, though for her it was only incidental to her relationship with Julian, the notion of making love to him was becoming positively exciting. But when it came to it, she withheld.

They had gone back to Julian's house off the King's Road, and he had poured more drinks, and filled the large Edwardian studio with the sound of Earl Hines. They sat on a huge squashy Chesterfield, and Julian's hands found his way beneath the high hem of her dress, over her stocking-tops to an opening that was as hot and ready as her eyes had suggested.

He surprised her with his dexterity, and she did not want him to stop. But even as she reached the point where stopping would be impossible, she thought of the difficulty this would cause when she finally met Liz.

Mothers, she was sure, could always tell with which women their sons had slept. For Julian to have a crush on an older woman was one thing; for them to have been lovers would be beyond toleration.

With a gasp, and protestations of genuine regret, she wriggled herself out of Julian's embrace, and got to her feet.

"Julian, you don't know what you're doing. I promise, I'm much too old for you, you can't do this; it's not fair."

Julian reacted with astonished frustration. "What are you talking about?" he cried in anguish. He undid his trousers to reveal an unequivocally aroused penis. "Does this look as though you're too old? You're crazy. You don't want to stop, so so don't, please."

Filumena walked a few paces away, and began to do up various of her fastenings that Julian had loosened.

"I do want to, but not yet, not already, when I've only just met you."

"Why are you sounding like some innocent juvenile? If you want it, go for it."

"No, I can't and I won't. Maybe soon, but not yet. I am sure about it, so don't try to persuade me."

Julian's self-confidence and erection collapsed. But he had enough experience not to let it show too much, so as not to mar his future chances.

"All right, then," he sighed, as he pulled up his zip and re-buttoned his trousers. "But we'll have to get out of here, or I'll die of frustration. And believe me, you're not too old. I've seen enough of your flesh to know that."

She laughed. "You are a funny man. And you make me feel very nice. I'm sorry to frustrate you, but control is good, too; it can make love-making very special, when the time is right."

Julian was still perplexed but decided to recover some lost dignity with an overstated display of chivalry. "Let me know when the time is right, then: I'll be as ready as I am now."

Certainties and uncertainties

From the window of his Cessna jet Pyon looked down at the tops of the Alps, fifteen thousand feet below. He shivered. It was as though the chill from the glistening white glaciers had seeped into the small cabin.

It was an unusually clear day, and the afternoon sun threw the peaks of the mountains into sharp shadows against one another. From this height, life on the valley floors was indiscernible, and the impression Pyon received was of a craggy deserted wasteland which matched his mood.

The few days in Paris with Natalie had been a short, enchanted interlude, which seemed, once again, unconnected with the mainstream of his life.

His visit to Naples and Amalfi had been a mistake. He had known, more or less, what he was going to find, or, rather, not find. He was told that Maria had gone on a short trip, they did not know where, she would be back at the end of the week. Caterina was at school in England, but his son, Gianni, was pleased to see him. He was in the care of the servants and Maria's doting mother. Old Signora Gatti viewed Pyon with more suspicion than usual, and the brothers were positively hostile. Sergio claimed that Pyon had brought dishonour on their family name. He muttered vague threats requiring him to make amends in some way which Pyon laughed off. He was used to the impotent *braggadocio* of his brothers-in-law.

"You know damn well," he told them, "that I've looked after your sister and the children very well. Of course I'm away a lot; that's part of my business, and if newspapers want to make up stories about my love-life, that's a risk of being rich and successful. And where is my wife? I can't believe she's simply gone away without telling anyone where."

"She has gone to recover from the shame you have caused her," Sergio growled.

"And doing it, no doubt, on a lavish scale with my money."

Pyon stayed only two days. He decided to delay the inevitable confrontation with Maria until he discovered what she had been trying to achieve.

He took Gianni out on *Speranza*, which lay in the marina at Naples. He took him to see Vesuvius and to the pleasure gardens. He devoted almost the entire two days to him, and Gianni warmed to his enthusiasm and ability to talk to him in a way he understood. But as Pyon drove away from the house, with the boy waving vigorously and tearfully from the front steps, while his grandmother scowled behind him, he felt a great sadness.

Even the regular reports he had been receiving of the Chemco bid, good though they were, did not cheer him. The Southern Hemisphere price was beginning to rise steadily. Chemco showed signs of panicking, and had stepped up their campaign of denigration. The attacks on Pyon himself had become more personal, and he was being portrayed to the American public as a combination of Machiavelli and Lothario.

He had made an announcement through his New York PR company that, when SHR had control of Chemco, Adnan al Souf was to buy the Agricultural Bank of Texas and all its recently acquired network of Savings and Loans banks in ten other states. This had unleashed howls of outrage which Pyon had expected. He had judged it best, though, to get over this obstacle as early as possible, not least to dispel any doubts about SHR's ability to fund such a highly leveraged takeover.

He and al Souf had been to New York to work on the various State and Federal banking authorities, and to prepare a public relations campaign with Bob MacFarlane. Pyon had no wish to appear himself, and anyway, MacFarlane advised against it, but al Souf allowed himself to be interviewed on television. His performance surprised and impressed the American public with a softly articulated urbanity which they understood.

Pyon was sure that, given time, al Souf's American lawyers could clear the hurdles to his eventual ownership, albeit with certain conditions, and this was another reason for starting this process now, the cost of which anyway was being borne by al Souf.

Confidence had returned, particularly in Europe, that Southern Hemisphere would succeed in placing their proposed huge issue of junk bonds.

From Pyon's perspective, he was winning. It would be a long fight, but provided he stuck to the plan he had put into operation, it should only be a matter of time – six months, a year, even – to quell the fears of a xenophobic public. The only factor that could go against him would be the announcement by Chemco of a successful trial of the AIDS vaccine which would send their price into the stratosphere. But there were a hundred other laboratories around the world chasing this particular golden goose, and there was a good chance that one of them would get there before Chemco. Better still, Chemco would get there first, but only after SHR had won control.

Sitting alone in the cabin of his private plane, Pyon was conscious of the uncertainties his relationship with Natalie was causing him. He recognised now that, uniquely, she had the power to divert him from the single-minded pursuit of his goal. He resented his inability to compartmentalise his life as previously he had always done. But he could not bring himself to resent Natalie.

He felt no more settled when he arrived at Heathrow. There he established through his office that there was no immediate need for him to go on into London and, making a sudden decision, he told Hanks to drive straight to Herefordshire.

As the Mercedes eased its way into the solid stream of

home-going commuter traffic heading west along the M4, Pyon telephoned his stockbrokers and Jeremy Fielder to receive a satisfactory update of SHR's position. Then he telephoned his mother.

"Hello, Mother," he boomed at her, "it's your boy here. I'm on my way out to see you, is that all right?"

"Would you turn back if I said it wasn't?" she asked.

"I would not. How are you?"

"Not too good. I've a touch of bronchitis, and my arthritis is bad, even in this good weather."

"You poor old wreck. I'll give you a good massage when I get there."

"That's the last thing I want from you, but I'm glad you're coming."

"Okay, Mother. I'll see you in a couple of hours."

Even from the air-conditioned, leather-upholstered insulation of the back of his car, Pyon could sense the lifting of urban pressures as they crossed the River Severn at Gloucester and started to wind their way through the small Herefordshire hills.

There was no particular frustration at being held up behind a tractor towing a silage trailer, or, in the small city of Hereford itself, being stuck behind a lumbering overloaded hay lorry. When they were through, and heading on into west Herefordshire, they reached the brow of a hill where the familiar sight of the ridge of the Black Mountains and the steep drop of Hay Bluff came into view.

Pyon told Hanks to pull up, and climbed out to walk a few hundred yards up a track he had not walked for thirty-five years. The sun was still high, but starting to drop down to rest in the Radnorshire hills to the north-west. Pyon looked across the small tumps and valleys which lay between, and the conical knap above Canon Pyon, from whence Jack Pyon's family had derived their name in pre-Norman times. Here, as a boy, he had hunted, stalked, fished and trapped. He could see places where he had tried out the horses he brought home from the markets in Hay, Brecon and Hereford. He wished he could transport Natalie back with him to this place and to those times, to show her the eager, happy boy he had been.

He could just see some of the outlying fields of his mother's farm – his farm, really – and he thought of Maeve, quietly controlling the crops and the stock in those fields for the last forty years and of how she had grown from a terrified servant-girl into the respected, slightly formidable old lady she now was. And, Pyon thought with a jolt, a frail seventy-year-old, whose mental strength disguised an increasing physical weakness.

He turned quickly back towards the car, and strode down the path to climb into the front seat beside his driver.

"Okay, Hanks, that's enough nostalgia, let's get on to Mother's."

"How is the old lady, sir?" Hanks asked in his respectful Cockney.

"I think she may not be too good. She's strong-willed, but not so tough. I may stay with her a few days. You go on back to London after you've dropped me. I'll probably drive myself back. I'll let you know."

"Okay, sir," the chauffeur replied doubtfully. "Is there a vehicle here?"

"Don't worry about it. I'll find something if I have to."

Shortly afterwards they reached the gates of the manor house, and turned into the long avenue of horse-chestnut trees.

Maeve stood in the stone porch, waiting to greet her son. Pyon leaped out and walked briskly to give her a warm hug.

"B'Jaysus, Mum, it's good to see you."

Maeve Pyon looked at her tall, handsome son, who seemed to her as fresh and full of energy as he had always been. "I wish it hadn't been so long, Christy." She returned his kiss on the cheek.

"It's only been a few months, Mother."

"When you've not so many left, each month becomes more precious."

"Don't be so morbid," he laughed. "All right, I'm sorry. You know how it is."

"That's not how it should be. But come on in before I start giving you a proper talking to."

Pyon pulled a face of mock contrition, and held the front door open for her. Over his shoulder he said, "Hanks, would you just bung those two small bags of mine in the hall, and take the big one back to London. And get yourself something to eat and drink."

"Thank you, sir. I'll see you in a few days."

Jack Pyon's heir

Maeve led her son through into her large light kitchen, where she spent most of her time now.

"Will you have a cup of tea?" she asked.

"I'd rather have a whiskey."

"I dare say you would, but you can leave it for a bit. Your liver must be in a terrible state."

"Tea it is, then."

Pyon sat in an ancient high-backed elm chair, and looked out of a west-facing window, across the quiet sunlit land while his mother made the tea, poured it and sat down opposite him at an old deal table.

"You know, Mother, it's bad for me to come here. I love it, but the peace and the quiet are like small, alien organisms eating away at my vitals. It would be easy to give in to it, and sink into a kind of timeless, irrelevant existence on the margins of real life."

"It would take more than a bit of rural peace to slow you down – God knows, I wish something would – but you'll have to start coming here when I'm gone."

"Why? Why should I have to take over? Why don't I just sell the place?"

Maeve shrugged. "You're Jack's heir. There have been Pyons here for at least eight hundred years. It's your duty to the continuity of the history of this place to carry on."

"But I'm not a Pyon."

"As far as the rest of the world is concerned, you're Jack Pyon's son."

Pyon looked at a photograph which still hung on the kitchen wall. It showed Jack Pyon standing by the edge of the Wye near Builth, proudly holding a twenty-four-pound salmon by its tail.

"He was a funny little fella," Pyon remarked. "It must have crossed a few people's minds that I'd be an unlikely offspring for a man like that."

"Not at all," his mother said "They would just think you'd inherited more from me than from him."

"Are you ever going to tell me who I did inherit my characteristics from, besides yourself?"

"I've told you, it would cause too much upset and would do no good. Don't think I haven't wanted to from time to time. But I never will. I'm sorry, but I know I'm right not to."

"He sure as hell wasn't an Englishman."

"I won't tell you one way or the other, so don't try and drag it out of me by elimination. As far as the world's concerned, you're Jack's son, and that's how I want it to stay."

Pyon understood the value his mother placed on the standing she had achieved after fifty years in this sparse rural community. And for that reason, he knew that ultimately he would have to take over responsibility for the estate. He also knew, as did his mother, that this would raise other problems for him.

"You'd better look after yourself, Mother. I am definitely not ready to get involved in this place. You know that I'll keep it really, don't you?"

"Yes. I know that. You mustn't let the fact that you were happy here prejudice you against it."

"For God's sake, why should I? I'm happy enough now."

"I don't believe you can be. You're a mess, Christy. What can you have been doing, going about with a girl half your age, showing yourself in public with her? What did you think that would do to Liz, whom you've treated like a doormat ever since you went off with the Italian woman."

Pyon sighed. "Don't do this, Ma. Things are a little tricky at the moment. But it's Natalie more than anything else who's kept me happy over the last year. I admit that Maria was a mistake. I made a bad judgement, and for the last fifteen years I've told myself I have to live with my mistakes. Meeting Natalie showed me what a pointless attitude that was."

"You could have put a lot right by going back to Liz. Liz is a fine, gentle woman. In the eyes of God, you're still married to her and she loves you still, though I can't think why. But she would be the right wife to bring back to this house."

"Maybe, probably. But it's too late. I can't turn the clock back. I can't unmeet Natalie, though she might well agree with you."

"If you had any goodness in you, you could. God would help you."

"I think God's given up on me by now."

"And you always had such faith as a boy," Maeve sighed sadly.

"Don't start that now, Mother," Pyon said with ill-disguised impatience. "You may not be aware that I'm right in the middle of the biggest deal of my life. I'll be among the top world players when I've pulled it off. Have you any idea what that will mean I've achieved?"

"Of course I know, but I'm not impressed by your making a ton of money if you can't keep your family life in order. It doesn't matter a damn if you're rich as Croesus when you can't make the people around you happy."

"D'you think I don't try? Hell, I do all I can to see Liz and give her whatever she needs, you know, for the horses and all. I see the kids enough. I helped Julian with his film, and I'm about to do the same again, I suspect. It's difficult with Caterina and Gianni; their mother's family are trying to set them against me. I know I've made mistakes. I don't need anyone to tell me, and when this deal's through, I'm going to set about rearranging things. But I'm not going to exclude Natalie. She's a very special person. When you meet her, you'll understand."

"I never want to meet her. You've never brought the Italian here because you knew I didn't want to meet her, and this is no different."

Pyon looked at his mother's tight anxious face, and heard the wheeziness in her voice. He put a hand across the table to take hers, and squeezed it.

"Don't worry about it. I promise I'll work things out for

the best. I know I've been a lousy son to you, but you wanted me to do well and you can't set someone a goal and then keep expecting him to take his eye off the ball."

"Yes, I wanted you to do well, Christy. After all, I gave up my whole life to you. But that didn't mean I wanted you obsessed with money-making, and exploiting and bullying. Look at all the destruction you've caused, tearing up beautiful river valleys to pull out cheap gravel; they're even talking of doing it here in Herefordshire, along the poor old Lugg – one of your companies, it is, and do you care? And Julian tells me you've another business in Brazil that's cutting down the rain-forests by the square mile."

"I don't know what the hell he's talking about. And as far as the gravel's concerned, if we didn't do it, the County Council would only give permission to someone else. But I didn't know we had applications in up here."

"I wish you would do something about it. But what I'm saying is that you've got everything out of balance. I know you don't mean to harm people, but you're so thoughtless. You seem to forget that there are other points of view besides your own. Just because you have the power to decide doesn't give you the right."

He looked at his mother, and thought about defending his position. After a moment, though, in a gentler tone, he said, "That's enough about me. How about you? Are you feeling up to taking me out and showing me your stock?"

She smiled at his ability, when he chose to use it, to play on another's susceptibilities.

"If you're interested, of course I am. Have you had enough tea?"

Pyon nodded and got to his feet. His mother rose and led him out through the back lobby. They crossed the old stable yard to a group of ancient stone bothies and beast-sheds on the far side of a high stone wall.

As they walked, Maeve said, "First I must show you my new toys, my *Bleu de Maines*. I bought a beautiful tup at the Brecon sale and two ewes from a man in Kent. He's in here." She led her son into an open-ended barn divided into pens by timber railings. A well-built ram of arrogant disposition glared at them. "Look at him. Isn't he handsome? Don't you love his velvety blue face?"

Pyon admired the ram, and stroked the curious wrinkly skin around its muzzle. "He's very fine, but a bit foreign-looking for my taste. You've still got the Ryelands, I hope?"

"Oh yes, of course. I got a new tup last year. There he is, over there."

They walked across the barn to a pen in which a large, rotund and woolly-faced ram ambled placidly towards them. Pyon noted the large fleece-clad testicles swinging between the ram's stocky rear legs. "He looks as though he could bother a few young ewes without any trouble."

"He covered all my Ryeland ewes and we've had some lovely lambs this year; a couple of very good ram lambs."

"Good, and what are you going to do with your blue fella?"

"I'll put him to half the Suffolk ewes this year. He should produce lambs with lovely back ends."

"Sounds nice for someone," Pyon remarked with a laugh.

"Don't be so puerile, Christy."

"Sorry, Mother. How about the cattle?"

"I wrote and told you, though I dare say you've forgotten. The Ayrshires are now a pedigree herd," she went on with obvious enthusiasm. "We took two rosettes at the Three Counties and I've high hopes for a two-year-old bull at the Royal Welsh. I'm so glad I made the change from Fresians."

"The Ayrshires certainly look a lot prettier."

"And they're giving me much nicer calves when I put them to the Hereford."

"And is the farm keeping its head above water, generally?"

"I've never lost money here, as you well know. It's been harder over the last five or six years, with the reduction of the corn intervention prices, but the sheep haven't being doing badly up till now. Fortunately, I don't have any expensive personal hobbies that the farm has to support and I still manage it myself."

"Isn't that getting you down a bit?"

"On the contrary, it's what keeps me going – that and my grandchildren, when I see them."

"Caterina said that she loved staying with you here at Easter. She said you were very kind to her."

"Poor child. She must have been very upset by what the newspapers said about you."

"I think she's got over that. And I've also just spent two days with Gianni, and tried to explain."

"How on earth could you expect them to understand? That's what I mean when I say you're thoughtless."

"Please, Mother, you've done your lecture. Let's drop it for the moment. Why don't we go and look at the dairy herd?"

Maeve glanced at her son's face, suddenly showing the tiredness of travel. "All right, Christy. But when we get back to the house, I'm going to make you a little dandelion tea, to calm you down; it's a wonderful old remedy for what they now call stress, what I've always called short temper."

"For goodness sake, Mother, what'll I be wanting with dandelion tea?"

"You can have it raw, if you like, in a salad, it works better like that."

Maeve Pyon led her son out of the sheep pens and down a track to the nearby paddock to show him her bulls. The conversation stayed with stock and farming, and Pyon warmed to the topic. He was sorry not to see any horses, but he did not say so, remembering that some of the earliest rows with his mother had been about horse-rearing, which she did not consider a serious agricultural activity.

When they returned to the house, Pyon took himself into the library and spent an hour on the telephone. He spoke only to people involved in the Chemco bid, and resisted an urge to ring Mauritius.

Ken Newberry greeted his call with surly complaint. "Where the hell have you been, Pyon? You should be here, or in New York while all this is going on. People expect you to be accessible."

"I'm in touch. It's no problem. I'm in Herefordshire if you want me over the next twenty-four hours, then I'll be back in London. This deal is going to take a long time, so there's no point winding ourselves up. But it's all going according to plan."

"Not entirely. There's a nasty little piece in the *Guardian* today, about disturbances in Transvaal."

"I know about that. As it's not true, the rumour will go away. It's only pulled the shares down a couple of points. Stop worrying, and I'll see you tomorrow."

Pyon disguised the uneasiness he felt about this obscure item of news surfacing in London. But, even as he replaced the receiver, he reassured himself that it was no more than an unfortunate coincidence.

Over a quiet dinner, alone with his mother, and during the next morning, Pyon discreetly, and with concern, tried to find out just how ill his mother was. He drove in a farm Land Rover to see Maeve's doctor in Weobley.

"She's a brave woman," the doctor said, "but not strong. She's developed a nasty chronic bronchitis which could give her a lot of trouble this winter. She shouldn't be going outside all the time, so you'll have to persuade her to get a foreman she can trust."

"That'll be hard. She's been overseeing everything herself for so long that she'd find it impossible to delegate."

"Well, if she doesn't, she could get seriously ill, and she'd hate that even more."

Pyon drove back thoughtfully. He stopped a quarter of a mile from the house, and walked into a field where the brown and white dairy herd grazed. The fences and the cattle they guarded were in fine condition. The crop of barley in an adjoining field showed signs of care and a good yield. The roadside hedges were neat and thick, and a small stand of oaks nearby had been expertly thinned. All the indications were of an estate run with knowledge and dedication. The land had become the outlet for all the affection which his mother had not been able to give to Jack Pyon, and which she obviously found difficult now to give to her son.

Pyon persuaded Maeve to have lunch with him at a small pub in the next village. The landlord of the pub and the few locals in the bar were astonished to see him, but they had no compunction about engaging him in conversation. Some of these people he had known as long as he could remember, and he was pleased to find how he enjoyed their reminiscences and microscopic knowledge of recent local history.

After lunch, he had arranged for a twin-engined charter plane from the tiny nearby airfield at Shobdon to fly him to Northolt, where Hanks would collect him.

His mother came to see him off at Shobdon, happy to drive herself the few miles back home. And as Pyon wished her goodbye, with both arms wrapped around her in a great hug, he sensed that his visit had gone some way to reassure her that his was not an entirely lost soul.

Amalfi

Maria Pyon stood on the terrace of her house in Amalfi and watched her brothers drive out through the wrought-iron gates. She did not wave. Instead, with an angry scowl, she turned and walked back into the large, cool salon.

"Maria," her mother said, "they are right. He should not see your children. You must divorce him."

Maria replied huskily, "Don't worry, by the time I've finished with him, he won't be seeing anything. But first, I must hurt him where he will hurt most."

"His children?"

"No. His children are just pale reflections of himself. He could do without them."

"I don't think so. But maybe money is more important?"

"No. He is beyond caring about money for its own sake. He doesn't work to make money, that's just a by-product. What he loves is to win. He has an image of himself wielding international power, world-wide influence. Above all else, he hates to lose."

"How can you do anything to hurt him? You're not involved in his business. He controls your income."

"Sure, he's always kept me away from anything to do with his work. He's never taken me to London, even. But luckily, I've a few friends of my own there."

"Is that why you went to London last month?"

"How do you know I went there?" Maria asked angrily.

"I saw the air ticket among your papers."

"Mama, I've pleaded with you not to pry among my things. I asked you to live here with me to support me, not to spy on me."

"How can I support you if I don't know what you're doing?"

"I'll tell you what I need to. I have to get closer to people in London, people he works with. This crazy deal of his to take over Chemco in America may make him overstretch himself. He's very vulnerable just now. I read in the English papers, his company must be seen to be very strong. So, I have an idea to make him invest in something, not too big, but which would be a bad mistake, and make his company look weak."

"How are you going to persuade him to do that?"

"I think I have found an ally. But don't ask me who, I'm not sure yet that I will succeed."

"You must be careful," Signora Gatti warned. "If he finds out, he'll be very dangerous. And when you went away, he came here. I'm sure he knew you were up to something. We didn't tell him where you were, though."

"He knows. He saw me."

"He saw you! In London? But surely he asked you then what you were doing?"

"No, he didn't. It was in a club. He was with his son, Julian. I guess he didn't want Julian to meet me. He's always kept those other children as far as possible from me. God! It's so insulting!" She blew through gritted teeth and shook her head. "But that's too bad. After I've taken the kids to Porto Cervo, I'm going back to London. You must stop Sergio and the others from doing anything, or they'll spoil my plan. Will you promise me you will control them?"

Signora Gatti shrugged. "You know what they are like, but they'll do what I tell them. But if you don't achieve anything in London this time, you must start to divorce him. We must not suffer the insult of his divorcing you because you have done something stupid."

That evening, Maria drove to Capodichino airport outside Naples to meet her daughter, returning from school in England.

When she saw her mother, Caterina ran out through the arrivals gate and flung herself into Maria's arms.

"Oh, Mama, I'm so glad to see you at last. It's been a horrible term. I don't want to go back."

"You won't have to, darling. It was your father's idea and it's just made you miserable. Especially because of what he's done."

"Don't be unkind about Papa. He came to see me at school and took me out. I was very worried about it, but it was lovely to see him. He was very nice. He explained how the newspapers like to write lies about him. He said he would come out and see us in Sardinia this summer. So please don't be cross about him, Mama. It was the other girls who were beastly."

Maria contented herself with saying, "The English are not kind people. They are hypocrites."

"But Papa's not English, is he? He says that he's Irish, and that's different."

"But not any better."

The Irish in Julian

"Do you think I have any Irish characteristics?" Julian Pyon asked his mother.

They were sitting on a sofa in the drawing-room of Clonegall House. Through the high, Georgian windows, they could see across a ha-ha to the parkland where a few mares stood in the shade of the great beech trees, whisking flies away with their tails.

Elizabeth Pyon looked at her son for a moment. "Yes. Your creativity, the perception that allows you to make films that people can relate to."

"But I feel that I have nothing in common with my father."

"Well, I can assure you that he is your father and, in some ways, you're not dissimilar."

"Don't be absurd; I'm his living antithesis."

205

"I wish you weren't so hostile towards him. He really does care about you. He wants you to do well, but he never wanted you to be exactly like him. He is aware of his own shortcomings. And you have to admire him a little for what he has achieved."

"No more than I might admire someone like Muhammad Ali, which I don't," Julian said dismissively.

"But he was very enthusiastic about your film, and he told me he was going to get involved with another one."

"Well, he might, I suppose."

"Don't completely alienate him. Your father likes the idea of relationships but he's not very good at them. He doesn't like the way they won't be controlled or conform to his ideas of logic."

"I am making an effort with him. You must have seen that when I came for dinner after Epsom, and I have seen him once or twice since then. As a matter of fact, I might be able to do him a favour that would help me very much."

"What's that?"

"There's a small Californian studio that's up for grabs. Have you heard of the Actors' Production Company?"

"Yes, of course. They made a lot of good films in the old days."

"They've fallen on hard times now. The studio's property assets are very undervalued, and superfluous to the size of operation it is. It's also got an amazing catalogue of classic movies. From my point of view it's an ideal vehicle for getting a completely different type of film made in Hollywood, with much more European influence. The other studios are shit-scared of anything unusual, and they just don't give people like me the breaks."

"How did you come across it?"

"Through a friend, Filumena di Francesci, someone I met at Enzo Fratinelli's. The current boss of the studio was an old friend of her father's. He's been in touch with me about doing a picture from an Updike novel, I've mentioned it to you. But he wants additional funding. I asked Filumena, and she said he was in a bit of trouble. It's partly owned by some shady American conglomerate, and they could be amenable to an offer for it. She said we'd obviously have to tread carefully, because he might take umbrage at the suggestion, and upset my chances of doing the movie."

"I'd talk to your father about it if I were you. It's what he knows about, after all."

"Yes, well, I thought I would. At least if I was responsible for him pulling off a major business coup, I'd feel less beholden to him for backing my projects."

"He's gone to America for a couple of weeks. Why not put it to him when he gets back?"

"I will. Are you coming over to London in the near future?"

"You don't need me to help."

"I know that, but I'd like you to meet Filumena; at least, she's said she'd like to meet you."

"Why should she want to do that?"

"I don't know, really, unless it's because she's fascinated to learn more about me. She's an enthusiastic admirer of my work."

"Of *Michael and Mustapha*?"

"Sure."

Liz was surprised. "What's she like, this Filumena?"

"She's clever, in an uneducated sort of way, and outrageously sexy."

"Have you slept with her, then?"

"No, not yet," Julian admitted.

"How old is she?"

"I'm not sure. Thirty-five, maybe. Does it matter?"

The idea of a liaison between Julian and the woman he described struck Liz as unlikely. She stood up and walked around to fiddle about with a large arrangement of flowers on a table behind the sofa.

"I'll try and come to London this week. Let me know when she's coming."

Encounters with Filumena

Julian sat on the sofa in his studio, gazing at the skylights, high above. By his side was an untidy sheaf of typewritten papers. He had been working on his film script, but now his mind had wandered to the inviting warmth of Filumena di Francesci's body. He was jolted out of his reverie by the shrilling of a telephone.

"Three five two four double nine one." His voice aimed to give an impression of efficient langour.

"Hello, Julian? It's Filumena. I'm in London. Will you take me out to dinner tonight?"

Julian quickly thought of how he could get out of a date with an old friend from his university newspaper days. He tried to disguise the excitement he felt.

"Sure, but it'll have to be late. I could pick you up at half-past nine."

"That will be marvellous," she said. "I'm staying at the Savoy." Then she added quickly, "I'll meet you in the lobby."

"Okay. See you then."

Julian felt his genitals become restless even as she settled into the passenger seat of his car. She was every bit as sexually arousing as he had remembered. He leaned across to kiss her, and she turned her lips to him.

"You look delicious, Filumena; like some Botticellian virgin."

"I am no virgin, though."

"Nor were Botticelli's, I suspect."

She laughed. "You're right."

Julian drove them to an Italian restaurant in World's End.

"They say the food's better here than in Italy," he said by way of explanation. He wanted heavily garlicked food and dark wine from the northern Italian hills.

Filumena was pleased to see Julian and not just because he represented an important part of her plan. She delayed getting to her real purpose, and encouraged his confident flirtation.

When their main courses of *fegato* and *vitello* had arrived at the table, she turned the conversation to the subject of Christy Pyon.

"Tell me about your father, Julian. Has he been an influence on you?"

"In a negative sense, yes, inasmuch as he's a lot of the things I wouldn't like to be."

"You really don't like him, then?"

"Not at all. I'm ashamed to say that at the moment I'm trying to keep a dialogue going with him because he can help with my film, as you know. And I think I might be able to talk him into buying the Actors' Production Company."

"Why should you be ashamed? He must have used people all his life to be what he is. So why not do the same?"

"It's hypocritical."

Filumena shrugged her head to one side in a gesture of pragmatism. "Always in history, artists have to be devious towards their patrons. The art is more important than a small lie."

"Yes. That was the view I took. I'll need some more details to show him. Do you think Johnny Capra would let me have them?"

"Sure. Leave it to me. I'll ask him. If he knows I am involved in some way, he won't mind. But you must not let your father know my connection; that's really important."

"Why?"

"Because . . . He probably won't trust the judgement of a woman – few businessmen do."

"He certainly won't rely on your judgement. Not that he's particularly chauvinistic – he simply doesn't listen to anyone, male or female."

"I don't want your father to know that this idea has anything to do with me; it's much better if he thinks it comes straight from you. Will you promise not to tell him?"

"Okay," said Julian, "you may be right. But you will get the details, won't you?"

"Of course."

For a while, Julian talked with boyish eagerness of what could be done with a studio like the Actors' Production Company. Under European guidance, he said, it could become a revolutionary force in world film-making.

Filumena sat and listened, and encouraged him. She tried not to think of the risks she was taking. There would be confrontation some time in the future, but she pushed that to the back of her mind while she contemplated the damage she could do.

Her next step was to meet Julian's mother. This would be risky too, but it had to be done. There was a pause as a waiter removed their plates. When he had gone, she said, "Does your mother feel so strongly as you about your father?"

"I don't think so. She was hurt when he went off with Maria, but she lives with it. She doesn't seem bitter. God knows why. I told you before, she's a loyal woman and she tends to treat him like an errant child. His new girlfriend has given her a bit of a jolt, though."

"How do you mean?"

"My mother was obviously upset when she had to divorce him, but I think she felt she hadn't really lost him; that Maria was simply a sexual adventure which would pass. But Natalie has obsessed him in a different way. He's using her to recapture his lost innocence."

Filumena's eyes became unfocused and bleak. For a moment she seemed a long way off. With a visible effort which puzzled Julian, she brought herself back.

"You know," she said, "I really would like to meet your mother. She sounds like a remarkable woman." But not as remarkable as I am being right now, she said to herself.

Julian glanced at her doubtfully, but nodded, "Okay."

Filumena realised that then her handling of Julian would become a major challenge.

But there was a more immediate challenge that night, when once more she chose to deprive Julian of a fulfilment he had confidently expected.

She insisted he take her back to the Savoy.

They would see each other the next day, she said, why rush it?

Julian saw her into the lobby and drove back to Chelsea in a state of frustrated bewilderment.

What did the woman want? It was obvious that she wanted him, and she was old enough not to have any hang-ups. She had been reticent about her own current relationships, but he was sure they were unsatisfactory. And there was this odd insistence of hers that she wanted to meet his mother.

Maybe he should get that out of the way; maybe that would answer some questions.

When she telephoned him early next morning, he was able to say, "I've arranged to have lunch with my mother today. D'you want to come?"

After a moment's silence, she said, "Sure. That will be wonderful. Where?"

"At her house in Mayfair."

He gave her the address, and asked her to be there at twelve-thirty. "And there's a preview of Nic Roeg's new film at the ICA. We could go to that afterwards, and then on to dinner."

"Okay," she said, with a calmness she did not feel.

Liz Pyon glanced around her drawing-room to make sure that everything looked right. It was absurd, but she wanted to impress this older woman of Julian's. She felt that she was about to be confronted by a rival. She had not experienced this with the earnest, humourless girls that her son had occasionally brought home before. And she had never seen Julian in such a state of agitation over a woman.

Julian had not arrived when the doorbell rang.

He had a key of his own, Liz thought, so it must be this Filumena.

She decided to let Hanks open the door and send up her guest.

When the woman walked into her drawing-room, Liz was first struck by how much younger she looked than she had imagined; then by her obvious attractiveness. And she could not dispel a vague sense of familiarity.

"Hello, you must be Filumena di Francesci. I'm Elizabeth Pyon. I'm sorry, but Julian hasn't arrived yet. Do come in and sit down." She held out a hand, and noticed the nervousness in the other woman's as she shook it.

"Hello, Mrs Pyon. I've been looking forward to meeting you," Filumena said in good English and a rich voice.

Liz looked at her closely for a moment, trying to remember where she might have met her. "Would you like a drink?"

"Martini, please, dry."

Liz rang for Hanks to get drinks, and turned back to her

guest. "My son hasn't told me much about you, but I gather you're interested in his films."

"Yes," the woman replied slowly, and, ignoring the offered seat on the sofa, walked towards a window. The sun caught her face at an angle which sharpened her features. At that instant, Liz knew who she was.

"My God! Why have you come here? What are you doing with my son?"

Maria Pyon turned sharply to face her husband's first wife, almost relieved. "You know who I am, then?"

"I do now. I knew I'd seen you before. Did you know that? Just once, very quickly in the back of Christy's car at La Napoule. It's as vivid to me today as it was fifteen years ago. You've changed, of course, but I knew I'd seen you as soon as you walked in." Liz gazed at Maria with horrified fascination. "Why on earth have you come here?"

Maria looked at her steadily, not challenging her. "I'll tell you why. My husband is still in some ways your husband. I am not so stupid I did not know he carried on seeing you when I married him, staying with you, as if he had never left you. That's why he has never let me come with him to London or to any places where you and I might meet." Maria tilted her chin, "So, let us call him 'our' husband. Our husband is a bigamist, not in law, but in fact. And now he is cheating on both of us."

Liz could not speak for a moment. She had always avoided such blunt articulation of the position, but she knew that Maria was right.

Hanks appeared and Liz distractedly asked him to pour a Martini and a glass of Apollinaris water. Maria chafed impatiently until he he had handed them both their drinks and left. When his footsteps had faded, she went on, "I won't be treated like this. It is the last insult, and you should feel the same. You must help me to teach him that he can't do this."

"You are aware, of course," Liz said, "that he's done this to me before."

"It was not the same, and it was a long time ago. You never really lost him, did you? This time, you will."

212

"But why have you brought Julian into this? It's intolerable! Julian is Christy's son, for God's sake!"

"Julian has also been badly treated by our husband. I think he doesn't love him. He will help us in our revenge."

"Oh, I hope not!" Liz said angrily. "And why did you have to seduce him?"

"I have not. He is a good-looking, quite fascinating young man, but I would not let him; I could not, of course."

Liz reluctantly believed her. "But why the subterfuge?"

"I had to find allies, and I wanted to meet you. I did not think you would see me if I just telephoned. I wanted to tell you that we are in the same boat. Together we can punish Pyon for his abuse."

"What the hell is going on?" A man's voice sounded angrily from the entrance to the room.

Both women spun round. Neither had noticed Julian's arrival.

He was clutching the door handle and his eyes were wide with astonishment. "Filumena, what are you talking about, punishing my father?" he demanded of Maria.

"Julian," Liz said quickly, "this isn't Filumena. This is your father's second wife, Maria."

Julian walked into the room and collapsed on to a sofa. He stared at Maria in horrified disbelief. "What the hell are you talking about, Mother? This is Filumena di Francesci whom I asked for lunch to meet you."

Maria shook her head, with a remorseful tightening of her mouth. "I was going to tell you today, I promise. I have good reasons for my plan. I had to get to know you before you knew who I was, you will see that."

Julian stood up and walked to the other end of the room. He turned back towards her, white-faced. "You've made a complete arsehole out of me! Fratinelli must have known you were scheming something. Was he in on it too?"

"Of course not. Is that what you're worried about, your image in the eyes of the great director? I just told him I thought it would be fun to meet you without your knowing who I was."

"Christ almighty, I've been a complete prat. I should have guessed that someone like you couldn't really be interested in my films." He walked towards the door. "You scheming bitch. I'm not fond of my father, but there's no way I'm going to be part of any plans to avenge your bruised ego." Before he left the room, he said to his mother, "Sorry to have wasted your time. Obviously you don't want to have lunch with this woman, but can you chuck her out? I can't stay here."

Julian walked out of the room and slammed the door behind him. He ran down the stairs two at a time, and rushed out of the house. He got into his car outside and drove blindly out of the mews.

The two women stood, twiddling their glasses.

"You'd better sit down," Liz suggested.

They placed themselves on sofas opposite each other.

"I think your approach through Julian has backfired, don't you?" Liz asked.

"Maybe, but I am talking to you."

"I don't think we have much common ground. Obviously, I'd like my husband back, and of course I'm hurt by this new affair of his. But I don't want to punish him. Anyway, what could *I* do?"

"You know all about his business, the people he works with, and that is where he can be hurt."

"Even if I did want to hurt him, which I don't particularly, if we damaged his business, you would suffer as well," Liz remarked calmly.

"No, I can gain, we can both gain. You must know he is doing a big deal in America."

"Chemco? Of course I do."

"And he is very exposed. Even for him it's a big deal, no?"

"So he says," Liz answered.

"We can make a lot of money by knowing what is happening, by being on the inside. You know the people on the inside, and some of them must have reasons not to like him. They would help, and they would help you to make some money of your own, instead of having to accept it from him. And I think maybe we can make him lose his fight for Chemco." Her eyes glinted. "And he would hate that!"

"I don't think I'm interested, Maria," Liz said evenly. "I

don't care whether Christy succeeds or not. I want no more of his money than he's already given me. I'm quite independent now. I agree that he's behaved selfishly in most things, most of his life, but that's because he's thoughtless, not because he's malicious. You do what you like, but I won't help you. And you can be sure that he can defend himself. He didn't get where he is by not watching his back. And it looks as if you've lost Julian as an ally."

Maria almost snarled with frustration. "Why do you want Pyon to go on abusing you, treating you like some highly paid whore?"

"I think I've said all I want to say to you. Will you excuse me if I cancel our lunch date? I obviously wouldn't have agreed to it if I'd known who you were."

Liz stood, and calmly walked towards the door. "Hanks will show you out," she said, without looking back.

Julian's car screeched to a halt outside his white stucco studio house. He leaped out, ignoring the yellow line on the side of the road, and strode up to his front door. Angrily, he brushed aside an innocent, trailing branch of wisteria that hung across it and plunged his key into the lock.

Inside, blinds still covered the high roof lights and the cavernous room was ten degrees cooler than the baking streets. Julian clumped across the bare floorboards and opened the top doors of an old Irish linen press. He pulled out a bottle of '71 burgundy and carried it into his kitchen to open it. He filled a half-pint goblet with wine and took a gulp. From a bread crock he took a long French loaf, broke it crudely and smeared it with butter and brie. He took the food and drink in awkward handfuls into the studio and put them on a large pedestal desk.

He sat down at the desk and tore off a mouthful of bread and cheese with his teeth. He glanced at the typescript which lay in front of him, and began to leaf through it. He had been working on it for two weeks and it was covered with his pencilled notes. The blur of letters gradually came into focus, and he became absorbed in the scene unfolding on the pages. Without looking, he fumbled across the desk-top for his pencil.

Here was a refuge from his humiliation and he entered it gratefully.

Three or four hours and a second bottle of burgundy later, he was abruptly drawn back to the present by the shrill bleating of his telephone.

"Hello." His voice was hoarse and non-committal.

"Julian. It's Maria . . . Filumena. Please let me talk to you."

He did not answer.

"Julian, please. I want to see you."

Her husky voice tingled his eardrums and sent a message flushing through his body to his genitals.

He glanced at the script. Its future depended on her.

And he wanted to screw her.

"Come here then, now." There was to be no argument about it.

"Okay," she said, breathless. "I'll be there in half an hour."

Julian went to the linen press again and fished around for a bottle of cognac. He poured two inches into a tumbler. He did not want to spoil this opportunity with over-hasty reactions.

The doorbell rang.

She was on his front step, her eyes wide and submissive.

He ushered her in without speaking. She brushed past him and the smell of her scent and her own secretions swirled through his nasal cavities to trigger primeval responses in his brain.

He closed the door behind her.

She stood in the middle of the room and shivered slightly.

"It's delicious and cool in here," she said, taking in the grand old Edwardian studio. "How clever to find such a splendid place."

"I found it, my father paid for it," Julian said without emphasis. "Now, would you like a drink? Brandy, wine?" he asked.

"Brandy, please."

He poured her one, and another for himself. He put both

glasses down near her on a low table of Indian *shisham* wood inlaid with teak.

He stood in front of her, a foot away. She looked uncertainly into his motionless eyes. Her face and bare legs still gleamed from the outside heat; their tan contrasted with the simple turquoise cotton jersey dress and Florentine shoes she wore.

He reached his arm behind her and stroked the nape of her neck and drew her to him until he could feel her breasts against his ribs. Between his thumb and forefinger he caught the tag of the zip which ran down the back of her dress and gently tugged. When he reached the point just at the parting of her buttocks where the zip stopped, he slid his hands up her back, beneath her dress to her shoulders and slipped it down her arms, over her naked breasts.

Gravity took over and the garment fell in a flimsy circle around her feet.

Julian gazed down at the smooth brown body, and the tiny triangle of silk fringed with small black curls that rose in her loins.

She reached out her arms to pull him back against her. She turned her shiny lips towards his. Their damp mouths met in a soft collision and melted greedily into one another. Her hands searched his shoulder blades, the small of his back, his buttocks, until she found the waistband of his trousers, unbuttoned, unzipped, delved into his pants and fondled his swelling flesh.

He drew his mouth away from hers and stepped back to lift her with his arms beneath her back and her knees. He carried her across an Afghan rug and laid her full length on the Chesterfield. He sat by her feet, and slid off the turquoise shoes. He leaned forward and she arched up her pelvis to let him slide her tiny pants beneath her bottom and down her smooth long legs.

She laid her head back, crooked her left knee against the back of the sofa and dropped her right leg over the edge. She closed her eyes and felt his tongue questing up her thighs with tantalising slowness until it flickered among her pubic curls. She lifted her hips in delicious anticipation. The tongue softly probed the warm slit until, with short, rhythmic thrusts, it touched her tender spot.

Her husky moans rose to a crescendo. She felt as if her loins were melting while she drowned in a flood of pleasure.

Julian sensed her stiffen, then relax into a luxurious, gentle squeezing of his tongue.

After a while, she raised her head and looked down at him between large, soft nipples. There was a groggy acclamation in her eyes that thrilled his vanity.

When she lifted her arms to beckon him to her, he fell towards her. Their mouths locked and their tongues vigorously stirred a cocktail of bodily juices.

She struggled her hands to his chest, ripped the buttons off his shirt and tore it off him. With their arms around each other again, they rolled off the sofa on to the rug. He was on his back. Maria released herself and crawled to his feet. She undid his shoes and pulled them off with his socks, then dragged his trousers and pants down his legs, laughing gleefully as his ripening erection sprang free.

She placed her knees either side of his thighs and lowered herself over him until her nipples brushed his chest. She reached a hand back between her legs to guide his shaft into her and lowered herself slowly on to it.

Her dark brown eyes gleamed mistily and there was a half smile on her lips. She lifted her hips and moved them back a little. Julian pulled her down towards him until her breasts were splayed like two suction pads across his chest. He began to lift his pelvis in a deep thrust.

"This time," she gasped, "we come together."

Julian's mouth found hers and their saliva mingled and smeared all over each other's faces. Tongues licked and teeth nipped, like puppies in play. He thrust up into her again, her hips came down to his and they met with a soft impact, cushioned by her fleshy mound. And again, with instinctive timing, each stroke faster than the last, each pass touching her own most sensitive place.

She lifted her head from his and came again. He felt it, and smiled, pushed his torso up beneath her and, still inside her, brought his legs round until he was kneeling and her feet were crossed in the small of his back. He put his hands beneath her buttocks, lifted her and carried her to his bedroom where he laid her on his seven-foot futon.

"*This* time," she whispered with a smile. "You deserve it."

This spur to his vanity, and the cognac, extended his energy and imagination beyond all previous limits. There was almost as much pleasure to be gained from the knowledge of what he was giving to this woman as there was from his own physical gratification.

After two vigorous, speechless hours, they both lay back exhausted, certain that it was the best either of them had ever known.

Maria stroked Julian's hairless chest, trailing her fingers through the sweat. She propped herself up on one elbow to look at him, and he saw a new regard in her eyes.

"It's incredible," she said. "I just didn't think you were so *sexy*. But you are a fantastic, strong lover."

With steady eyes, he asked, "Better than my father?"

"Of course you're younger, more eager."

Julian laughed, and chose to grant himself the benefit of her ambiguousness. He did not really care. But he, too, could not avoid seeing her in a new light. He could not despise the giver of so much pleasure.

So they talked easily of small things and ideas, with the intoxication that comes with good love-making. In this afterglow there were few obstructions to the flow of communication.

They made love some more and their pleasure increased with their growing knowledge of each other's special likes.

It was after ten, and midsummer dusk had fallen before they ventured out into the street. Julian's car had been clamped. They laughed about it and walked up towards the King's Road to have dinner.

Among the quiet bustle of a chic Italian restaurant in Park Walk, they felt apart from the other eaters, still cocooned by the afternoon's special intimacy.

Maria thought it safe now to refer to the Actors' Production Company.

"Did you talk with your father about Johnny's studio?"

Julian glanced at her sharply, trying to evaluate a suspicion which still soured the otherwise sugary aftertaste of their love-making.

"Maria, you've got to tell me the truth now. This deal with Johnny Capra isn't something to do with you trying to punish my father, is it?"

"Julian!" She was appalled that he could even consider it. "You're someone with a lot of talent, but you need the use of your father's money to realise it. So, use it. If you do a deal on the studio and it's a success, and he makes money as a result, that's too bad. But at least you will be the important part of that success. Listen, if you can find someone else to pay for it, that's fine by me."

"No. You're right. We'll use my father."

"You realise now why I said he mustn't know about my involvement, nor should your mother, or your sister – anyone at all. It's a big deal for someone like you to bring to Pyon, but you must show that it is your idea."

"Sure, that's obvious. But I'm going to need as much detail as possible to get him interested."

"I already asked Johnny. He's going to fax all the information to my hotel – it's better like that. He doesn't want too many people to know about his problems. He's worked hard and he's a proud man."

Everything seemed possible to Julian just then. He wanted to trust Maria, and he believed her. He believed that a 28-year-old, novice film director could take on the Hollywood establishment and beat it with integrity and ideals.

Maria did not disabuse him.

Maria and Julian spent the next three days with one another.

Maria – anyway more than glad to be made love to by him – was able to maintain his enthusiasm for the Actors' Production Company. When twenty sheets of scanty information arrived from Johnny Capra, they went through them together, and worked on the kind of proposal he should put to Pyon. They spoke of Pyon as if he were a stranger, not a father or a husband, and so diminished the bizarreness of their own relationship.

Julian also pursued the film project with unprecedented optimism. He made calls to potential producers, cameramen and others who would form part of the package he could take to APC. Maria's readiness to talk and hear about the script and Julian's treatment of it convinced him that her commitment was genuine.

Work on the film and the studio deal was interspersed, at any time of night or day, with sessions of vigorous erotic adventure. Julian surprised himself with his own energy. The more he expended in love-making, the more he seemed to have available for the pursuit of his career.

After three days, Maria left for Italy. Julian took her to the airport, but when he had kissed her goodbye – and she had discreetly squeezed his balls – at the departure gate, he raced back to London, thinking only of the meeting he was about to have with his father.

Research

Julian insisted that they meet at Pyon's office – it was a business meeting and should be conducted under normal business conditions.

"There are no such things," Pyon had said, but agreed that Julian should come to the Southern Hemisphere building.

For a few moments, when he first walked in, all Julian could think about was his father making love to Maria, and he rather enjoyed the private knowledge of this bond between them, and he thought of Maria saying, "Of course you're younger," and he knew that meant "better".

Pyon greeted him effusively, and waved him over to a large, leather chair that was in a group around a low table at one end of the room.

"Drink?"

"Sure. Have you got any wine?"

"Of course I have wine. Dom Perignon? Château-Lafite? Montrachet?"

"That'll do."

Pyon opened an elaborate chilled wall cabinet, and took out a bottle which he opened and poured himself.

They sat opposite one another, either side of the low walnut table, upon which Pyon placed his gleaming brogues.

"So, you've a property deal for me; in the States, you say?"

"Yes. More than a property deal, actually; a chance to buy into a Hollywood studio, with a lot of underused land, the rights to a catalogue of amazing old movies, and a television station in Australia." Julian looked at his father to gauge his reaction.

Pyon merely lifted an eyebrow. "This would be APC, the people who have asked you to direct a film for them?"

"That's right. When I pressed them about my finding outside money for it, they admitted that they had major cash-flow problems. They owe a lot of money on several big pictures that didn't take off. They're desperate, but the rest of Hollywood's in such turmoil, no one there wants to touch it."

Julian tossed a pile of facsimiled sheets on to the table. Pyon leaned forward, picked them up and began to leaf through them.

Julian went on quickly, "As you can see, they've some tremendous assets to offset their liabilities. Trouble is, they don't have the income to service the loans. It's a shame, because they were once a great studio."

"Sentimental regrets don't come into it. The commercial world is like the tropical rain forest; the vigorous and adaptable survive, the rest atrophy and provide nourishment for the survivors."

"Graphic metaphor, Dad, but there's a chance to save this one, and there's scope for some of your creative unbundling. They don't need half the studio lots. And the Australian TV station has been a distraction. They were hoping it would provide work for the studio, but they've ended up having to buy in most of their programmes."

"It sounds a regular tale of incompetence and mismanagement. How the hell did this Johnny Capra get into it?"

"He was a powerful distributor. He had connections with a lot of the smaller cinema chains. I imagine he thought he could make a better job of producing pictures that punters wanted to see. He had a few good ideas, but nothing took off. He's in it up to his neck now."

"So it seems."

"Well, what do you think?"

"What do I think about what?"

"About my proposal, of course."

"I don't think anything about it. This pile of bumph is probably telling me half the story."

"But could you be interested?"

"That's entirely hypothetical."

"All right, but do you find the deal as it's presented there attractive?"

"Of course it is. It's designed to be. But I doubt that it bears much relation to the true situation. It's no good coming to me with all this crap, wanting a reaction. I expect to be shown the facts, independently researched, backed up by outside accountants and lawyers. Have you even been to this place? Have you seen the properties? Have you checked out their rights to the titles they're claiming?"

"No. Not yet. I didn't want to waste time and money unless I knew you were interested in principle."

"I am not interested in forming any views on the strength of a few pages of half-baked sales literature. If you want to know what I think, do the research, check it out thoroughly, then come back to me, and I'll look at it."

"Since when did you research your deals? When you first started horse-coping, did you go out and investigate and decide that what the public wanted was sixteen-hand, chestnut geldings? Of course you didn't. You just bought what you thought you could make a turn on. Don't give me all this research bullshit." Julian's frustration was getting the better of him. "You've always told me that you relied on your gut reactions."

"Don't get so excitable. I don't want to put you down, Julian, and I've no objection to your coming to me with a deal, but I have a much more experienced gut than you. I've been at it for over thirty years."

Julian stood up angrily. "Can't you accept that for once I might know more about something than you do? If we don't get a move on, someone else will snap up the deal." Julian was slightly embarrassed by what might be misconstrued as greed. "It's not the money to be made that I'm interested in, it's the chance to inject a bit of creativity into American movie-making."

Pyon laughed. "What the hell makes you think you know what the public wants to see? The reason the Americans dominate world cinema and television is that they're better at putting bums on seats. They make watchable films. Sure they have failures, but the top-grossing movies are nearly always American. You're kidding yourself if you think you know better. And after all you've only had the one, very minor success yourself."

"Listen, there's a whole movie audience which is being ignored – the baby-boomers. They like going to cinemas, but they don't want to see Michael Jackson or *Batman* or *Gremlins*. They want something that demands a bit of them. And that requires a more sophisticated approach, a more *European* approach."

Julian had picked up his glass of wine and was striding around the room. "I know I'm right, and the Americans don't know how to do it, not the ones who control the money, the studio bosses, the men in sharp suits; they don't have an ounce of creativity between them."

"Few people have lost money simply because they under-estimated public taste. You're talking about a minority audience, and I don't say that there isn't a place for specialist film-making. But in the main, Joe Public is an idle fella. He doesn't want demands made on him."

"You could at least have considered what I'm putting to you, as a business deal."

"Don't get in a state. You wouldn't want me to give you special treatment, would you? All I've said is come back to me with some hard information, not some rosy picture painted by a desperate man who's obviously drowning in debt."

"Right, I will, and if you don't like it then, I'll take it elsewhere."

"That's up to you," Pyon shrugged. "But at least I'll give you a hearing."

"I'll see you when I get back from Los Angeles."

"When are you going, then?"

Julian slammed down his empty glass on the table. "Right now. Thanks to my relationship with the studio as a director, I have an advantage that I don't intend to lose before someone else realises the potential."

"You don't think, maybe, that this fella's talked to a few other people besides yourself, then?"

"I'll tell you when I get back."

"Best of luck to you." Pyon took his feet off the table and stood up. "And I do mean that, Julian. I'm only marking your card. And I should warn you – for every ten deals you try to get started, maybe only one ever comes to anything."

Julian glared at him a moment before storming out of the room and slamming the door behind him.

A warning for Laura

Laura Pyon blinked her eyes open and tried to stretch within the constraints of an economy seat on a Venezuelan Airlines 747.

She shook her straight black hair from her face and glanced down at the Mary Wesley novel that had lain open at the same place since she had left Caracas. She had resisted all attempts by the cabin staff to feed her, and now as they were beginning their descent towards London, she was regretting it. She looked out of the window and saw only a layer of thick cloud, into which the plane was about to plunge. She turned to look at the passenger beside her whom she had scarcely noticed until then. He was a small, balding man, wearing a plain white shirt with the top button undone and a bogus club tie with its knot slipped down a few inches. He gave her an uncertain smile. She returned the smile, and spotted that he had an unopened packet of biscuits on his tray.

"I seem to have missed breakfast," she said to him. "Could I have those biscuits if you're not going to eat them?"

The man handed them over willingly. He had been trying to catch her eye ever since they had settled into the plane in Venezuela.

"You do seem to have been sleeping most of the time," he said conversationally, in a small nasal voice.

Laura, munching one of his biscuits, turned her blue eyes full on to him. "Yeah. I hate long flights, they're such a drag."

"Have you been in Venezuela on holiday?"

"Sort of."

"Must be a good place for a holiday. I've been working out there myself."

Laura turned back to her book. "Have you?" she said.

He did not notice her lack of interest. "Yes, offshore oil exploration. I travel around quite a lot. I'm on the costs side of it."

Laura yawned. "Really?"

"So, what have you been doing with yourself, then?" the man persevered.

"I came up in a truck from Brazil. That's why I'm so bloody knackered. I don't seem to have done anything except drive and fuck."

The man's jaw dropped and he flushed with excitement. Laura saw him glance at his watch, and laughed to herself – he was working out how much time he had to get off with her.

"I expect we'll be landing in about ten minutes," she said.

"Yes," he said with disappointment, watching the fantasy fade as quickly as it had come. Then, optimistically, he asked, "Where have you got to get to from Heathrow?"

"Into London, I should think. I haven't decided yet."

"I live in London, well, Sidcup. I could give you a lift. My car's in the long-term. We could stop and have a bit of lunch. You haven't eaten anything for twelve hours."

Laura looked at him and thought, you cheeky, presumptuous little man. She thought of the tough, uncompromising and curiously vulnerable man she had left behind in South America. Men could lay claims to women's minds and bodies on the flimsiest of grounds.

"That's kind of you to offer. I'll let you know when we've landed," she said.

That seemed to satisfy him, and he kept up a continuous banter which she ignored until they were filing off the plane. He almost ran to keep up with her as she strode down the corridors of the concrete and glass tubes that led to the baggage claim halls.

To his relief his case lurched out of the rubber-flap mouth before hers. He piled her big, khaki canvas bag on to a trolley with his, and pushed them through the green channel, without attracting the notice of the customs officials.

Outside the arrivals gate, just beyond the rail, Hanks was waiting. He spotted her immediately.

He waved to catch her attention.

Laura's self-appointed porter did not see. She continued to let him push her bag until Hanks was by their side, touching the peak of his chauffeur's cap.

"Welcome back, Miss Pyon."

"Hello, Hanks. I wasn't expecting to see you."

"Your father insisted, Miss. Can I take your bags?"

Laura turned to the oil cost-accountant.

"Thanks for your help," she said. "I won't be needing a lift, thanks."

She heaved her bag off the trolley and handed it to Hanks who hoisted the strap over his shoulder.

Laura's fellow traveller watched with open-mouthed disappointment as they wove a path through the crowd.

"Mr Pyon said to drive you straight to Nethercombe, and he'll come down later in the helicopter," Hanks said when they were in the Mercedes.

Laura considered this. "Okay. Why not? I could do with a couple of days' rest. Are my grandparents expecting me?"

"I couldn't say, Miss, but I should think your father would have told them."

Laura sank back in her seat, and closed her eyes. She did not wake again until the car was winding its way along the narrow lanes, through the gullies of Exmoor towards her mother's childhood home.

She looked out fondly at the familiar landscape. The

sombre sky that hung close over the tops of the hills was a welcome contrast to the humid sunshine of the rain forest. She preferred being here to scrambling around the edges of the Angel Falls with a man obsessed by the need to prove himself a man.

A few days with her grandparents – unchanging, understanding, uncondemning – would suit her very well. She was less sure about seeing her father; he might remind her of her abandoned adventurer.

Lord and Lady Barnstaple were delighted to see Laura. They loved hearing the stories of her travels – journeys that they were now too old to make. They fetched maps and atlases to follow her routes, happy to relive her experiences through her animated descriptions of the people and places. They could excuse a lot of outlandish behaviour in a goodlooking young woman in her prime.

After lunch, Laura asked if she could take one of the hunters from its paddock, and hack across the nearby hill. The wind had backed to a brisk south-easterly and was brushing the low clouds off the horizon. By the time she reached the rounded summit of the tor, the sun was beginning to break through. It lit the valley where Nethercombe lay in its park and glinted off a lake which had been planned by an early Victorian Lord Barnstaple amidst copper beeches, wellingtonias and rhododendrons.

It was a scene that was unassailably peaceful and safe, and it made Laura wonder why she could not settle for an existence in a place like it. But she knew that a few days – a week at the most – would be as much as she could stand, before her restlessness moved her on.

The horse she rode, resigned to having his summer holiday disturbed, stood patiently, glad to rest his unfit muscles after the long climb. But the reverie of horse and rider was jolted abruptly by the arrival of a helicopter, swooping over the shoulder of the hill, to descend sharply towards the lawns in front of the house.

The Jet-Ranger slid neatly between two spreading blue cedars and landed on the finely mown grass. Pyon jumped out and strode briskly from beneath the rotors. He was barely clear of them when the pilot eased out the throttle, and the helicopter was up and on its way back to London.

Lady Barnstaple walked through the French windows from her drawing-room on to the broad terrace above the lawn, and waited for Pyon to climb up.

"Hello, Marjorie," he said and jumped up the few steps to greet her with a kiss on the cheek. "How are you?"

"I'm fine, Christy. It's nice to see you, but surely you're very busy at the moment?"

"I wanted a chance to talk to Laura quietly. It's very hard to keep her attention these days and there are fewer distractions down here. I also wanted to see Alaric. I hope you don't mind my inviting us."

"Not really. Actually, it's been lovely to see Laura; she's such a bundle of energy, and so funny."

"Does she seem well, then?"

"Oh yes. The man she went to Brazil with seems to have turned out to be a bit of a trial. Mind you, I don't suppose she's interested unless they are. Anyway, I think she just left him there, but she doesn't seem particularly upset."

"She's a pragmatist, is Laura. She never did weep for long over anything."

They had walked back through the French windows and Lady Barnstaple asked him if he would like to sit while she got some tea.

Pyon nodded, but continued to wander around the room when she had left. He inspected the pictures, noting with envy a couple of recently cleaned Herrings, and wondered where his daughter was. His hostess told him when she returned with tea things on a tray.

"She can't sit still for two minutes, can she?" Pyon sighed. "I'll try and have a word with her later. I have to leave early tomorrow, I'm afraid."

They conversed, with a slight awkwardness that Pyon could not ignore. Lady Barnstaple guessed what he wanted to talk to Laura about, and she admired him a little for doing it on Liz's home territory. They were both relieved when Lord Barnstaple walked into the room and greeted Pyon with his normal affability.

"I thought you must have been responsible for that bloody noise," he said, "but there's no chopper out there now."

"He had a few other things to do. He'll be back for me in the morning."

"Anyway, nice to see you, Christy. Marjorie told me that you wanted to have a word."

"Yes, if you've the time."

"Don't be ridiculous. I've got all bloody day and night. My agent thinks I'm too senile to make a decision about so much as a fence post, and I can't be bothered to argue with him. If you'd like a proper drink, come on through to the library, if you don't mind, Marjorie?" He turned to his wife.

"No, of course not."

Lord Barnstaple's library was a real library with thousands of books on hundreds of subjects. It was furnished with a grand old desk and a few threadbare armchairs. A table in one corner held an army of bottles.

"Black Bush for you, Christy?"

"Please."

Lord Barnstaple poured half a tumblerful and a scotch for himself.

"Sit down, Christy."

"If it's all the same to you, Alaric, could we take a stroll outside?"

"Certainly, though Marjorie gave up listening at keyholes years ago and what staff we have left are either foreign or deaf."

They walked out through a door that gave directly on to the terrace and headed down a path that led to the lake.

As neither had spoken, after a few yards, Lord Barnstaple said, "Well, how are my Southern shares going to do? Is the great takeover looking good?"

"We'll get there, no question, but the lawyers aren't going to yield up a beanfeast like this too easily. There's no real case against al Souf's ownership of the Agricultural Bank of Texas, but with all the trouble they've been having with the Thrifts, no one wants to be seen to be careless, and the bloody regulators are going to take their time. The trouble is that I can't really backtrack on our announcement that al Souf is buying them, because it will shake the credibility of the whole deal. Nor can we tout the deal around to any other more obviously acceptable players because al Souf would have my bollocks."

"So it's just a question of waiting?"

"That's right."

"Should I buy some more?"

"I can only say what I've said publicly. The deal will go through eventually, at which time the price will probably drop back a few points. But I'd say it was a good long-term proposition."

"The press have not been kind lately, have they?"

"No, but thank God they seem to have quietened down a bit since they got so excited about Cannes. As a matter of fact, that's more or less what I wanted to talk to you about. I know you're no longer my father-in-law, but I feel you might be prepared to listen. What I have to say will affect Liz, and I only want you to know that whatever happens, I will do everything possible to avoid hurting her."

Lord Barnstaple said nothing, and waited for Pyon to go on.

"I am going to have to divorce Maria. Not now, but after the Chemco bid is successful. I've tolerated some terrible behaviour from her over the years because I wanted to avoid the trouble it would cause Caterina and Gianni. I'm not unaware of what my divorce from Liz did to Julian."

"And to Liz," her father added.

"Yes, of course, and to Liz, though you know I've always done my best to soften the blow."

Lord Barnstaple acknowledged this with a slight nod.

"But Maria's gone mad about this business with Natalie – the girl I took to Cannes."

"Is that still going on?"

They had reached the lake now, and they both leaned on a rustic wooden rail that overlooked a small jetty. Through a great beech tree above them, the sun cast a dappled beam on the water. A few mallard drifted away, not concerned, and a pair of coots nodded among the foliage of a waterside rhododendron.

Pyon did not answer Lord Barnstaple at once. Looking down at the untroubled waterfowl, he said, "Yes. It's still going on. She is an exceptional girl, and I can't deny that I'm involved with her, quite deeply."

"Liz is going to be hurt, you know, if she finds this out."

"She will find out, in due course. That's why I'm talking to you. I still love Liz, you know, but like a very close sister. I don't deserve what she still gives me, I know that. I've been very lucky."

"But this time it will be different," Lord Barnstaple said. "You see, she never really saw Maria as competition, even though you went off and married her. It's strange. I talked to her about it shortly after she caught you in the south of France. Even then, she wouldn't let me say a thing against you."

"Look, Alaric, I'm talking to you as an old friend, as well as Liz's father. I don't know what the hell I expect you to say that's going to help her, or me, for that matter. I just wanted to tell you."

"Christy, you're fifty. You can't expect me to condone your being infatuated like some spotty teenager with a girl less than half your age. From the photos in the paper she looked a real stunner, and I couldn't care less what colour she is, but you're just too old to do this kind of thing and retain any dignity."

"I never was too concerned about dignity, but I am concerned about Liz, though I know that must sound like hypocritical bullshit, but . . ." – he paused – "I don't know, I thought maybe, coming from you, she might understand that I don't want to harm her."

"Why not tell her yourself?"

"I'm useless at that sort of thing. I always have been. Give me a room full of ten thousand people to talk to any day."

"I thought you weren't too keen on that sort of thing either."

"Yes, but not because I'm shy. In the old days, when I used to do my own press conferences, I loved it. But I got sick to death of the hacks misconstruing my every word and action, so I decided to deny them all access."

"Until Cannes," Lord Barnstaple added.

"That, as you know, was a serious slip-up. And look at the trouble it's caused to my family, as well as my business."

"Are you saying that you wouldn't be considering marrying Natalie and divorcing Maria if the press hadn't caught you?"

"I don't know," Pyon said with a shake of the head.

Lord Barnstaple lifted himself up from where he'd been leaning on the railings. He looked across at the rising moorland, avoiding Pyon's deep blue eyes.

"For a man with a world-wide reputation for instant, bold decision-making, you seem to be remarkably unsure of what the hell you're doing. And frankly, it's up to you to tell Liz whatever you want. I don't think I can help. I'm sorry, Christy, you seem to have got yourself in a mess, and at a very critical moment in your business. The best advice I can give is, drop this Natalie, and try to remain on civilised terms with your present wife."

Pyon also straightened himself, and started to walk back up the path by which they had come. After a few paces, he stopped and turned steady, piercing blue eyes on Lord Barnstaple as he slowly shook his head.

"That is simply not an option."

Dinner at Nethercombe that evening was eaten in a strained atmosphere. Laura lightened this a little with descriptions of her travels in the Orinoco basin. She also energetically proclaimed her new green enthusiasm for the tropical rain forests and their archaic inhabitants.

There was a moment of tension, though, between her and Pyon.

"Of course," she said, "the rain forest and the way of life of its people is under colossal pressure from big business. In fact," she threw an accusatory glance at her father, "I think one of your companies is involved in tree clearance."

Pyon shrugged. "Could be. We have some interests in Brazil and Guyana, but mining and chemicals mostly."

"And timber, in case you didn't know."

"Maybe, but I hear what you say. I'll look into it," Pyon said with a finality she recognised as a conversational dead-end.

That seemed to satisfy Laura for the moment, and she expanded in more general terms her worries about the demise of the tropical forests.

But her bio-clock was still confused. She excused herself soon after dinner and went to bed at ten o'clock.

At six the next morning, she woke to find that the soft south-easterly wind had swept all the remaining clouds off the hills. A confident sun had just appeared between a cluster of scots pines on a nearby ridge.

She threw back her sheets and swung her legs out of bed. Within minutes she was washed and wearing jeans, T-shirt and trainers. She tiptoed downstairs and let herself out of an unlocked back door. The wind gently moved the long, upright branches of a cluster of aspens, planted by an earlier Lord Barnstaple for the soothing rustle of their silvery leaves. A blackbird fled from the bushes with a sharp *chit-chit-chit* of alarm, and the smell of the dew still hung in the air.

She could hear Boris, the old hunter, stamp a hoof in his stable. She had put him there the evening before with a plan to take him out again this morning.

She strolled up a path that led behind a walled garden to the stable block. She sniffed the air as she went, feeling fit and full of good resolutions. She walked under a clocktower arch into the stable yard, where Boris greeted her with a whinny from his box on the far side. She walked over to him to stroke his forehead, and the underside of his chin, while he nuzzled her for the food he assumed she had brought.

"Greedy old bastard," she murmured, sucking up into her nostrils the pleasing smell of horse and damp straw. She fondled him for a while until his nuzzling became more insistent.

"Oh, all right. I'll find you something."

She turned and started to walk to the feed store. She noticed the incongruous smell of Havana tobacco. Then she saw her father.

Pyon was sitting on a stone mounting block, just inside the arch, smoking a large cigar.

"Hello, Dad. What the hell are you doing here, at this time of day?"

"I was having a quiet smoke, until you barged in. I'm

always up at this time of day, not that you'd have ever noticed that."

Laura walked over and sat on the step of the mounting block. She put a hand on his knee.

"I hope you weren't hurt by my having a go at you last night about the jungle, when I hadn't seen you for months. I know you can't know everything that's going on."

"You're right to be critical. I've told you I'll look into it and I will."

"I believe you, Dad. It's nice to catch you on your own. I didn't think you went anywhere these days without your entourage – all those secretaries and chauffeurs and gofers."

"I don't get a lot of time to myself, but I'm very glad to see you. My chopper's coming at eight, and I'm back to London. I wanted to talk to you some more, and then you went off to bed! But, here you are."

"What did you want to talk about? Not another sermon about Gervase, I hope."

"Sounds as though you don't need that now. What went wrong?"

"Nothing really. I just discovered that he was a bit too like you – arrogant and full of himself. He doesn't like other people involved in his decision-making."

"Now," Pyon said with a smile, "you don't mean that, not about me."

"Don't I? Anyway, what did you want to talk about?"

"I was wondering . . ." Pyon took a long draw on his cigar, "if you'd heard anything about me and a girl, while I was in Cannes with Julian?"

Laura looked blank. "No. I read in Brazil that Julian's film got an award, and some high praise. I was really pleased for him. But the only mention of you was as co-producer."

"B'Jaysus, you must have been out in the bush. I thought the whole world had read about it."

"About what, Dad?"

"There's a fine young woman I know – a very good sort – who said she would like to go to the festival in Cannes, so I took her. As you know, I've managed to avoid any personal publicity since . . . me and your mother divorced, and not many people know what I look like. So, I was getting a little careless. But this girl is something of an eyeful, and one of the photographers snapped her. Anyway, they found out it was me with her, and splashed the shot all over the place – in Europe, in America – and they've been hounding me ever since. Not with any success, I might say. I thought I ought to make the position clear to you."

Laura stood up, and faced him where he sat on the block.

"And, what is the position?"

Pyon struggled to meet her flashing, angry eyes.

"Jesus, I don't know, now it comes to it. Don't look at your father like that. There's a situation, now. Maria's gone mad. She's had a go at Julian, trying to set him against me. She's going to cause trouble in some way. I don't want her to get at you."

"There's no chance of that. I can't stand the silly cow. As a matter of fact, I'm planning to go out to Sardinia to see poor little Caterina and Gianni. I promised Caterina I would this summer."

"Good God, you can't go to see them. There'll be an almighty scene." Pyon stood up to emphasise.

"It's a bit late for you to tell me what I can and can't do. You haven't done much for those kids, and they are my siblings, you know, so I'm going to."

"Look, Maria's brothers are very tricky. Sergio's a terrible mad little prick. You wouldn't want to be getting into any arguments with him. You cannot go." Pyon was almost shouting now. "I absolutely forbid it!".

Safari in Mauritius

Harry Hackwood looked east across the Indian Ocean from the window of an Air Mauritius plane flying south across the equator. A few hundred miles away, the curved surface of the world was coated with thick white vapour, like icing on a cake. Nearer, below him, the sea gleamed grey-green in the early sun, beneath isolated puffs of cloud.

He glanced at his watch and scowled as he wriggled his large behind in the narrow seat. Beside him, slumped against his shoulder, was the head of his colleague on this mission. Even in sleep, Bruno Testa's Roman face displayed his famous arrogance.

Harry wondered what it would be like to work with this legend, this king of the paparazzi. He was still astonished that his editor had agreed to the expense of the trip, and of engaging a free-lance of Bruno's reputation.

The tip-off had been flimsy; a quiet London voice on the telephone: "Christy Pyon's girlfriend is called Natalie Felix, and she comes from Mauritius."

That was all.

Harry had made all the usual calls to the numbers on Pyon's file. He was evidently in none of the likely places, in Europe, London, Ireland or New York.

Harry had telephoned, of course, as a financial journalist, and had received polite replies from the various PR companies that acted for Southern Hemisphere. But one number, extracted from an off-guard secretary in Pyon's Mayfair office, had caused a reaction in his gut.

It was a London number, but when it was answered, it sounded to Harry like an overseas line, and the curt denial of any knowledge of Pyon's existence was delivered in a curious French accent.

He had waved his hunch under the nose of his boss, Nigel Judge. Fleet Street's uncontested champion of the gossip columns attributed their good fortune in receiving the tip to his own high-profile infamy, and had bitten hard.

Bruno Testa did not know where they were going until he met Harry at the airport.

A hot place, a beautiful woman with an unspecified famous man, a fat fee, and the right to sell his pictures wherever he liked, after seven days' exclusive use by Harry's paper. That had been attractive enough. Mauritius was fine by him.

"How big is this place?" he asked Harry.

Harry looked at the guide. "About forty miles by thirty."

"That big? And how many people live there?"

"A million or so."

"And all you've got is a girl's name?" Bruno said angrily. "We could be there for weeks!"

"We've got the man's name, too." Harry smiled. He was confident of his sleuthing skills. The plane was starting its takeoff from Heathrow. "Which I'll be able to tell you as soon as we're up. Would you like to know?"

"Of course I would," Bruno's Italian accent became more pronounced in his testiness, "*deek*-head."

Harry gave him another chubby smile. The plane left the ground.

"Christy Pyon," he said smugly.

"Fuckin' *hell*!" Bruno was impressed, then sceptical. "He spends his whole life dodging. He's going to be impossible to find!"

"You leave that to me," Harry said.

It had been a long dreary flight, leavened only by the smiles of lovely creole stewardesses. The two men had spoken little. Bruno flipped through a copy of *Hello* and dozed. Harry drank too much brandy and sweated.

The rising sun caught Harry's slightly bulbous, Anglo-Saxon features, and turned his dark blond hair to pale orange. The strain of carrying two stone too many for too long, and his receding hairline made him look older than his twenty-eight years and disguised his ambitious energy.

With relief, he saw the island of Mauritius come into sight. It was bigger than he had expected and very green, with strange, jagged little mountains. As they flew over it, he gazed down, like a hawk searching the land for prey among the millions of hectares of sugar cane.

They shuffled off the plane and across the concrete apron of Sir Sewoosagur Ramgoolam Airport in a fierce, humid heat. In the cool of the immigration hall they were greeted by a sign announcing that drug-traffickers were liable to the death penalty. Bruno paled, and mentally searched his bags and his pockets, before relaxing.

After a half-hour crawl between zealous customs officers, they emerged once more into the heat. Harry eyed the waiting taxi-drivers for a few moments before selecting a jovial-looking, dark Creole with a white Honda.

As the driver, who introduced himself as Paul, loaded their bags and Bruno's chequered aluminium camera cases into the boot, the photographer looked disparaging.

"This car's too little," he declared.

"It's inconspicuous, like most other cars on the island if what's here is anything to go by. We may need that."

They heaved themselves into the back seat, and Paul turned round to ask them where they wanted to go.

"We may need you for a few days, and maybe at night, maybe all night. Is that okay?"

Paul beamed. "Oui, m'sieur. However you like."

"Good. Okay, first we'll head for Port Louis."

The driver nodded and they sped away from the airport.

Bruno looked surly, with his long legs wedged against the back of the passenger seat.

"What's your plan?"

"I thought I'd start with a few enquiries around the banks in Port Louis, that's the capital, and then make a visit to the British Embassy. I think Pyon's got a place here, or at least a presence, and he must have financial dealings. A *grande fromage* like him doesn't move into a place like this without anyone knowing."

With no apologies for listening to their conversation, Paul interrupted.

"British Embassy in Floreal, on the high land. All rich peoples live there; not so hot. It's on the way to Port Louis. You wanna go there first?"

"Sure, good idea," Harry said, and then as a long shot, "Do you know if an Englishman, a big businessman called Christy Pyon, has a house there?"

Paul shook his head. "Don't know, m'sieur."

Bruno looked at Harry. "What about the girl?"

Harry shook his head, but asked, "Do you know a girl called Natalie Felix?"

"Sure, m'sieur. She's a teacher at the convent in Curepipe."

"A teacher? No, that can't be the one. Would it be quite a common name?"

"Her father called Phillipe Felix. He's good man, work

hard for the creole people in the MMM – the Mouvement Militant Mauricien." Paul shrugged. "Maybe others called Felix, I don't know. What she do, this girl?"

"I'm not sure. Probably nothing much. She's very beautiful."

"Natalie Felix is very beautiful," Paul said.

"What, the schoolteacher?"

He nodded enthusiastically. "Sure. I seen her. She teach my brother's little daughter."

Bruno scowled. "They got different ideas about beauty. She *can't* be a teacher."

"It's worth a try," Harry said. "She may be a relation, or know about another Natalie Felix." He became excited, and said to Paul, "Can you take us to the convent first? Is it on the way to the embassy?"

"Sure, but school's on vacation."

Unmarried, childless Harry had not considered that. "Never mind," he said. "There may be someone there who can give us her address."

They had left the coastal plain, where the potholed road ran through endless open fields of sugarcane, and they had climbed fifteen hundred feet on to the central plateau of the island. Small, craggy hills protruded from tropical forest and tea plantations. The road became a newly-metalled highway now, the island's only main artery, fringed with bougainvillea and poinsettia of orange, red and mauve.

Abruptly, they turned off it into the outer fringe of the central conurbation. The road was lined with trees, small neat bungalows bedecked with flowers, and, every so often, a little shrine to Shiva or another of the Hindu gods.

In a few minutes, they reached the centre of Curepipe, and the imposing, basalt church of Sainte Thérèse. Paul swung the car down beside it, and drew up outside a pair of gates that gave on to an untidy garden and a building that was obviously clerical. Ugly flat-roofed classrooms had sprouted from the nineteenth-century gothic arches, giving the place a functional air.

Harry eased himself out of the car with surprising nimbleness.

"I'll do this, Bruno. You'd scare the shit out of them."

He strode up the drive to the gloomy, studded double doors and tugged a cast-iron bellpull.

A small Indian maid opened the door on to a gloomy hall with highly polished, dark red floor tiles.

"I would like to see Reverend Mother, please."

The maid nodded, closed the door behind him, and scuttled off.

After a minute or so, a tall, French nun glided into the hall."

"Bonjour, monsieur?"

"Good morning, Reverend Mother," Harry replied in English, with a warm smile of apology. "I'm sorry, my French is not too good."

"That's all right," the nun said. "What can I do for you?"

"My name's Hackwood. I'm a master at a Benedictine school in England, and I'm spending my summer holidays studying education in the . . ." he paused, ". . . third world," he added hopefully.

"I see," said the nun.

"Yes, and a chap at the embassy said that one of your teachers had some strong views that might interest me." Harry fished a scrap of paper from his pocket and appeared to scrutinise it. "A Miss Felix."

The Reverend Mother looked surprised. "Miss Felix? She has strong views, with which I don't always agree, and she will be a good teacher, but she is only new, and teaches the young children."

"Ah, well. That's probably why this chap gave me her name. I'm particularly interested in the teaching of young-sters. After all," Harry laughed, "that's where the process of education begins, don't you think, Reverend Mother?"

She nodded but said, "I'm afraid, as the girls are on holiday, Miss Felix is not here."

"No, of course, but I was hoping you might be able to give me her address."

The nun assessed him for a moment, then began to walk towards a door off the hall. "Come with me."

They went into a small office. The Reverend Mother delved in the drawer of a desk to find a book. "Here it is," she said, indicating the hand-written information on one of the pages. "It's no secret; her father's well-known on Maurice. But I think she will be away. This is her parents' house."

"That'll be fine. I'm sure they won't mind telling me where she is." Harry eagerly copied the address into his notebook.

The nun led him back into the hall and to the front door, which she opened for him. "Goodbye, Mr Hackwood. I hope you are successful in your researches. God bless you."

"Yes, indeed, Reverend Mother. Thank you *so* much."

Harry walked back down the drive with as much dignity as he could manage, while his heart pounded with excitement.

When he reached the car, he leaped in jubilantly. "Got it!"

"Got what?" Bruno asked.

"Her address, of course." He turned to Paul. "Is Quatre Bornes near here?"

"Oui, m'sieur. On the way down to Port Louis."

Harry tore Natalie Felix's address from his notebook and handed it to Paul.

"Take us there now, please."

"Not to the embassy first?"

"No. No need."

Bruno was less certain. "I'm not so sure this is the right girl. Pyon can't be having a scene with a teacher, for God's sake!"

"Why the hell not? Her father's obviously somebody round here and, anyway, maybe he's got some kind of misplaced Oedipus complex, or maybe he likes her to tell him off and stand him in the corner, or give him a good flogging with a gym shoe."

"Don't be ridiculous! Not Pyon," Bruno said.

"All right, but if she's as tasty as she looked in that Cannes shot, I wouldn't give a toss what she did for a living, and I don't suppose Pyon does either. I've a real feeling that this is the one."

They were bouncing down the hill towards Quatre Bornes, which was a lower extension of Curepipe and Floreal. Bruno had extracted one of his cameras from his case, and a thousand-millimetre lens about a foot long which he was polishing diligently.

When they reached the end of the road where Natalie Felix lived with her mother, Harry told Paul to stop.

"Okay, Paul. Drive down until you find the number, and pull up a few yards further on. Bruno, you duck down out of sight, and for God's sake, don't wave that bloody camera about."

"I gotta have it ready. Maybe the only chance at a shot."

"Well, only use it if she's obviously sussed us and is doing a runner."

They drove past the house, a neat little bungalow, built like all the others, of painted breeze-block. The garden was packed with flowers and a tiny grotto to the Virgin Mary.

"Phillipe Felix can't be a very corrupt politician," Harry observed.

"According to the guide, the MMM was only in power for six months, six years ago, so he didn't have much chance," Bruno answered cynically.

They saw that the front door was open, and Harry's heart quickened again.

Paul stopped the car twenty yards up the road, and Harry climbed out.

He walked back and let himself through a small front gate. He ambled up the drive and tapped on the open front door.

A tall, handsome creole woman appeared, and looked at him suspiciously.

"Good morning. Mrs Felix?"

The woman nodded.

Harry gave her a broad beam of a smile. "I'm sorry to disturb you, but the Reverend Mother gave me your address to contact your daughter, Natalie."

"Reverend Mother?" The doubt in her eyes diminished.

"Yes. My name's Hackwood. I'm a teacher at a Catholic school in England, and I'm finding out about education in Mauritius. I was recommended to talk to your daughter. Reverend Mother says she has some good ideas."

"Does she?" Mrs Felix looked a little surprised, but not displeased.

"She certainly does. I wonder, is Miss Felix at home?"

"No. She's out on one of the islands." She stopped suddenly and looked guilty. "I mean, she's not here, but she said she would come after lunch today. Her sister has been ill."

"I'm sorry to hear that, but perhaps I could come back and see her then?"

Mrs Felix looked uncertain. "It will be better if you tell me where she can get you. I will tell her and she can tell you if she wants to talk to you."

Harry disguised his frustration with a smile. "That would be marvellous. Only if it's no trouble to her, of course. You will tell her that, won't you?"

Mrs Felix nodded. "Where can she telephone you?"

"Er," Harry thought swiftly, "at the British Embassy."

"You're staying at the British Embassy?" Mrs Felix asked doubtfully.

"Well, no, not exactly, but she can leave a message there for me. I'm going to be travelling around quite a bit, you see."

"I'll tell her," Mrs Felix said.

"That's marvellous," Harry effused, "that's *very* kind. You've been *very* helpful."

The woman smiled awkwardly.

"Well, goodbye, and thank you again."

Harry squeezed himself back into the car.

"Right, what's the time?"

"Ten o'clock."

"Not bad, eh? Two hours and I've tracked her down already."

"Was she there?" Bruno was excited now.

"No, but she will be after lunch, her mother said. Apparently she's out on one of the islands," Harry revealed casually.

"You think, with Pyon?"

"Maybe," Harry said in a way which meant that he was certain. "Anyway, if we come back after lunch, we should be able to follow her when she leaves, and see where she takes us. I got the impression from her mother that she's only popping back to see her sister who's ill."

"What else did her mother say?"

"She was guarded at first, which I take as a very hopeful sign, but Reverend Mother's recommendation looked after that. And she felt guilty about telling me where Natalie was."

"But she didn't tell you which island?"

"No. That's no problem, though. Now, I'm starving. Let's go and get something to eat."

"It's better to find a hotel first. I need to change. I'm so sticky."

"All right," Harry said grudgingly, "but then I must eat." He turned to Paul and asked him to take them to the best hotel in Curepipe.

An hour later, fresher and more comfortable, Harry and Bruno joined up in the foyer of the spartan concrete building that was the town's commercial hotel. Two cameras and several lenses dangled about the photographer's shoulders, and Harry carried a pair of binoculars, a small tape-recorder and a notebook.

Harry had done his homework.

"Apparently the best restaurant on the island is a place called *Au Gourmet*, and it's a few minutes from here, so I've booked a table for lunch."

"Harry, we can't sit around to have lunch. This girl is coming to her mother's."

"That's not till after lunch. She's bound to be there a while, so we'll get Paul to wait outside and come and get us as soon as she arrives. She'll smell a rat if she turns up and finds a pair of dodgy-looking Europeans like us hanging about."

"You're crazy. We could miss her. It could be our only chance."

"Look. I know what I'm doing. I saw the mother, not you. And I'm dying for a decent meal."

Bruno gave up with a hopeless shrug. "If we miss her, I kill you."

"Fair enough," Harry said happily.

They arrived at the old colonial clapboard mansion that housed the restaurant shortly after twelve, too early to eat, but the elegant French *patronne* was happy for them to have a few preprandial drinks, and Harry managed to swallow three large gins before their lunch arrived.

They ate an *hors d'oeuvres* of boudin, various fish and octopus with a peppery dressing – a stimulating blend of French and Indian cuisine. After that, they were served *sacrechien*, a white fish wrapped in spinach leaves with fine shredded vegetables and a magnificent sauce. They also ordered three bottles of the best Chablis, most of which Harry drank, before he changed to cognac when they had finished eating.

Over the meal, they studied a map of Mauritius and its offshore islands. There were a dozen or so, most within the island's encircling coral reef, but the map gave no indication of habitation on any of them.

Bruno was beginning to get twitchy. Every few minutes he looked at his watch and his face tightened.

"This bloody girl will have come and gone. Where the hell is that driver? It's your fault, you greedy bastard. How can you sit there stuffing yourself and getting pissed? This is a *big* story."

Harry nodded, his mouth full of bread and goat's cheese. "Ughm." He swallowed. "And it's my story. Everything's under control." There was a tap on the window beside them. "There, what did I tell you?"

Paul's smiling face looked through at them.

"She come," they heard him say.

Harry sprang to his feet, knocking over a collection of empty glasses, and barged his way through the restaurant to thrust at the startled *patronne* some money which he reckoned would cover their bill and more, and scurried out through a peeling verandah, down a flight of steps to the waiting Honda.

Bruno was already installed, nursing his cameras.

"Hurry, you fat bugger. We'll miss her."

"Get going, Paul," Harry said cheerfully, and the car shot off down the sweeping drive.

Once again, they arrived at the top of the road where Mrs Felix lived. They turned into it.

Heading towards them bucking and lurching along the crumbling road, was a black Range Rover.

"Maybe that her car," Paul gasped.

"Okay," said Harry calmly. "Don't panic. Just cruise to the next opening where you can turn, and we'll get behind her."

The big black vehicle was passing them now, and they had a quick glimpse of the driver.

"Was that her?" Bruno asked.

"I don't know. I couldn't see enough," Harry replied impatiently.

"That Natalie Felix, for sure," Paul said.

"In a bloody Range Rover! You can bet your life teachers don't earn enough to run a mini here. That *must* be Pyon's Natalie!" Harry yelled triumphantly. "Come on, Paul, you can turn here. I'll watch which way she goes on the main road."

Paul drove into a small turning off the lane, then backed out, facing the other way. They were in time to see the Range Rover swing left at the top of the lane.

The little Honda flew across the holes and ruts, and shot out on to the main road. They were only two cars behind Natalie.

"Well done," Harry said to a beaming Paul. "Stay a couple of cars behind as far as you can. Don't get too near to her."

"How the hell are we going to keep up with her in this bloody car?" grumbled Bruno. "I told you it's too small."

"We keep up, m'sieur. No one drive too fast in Maurice. Roads no good."

"What if she turns on to that big highway?"

"We keep up," the driver reiterated confidently.

The small white car dogged the large black vehicle through the sprawling township until they reached the Port Louis road. To Harry's relief, Natalie drove straight across it.

Paul was enjoying himself. He did not know why these two Europeans should be chasing a beautiful young schoolteacher across the island, but, as instructed, he tried to keep at least one other vehicle between them and Natalie. And she did nothing to suggest she had noticed them.

Harry and Bruno relaxed. It was clear from the map that,

if Natalie was heading back to an island, it was on the east coast, and at least half-an-hour's drive.

They passed through a few villages and the small town of Flacq. They found themselves just a few feet behind the Range Rover as the busy market brought them to walking pace. The two journalists crouched in the back of the car, feeling that somehow their quarry would recognise them for what they were. But she did not so much as glance in her driving mirror, and was soon heading out of town to the north.

They consulted the map.

"She must be going to one of these islands up here," Harry said. "There isn't any sign of habitation there. Does anyone live on any of them?" he asked Paul.

The driver shrugged. "I don't go there for long time."

They were still not yet in sight of the sea, and the road continued inland for another ten miles or so. They crossed a river, and turned sharply to the right, past a vast, dusty sugar refinery, and down towards the coast.

For a few miles they ran parallel to the coast. The sun glinted off the smooth lagoon, glimpsed between the shoreline fringe of casuarina trees. Gradually, the road struck inland, between waving eight-foot walls of sugarcane. Abruptly, their quarry turned off the road to the right a few hundred yards ahead.

"Slow down! Slow down!" Harry hissed.

They drew up some yards short of the gap where the Range Rover had disappeared. Harry and Bruno scrambled out and Paul turned the motor off.

There was no other traffic on the road, and the sugarcane deadened any distant sounds. The two men crept forward and peered down a dirt track. There was no sign of the black vehicle. After about twenty yards, the track curved away to the left and was lost among the cane. Hugging the edge for cover and shade, they walked down the path as silently as Harry's bulk and binoculars and Bruno's dangling cameras would allow.

As they rounded the bend, they stopped.

The Range Rover was parked under an open-sided, palm-roofed shade. Beyond it was a small boathouse, with a short jetty into the shimmering lagoon.

Harry held his breath, and Bruno, with a predatory smile on his smooth face, gingerly lifted a camera to his eye.

Two people, Natalie and an Indian dressed in white like a European sailor, made their way along the jetty to a glossy teak Riva launch. They climbed down and a few moments later the boat's engine burst into life. The deep gurgling echoed off the flat water and the Riva nosed out. It picked up speed and made deep furrowed vees in the shallow, blue-green water.

Harry and Bruno watched the craft head straight for a white beach and a small landing stage on an island opposite them, within the lagoon and about a mile off shore.

Harry clapped his binoculars to his eyes like a hunter with a rifle.

The vegetation of the island seemed particularly lush. It gave the impression of a long-neglected botanical garden. Apart from the ubiquitous casuarina and mango trees, there were stately royal palms, long spindly hurricane palms, dangling, aerial-rooted banyan trees, a fat-bottomed boabab tree and, amidst all these, huge splashes of vivid bougainvillea, poinsettia and frangipani.

And through the tops of the trees, the sun caught the grey-tiled roof of a large building.

"Eureka!" Harry shouted against the dwindling sound of the motorboat.

"Shut up, you fool!" Bruno hissed, and yanked the glasses from Harry's hands, tugging his neck with the strap. But as he gazed through the binoculars, he whispered, "You're right, Harry my friend. We got 'em."

Ile Vermont

Christy Pyon was in the room that was his office on the *Ile Vermont*. He sat in a large, swivel desk chair with his back to the window. The room was lit only by the fading day. In this pink and golden light, the characters on the great canvas which faced him assumed a mystic air of which Edward Burne-Jones, their creator, would have been proud.

These mythical, untouchable characters always made Pyon conscious of his flesh, his worldliness, his sins. Seeing them was like making his confession, but without the inconvenience of a confessor who probed and made demands on his privacy.

A few moments' guilt was enough. Abruptly, Pyon swung the chair back to his desk and switched on the light. He reached across the expanse of Morocco leather for a bottle of Black Bush and refilled his glass.

He picked up a file of papers, neatly bound and entitled "The Actors' Production Company Inc. Proposals for Procurement and Operation" and slowly flipped through the pages.

It would go a long way to placate Liz if he were to help Julian. It would certainly placate Julian.

To Pyon's pleased surprise, Julian had done his work thoroughly. He had checked the accuracy of all the claims by APC about their assets and liabilities, and this had thrown a few new, negative factors into the ring. But, on the whole, the deal still stood up. Julian's proposals for the disposal of surplus assets and the operation of what remained were, with a few adjustments, realistic. He must have taken advice from expensive people to have toned down his original aims as much as he had.

But Pyon shook his head – he did not do deals unless all his instincts told him they were right. And there was still an odd smell about this one.

Slowly, he opened a drawer in the desk, and placed the file in it. He switched off the desk light and stood up. He gazed out of the window and watched the flapping fruit bats in the dusk, scurrying between the tops of the trees to plunder his island.

When he left the room, he closed the door on thoughts of APC, Julian and Elizabeth.

He nodded good night to the two women in the outer office, still hard at work on typewriters and fax machines, and went through the house, out on to the verandah that ran either side of the great front door.

Natalie sat with her feet on the balustrade, stitching.

"What's that you're making?" Pyon asked.

She looked up with a smile, displaying one of Pyon's shirts. She was sewing an appliqué scene – palms, sun and a dodo – on to the back.

"Your clothes are too boring, so I'm brightening them up."

Pyon laughed. "Jesus, they'd love me in that in the Bank of England. They never could trust a man in a dodgy shirt."

He leaned down to kiss her forehead, and drew up a cane chair beside her. "In six months' time, when Chemco's in the bag, I'll come back and live here with you, and you can sew dodos on the back of all me pin-stripe suits."

She smiled and stroked his cheek. "I don't believe you."

"You'll see," he said quietly. Abruptly, he stood up, and, with a change of voice, said, "But right now, let's eat, swim and make love, for tomorrow I have to leave."

Harry Hackwood winced as he stretched his legs among the branches of the mango trees that surrounded him.

"Shit. I hope we don't have to sit like this for too long. I've got pins and needles in muscles I didn't even know I had."

"Stop complaining," Bruno Testa snapped. "I've waited ten, twelve hours in the same position to get a shot. We've only been here half an hour."

They had arrived at the north end of the *Ile Vermont* shortly after dusk. A tiny fishing boat, under sail, and a compliant, knowledgeable boatman had taken them to that part of the island least visible from the house.

The boatman had also told them on which beach they were most likely to see Pyon and his girlfriend.

They had struggled through dense vegetation on the east side of the island, then crossed below the house to settle themselves on a small, mango-clad promontory that overlooked the western beach and the island's landing stage.

The last trace of day had disappeared beyond the spiky tips of the mountains on the mainland opposite them, to be replaced by a waxing moon, high above them, and a generous sprinkling of bright stars. The lagoon shimmered, and the sand was silver-white. Palm tops waved in the gentle south-east trade wind like giant black spiders hopping back and forth on the horizon.

"I hope that bloody boatman wasn't winding us up, telling us that Pyon and the girl often skinny-dip in the dark." Harry was less optimistic in these uncomfortable conditions; he was used to waiting for his quarry in nightclubs and restaurants.

"You say he must go back to the States tomorrow, so, he'll want to have all the good times he can." Bruno understood a man with a busy schedule.

"I don't *know* he'll be going back, but his takeover is at a critical stage. There's a lot of pressure on the various state banking authorities to put the kibosh on the deal. He's going to have to go back soon. At least, that's what my man in the City says." Harry stretched again and listened to his stomach rumbling. "Christ, I wish we'd brought some food with us."

"You always want to eat, Harry."

"Well, it's at least seven hours since we last had anything."

"I don't like to eat when I'm on to a hot story; it just makes me want to shit."

"Shhh!" Harry grabbed his arm. "Someone's just come out on to the beach by that little bathing hut," he whispered.

He lifted his binoculars to his eyes and peered through the curtain of mango leaves. Two figures were easily discernible in the moonlight. They were walking hand in hand up the beach towards Harry and Bruno. Soon, the two watchers were able to hear murmuring voices above the quiet lapping of the lagoon.

"Is that him?" Bruno whispered with excitement.

"Yes, I'm sure it is."

The figures were identifiable as a tall man and a slender woman, both wearing beach robes. They had stopped, and were facing each other. The man wrapped his arms around the girl who responded by pressing her body to him.

Harry held his breath and strained his eyes in the dark as he watched. The robes fell to the sand, and the paler skin of the larger figure showed white in the moonshine.

A rumble of deep laughter drifted down the beach, and

the man lowered the girl on to the silver cushion of the sand.

With the excitement of the professional voyeur who loves his work, Harry gazed at the rhythmic surging of the amorphous mass, dark against the silver sand, and heard faint gasps and murmurings.

"Holy shit! I don't believe it! Pyon and a dusky schoolteacher, fucking under our noses. What the hell are you doing?" Harry turned angrily to Bruno who was lining up a camera with a long-distance flash on the scarcely visible scene. "You can't take a shot now! You'll only have one chance, and we'll never get off the island. Don't be bloody crazy!"

Bruno knew the truth of it, and his shoulders dropped. "Okay, okay. But maybe we have to try. We may not have another chance."

"We'll have something tomorrow. If he leaves, he's going to have to come out, and he'll want to kiss her goodbye, or something. And the boatman's brother said they often swim in the mornings. We'll have to sit it out until then. Oh my God," he groaned in a whisper, he had resumed his surveillance of the two love-makers. "They're really going for it now."

The sounds reached a crescendo, and died away as the heaving shape subsided into sporadic movement.

Bruno and Harry remained silent, aware that their victims' hearing would be more acute now. After five minutes, they could see the dark mound separate into two figures who stood up and walked down towards the shore.

Talking quietly, and with frequent pauses for displays of affection, the man and the girl waded out into the shallow waters of the lagoon until they were fifty yards off shore. There, they began to swim, making small ripples across the flat silvery surface of the water.

Bruno and Harry watched them in silence until they had disappeared around the small headland.

The photographer expelled a great sigh of frustration. "Tomorrow, Harry, we gotta get something tomorrow or I kill myself."

"We will, we will. Have I been wrong so far? The only

problem is waiting here all night. This has got to be the right place. But I must eat."

"Okay. When I go to meet the boat at midnight, I'll tell him to come back after dark tomorrow, and I'll bring back some food."

"From where? Are you going to raid the kitchens?"

"Of course not. This place is full of fruit trees. There's enough to keep you for months."

"If I were a vegetarian."

"For one night, you can be a vegetarian."

Harry awoke refreshed.

He had fallen asleep, perforce sober and well fed, on a makeshift palliasse of leaves and small branches. Bruno had shown unexpected resourcefulness the previous evening. He had gathered a substantial meal of banana, papaya, jack fruit and jamalaque. Harry had not picked so much as a blackberry since he was a small boy and he marvelled at the abundance of edibles that nature offered for the taking.

Now, flicking his eyes open in the slanting sun which beamed through the mango branches, he saw Bruno hunched over a camera with a lens eighteen inches long, which he was fixing to a tripod while he munched a banana. The Italian's face showed his concentration as he prepared for what he hoped would be the biggest shot in his career.

"Morning, Bruno," Harry said huskily.

"The bambino awakes. Feel better?"

"Yeah, I feel great. But is it worth giving up booze and becoming a vegetarian?"

Bruno passed him some bananas. "Here's some breakfast."

Harry ate them gratefully. He looked at his watch. It was just after seven o'clock. "I wonder what time Pyon will come out for his morning dip? I could do with a swim myself. It's very inviting," he said with his mouth full, looking at the morning sun glinting off the placid water. Out in the lagoon, there was a loud splash. He tensed up. "What's that?"

Beside a quickly fading circle of ripples, he caught another flash of silver as a large fish leaped and fell back into the water. Harry relaxed and watched the ripples disappear. Just then a new movement in the blue-green sea in the corner of his eye made his heart thump like a steam hammer.

"Bruno," he hissed, "someone's swimming round into the bay."

As Harry reached for his binoculars, Bruno put his eye to the camera on the stand and swung it round towards the mainland.

"It's them!" he hissed.

Two heads and, occasionally, two pairs of shining buttocks slowly ploughed two vees across the surface of the lagoon.

The swimmers turned in towards the shore, and Harry began to hear their voices. They stopped swimming twenty yards from the beach, and stood with the sea around their waists.

Harry gazed and sighed ecstatically.

Pyon and Natalie were both clearly visible, and as they waded hand in hand towards the beach, their complete nakedness became apparent.

Harry murmured into his tape-recorder; Bruno's camera clicked and whirred.

Pyon stopped. He turned to face Natalie, looking down at her with a big, happy smile on his face. He put his arms around her and they kissed one another with their whole bodies. Beads of sea water ran twinkling off their backs and the low sun sparkled on the wavelets lapping around their knees.

His deep, soft laughter drifted across the quiet lagoon, and the two bodies separated. His physical excitement was obvious as he and Natalie walked the last few yards to the beach.

Bruno's breath hissed between his teeth as he finished a roll of film and changed cameras.

"Shi . . .t!" Harry whispered. "She is *luscious*. What a lucky bastard. I can't believe it!"

Bruno did not answer. He was totally absorbed by the scene on the beach.

As if they were in their own, utterly private Garden of Eden, Pyon and Natalie were making love.

"Holy cow!"

The harsh, Glaswegian vowels echoed around the newsroom.

MacTavish, the picture editor of Harry's paper, gazed with awe at the dozen black and white prints spread out on a table in front of him.

"Those are the most sensational shots I've ever seen."

Harry beamed; MacTavish had had a long career in mucky journalism.

"A'course," the Scot went on with regret in his voice, "we won't be able to use the full frontal ones of his hard-on, even the *Sunday Sport* daren't use plonkers above the horizontal." He turned to Bruno, who stood behind him with a quiet, triumphant smile. "My God, laddy, you can name your own bloody price from the continental magazines for these."

Bruno inclined his head in a slight nod.

"Has the boss seen these?" MacTavish asked Harry.

"No. I haven't managed to get hold of him yet."

"I'll tell Julie to get him here as soon as possible. We've got two or three pages here."

Gleefully, Harry watched the story unfold on his VDU. It had everything that would appeal to the self-righteous, voyeuristic character of his paper's readership. He painted Natalie with kindly strokes; the innocent convent girl from the far-away island. The pictures would show other aspects.

His telephone bleeped.

"Hackwood," he bubbled.

"Hello, Harry." It was the same flat London voice that had sent Harry to Mauritius. "When are you going off on your travels?"

"I've been."

"Already?" The voice displayed some excitement. "Did you find anything?"

"Yes, thanks. I'm writing my piece now."

"And will it be illustrated?"

"Quite lavishly, as a matter of fact."

"That's very good news. When will it be out?"

"First edition, about eleven tonight."

"Thank you, Harry. I thought I could rely on you."

The line clicked dead. Harry continued to hold the phone in his hands for a few minutes. There was, he thought, the beginnings of another story here.

The editor arrived in the news-room, ever wary of his journalists' claims to major scoops. But when he saw the pictures he was rigid with excitement.

"Christ almighty, Harry! I think you've pulled it off. There's nothing he can do to argue with these. We won't be able to use the really rude ones, but . . ." He shook his head. "What a cracker!" Then, back to normal. "Okay. We'll put a teaser on the front page. This one." He indicated a shot of Pyon and Natalie waist-deep in the water, grinning happily and holding hands with each other. And we'll fill the two centre pages with the others. And Harry, we'll want the spiciest copy you've ever produced. What background have you got on the girl?"

"Plenty. We went to her parents' house, to the convent she works at, and I met several other people who know her. She sounds like a really nice girl. What angle do you want? Dirty old man or happy lovers?"

The editor considered this. "Our City page is supporting his bid for Chemco, so we'd better go with the happy lovers, especially as she's a Catholic schoolteacher."

"It'll still do him a lot of damage in the States. It's just what they want there – good, incontrovertible muck."

"Well, too bad. Anyway, most men will envy him, and a fair number of the women will wish it was them. I'll sub your piece personally. Well done, Harry, and thank you, Bruno. You've almost justified your obscene fee."

"This little deal of yours"

In the private office of his house in Mayfair, Pyon cocked an eye at the teletext screen.

There was an item about the APC studios.

The Australian wheeler-dealer, Doug de la Tour, was having talks with the studio's parent company. It was rumoured that he badly wanted the Australian TV station to bolster his existing Antipodean media empire.

Doug de la Tour was one of the recently emergent entrepreneurs from across the world who had come in and taken so many European and American companies by surprise. Pyon had inevitably crossed swords with him many times before and with considerable acrimony, but the score between them so far was about equal. Here was a chance for him to whip the carpet from right under de la Tour's feet.

Pyon was especially pleased to have seen this item just then; he was expecting Julian at the house to give an answer to his proposal. De la Tour's involvement outweighed other misgivings.

A coincidence, he thought; but then, life had frequently supplied him with timely coincidence.

Pyon picked up his telephone and asked for a Los Angeles number.

Julian came into the room warily.

His father's tone when he had arranged to meet him had not boded well. Nor had the venue – the house rather than the office. But Pyon greeted him effusively.

"Julian, my boy. Good to see you, and I'm very impressed with what you achieved in the States. I've had a thorough look at the deal, and I like it."

Julian felt a surge of gratitude. "That's great, Dad. I knew you'd like it when you saw the whole potential." His confidence returned. "You're looking very tanned and well, by the way. Where have you been?"

"Oh, just here and there. I've had to do a lot of running around, trying to knock some sense into the heads of the American authorities and institutions, but I managed a few days off in the sun. Now, as for this little deal of yours. They've assets that they value at $140 million and liabilities, mostly loans, of $80 million. I'm prepared to take on the loans, provided they're restructured, and offer them $30 million in cash."

Julian looked crestfallen. "But, Dad, that's thirty million short! They won't look at it."

"D'you want a bet? We're on a plane tonight. I offered yer man $20 million over the phone and he's ready to talk about it tomorrow."

"Good God!" Julian was impressed, but he added peevishly, "You might have talked to me first, after all, it is my deal."

"Oh, might I? And what would you have suggested different, apart from offering more? They're desperate to deal, and they don't want a great protracted discussion with de la Tour moving the goal posts every few days. But we've got to move fast."

"Okay." Julian laughed. "Fine by me. When are we off?"

"Hanks will pick you up at seven-thirty. Get yourself packed for a few more weeks in California."

Christy Pyon and Julian were booked into the Beverly Wilshire for their first night in Los Angeles. Pyon proposed that the next day Julian should set about renting a house somewhere convenient for the studio, which would give them more privacy.

They arrived at breakfast time and went straight to the APC lot to a meeting that had been arranged with Johnny Capra.

Southern Hemisphere's American lawyers had sent out two representatives from New York to deal with the formalities. Pyon reckoned that he could negotiate the price down to his target, but could not let it take too long.

His first words to the agitated seller did not convey this. "It's good to meet you in the flesh, Johnny, and great to be in LA again. I'll enjoy a few weeks here."

A big handshake, an arm around his shoulder and a broad, relaxed smile alarmed the American.

"A few weeks? Won't you be needing to get back to your Chemco deal?" he asked.

"I can do as much here as anywhere," Pyon said lightly, and the haggling started.

Negotiations were easier than Pyon had expected. He

guessed that this was because Johnny Capra was under acute pressure from his banks. As always, Pyon took most of the initiative in the discussions, but now he refrained from offering a firm price. He set about overwhelming the other side with general and particular objections on which he insisted on having answers. He went through each of the major assets of the business, chipping away at them one by one, demanding and receiving piecemeal concessions. It was a process designed to wear the opposition into submission, almost out of desperation to get the thing over with. It required a more patient man than the excitable Johnny Capra to resist Pyon when he was going full ahead.

Capra made a passing reference to the interest that had been shown by Doug de la Tour. Pyon shot that down.

"I don't give a damn who else is interested, or how they value your corporation." He had established his own valuation, and that was the only basis on which he would talk.

The two negotiating parties were ill-matched. Pyon had the weight of personality and his well-known capacity for instant decision-making on his side. His lawyers sat silently, noting each concession made by Capra, and Pyon reached the position he wanted before lunch. They were to eat at the studio, so he decided he may as well press on afterwards, and see how much further he could get.

By late afternoon, the deal was done. Pyon agreed to pay $28 million in cash, and SHR would assume liability for the outstanding loans of $80 million. The lawyers were instructed to draw up the contracts, and everyone shook hands with each other. Pyon was certain that he had a bargain.

He and Julian were driven back down Laurel Canyon to Beverly Hills in a Mercedes limousine. Pyon was exultant and Julian overawed by the shock that the deal had actually been done. He was also impressed by the determination and thoroughness with which his father had pushed it through.

Now that it was done, Julian was more relieved than he liked to admit to himself that Pyon was to take overall control.

They drew up in front of the Beverly Wilshire and a porter leaped forward to open the car door. They strolled up the steps, still congratulating themselves, and into the lobby.

Suddenly, they were surrounded.

Two dozen men and a few women jostled around them, toting notebooks, tape-recorders and cameras which clicked amid a cacophony of questions.

"Christy! Christy! Are you going to marry Natalie?"

"How long have you been going with her?" – American voices.

"Mr Pyon, have you got any comment to make about your relationship with Natalie Felix?" – an English accent.

The questions continued without any of the questioners waiting for answers.

The doorman and two lobby clerks rushed up to hustle the newsmen out, angry that they had been fooled.

Pyon stood his ground, smiled blandly and said nothing.

"Sorry lads," he laughed after the departing crowd, "you'll have to wait until you hear it all on the Johnny Carson Show."

He and Julian were ushered to a lift by an embarrassed young manager.

"I'm sorry, Mr Pyon. I don't know how they got to know you were staying here. It wasn't one of our people, for sure. You won't be disturbed again."

"I'd better not be," Pyon growled. The young man entered the lift with them, and went up to the fifth floor to show them to their suite.

When he had left after a further deluge of obsequious regrets, Pyon turned to Julian with his eyes blazing. "For fuck's sake, try and find out what this is all about!"

"How the hell am I supposed to do that?"

"Use your initiative, Julian. Some story must have come out. Why the hell it should now, God knows, but just get out there and find out."

"Have you seen Natalie recently?"

"As it happens I have, but there's no way anyone could have got hold of anything substantial. Now for God's sake, get going."

"Why don't you ring your PR people? They should know."

Pyon looked at him a moment. "Okay. You're right. Sorry for bollocking you. It's nothing to do with you."

He picked up the telephone and asked the operator to get him a New York number.

A few seconds, and he was barking into it. "This is Pyon. Get me MacFarlane." Another pause. "Bob? Yes, this *is* Pyon. I'm in Beverly Hills. I've been at a meeting all day and I've just arrived back at the Wilshire to a pack of slavering hacks."

Pyon was silent for the thirty seconds or so that it took the public relations boss to tell him. His face collapsed and whitened in a way that Julian had never seen.

"Holy shit!" he said finally. "You'd better get your ass out here as quick as you can. You're going to have a lot to do, and the sooner we start, the better."

Pyon put the telephone down and turned to Julian. "Go down and get the English papers. I can't ask room service. They'll wonder why the hell I don't already know what's going on. And be discreet."

Julian nodded and left the room to go down to the lobby.

He reached the paper shop, searched through the rack but could not find what he wanted.

He asked the girl behind the counter, "Do you know if you've got a *Daily* . . ."

"Is this what you're after, Mr Pyon?" an English voice said behind him.

Julian spun round to find a man of about his own age, stout, tanned, wearing jeans and a white shirt, and brandishing a folded copy of a British tabloid. He offered it to Julian, who took it without hesitation and unfolded it.

The photograph took up a third of the front page.

It was a crisp clear shot, taken under good conditions. His father looked fit, handsome and happy. Natalie looked sensational. They could have been advertising a big, glossy movie.

Julian was stunned by conflicting emotions.

Outrage on his mother's behalf.

Outrage on his father's behalf.

He gazed at the picture. He paled and his jaw slackened.

It was a few moments before he could concentrate enough to read the copy below the photograph.

"Tycoon Christy Pyon gets away from the pressures of his bid to take over the mighty Chemco Corporation. Keeping him company on his desert island hideaway in the Indian Ocean is Mauritian schoolteacher, Natalie Felix – Full story and pictures, p. 7 & 8."

With trembling hands, Julian clumsily riffled through the paper to the indicated pages. He was confronted by three photographs – sharp in focus, well framed, beautifully shot – that were little short of pornographic. With a feeling of numb horror, he slowly absorbed each one.

There was some copy, too, but he could not bring himself to read it. As if from a distance, through a fog, a voice interrupted his thoughts.

"Bit naughty, aren't they?" It was the man who had given him the paper.

Julian looked up and saw him for the first time. The tubby man was slightly familiar. Where had he seen him? He knew him vaguely, he was sure. Then he began to remember.

School, Ampleforth, Harry Hackwood, memorable for his girth even as an eighteen-year-old schoolboy; now a familiar face in a hostile environment.

"Christ, Harry Hackwood?" Then he was jerked by a more recent memory, and his eyes flew back to the paper, to the by-line at the top of the copy. "Shit! You bastard. What have you done? For God's sake, didn't you realise Christy Pyon was my father?"

"Of course I did. That made it all the more fascinating."

"But for Christ's sake, don't you realise what you've done? We're just about to take over a studio here, and this story could kill the deal stone dead."

"Don't be ridiculous, Julian, I haven't said anything nasty about your father. Ninety per cent of the men reading this will be thinking, I should be so lucky, and I dare say most of the women."

"What about Chemco?" Julian shouted.

"Take it easy, Julian. People are beginning to look. If you want to talk, why don't we go somewhere private? I've got a room here."

"I'll bet you have, and I'll bet the paper doesn't mind paying. If you think you're going to find anything else to print by hanging about here, forget it."

Julian stormed off to a waiting lift.

Pyon was pacing up and down when Julian reached their suite. "Where the hell have you been?" he growled as he reached for the newspaper.

He glanced at the front page, smiled, then turned to the inner pages.

He displayed no emotion as he studied the photographs and read Harry Hackwood's copy. Still reading, he wandered over to the nearest window. After a while, he lowered the paper and turned to Julian.

"It could be worse," he said.

"What do you mean – it could be worse?" Julian was appalled. "There you are, fucking on the beach for the whole world to see! What the hell do you think that's going to do to your reputation? For God's sake, the American press will go apeshit over this and your Chemco deal. It's exactly what they want. Not that I care about Chemco, but what about our studio deal?" He paused. "And what do you think it'll do to Mum?"

"I'll grant you, your mother won't be best pleased, but I think she'll understand."

"Of course she won't understand, you bastard. She still bloody loves you. Don't you give a toss for her feelings?"

"Look, son, I didn't ask for this," Pyon shouted back. "I've always taken every precaution to be discreet. How the hell these fellas got those shots, God knows. Of course her pride'll be hurt, but she'll get over that. Damn it, I've been divorced from her for fifteen years!"

"She's been too tolerant for too long. She won't be after this, I can tell you. You must be mad to behave like this." Julian thrust his finger at the photos.

"Sure you wouldn't fancy a bit of it yourself?"

Julian stared at him. "You're amazing! For years you've been obsessed with privacy, and now, when you're snapped in *flagrante delicto*, you give yourself a pat on the back because it's with a woman half your age whom, you imagine, every other man in the world would like to screw. It's a great big advertisement for Pyon the macho stud. Well, it's going to cost you, and don't think you can back out of the APC deal now!"

Pyon shook his head contemptuously. "It makes absolutely no difference to any deals I'm doing. All this says," he waved the paper around, "is that I've a relationship with a beautiful and totally respectable girl. There isn't anything so rare or reprehensible in that."

"If you think that's how the public will react, you're mad. You know how they love to kick a man when he's tumbled off a pedestal he's made for himself. You're a perfect target. They'll have a bloody field day. In the meantime, you'd better let me deal with Mother and Laura. God knows, I can't make excuses for you, but I'll try and soften the blow."

Pyon did not let his son see his gratitude. "As you wish. Of course I'll go and see your mother as soon as I can. Laura will be more difficult. She's gone to Rome for a few days, and then she's going to Sardinia, though I tried to stop her. If you can get hold of her, tell her not to. Maria'll not be good company. She'll be jumping around like a wild cat with hornets up its arse. And I don't trust those brothers of hers."

"Chemco's people are jumping for joy"

"Mr Pyon? Is that you?"

In Jeremy Fielder's voice there was a quaver detectable even down the international telephone line.

"Yes, Jeremy," Pyon said evenly.

"The news isn't good here. There was some very heavy selling overnight, and it went on all day."

"I have seen the latest price, thank you, Jeremy."

"But what shall we do?"

"Stop panicking, for a start. We're not going to get a ruling on the bank for at least another three months. There's plenty of time for the price to recover. That's when we need it to be strong."

"But will it recover?"

"Of course. This is a nine-days wonder. Everybody will have forgotten in a month."

"I'd feel a lot happier if I knew who sold. It started in New York late the day before the . . . thing was published."

"I had noticed that, too. I'm coming back to London now. I'll sort it out myself. Just keep calm. It's more than likely a few journalists earning a little bonus. It's obvious that our price'll go back up."

Fielder did not detect the fury that gripped Pyon.

Fury at himself, at Julian for having been right, and at whichever of his support party had welshed.

Pyon left Julian in California with full authority to sign the formal documentation for the purchase of the Actors' Production Company, its studios, catalogue of titles and Australian TV subsidiary. He caught the first morning flight to New York, where he transferred to Concorde.

He walked into SHR's Mayfair offices shortly after midnight. Morry Weintraub was waiting for him.

Weintraub's eyes, normally expressionless, glared with sullen and resentful anger.

"Hello, you miserable old sod," Pyon greeted him with a laugh.

"Would you mind telling me what is going on?"

"Are you worried about our price?"

"Of course I am. I bought at five dollars, and they're trading at just over three. I'm six million dollars light at the moment."

"What are you worried about? You've my indemnity against any loss."

"If the SHR price crashes completely, you'll be in no position to be honouring indemnities, especially unwritten ones."

Pyon's eyes turned on him, flashing like a pair of police-car beacons. "Now listen to me, my friend. I have never welshed on a deal in my life. The price will recover anyway, and it's not me you want to blame for the drop."

"I suppose it wasn't you splashed all over the papers, fornicating with a sooty on a South Sea Island."

Pyon could not help a bellow of laughter. "Your geography's not too good, nor is your anthropology."

"Never mind that. It sent the price tumbling."

"The price started tumbling before the paper hit the streets. Someone knew, and used it. It could be one of the arbitrageurs." Pyon paused, and put his head to one side. "Or it could be one of our party."

Morry Weintraub looked outraged, but before he could speak, Pyon went on, "Either way, it's a bogus movement."

"Oh no it isn't. The American media are on to it, and Chemco's people are jumping for joy."

"You'll have noticed that their price fell back too?"

"Obviously, if you're seen to be out of the ring."

"Well, I'm not, and you'll just have to trust me."

"I don't think I can afford it. I should cut my losses and get out now."

"Then, of course, my guarantee becomes invalid." Pyon shrugged.

"I've already told you what I think of that. There is another thing. What's this I hear about you – or rather SHR – buying some bankrupt film studio in America?"

"Southern hasn't totally ceased to operate, you know. It is the company's business to buy and unbundle messy businesses. That is how we make our money. It's a small deal anyway, and we should see back the whole purchase price by selling their Australian TV station to Doug de la Tour."

"I'll believe that when I see it. From you, de la Tour will be reluctant to accept it as a *gift*. And what experience has your son of running a film studio?"

Pyon winced slightly.

Weintraub spotted it and persisted. "It's a piece of flagrant, irresponsible nepotism."

"You're entitled to your views, of course, but naturally, I haven't left Julian there on his own. He knows a lot about making movies, and, as you know, he's had some acclaim for it."

"One prize for an obscure little arty farty piece of homosexual propaganda."

"Well, there it is. That's what I've done. My track record in corporate reorganisation speaks for itself."

"Maybe, but this is the first time you've been motivated by anything other than a good clean profit, and that worries me."

Pyon put his arm around the shoulders of the agitated Jew. "Now look, Morry. There's nothing to worry about. We've a long wait before the federal and state banking authorities give rulings on al Souf's ownership of Chemco's banks. That'll go our way, I'm certain. I'm not saying I'm happy about our price taking a hammering, but provided we don't panic, it'll come back up. So you just hang on in there. As a matter of fact, with the price where it is, if I were you I'd buy a whole lot more."

Pyon looked the other in the eyes, daring him to argue.

After a moment's silence, Weintraub shrugged and shook his head. "I don't know why I listen to you, Pyon."

"Because you've always made money out of me, and you always will."

"I just hope the other members of your little party have as much faith."

After Weintraub left, banging the great front door of the building behind him, Pyon waited a few minutes before leaving himself. He told the dozing night-porter to let him out of the back door, and made his way round to Liz's house in the mews. He knew she was in Ireland. Pyon was relieved. He was prepared to face her, but not yet. There were too many other problems to be dealt with that could not wait.

But he did want to ring Natalie. He had not done so since the photographs had been published in London the day before. They would certainly have reached her in Mauritius by now.

He rang the *Ile Vermont*. After a dozen rings, the telephone was sleepily answered by his housekeeper.

Natalie was not there. She had left in the morning, after the driver had brought up the English papers which arrived by the daily flight from London.

Reluctantly, Pyon dialled the number of her parents.

On the two occasions he had met Phillipe Felix, the

politician had made it clear that, as far as he was concerned, Pyon was unqualified for the relationship he had with Natalie. It was unlikely that recent events would have changed his view.

Luckily, Natalie answered.

"It's Christy," he growled.

"Oh my darling," she gasped with compassion, "what have they done? Who has done it? I think I know. Two men went to the convent and then here, asking for me. My mother only told them I was away on one of the islands. It's awful, what everyone is saying here."

"I'm sure it is, and I'm so, so sorry that what we have between us should have been exposed to this kind of horrible, gutter reporting. Still," he chuckled, "you looked very well in the pictures."

"Please, Christy, don't laugh about it, not yet. My family are very upset, and the nuns are furious."

"Sure, I understand that, my angel. I'll sort everything out, though, don't you worry. Just keep your pecker up, and remember I love you. But I won't come over for a while. It's caused a few hiccups in the deal I'm doing. But you be sure to ring me, if you need to. My secretary here will always tell you where I am, or tell me you called, okay?"

"Okay, Christy, and I know how much trouble it must be for you. I think of you nearly all the time."

"It won't take long, I promise. Goodbye for now, my lovely little piccaninny."

"Goodbye, you big hairy monster."

Pyon smiled at this display of spirit as he replaced the phone. He knew that he was right to have risked so much for her.

Violence on the Costa Smeralda

Laura Pyon leaned back against a hummock of marram grass on a high, empty promontory of Sardinia's Costa Smeralda. The sun was nearing the top of its arc, fierce and unimpeded in a deep blue sky, but a fresh wind rippled the grass and shook the scrubby bushes, and cooled Laura's well-tanned skin.

The wind blowing off the sea brought no sounds other than its own soft murmur. The few cars that wound along the narrow coast road below her seemed to achieve their motion with soundless motors. They looked to Laura like toys from a Lilliputian world, containing funny little people engaged in plans and relationships of complete insignificance beside the violent and far-reaching eruptions that were about to envelop her family.

Her only real point of reference was a large white villa, set up above the bay that curved in from the stubby headland on which she sat.

A maid at the house, a small, anxious woman, had told Laura that Maria Pyon and her two children would be back for lunch. She did not know where they had gone that morning.

Laura, watching for their return, wondered whether Maria had seen the English newspaper that had arrived late the day before, and the two pages devoted exclusively to her father's activities in Mauritius. She doubted it, unless they had been into Porto Cervo and been told, or someone had telephoned from England. But she hoped so; she did not want the unrewarding task of breaking the news.

The children had been delighted to see her on the previous day. She had driven Caterina and Gianni to the marina and taken them off in a small sailing boat for a picnic on one of the islands. Their enjoyment of this simple pleasure was gratifying and made the tussle she had had with Maria worthwhile. Of course, Maria's objections to her taking the children for the day were tempered by relief at getting them off her own hands.

Laura saw Maria's Daimler appear on the shoulder of the next headland. It turned off the road on to the long, dusty drive that led up to the house. She scrambled down the hill to her rented Fiat, jumped in and bounced down a rutted track while her heart pounded at the thought of confronting Maria.

Maybe, she thought, her father was right. She should not get involved with these people, and if she was honest, the motives behind her concern for her two siblings had as much to do with her asserting herself over her stepmother as it had with their welfare. But her blood was up, and pumping adrenalin to the tips of her fingers. She was ready for a fight.

Maria's greeting was almost civilised.

"Hello, Laura. Have you come for the kids? They did enjoy their trip with you yesterday."

She hasn't heard yet, thought Laura, and I'm not going to tell her.

"I'd love to take them again, if you haven't got any other plans for them."

Maria shrugged. "They just say they are bored all the time with me."

"They said they wanted to play tennis today. There's a court where I'm staying at Cala di Volpe. We could go there."

"Sure, why not? Do you want to have lunch here first? There are a few people coming."

After a moment's hesitation Laura said, "Yes, thanks. Who's coming?"

"My brother Sergio and his wife. Enzo Fratinelli's coming from Porto Rotondo with a few others, I forget who."

Laura sat out on the terrace with a drink and talked to Caterina. But as she chatted and laughed with the shy teenage girl, she was wondering how she would deal with Maria when Pyon's latest publicity reached her. She also wondered about Enzo Fratinelli.

Her mother had told her that Fratinelli had introduced Maria, with a bogus identity, to Julian. Julian had been infatuated, Liz said, then furious when he had discovered who she was. It had all been a plan of Maria's to get to Liz, to persuade her to join forces in delivering some kind of chastisement to Pyon.

When the famous film director arrived, and was introduced to Laura, he glanced at Maria with a look of surprise, then amused cynicism.

Laura and Fratinelli found themselves alone on the terrace.

"Is my stepmother an old friend of yours, Signor Fratinelli?"

"Enzo. Call me Enzo, please, or you'll make me feel very old. I've known Maria since she was born. Her father was an old crook, but full of vitality, and I liked him very much. Maria is a wicked bitch, but I am like her uncle. You can't wipe away these connections. To be truthful, if she had married a more controllable man, an Italian, for instance, she wouldn't be so bad." He shrugged, "Maybe."

"Why did she want to meet my brother Julian?"

"I didn't ask her. But I imagine to damage your father in some way. I don't think it came to anything, thank God."

"Why thank God?"

"She could chew him up and spit him out. He's a talented boy, but too sensitive."

Laura considered this a moment. "Have you heard about my father's latest escapade?"

Fratinelli nodded, with a smile. "Sure, but Maria hasn't, has she?"

"No."

"Be careful when she does."

Three other people who had come with Fratinelli walked out on to the terrace, followed by Maria and a maid carrying a tray of drinks. The others were also film people, English and Italian, and the conversation turned to movie gossip.

Laura could not concentrate. She constantly glanced at Maria, as if at a bomb about to explode, and wondered whether it would be wiser to run for cover now.

But she stayed. Sergio Gatti and his wife arrived. He regarded Laura with surliness, and refused to speak to her. That was normal, though. It was obvious that he had not yet seen the newspaper either.

As soon as lunch was over, Laura drove away with the two children to the house in which she was staying, up the coast from Porto Cervo.

The small stone house was little more than an extended shepherd's lodge, and one of the few original dwellings on the Costa Smeralda. It belonged to an old admirer of Laura's who had frequently asked her to stay in Sardinia. He was delighted that she had finally come, even though she had made it clear that she had no plans to sleep with him. He had, anyway, left for Rome the day before, so Laura had the house to herself.

She played tennis with Caterina and Gianni, then took them down to the harbour in Porto Cervo to see some friends on a spectacular old three-masted schooner. Gianni enjoyed himself, clambering up among the rigging, while Caterina coyly fended off the advances of an amorous fourteen-year-old.

Later, when she took them back to the villa, there was no one there besides the maid, who seemed more nervous than normal while telling Laura that Maria had left two hours before with her brother and had not said when she would be back.

The children were resigned to being left there on their own, so, with only slight misgivings, she drove back to Cala di Volpe.

That evening Laura had dinner with her friends on the schooner. She went home shortly after midnight and sat up in bed reading for a while before she turned out the light. She lay thinking of her father and his children; she hoped that the father of her own children would do a better job than Pyon had with Caterina and Gianni. Eventually, she slept.

An hour later, she woke, tense and straining her ears. Into her muddled dreams had intruded a muffled thud and a harsh creak of breaking wood. Fear prickled over her skin. She could not dismiss, as she would normally have done, an acute awareness of her feminine vulnerability.

A clear night showed through the skimpy, fluttering curtains. In an instant, Laura had climbed out of bed, making no sound. She did not feel the cold stone floor on her bare feet as she padded a few paces to stand behind the door. Fear and the night chill made her shiver in her short cotton nightdress as she looked around for a weapon. She picked up a large, crudely turned vase from a table beside her, grateful for her host's bad taste and the potter's lavishness with his clay.

She judged that there were two intruders in the house now. They were attempting to open each of the doors as silently as they could, but old iron hinges squealed and ill-fitting doors scraped against their jambs.

She saw the handle of her own door turn slowly. Every hair on her body lifted from her skin and her mouth was suddenly dry. She pressed herself back against the wall and raised the ugly pot above her head.

A head of black, wiry hair, just visible in the pale light, appeared around the edge of the opening door; then a distinctive, curved nose and an angry chin.

The man's head was almost motionless as he peered into the gloom, trying to judge whether or not the bed was occupied. Laura took a pace forward, aimed carefully, and swung the vase down like a navvy wielding a sledgehammer.

There was a hollow thud as it struck the wiry head. With a groan and a whimper, the man sank to the floor. His head hit the stone flags with a sharp thump.

Laura still held the unbroken pot in her hands, and promptly stepped back behind the door, panting, terrified, but ready for the next intruder.

He flung the door open. The handle pounded into her stomach, winding her, pinning her against the wall. She lost her grip on the vase, which fell to the ground. This time, it did not survive. Shards of heavily glazed earthenware scattered about the room. The door swung back, and a pair of gloved hands grasped Laura's throat. She wanted to scream, but she had no breath in her lungs. Her knees collapsed beneath her, and she felt herself slip helplessly down the wall.

The man's face was inches from hers. His breath was thick with olive oil and aniseed. He hissed through clenched teeth in Italian, "If you've killed my brother, we'll kill yours."

Laura could think only of getting oxygen into her searing lungs. With a desperate surge of energy, she lifted her hands to grab his wrists and tugged furiously. His grip slackened enough for her to gasp some air. He caught hold of her forearms and dragged her into the middle of the small room, and flung her down on the bed. Before she could recover her breath, he was on top of her. She struggled furiously but he pinioned her arms to the sides of the bedhead. His bony body and a big belt buckle jabbed into her soft flesh.

"Don't fight me, bitch, or I'll tie you to the bed."

Laura stopped moving. Only her breasts heaved as she tried to catch her breath.

"That's better," he said, and took one hand from her wrist to draw her flimsy nightie up to her waist.

Laura was breathing steadily now. She controlled her repulsion, knowing that he would have to release her other arm to undo his fancy buckle. She lay still, and offered no resistance.

Confident now, he did as she had hoped. He knelt above her, straddling her hips, and slid his trousers a short way down his buttocks.

With all the power in her healthy thighs, she stabbed her knee upwards into his groin. His testicles were driven hard and agonisingly upwards. At the same time, she brought her right arm up and punched him in the stomach with animal fury. He yelled and grunted, and became limp with pain for the few seconds she needed to push him off the bed.

She leaped free, and fled from the room, not knowing what to do or where to go. She checked herself, made an impromptu plan and grabbed her car keys from the hallstand. She stumbled out of the front door, which was swinging lockless on its hinges, and ran up the stony track, heedless of the pain to her feet. In the bright but moonless night, in this lonely hinterland of the carefully developed coast, there was not a light to be seen, nor a sound to be heard above the harsh trilling of the cicadas.

Her car was parked at the top of the track by the side of the deserted road. It was only as she reached it that she saw the dark shape of a large jeep, blocking her exit.

She ran round to it to open the driver's door. Before she reached it, she was grabbed by a pair of huge arms which squeezed around her like a python round a gazelle.

"*Scusi, ragazza.* You're coming with us."

This man was evidently some kind of minder. He was enormous, over six feet six with a torso to match. His deep relaxed voice displayed total confidence in what he was doing.

Now the man who had tried to rape her was panting up the track towards the cars.

"Did you stop her?" he demanded in a shouted whisper.

"Sure, Luca. I got her."

"Good! She's got a lot to pay for. Gino's still out cold,

down at the house. We'll have to get him out of here fast. Just tie the bitch up like a chicken so she can't move and put her in the back of the wagon."

Gagged with an oily rag and bound with a tow-rope, Laura lay helpless among a mess of feathers and empty cartridge cases in the back of a big Japanese jeep. One of the rear doors was flung open and she could hear a lot of grunting and heavy breathing, followed by the sound of somebody being dumped on the back seat.

The door behind her was opened, and she found herself looking into the blazing eyes of the man she had tried to emasculate.

"I hope you're uncomfortable, you bitch. But if you're not, don't worry, you soon will be."

He slammed the door shut, and she heard the two men climb into the car. Whichever of them was driving soon made a point of flinging the vehicle around every bend, and Laura was so tightly trussed that she could not use her legs or elbows to brace herself into one position. She was hurled from side to side, bruising and cutting herself against various pieces of rubbish and tools.

The journey lasted hours. Laura could not hear what her abductors were saying over the noise of the engine and the transmission, but the angle and speed of the vehicle suggested that they were climbing.

She realised what was happening and forced herself to stay calm. She finally managed to wedge herself between what felt like a tool-box and a spare wheel. After a while, with her head resting on a piece of old sacking, she fell asleep.

She awoke to find herself being carried effortlessly, like a small child, in the enormous arms of the minder. The sky was tinted with dawn pink, and all around was a horizon of jagged hills. Immediately above her, a large, unshaven chin was discernible in the early light. She looked around as she was borne up a steep track.

They were in a small mountain valley, empty of sound beyond the mewing of some high birds of prey and the whine of a sharp breeze. Laura twisted her head and saw that the path they were on led up to a stone farmhouse. It looked as though once it had been a big establishment, but was semi-derelict now. At one end, the roof had caved in, and the range of barns that surrounded it had long since ceased to offer protection from the weather.

Glancing back the way they had come, Laura could see the jeep and, beside it, her two attackers. The one she had hit over the head had recovered. At least, he was standing without support, smoking a cigarette. Both men were speaking in voices inaudible to her, with angry gesticulations and glances in her direction.

The giant who carried her reached the courtyard of the house and kicked open the front door. It swung inwards with a long groan, and Laura was carried over the threshold.

They went through a dusty hall, into another room that was, by contrast to the rest of the place, clean and lavishly furnished.

Laura was dumped on a long low sofa of black leather and chrome. The big Italian twisted her round so that she was able to sit as normally as her tied legs and wrists would allow. He looked down at her.

"If you're a good girl, I'll untie your hands later," he said in a thick Neapolitan accent which Laura only barely understood. She gave him a brief smile of thanks, but turned the smile to a grimace of contempt when she heard the others walk across the hall towards the room.

The younger, better-looking of the two, whose ego had been violently affronted by his failure to rape her, stared at her with vitriolic malevolence.

His brother appeared to hold her in some esteem for having outwitted him. It was he who spoke first.

"Do you know why we have brought you here, Signorina Pyon?"

Laura shrugged. "To add a bit of excitement to your dreary lives?"

"No, Signorina. I am Gino, and this is my brother, Luca. This is just a job for us. Your father has behaved very badly. He's upset too many people, and he's too greedy. Our bosses want him to be punished. We are going to extract from him a very large fine, large enough to teach even him some manners. And, until he's agreed, and paid, you will be staying with Alphonso here."

He jerked a thumb at the placid giant who had sat himself in an easy chair to read a cartoon book.

"Alphonso may look kind, but he's very loyal to our family, aren't you, Fo-fo? He was an orphan and we brought him up," he added by way of explanation. "Weren't we lucky to find such a big one?"

Alphonso glanced up and stared at Gino, nodding his head, then turned back to his cartoons.

"So, you won't want to go anywhere without asking him, will you? He goes wild when he's angry, but he won't harm you if you do as you're told. We don't want to send you back to your father damaged in any way, no more than is necessary to help him make up his mind. He loves his beautiful daughter, doesn't he? So I don't suppose it will come to that. We'll say goodbye now." Gino glanced at his watch. "There's a nice party in Rotondo today and we don't want to miss it, do we, Luca?"

Luca had remained motionless during his brother's monologue. He continued to stare at Laura. "No we don't," he said huskily, "but some time, you and me are going to have a party, darling." He walked to the sofa where she sat, leaned down and kissed her savagely on the lips. Laura, taken by surprise and with her hands tied behind her back could not avoid it, but when he backed off, she shook her head with a face of disgust.

Gino grabbed his brother angrily. "For God's sake, Luca. We haven't brought her here to satisfy your nasty habits. We must do this honourably, in the way the old man would have done."

Laura was still quivering with horror, but felt some gratitude to Gino.

"Who cares?" Luca growled. "She's just an English whore."

"Don't come here, don't touch her, Luca, I warn you." He turned to Alphonso, sitting unconcerned across the room. "Okay, Fo-fo. We're going. Lock her in the back room. Feed her and let her go to the lavatory. But keep her tied. She's harder than she looks. And I don't want her damaged."

"No problem, boss," Alphonso grunted.

Gino addressed Laura. "If you co-operate, you'll be all

right. We want to punish your father, not you. If he loves you, you'll be out of here in a week or two."

Laura said nothing, but looked at him steadily.

Dear God, she prayed, I hope Father loves me enough.

"I won't forgive you, if you don't do everything you can"

Elizabeth Pyon walked into the house, almost content after a day's peaceful but, as it happened, fruitless fishing on the Slaney. When she needed to escape from outside pressures, she liked to spend a whole day on her own by the river, taking a picnic lunch with her to eat in the small stone fishing hut.

The telephone was ringing on a small table in the back hall. She picked it up, annoyed at its intrusion on her calm day.

"Mrs Pyon?"

"Who is that?"

"This is Harry Hackwood from the –"

"I know where you're from, Mr Hackwood, and I don't want to talk to you."

"Mrs Pyon, obviously I'm very sorry to have to intrude at a time like this, but the public should get an accurate idea of your reactions. If you won't tell us directly, other papers will just make it up."

"I think there has already been quite enough written about my reaction to my ex-husband's activities, not least some very speculative articles of your own."

"But, Mrs Pyon, I'm not talking about your husband –" He stopped. "Oh my God, haven't you heard the news?"

Liz stiffened. "What news?"

"About your daughter?"

"Laura? What's happened to her?"

"I'm terribly sorry," Harry blustered, greatly embarrassed, "it didn't occur to me that you wouldn't know."

"I wouldn't know what, for God's sake? What's happened to Laura? Is she all right?"

"Yes, as far as we know, she's all right, but she's been kidnapped."

"Oh, no! Oh my God! Who by? Where from? I knew she shouldn't have gone to Sardinia."

"Why do you say that, Mrs Pyon?" Harry asked sharply.

Liz did not answer for a moment. She put the telephone receiver on the table, and breathed deeply to regain her composure. She heard Harry's voice squawking up from it: "Mrs Pyon? Mrs Pyon, are you there?"

She picked up the receiver. "Yes, Mr Hackwood, I'm here," she said as calmly as she could. "I've been out of the house all day; I've only just come in, so I had not heard. Would you kindly tell me what you know without any journalistic embellishments."

"I'm afraid there isn't much yet, Mrs Pyon. Laura has been staying on the Costa Smeralda, in the house of a friend, a man called Tony von Lichenstein. He went to Rome for a couple of nights and when he returned at lunchtime today, he found that the house had been broken into, and signs of a struggle. Laura's bed had been slept in, and a car she had rented was still parked beside the road, with the keys on the ground beside it. He reported it to the police, who immediately concluded it was a kidnap, but they've had no communication yet from anyone. Apparently that's normal – you don't hear from them for a day or too."

"But it might not have been a kidnap," Liz stammered. "What about rape, or murder?"

"In Sardinia it's more likely to have been a kidnap. Laura's father is known to be a very wealthy man."

"Especially since your revelations."

"Mrs Pyon, it was common knowledge before that."

"I haven't the slightest doubt," she interrupted, "that there's some connection with the current scandal surrounding my ex-husband, for which you were largely responsible. You want my reaction; there it is. Thanks to your sensational muckraking, a perfectly innocent young woman has been abducted. If you people only knew, or cared, how much damage you cause maybe you'd think twice before wallowing in other people's misfortunes or misjudgements, but I doubt it. Thank you for letting me know the news, Mr Hackwood, and please don't ring me again."

Liz banged the telephone down, and with all the strength ebbing from her legs, she lowered herself on to an uncomfortably carved Queen Anne chair. She put her face in her hands, overwhelmed by the events of the last few days, and she sobbed.

Tom Brophy had been searching everywhere for Liz since the news had reached Clonegall House shortly after lunch. Now he put his head around the door from the kitchen passage and saw his employer as he had never seen her before.

"Oh Jaysus, missus, you've heard already, then?"

He clumped over to her, and laid an arm on her shoulder in a gesture he had never dreamt of using before.

She glanced up, and her red, tearful eyes gratefully acknowledged the affection in the old groom's eyes. She nodded and her lips and eyes tightened in another spasm of realisation. She sniffed and put a hand on Tom's grimy arm. "One thing after another, isn't it, Tom?" she said.

"It's a terrible thing, but, please God, she's all right. They said on the news that the police reckon she'll not be harmed, if they want a ransom."

Liz looked at him bleakly. "Pyon will never pay a ransom. He's often said so."

"Sure and he will, for his lovely daughter. He's a good man. He'd not want any harm to come to her."

"It's good of you, Tom, but I'm not so sure. Did Cathy say that Mr Pyon had phoned?"

"I believe she did. I'll ask her. Will I tell her to bring you a cup of tea? You'll be needing one."

"Thank you, Tom. You've been very kind. I only wish you were right about Mr Pyon."

"I'll talk to him about it, missus. He always listens to me about the horses."

Liz gave a small smile at Tom's faith in his influence over her impregnable ex-husband.

Pyon had been telephoned directly by the chief of police at Sassari. He had immediately tried to contact Liz, and cursed her habit of going off without telling anyone where.

And while he was churning with anxiety for Laura, he cursed the pig-headed stubbornness which his daughter had inherited from him. He had warned her there would be trouble in Sardinia.

Maria had been trying to contact him for the last twenty-four hours. He had not deliberately avoided her, but he had made no effort to ring her back. Press from all over the world had been pestering his offices since lunchtime, and his PR people were reeling under the double hammering they had taken that week.

Speculation about what would be asked of Pyon for the return of his daughter was now in the realms of fantasy. Reporters on the television, radio and in the evening papers had wallowed in the enormous sums attached to Pyon's name that had been bandied about only a few days before.

Pyon refused, as ever, to appear or be directly interviewed. He issued a statement which the head of his London public relations company read to the press on the steps of the Southern Hemisphere offices.

"Mr Pyon has not received confirmation that his daughter, Laura, has been kidnapped. In the event that a demand for ransom is made, it will not be met. Mr Pyon has personal assurances from the chief of police of the island of Sardinia that every available resource is being applied to the recovery of his daughter, and the apprehension of her abductors."

But the pressmen had stayed, a cluster of men and women on the pavement outside the Mayfair building, leaping forward with notebooks and cameras at the ready every time the front door was opened.

Pyon left by the back entrance and the alley that led to the far end of the mews where his house was. Hanks was waiting for him, and whisked him away unnoticed to the heliport at Battersea.

When he landed at Clonegall, the first person out to greet him was Tom Brophy.

"Mr Christy, for sure Mrs Pyon will be glad to see you. But, can I say something to you first? She's thinkin' maybe you won't be paying any ransom, but I told her of course you would. I'm right, am I not?"

"Tom, we don't know for certain she's been kidnapped. When someone tells me what they want, I'll be able to give you an answer."

Tom was relieved. Pyon's answer was better than a downright "no".

Inside the house, Pyon strode through the long corridors to Liz's sitting-room.

When he walked in, she was standing, evidently having just risen from her chair. Her normally neat brown hair was dishevelled, and her nose was red from crying. Pyon quickly crossed the room to her and folded her in his arms.

"Oh, my darling Liz. I'm so, so sorry this has happened. Our lovely girl." He paused and smiled. "By God, though, I'll bet she's giving them a hard time."

Liz snuffled at the joke, and Pyon stood back to take her face in his hands.

"Look, angel, the police there aren't going to sit on this. It's a major embarrassment to them. They're already combing the island, and running enquiries all over the coast. And if these people are cornered, they're not going to make their situation worse by harming her."

"But if they're cornered, they could be dangerous, and use her as a hostage?"

"Hostages are only any use as long as they're alive, so are kidnap victims. Don't worry too much."

"Good God, Christy. Of course I'm worried, and anyway it may not be a kidnap."

"I'm sure it is."

"You know you didn't want Laura to go and see Gianni and Caterina; you don't think this has anything to do with Maria?"

"Maria's family are tricky, but they're not that crazy."

Liz wriggled her hands free of Pyon's and walked across the room to look out on to the park.

"Somehow, though," she said, "I feel that this is all connected with your recent activities. I didn't want to see you three days ago when those awful photos were in the papers. I felt that they were the final insult, and I'm not sure that I can really forgive you, but I certainly won't forgive you if you don't do everything you can to get Laura free."

"Liz, I love her as much as you do, you know that. Of course I'll do everything I can."

"You'd better, Christy Pyon." She turned and looked at him with defiant eyes. "You'd better, or God help you."

Pyon stayed that night at Clonegall House, in a guest bedroom. He left early the next morning for London, then Sardinia.

In the afternoon, Lord and Lady Barnstaple arrived at the great Irish house and, without forewarning, Julian.

TV appeals

Southern Hemisphere's purchase of the Actors' Production Company was due to be completed that week. All the documentation had been drawn up, and both sides wanted to get on with it. Julian, privately, had become suspicious about Johnny Capra's wish for hastiness, but he was reluctant to tell his father in case that put the lid on the whole deal. Anyway, Julian could not put his finger on any one element that was suspect and, he argued, if the deal looked good enough for his father, it was good enough for him.

Then the news of Laura's disappearance exploded like a bomb beneath him. He told the lawyers to hold everything while he went to Europe. They said they understood; it made no difference to them. But Johnny Capra became agitated.

"Don't fuck me about now, you mother," he had said, glad to show his dominance over Julian if not Christy Pyon. But he was persuaded to relent and accept that a kidnapped sister was reasonable grounds for delaying the deal. "Only a few days, mind, or I'm on to de la Tour."

Gloom pervaded Clonegall House.

The only topics of discussion were Laura's plight and, tangentially, Christy Pyon's highly publicised affair.

News reached them, through a liaison at Scotland Yard,

that a demand had been made. There was no doubt about its authenticity, though it bore several signs of an amateur operation. Despite this, the way in which the demand was made was designed for maximum dramatic effect.

A courier had walked into the studio complex of Italian National Television to deliver a videotape to the duty news editor.

After a delay of several hours, while the police and Laura's family were consulted, the tape was shown on news broadcasts throughout Europe and in America.

Laura was seen sitting on a black leather sofa in what looked like a smart urban Italian apartment, though no windows could be seen. On the sofa next to her was an enormous man in a black hood which entirely covered his face apart from two holes for his eyes. He held an automatic pistol a few inches from her temple.

The camera zoomed in clumsily until Laura's face filled the screen. It was a few seconds before she was in focus, then she was prompted to speak.

Her eyes looked steadily into the camera, betraying no fear. She spoke evenly, without expression, delivering rehearsed lines.

"I am Laura Pyon, the daughter of Christy Pyon. I would like to tell my parents that I am unharmed and being well looked after. I am being held by the *Organisazione per Sardegna Libra*. It is impossible to find me, and I will be kept until my father complies with demands made by the OSL for my safe return. The OSL requires $500 million, which they estimate as half my father's personal wealth. They will advise how this is to be paid, and they are not open to negotiation. Any attempts to find me will result in my death, and for each week of delay in meeting the demands, one of my fingers or toes will be removed and sent to my father."

The picture faded and a reporter in Sardinia babbled earnestly into the camera.

Liz, her parents and Julian sat in stunned silence. Julian got up and turned down the volume on the television.

Lord Barnstaple spoke first. "One thing's for sure, Laura

doesn't believe them. I'm absolutely certain she winked as she mentioned the, er . . . toe business."

"You're right," said Julian. "She wasn't at all scared. She couldn't possibly have said all that crap if she thought it was true. These guys have gone for total overkill – half a billion dollars, for Christ's sake! And what the hell is the *Organisazione per Sardegna Libra*?"

"Shut up, Julian," his mother said quietly. "Laura may not have shown it, but she's terrified. She's quite capable of disguising."

Liz was interrupted by the telephone at her side.

It was Pyon calling from Sassari. "Have you seen the broadcast yet?" he asked.

"Yes, just now on the news."

"The police think it's all Mickey Mouse. The kidnappers have been in touch again. They want a sack full of diamonds," – Pyon laughed – "for God's sake, to be dropped down a pothole near Dorgali, halfway down the east coast. And they contacted me directly, not through the police. They want to talk to me first. I've to meet them out at sea, on my own. It's the craziest kidnap I ever heard of."

"For God's sake, Christy, how can you laugh about it? It's Laura's *life* you're talking about. If you fool around with these people, they'll kill her. You must do everything they say."

"Liz, Liz, of course there's a risk, I don't deny it, but I really don't think they know what they're doing."

"All the more reason they may panic and kill her! Look, I'm coming out there. I can't just sit here in Ireland, doing nothing."

"There's nothing you can do here either."

"Oh yes there is. I can make sure that you don't get Laura killed by antagonising these people. Can you organise a plane for me?"

Pyon did not answer for a moment, then, with a sigh, he agreed. "Okay, I'll send the plane to Cork to get you. They'll be in touch when they've a time. But I'd much rather you didn't come."

"Just remember, Christy, there's more than just a deal to

be lost here if you start trying to throw your weight around – there's Laura's life. Please, please promise me you'll do whatever they ask."

"I'll give you my word I'll do everything I can to get Laura back. I *will* get her back, for God's sake."

"I've told you, I'll never forgive you if you don't."

When she had put the phone down, she sat and shook for half a minute. Her parents watched, but did not speak. Julian came and sat on the arm of her chair.

"Don't go, Mum. There's no point. What can you do? We'll have the plane on standby so that the minute they've got her out, you can go and get her. Father's an experienced negotiator, and he's got the police behind him. Just trust him."

"I can't, I can't," Liz wailed. "For him it's a *deal*. But he can't negotiate on the price of his daughter's life. I know he'll let his ego get in the way. He won't let himself be beaten. I *know* what he's like."

Pyon wrapped his thick waterproof jacket around him more tightly against the fierce north-easterly that regularly whips the Sardinian coast. He was five miles off shore now, on his own in a twenty-five foot launch that was not designed for heavy seas.

The kidnappers had been in touch with him by phone. They were not hoaxers. Without access to Laura they could not have known that her first cuddly toy had been a horse called Hercules. He had agreed not to tell the police; he could not afford to upset these people until he was certain who and what he was dealing with.

Pyon looked around in the early light, but could see no other vessel. His navigation was accurate, he was sure, and the time was right. Looking back towards the coast, there was no sign of another approaching craft. He slowed to a few knots, sufficient to keep his position against the running sea, and cursed the events that threatened the most critical deal of his life.

He blamed himself. His carelessness and his fatuous marriage to Maria. He had made so few mistakes in his life, but those few were putting in jeopardy the pinnacle of his ambition.

And in front of his eyes all the time was a vision of Laura.

Laura's wicked, big-eyed two-year-old grin. Laura's chin set in stubborn defiance, only a few weeks before. The indomitable independence which she had inherited from him, which he understood and loved. And which he had no intention of losing.

The wind dropped quickly with the coming day, and his unhappy thoughts were diverted by the sound of a helicopter. He soon saw it, flying low from the east.

The aircraft swung around and circled the launch. Evidently satisfied that it was Pyon, the pilot brought it to hover thirty feet above. A door was opened, and a ladder unfurled. A man in a leather flying jacket clambered out and slowly descended. When he stepped off the last rung, he signalled to the pilot, who took the helicopter back up to a hundred feet, pulled in the ladder and sped off to the south.

"Okay." The man spoke with a strong Italian accent. "We go south too. We've got half an hour."

Pyon inclined his head and turned the boat.

The Italian sat on the bulkhead, facing Pyon, no more than a foot away so that he could be heard over the motor and the hissing spray. "Right, if anything happens to me, the girl is dead."

"Nothing's going to happen to you."

"It better not. My name is Gino. I work for the Gatti family. I organised the kidnapping of your daughter. The Gattis have been unforgivably insulted by what you have done. Your wife is the subject of a public scandal that has nothing to do with her. You have treated her with no respect. You have done it to her mother; you have done it to the memory of her father. You can't do that to any member of the Gatti family and expect no reprisal."

Pyon's face showed no reaction. He continued to steer the boat with his eyes fixed on the heaving waves ahead.

"You people are living in fairyland. Do you know how ridiculous Gian-Battista Gatti would find this if he were alive? Of course the Gattis haven't been insulted. Sure Maria's vanity has taken a bruising, but do you really think she's always been snow-white? She tried to seduce my son, for God's sake. This ransom is a joke. You haven't got a cat in hell's chance of pulling it off. You won't be surprised to hear that I've certainly no intention of throwing half a billion dollars' worth of diamonds down a hole in the cliffs."

"Listen, my friend, we are serious." Gino tried to adopt an air of menace. There was an angry desperation about him which suggested that matters were well out of his control. Pyon guessed that the younger, more impulsive Gattis had taken a pre-emptive initiative, on the spur of the moment and without consultation.

Pyon stared impassively at Gino, and watched his face collapse.

"You know how they are," Gino went on, as if to confirm Pyon's thoughts. "They're crazy. You won't see Laura again, I promise you, unless you do as we ask."

"Give you $500 million worth of diamonds?" Pyon laughed and shook his head.

"Look," Gino said with anguish, "this is not a joke. Okay, the half billion is crazy. They'll take a hundred million, as long as no one knows they agreed to it, but also, you must agree to a Papal annulment of your marriage to Maria, on the grounds that you were committing bigamy in the eyes of the Church. Not right away, that wouldn't look good, but in six months, and you must take all responsibility for it, and you must settle $50 million dollars on her."

Pyon shrugged. "There may not be $50 million for me to settle. Thanks to you fucking idiots, the value of my company has halved in the last two days, and it's still plummeting. The bid for Chemco is completely buggered."

"You were already in trouble because of your black whore," Gino sneered.

Pyon took one hand off the wheel and leaned forward to grab the Italian by his throat.

"Listen to me, you scumbag. Don't you ever talk about her like that. You're not fit to whisper her name."

He pushed the Italian on to his back and released him. Gino slithered across the foredeck and just saved himself from being pitched into the sea by clutching at the lifebelt anchored there. He pulled himself up to face Pyon again.

"You really want your daughter sent back to you in a plastic bag?"

"If anything happens to her, I'll have the lot of you killed," Pyon said calmly. "I'll make you one realistic offer, and it'll be my only offer. Just to save your miserable faces, I'll pay $5 million. I'll also agree to an uncontested annulment in six months, but Maria will have to settle for whatever the courts give her. D'you understand? That's it."

"Five million! They'll never take it."

Pyon continued to look ahead. "Well, there it is."

"If they do," Gino whined, "and our part in this is ever revealed, next time it'll be you who's taken, and it won't be for money."

"Good God! Do you think I want the world to know I did a deal with a bunch of arseholes like you lot? No one's ever going to hear about it from me, that's for sure."

In the distance, just above the horizon, they saw a glint of shining metal before they heard the returning helicopter.

Gino glanced at it nervously. "Okay, Signor Pyon. I'll try and persuade them. You've caused them a lot of harm. But just remember, if they accept this ridiculous offer of yours, all the terms must be met, or . . ." He pulled his finger across his throat.

"Sure, Gino. Sure. But I want your answer within two days, or there's no deal. Understood?"

Laura heard the key turn in the lock, and the bolts being drawn back. She watched the door with horrified fascination. Sooner or later they were going to realise that her father would pay nothing, and that would surely be her death-sentence.

Luca's thin, ferret face appeared round the door. Gino was right behind him.

"Your father doesn't love you too much. Gino's just been with him. You wanna know what he thinks you're worth?"

"I couldn't give a toss," Laura replied, trembling inside.

"Five million dollars, that's all."

Laura nodded her head to one side and looked impressed. "He's offered as much as that, has he? I'm amazed. That's the most you'll get out of him, so you may as well take it. I told you half a billion was straight out of cloud cuckoo land."

"Don't be crazy," Luca sneered. "What do you think we are, some small bandits or something?"

"Some small something, I should say."

"Listen, Gino told him, a hundred million or you're dead."

"Well, you're even more dumb than I thought. If my father's seen you, he'll find out who you are and the minute he knows I'm dead, he'll tell the police."

"You think they'd get anywhere? No body, no nothing to prove it. Just his word. No, that's not a problem." He came right into the room and walked across to the bed where she sat. He took her chin in his hand. "Now, we're going to put your face on television again. You were a big hit last time, all over the world." He grabbed her wrist and jerked her to her feet.

In the main living-room, where she had spent most of the last five days, the makeshift lights and video camera were set up again.

Alphonso stood on the other side of the room, clutching his black hood in one hand, and a gun in the other.

Gino was behind the camera. "Okay, Luca, leave her alone. You want to put some make-up on, look pretty for the camera?" he asked Laura.

"Yeah."

He presented her with an elaborate box of make-up, and a hairbrush.

She spent a few minutes, applying a little colour to her cheeks and eyelids, and brushing her unwashed hair. She needed the time, and the make-up, to give her confidence for the ordeal.

When she had finished, she said, "Okay, who's got the script? I hope it's better than last time."

Luca thrust a sheet of paper at her, and an Italian tabloid dated that day. "You got to hold that up while you speak."

Alphonso took his place on the sofa beside her, shrugged apologetically and put the gun to her temple.

Laura took a deep breath and looked into the camera.

"Okay. Begin," Gino said.

"I am Laura Pyon, daughter of Christy Pyon. My father has made a derisory offer for my return. The *Organisazione per Sardegna Libra* are deeply insulted. Unless the demands we have already made are met within two days, I will lose a finger."

Gino gestured frantically from behind the camera to get her to raise her index finger. With a look of bored embarrassment, she did so.

"I have not been harmed yet, so please, Daddy, could you arrange to pay the money before I am?"

Gino stopped the video camera. "That's good," he said. "Maybe we should charge the television companies, eh, Luca?"

Laura reverted to Italian. "Maybe you should, because you won't get any more out of my father."

"He doesn't want his lovely daughter to die."

Laura looked at the two brothers with disdain. "Frankly, I'd rather die than have you little pricks earn anything out of it."

"Shut your mouth, you dirty bitch," Luca hissed. He took a few paces towards her, but Alphonso held his hand up.

"Leave it, Luca, leave it."

Gino took the cassette from the camera and pushed the equipment to the side of the room. "Fo-fo, when she's had some food, put her back in her room, and don't move from the house. We gotta be careful. Police have been down in Nuoro asking questions."

"Okay, boss." Alphonso nodded as they left. When their footsteps had faded on the path outside, he pulled off his hood and threw it across the room. He stuffed the automatic into his trouser pocket.

"Little pricks," he laughed. "You're right."

Alphonso

Laura had found her guard to be unexpectedly kind. He had taken to letting her wander untethered about the two rooms, the small kitchen and bathroom. At nights he slept on the sofa, but before that he would chat to Laura for hours, or watch the television with her. He asked her to teach him English, and he was intrigued by what she told him of her experiences around the world.

It emerged that he had not much regard for his bosses. They had always treated him as if he owed them his life. Up until then he had been happy to go along with it. He was always fed and housed and given plenty of pocket money. It had simply never occurred to him to upset the status quo and defy them.

But at first he had been puzzled, then impressed with Laura's treatment of them, even though she was at a complete disadvantage, and, physically, at their mercy. He had begun to admire her uncrushable spirit. Beyond this, he thought she was one of the loveliest women he had ever met.

Alphonso continued to smile at his small, bold captive. "Let's eat," he invited.

"What is there?" Laura asked, relaxed and matter-of-fact now the brothers had gone.

"Come and choose."

They went into the kitchen, where a deep freeze was packed with meat, vegetables, sauces, milk and bread. In a cupboard next to it, there were piles of pasta, tinned tomatoes, herbs and salami – most of the things to be found in any Italian larder.

"You deserve a rest, Fo-fo. I'll cook dinner tonight."

"Hey, great idea! I'll get some wine and we'll make a party of it."

Laura gathered what she needed to produce as good a meal as she could. She relished the bizarreness of cooking for a giant man who a short while before had been holding a gun to her head. But her hands trembled as she sorted pans and prepared the food. The bravado which Alphonso so much admired in her disguised a deep fear and the unbearable doubt that her father would concede anything to her paranoid kidnappers.

But she was convinced now that at least Alphonso would not hurt her. They had spent five days together, alone except for the two visits the brothers had made to video-tape her "appeals". The hope was growing within her that she might be able to persuade him to help her. So far, though, she had been careful not to test his loyalty to Gino and Luca too obviously or too soon.

When Alphonso had gone to get the wine – from a store room in another part of the house, Laura assumed – he had not bothered to lock the door behind him as he normally did. When he returned and came into the kitchen, she looked up and smiled, unthreatened, like a young wife cooking fondly for a husband returning from work.

They sat at a marble-topped table in the main room, on chairs with tubular, chrome frames. Alphonso ate appreciatively.

"You cook well, like an Italian woman," he mumbled through a mouthful. He poured wine into two glasses, and lifted one to his mouth with a wink.

Laura took a drink as well and the light Sardinian wine nourished her confidence.

"It's easy with all the right ingredients. Where did all this food come from?" she asked.

"I had to go and buy a truck full of stuff the evening before the boys came to get you."

"I'm amazed they thought that far ahead. Is it a long way to any shops from here?"

Alphonso laughed. "I'm not supposed to tell you, but," he heaved his shoulders, "about thirty kilometres."

"Where are we, then?"

"I don't know the name of the place. It's up in the mountains. This valley is completely empty. There's only one way in, and the boys did a deal with the local guys to guard it. They're going to get some of the money." He stopped, suddenly embarrassed.

Laura persisted. "But whose place is this?"

"It's Gino's, I think. His mother was from Nuoro and he bought it some time ago."

"What's it used for, then?"

"I don't know. A bit of hunting, maybe. I never came here before. It just looks like a heap from the outside. It's all falling down except for these rooms. There's a generator just up the hillside, in a cave, and there's water from a spring. But from outside, you can never see any lights on in the house. Look," he gestured around, "there are no windows in any of these rooms. That's why they're sure you won't be found. None of the locals who know about this place are going to talk. They're too scared."

"Do you often have to do this kind of thing?"

"No. Usually I just drive the cars, and Gino likes me to come with him to meetings and things. I have to stand and watch his back. But no one ever tries anything. Most of the business they do for the boss is legitimate."

"Why have they decided to become kidnappers now, then?"

Alphonso looked at her for a moment. With a slight shrug, he appeared to come to a decision. "I'm not supposed to tell you who the boys work for, but what the hell, you're going to find out sooner or later. Just don't tell them I told you, okay?"

"Okay," Laura said, wondering what difference the identity of her kidnappers would make.

"It's the Gattis. The family of your father's wife."

Laura was dumbfounded. It had crossed her mind that they might be involved, but she had dismissed the possibility as being too remote, even for the excitable Gattis. They were, after all, the owners of a substantial and, as Alphonso had said, legitimate shipping business.

And as she turned the knowledge over in her mind, her

fears increased. This made her situation worse. She had not been taken just for the money. She had been abducted to settle a score. The price her father was to pay could well be her life.

She gazed at Alphonso and, this time, he did see the fear in her eyes.

"But Fo-fo, they must be crazy. Surely my father will know it's them?"

"Sure he does. But don't worry too much. They don't want to kill you, I'm certain. They just want to make him pay, and to release Maria from her marriage to him."

"But he won't pay! No more than he's offered, and God knows that's more than I expected. My father hates being backed into a corner. It's the worst possible way to negotiate with him."

"Even for his daughter's life?"

Laura shook her head as tears seeped into the corner of her eyes. "God knows. I wouldn't count on it."

Alphonso put his hand across the table and wrapped her hand in his huge fist. "Don't worry, little beauty. I may not be so smart, but I'm the muscle round here. Whatever else they do, I won't let them kill you."

An ill wind

Ken Newberry parked his Jaguar in his space in a Grosvenor Square car park and walked blithely in the sunshine to his office in the Southern Hemisphere building. Laura's kidnapping had been an unforeseen stroke of luck.

Newberry was, in fact, rather fond of Laura; she was the only person he knew who could argue with Pyon and survive. But there was no question about it, whoever had taken her had done Newberry a big favour.

SHR's price, already heavily depressed by Pyon's naked beach activities, had been hammered almost into oblivion by the world-wide publicity given to the ransom demands.

The support party was showing signs of serious panic and disintegration. Al Souf, Jackson and Weintraub between them had lost more than fifty million on their SHR shares. To compound this, the holdings they had built up in Chemco had also diminished in value, as the chances of Southern's takeover looked increasingly unlikely, and Chemco's own price had dropped back to its pre-bid level.

Ken, though, was happy. He had sold every single SHR and Chemco share he had, right at the top of the market. Now SHR's price stood at $1.50, less than half their asset value. When they reached $1.00, he would start buying again.

There was promise from another quarter. He had phoned Jeremy Fielder's office the evening before and had been given some interesting new information. Fielder had just got back from the States, from San Francisco.

Ken had looked for a connection, and quickly found one. A group of Chemco's AIDS vaccine guinea-pigs, about fifty of them, were being monitored in San Francisco.

He judged that Chemco's price could take a sharper tumble in the not too distant future.

In his office, Newberry phoned Lenny Shemilt.

"Hello, Lenny. What have you been up to, you naughty boy? I've been trying to get you since nine o'clock last night."

"Visiting my grandmother. What do you want?"

"Can we meet, sharpish?"

"It had better be urgent. I'm knackered."

"You'll be glad you came."

"Okay. Usual place in half an hour?"

"Yeah."

Shemilt strolled from Carlos Place through the quiet leafy gardens behind the Jesuit church in Farm Street. He gave a convincing smile of surprise when he saw Ken Newberry approach from the opposite direction. They shook hands and exchanged some small talk – two friends in a chance meeting – before sitting on a bench tucked away beneath a tall plane tree.

"D'you have any Chemco left?"

"Yeah. Far too bloody much of the stuff." Shemilt's Levantine sibilance emphasised his demotic English.

"Dump them now," Newberry said. "You can buy them back very cheap next week."

"But will they come back up again?"

"Eventually. They're bound to."

"Eventually, everything's bound to. Still, I'll dump what I've got. At least I unloaded Southern in time – especially with this crazy ransom business. Pyon's got to be up the shit creek now. What about his other friends?"

"They're nervous. Of course al Souf pretends he isn't, but Morry's running around like a chicken without a head."

"Who the hell are these people who have got Pyon's girl? Five hundred million dollars? It's rubbish," he said disparagingly, as though it was Pyon's doing.

"They've got a bit of front, haven't they?" Newberry laughed. "No one seems to know what this organisation of Sardinia Libra is. A bunch of Mafia jack-the-lads, I should think. Pyon won't give them a pot to piss in. Pity about the girl, though; I always liked her. Still, as long as they keep putting her on telly pleading for the money, Southern's price'll go on tumbling."

"What a fuck-up, eh?" Shemilt smiled.

"That all depends which way you look at it, dunnit?" Newberry said with a smug grin.

Natalie

On the evening after Laura was taken from the house in Sardinia, the news had not reached Mauritius.

Reverend Mother walked calmly across the lawn of coarse, springy grass among the flamboyants and banyan trees in the old gardens of the convent at Curepipe. Beside her, with longer strides, walked the dejected Natalie Felix.

"It's not for me to judge you, Natalie," the nun said quietly. "God will show you the right way in his own time. I believe you. You love the man, you want his children, he makes you happy. All these are in themselves good things. But he already has a wife in the eyes of God, two in the eyes of the world, and four children. He may not be a wicked man, but he must be thoughtless and selfish to do what he has done to those people. But I am not judging you.

"However, the parents of our girls cannot expect them to be taught by someone whose naked body, engaged in a private, sacred act that should only take place between husband and wife, has been shown in newspapers all over the world. We cannot condone it. You understand that, I know, don't you, Natalie?"

Natalie nodded, and bit her lip. To have the love and tenderness there was between her and Pyon described like this, by this good woman, was painful. Her mother had been less forgiving and her father could barely bring himself to speak to her. But Natalie had prayed that she would not lose her job. She prayed that the children would not be encouraged to despise her now, as if she were some kind of criminal – a fallen woman to be pitied.

"But Mother, it doesn't seem fair that to love someone should be a sin. We were always taught that it was good to love."

"There is a difference between love and lust, my child."

"I know that. Do you think I've had any other relationships like this? Do you think they just come and go? They don't. This is the only one I've had. I've been so happy with him. I know he's not a saint, but I promise you, Mother, he is a good person. Sometimes, though, it's as if he were two people and maybe one of those people is bad, but he knows that, and I think he longs to get rid of that person; but that's very hard to do. When he was here last week, he said that he wanted to marry me and live here. And then this horrible man came and tricked you and my mother into saying where I was. It will be very difficult for Christy now. He phoned me to say it made no difference. But whatever happens, I trust him."

"How could he marry you and live here?" the nun asked simply. "He's already failed two other women, and maybe others besides. You must be realistic. In five or ten years he would probably have gone."

"No, Mother, he won't. I know that he won't let me down. I'm very sad that I can't teach my children any more. I've

loved it, and I think I've helped them. But I do understand.
Just so long as you believe me when I tell you that I know
I'm not wrong."

The nun stopped and turned to face Natalie. She took
hold of both her hands and squeezed.

"I do believe you, Natalie, and the children will miss you.
We won't refer to what has happened, and if ever you want
a reference for your gifts as a teacher I will offer it gladly.
I know you have it in you to give a great deal. But I don't
think there's any more I can say. So, God bless you, Natalie,
and may He guide you to wisdom and happiness."

With a gentle smile, Reverend Mother released Natalie's
hands, and walked away towards the convent.

Natalie stood for a while, gazing with misty eyes at the
serene gardens she knew so well. Slowly, she walked back
towards the gates, down the drive where she had first waited
for Pyon to come and take her to lunch.

How much had changed. How much she had learned, and
how much she had experienced since then.

Outside in the road stood the black Range Rover,
incriminating symbol of her altered circumstances. But
the material things that were the by-products of Pyon's
obsession with winning meant nothing to her, though no
one else believed that. Her mother, her old friends, her
colleagues at the convent all assumed that Pyon's wealth
must be a factor in her attraction to him. But it was not, any
more than his shirt or his shoes or the hair on his chest. His
wealth was simply one element in his persona. Pyon would
have been every bit as impressive to her if he had nothing;
it was that inherent bigness that she admired.

She clambered into the vehicle and, resolutely, drove back
to her parents' bungalow in Quatre Bornes.

"Maman, don't worry. I'll go. You won't have to suffer the
embarrassment of seeing me around. If you can't understand
that what happened was something I'm not a bit ashamed
of, then we have nothing to say. Anyway, you've known
perfectly well that I've stayed on *Ile Vermont* with Christy.
You never objected before. It's only now all your friends
know that you're complaining. It's so hypocritical."

"It isn't only me who's embarrassed. Obviously it's very difficult for your father. He finds it hard enough to get support from the Hindus without having his daughter getting into this kind of trouble. Anyway, I did object before, but at least I didn't have hundreds of people looking at me in church, feeling sorry for me, talking about you as if you were a *putain*."

Mrs Felix looked at Natalie, and her heart filled with sorrow that her good and beautiful daughter should have become a source of pity among her friends. "I don't want you to go. I just want you to stop seeing him. He belongs in a different world to you. He's famous and rich. He can do what he likes, but it's different for people like us."

"It isn't. Christy's a human being, exactly the same. Things make him happy or sad. He cares about me as much as I do about him. I teach him things; he asks me what I think, and he listens to what I say. I'm not going to give him up. He probably needs me now more than he's ever done since I first met him. I'm not going to let him down. I'll stay on *Ile Vermont*, so that he can reach me when he wants to. But this time, please don't tell anyone I'm there."

Her mother looked at her and tears welled in her black eyes. "I don't want to lose you, Natalie."

"You won't, Maman, just as long as you try to understand. I've thought about what I'm doing, and I know it's the right thing. If I have to go away from Mauritius, I'll come and see you first, I promise."

Her mother was resigned. "I trust you, Natalie, and I'll pray for you every day." She stretched up to kiss her daughter, and squeezed both her hands.

Natalie returned her kiss, turned abruptly and walked out of the little house, down the short path to the garden gate. Without looking back, she climbed into the Range Rover and drove off in a cloud of dust.

Negotiations

In Sardinia, the usual cluster of reporters was waiting for Pyon outside the hotel he had made his headquarters. He considered going in by the service doors, but decided to face them. As his car drew up, he opened the back door and was out almost before it had come to a halt.

"What are you going to do now, Christy?" they shouted.

"Are you going to give them the money?"

"Are the police getting anywhere?"

Pyon calmly stood his ground, like a big rock in a choppy sea. He had only to lift his eyebrows for the clamour to die down.

"You'll have to ask the police how much progress they're making. As to the money, we are in contact with the kidnappers and negotiations are going on. I have made it clear that I will not pay anything at all until my daughter is safe."

"But they're not going to release her without the money, Pyon. Don't you care what happens to Laura? What does her mother have to say about it?"

Pyon rounded on the English woman who had asked the question. "D'you think mothers have a monopoly on parental affection? It's because I love my daughter that I won't part with a halfpenny until I've got her back alive." He held his hands up either side of his head. "And that's all I've to say right now. Thank you, gentlemen, ladies."

He swept through them like a bull through a flock of sheep.

Inside, the manager was waiting for him and ushered him to an empty lift.

Upstairs, alone in the drawing-room of his suite, he kicked off his shoes, flopped into a big leather swivel chair and stretched his legs on to a stool. From here he could gaze out through a wall of glass towards a torpid sea, stained pink and gold by the setting sun.

The day had not gone well.

Liz had telephoned him in the morning. She had seen Laura's second televised plea.

At first, her voice was even, as controlled as it always was. As Pyon had tried to tell her that he must negotiate, that he had to state publicly that he would not pay, her voice faltered as she could no longer hold back the tears.

"Christy," she was sobbing now, "they're going to hurt her. They mean it, can't you see that? For God's sake, you're not dealing with some company you're trying to buy cheap. This is Laura's *life*." Her words were lost in a tearful moaning.

Pyon had known that she would react like this to his style of negotiation. But only he knew with whom he was dealing; to reveal this aspect to anyone, including even Liz, could be fatal to Laura.

"Liz," Pyon said firmly, "you must trust me."

"I don't. You won't pay because you don't want to be seen to give in, and tarnish the reputation of Pyon the hard man. I know it, and if you're honest, you know it. I've had enough of your self-obsession, now that it's putting at risk your own family's lives. I warned you, Christy, if you didn't do everything they asked to get Laura free, you'd regret it." Liz's voice was calmer now, in control and with a sharp edge to it. "And by God, you're going to."

With a crackle, the line from Ireland had gone dead.

That was this morning. Then the kidnappers had been in touch, not with the police or Pyon, but with the Rome television studios.

The message was, $500 million or no Laura.

Pyon knew for certain they would settle for a fraction of that. But they had a lot of face to lose. It was their egos, not his, that were fouling up negotiations.

But to his intense frustration, they had made no arrangements for his response. Pyon could not simply arrange to meet the Gattis. Maria had flown back to Amalfi with the children, and as far as he could tell, her brothers were there too, or in Naples. But to take the initiative in meeting them now, and risk anyone – the police or the press – speculating about their involvement would be the surest way to kill Laura.

Pyon continued to gaze at the sea. The strength ebbed from his body. For the first time in his life he was helpless.

He picked up the telephone from a table beside him, and dialled the *Ile Vermont*.

"Hello, angel. I was hoping you'd be there."

"Christy. Thank God you've rung. I've been waiting here, hoping you would ring for the last four days. When I heard about Laura, I tried everywhere to get you, but no one would tell me where you were."

"I'm sorry, darlin', I should have rung you before. I'm in Sardinia, trying to get some sense from these creeps who have her."

"What's happening?"

Pyon sighed. He was not in the habit of saying exactly what he meant. He forced himself to tell the truth.

"It's not going well. I'm sure I can get her out, but for the moment they're sticking out for a hundred million, and I don't have a hundred million."

"The news said five hundred million. It sounds completely crazy!"

"It is completely crazy. I can't tell you why, and I can't tell anyone else. The rest of my family think I'm holding out because I won't pay. I've already made some commitments, but I can't talk about them. It's a very tricky situation. And business," he laughed, "that's become a farce. My company is worth a quarter of what it was two weeks ago. I've let a lot of people down."

"Oh, Christy. I've never heard you so miserable."

"No, life isn't much fun at the moment. But what about you, though? Has it been terrible for you?"

"I can't stay at home, unless I promise my parents that I won't see you again, so I thought I'd better come here until you told me what you want me to do. And of course, I've lost my job at the convent."

"That's terrible. You loved it so much. I'll bet the kids will be sorry."

"I think they will be. I understand Reverend Mother's decision, though I was very sad about it, but there's nothing I can do. All I want to do now is help you."

"Just knowing you think that helps. I won't be able to come to *Ile Vermont* for some time. I must stay here until Laura's free, then I'll have to go to London and the States to sort out the bloody messes there. If you came to Paris, it would be easy for me to see you. Would you mind staying there? I'll get an apartment organised, to give you a bit of privacy. You understand, don't you, that in the circumstances, it's better if we're not seen in public too much."

"Yes, I understand. I'll come to Paris. At least I'll be nearer."

"Great. Get Min to fix you a flight and book you into the Meurice for the moment. I'll ring you there in a couple of days. I promise I'll come and see you as soon as I can. D'you promise you'll be all right?"

"Of course. But try and come soon; you sound miserable, and for once I might be able to do something to help you."

"There's no doubt about that, angel. I can't wait to see you again."

Pyon put the telephone down feeling happier. It was an unfamiliar pleasure to need someone, and to have that need fulfilled.

More positive now, he dialled Jeremy Fielder in London.

"Jeremy? Christy Pyon."

"Hello, Mr Pyon."

"Well?"

Fielder knew that Pyon was not asking after his health. "I've set things in motion in San Francisco, quite cheaply, actually."

"Good. But hold it up until our shares have bottomed out. I reckon they'll start rising as soon as I get Laura back."

"When might that be, Mr Pyon?"

"Soon enough. You've not told anyone about the plan?"

"Only Leo Jackson, and it was his scheme anyway."

"Sure. He's not going to tell anyone either. I'll let you know when to get it off the ground. Goodbye, Jeremy, and keep up the good work."

Julian managed to dissuade his mother from going to Sardinia.

"You'll only feel worse, being near it all. There's nothing you can do. I'll stay in Clonegall with you until Laura's freed."

And he had, for seven days, while news of Pyon's "negotiations" filtered back, through the police and through the television news.

Liz had their main telephone line disconnected and relied

305

on the modem line. The reporters who had turned up on the doorstep had been gleefully discouraged from staying by various of Tom Brophy's younger, fitter nephews. Cushioned from the world outside by her family and friends in the scantily populated pasture land below the Wicklow hills, Liz subsided into a state of half-life. A diminished sense of time protected her emotions from the more vicious realities.

Only when she spoke to her ex-husband, on whom she was relying for Laura's deliverance, did the horribleness of events become sharp and inescapable. In her mind, Pyon became not simply one element in the drama, but the prime cause of it. He bore all responsibility for Laura's abduction.

When she finally told him over the phone that he would regret his reluctance to meet the kidnappers' demands, she meant it. And delivering her judgment brought the world sharply back into focus. Here, at last, was something she could do.

When Julian spoke to Johnny Capra, to tell him that they would have to delay the purchase of APC indefinitely, until Laura was found, Capra had issued an ultimatum: sign within seven days, or the deal is off.

"Do it," Liz said. "You have your father's power of attorney to sign, don't you?"

Julian nodded without looking at her. He was not sure of her motives. He and Liz were walking back from the river across the broad meadow where the mares summered.

Liz went on, "Then use it. I hope you make a success of it, but frankly, if you lose the bloody lot, I shall laugh."

"Of course I'm not going to lose it. I admit that there's something odd about Johnny Capra's urgency, but," he shrugged, "Pa didn't spot it, so I suppose it can't be too serious."

"Look, Julian, get over there now. I'll be all right. I feel a lot better now that I know where I am. I've done all I can to persuade your father, and he's taken no notice. I've reached the end of my tether with him. I've forgiven him every bloody transgression, every bit on the side, every insult I've suffered through his oversized, indiscriminate libido, and

I'm going to make him realise he's taken me for granted for too long."

"Mum, for God's sake, that's not going to get Laura back."

"Laura's only hope now is luck. That's why I'm so livid with your father. The daughter of one of the self-professed richest men in the world should not be relying on luck."

"Dad's never claimed to be one of the richest men in the world."

"He's never denied it, either. Anyway, he won't be for long."

"Don't do anything too stupid, Ma. Why not wait and see if he gets Laura out?"

"Julian, I've got to focus my mind on something, and giving your father a bit of the comeuppance he deserves will do very well."

They had reached a gate which gave on to the drive up to the house. Julian went forward to open it. He stopped when he reached it and turned back to face his mother. "I've never heard you being vindictive before, and I'm not sure that it suits you."

"When you have a daughter kidnapped, tell me how you feel."

"All right, I know what you're saying. Laura's my sister. She and I may not be similar, but we're close enough. I don't want to lose her either, you know. And I reckon Dad's playing it cool because that's the best way to be sure of getting her back. Whatever else you may think of him, he must be one of the world's best negotiators."

Liz looked at him witheringly. "I'm surprised at you, of all people. This isn't about some bloody old horse in the market, for heaven's sake." Her voice began to shake.

Julian did not persist. "Okay, if you're going to be all right, I'll go over and finish the deal."

Before Julian left for Los Angeles that evening, he drove up to see Tom Brophy in his three-roomed, whitewashed cottage.

"Can I come in and have a word, please, Tom?"

"O'course you can. Will you have a drop of Paddy's?"

Julian disguised his reluctance. "Yes. Thanks very much."
Tom poured half a tumblerful of the gold-orange liquid.
"Now, what's it you want?"

"I'm going back to the States for a week or so. My mother
is convinced that she can manage without me here. I'm not
so sure. She's feeling very bitter about my father."

"Well, why wouldn't she? It's a pile o' money they're
wanting, for sure, but what's that to a lovely young girl's
life?"

"I don't think it's as simple as that. And anyway, he
just doesn't have that kind of money. The papers always
exaggerate these things to make their stories as big as they
can. But I still think Dad will get her out."

Tom shook his head. "It's a terrible situation. All the
village are praying, but the Almighty is going to need a
little more co-operation from your father."

"Well, I don't know. What I wanted to ask you was to
keep a close eye on my mother. She trusts you most of all
the people here. Would you pop in and see her from time
to time, and just say something – anything to give her a bit
of hope?"

"But I would anyway, Julian. She's a special woman, is
your mother."

"Thanks, and if she says she's going to London, please
try and talk her out of it somehow."

Tom arrived as normal at the stud at half-past seven next
morning. He led eight mares out to the paddocks, and did
their boxes, before going up to the house for his first tea
and biscuits.

When he reached the kitchen, he told the housekeeper
that he was going to find Mrs Pyon first.

"You'll not find her here. Mick drove her down to Cork
this morning to take the plane to London."

"Oh, Jaysus. I promised young Julian I'd not let her go."

"And how were you going to stop her, you old fool?
You're a stud groom, not her nanny."

"She shouldn't be going off to London, not with all this
going on. She should have stayed here, where we can look
after her."

"Well, she's gone, and I haven't seen her looking so sure of herself since Laura was taken."

Outside Terminal Two at Heathrow, Maria, the second Mrs Christy Pyon, had a Rolls and a chauffeur waiting to meet her. They swept up the M4 towards London, a world apart from the thousands of commuters crawling in the other direction at the end of the day. They glided up on to the raised length of road that snaked into the heart of London. The early autumn evening sun was behind them. It turned the glass-clad office blocks that lined the motorway into pillars of dazzling red and gold.

But Maria, sunk into the soft leather of the car, saw none of this. Her mind was filled with the punishing of Christy Pyon. And the damage she could do with the help of her new ally.

Councils of war

For a second time, Elizabeth Pyon waited in the drawing-room of the Mayfair house for Maria Pyon.

This time she knew who was coming, and she wanted to see her.

Not because she liked the woman whose existence had at first tormented, then deeply irritated her for fifteen years, but because here was another woman with as much reason and an even greater wish to do down their common husband. There was already, she felt, a firm bond between them, unalike as they were.

This time when the doorbell rang, Liz went down to open it herself and greet her guest.

For a moment, Maria stood on the doorstep and the two women appraised each other.

Maria saw a quietly dressed Englishwoman of old-fashioned, confident good looks. There was an air of calm determination about her which was reassuring.

Liz saw a ripe, flamboyant Mediterranean beauty, who radiated egotism and a strong-willed resourcefulness. She opened the door wide and gestured her in.

They did not speak on the way up. In the drawing-room Liz said, "Martini?"

Maria shook her head. "No, thank you. Just coffee."

"I'm afraid I'll have to go to the kitchen and do it myself at this time of night. Come with me. We'll talk there."

They went down, and settled round a square pine table in what seemed like a large country kitchen. Herbs and hop-bines hung over a big black range. The elm chairs in which they sat were rustic and comfortable. It seemed an unlikely place for two women to hold a council of war.

Of the people who were involved in Pyon's deal, apart from Adnan al Souf, Liz knew Leo Jackson best. She arranged to see him first.

Maria was staying, for convenience, in the Dorchester. Liz took Leo there to meet her in her suite. When he arrived, he did not know who Maria was or what he had been summoned to discuss with these two women. But he was happy; he fancied both of them.

Liz introduced Maria, and Leo's jaw dropped before he could bring it under control. He had often wondered about the second Mrs Pyon, whom Pyon had so carefully and for so long avoided introducing to his English connections.

Leo was impressed, and his instincts quickly gave him an inkling of why Liz and Maria might be together.

"Poor old Christy has finally overstepped the mark, then." The statement was half a question.

Liz nodded.

"Presumably," Leo said, "it's his very public reluctance to come up with anything for Laura that's upset you. God, I don't blame you. I've seen Laura on television both times. She's a bloody brave girl, Liz." He put a kindly hand on Liz's arm. "Anything I can do to help you to persuade Pyon to get her free, I will."

"It isn't only that," Maria said.

"And I'm not giving up hope on Laura," Liz added, "but

whatever happens, I don't think I can ever forgive Pyon for doing this to her, or to me."

"So what do you want me to do?" asked Leo.

Liz took control. "Let's sit down with a drink first."

Maria found what they wanted on a drinks table, and the three of them settled into the big, squashy sofas with which the Dorchester provides its guests.

"Christy has taken both Maria and me for granted for a very long time. We've both put up with a great deal, but the events of the past fortnight are the last straw. I'm certain that the awful publicity over the Mauritian girl triggered Laura's kidnap. The papers were full of exaggerated stories about how rich he is. You've probably got as much idea as I have about the value of Pyon's various businesses and assets, but I doubt if they're half the billion dollars the media claim."

Leo shrugged. "It's impossible to say. One never knows how much he's borrowing at any one time. At the moment he's stretched because he's bought a pile of Chemco, and I'm afraid that deal is going very badly. I know, I've been helping him."

"That's why I wanted to see you, Leo." Liz paused, and stood up to emphasise the announcement she was going to make. "We don't want to start anything just yet, because that could jeopardise Laura's chances, but, ultimately, we, both of us, want to see Pyon ruined." She looked hard at Leo to let her words sink in. "We want to deprive him of Chemco, but before that, we want to stretch him beyond his limits. I've known Christy for over thirty years, and acquisitiveness is like a disease for him. He's obsessional and compulsive in his drive. That's why he so often wins. But I've never seen him quite so determined as he is over Chemco. It must be killing him to be sitting in Sardinia, dealing with the police there. I think the only reason he's stayed there is that if he left, the press would make such an outcry Southern's price would fall even further."

"I don't know if that's fair, Liz . . ."

"Well I do, Leo. You can't defend his position, and you know it."

"All right, Liz, but as you say, we can't do much at the moment, for Laura's sake. Anyway, things are bad enough as it is. It seems to me that the first thing to do is to try to get him to pay up something for Laura. Obviously the demand for half a billion is just a joke, a traditional Mediterranean way of beginning negotiations. I would say that they'll probably take no more than a tenth of that – still fifty million – a horrible lot of money, but I should think Pyon could manage that if he had to, without going belly up. Mind you, it would probably kill his Chemco deal stone dead, if it isn't already."

"That's why he won't pay, I'm sure of it."

"Liz, I think he loves his daughter very much, maybe even to the extent of blowing this deal."

"If losing Chemco is the price he is prepared to pay for getting Laura back, then I've misjudged him, and I would forgive him." She glanced at the quick flash of irritation in Maria's eyes. Liz's voice and body sagged with bleak hopelessness. "But I know I'm right."

When Natalie Felix arrived at the Meurice, there was a message waiting for her from Pyon.

The next morning, she was on a plane to Rome. From Leonardo da Vinci airport, she took a taxi, having made sure first that she had not been recognised by the driver, to a farmhouse among the vineyards outside Frascati. She was expected, and greeted warmly by an old Italian man and his wrinkled, smiling wife who appeared to be housekeeper and guardian of the place.

Pyon left the television studios in Rome by a back entrance and climbed into a car which he had rented and arranged to be there. His televised appeal to the kidnappers was allegedly going out live in twenty minutes' time, but it was already on tape. There was a small group of reporters outside the gate, but they were not expecting him yet and took no notice of the anonymous little blue Fiat Uno.

Pyon made a few manoeuvres on the road heading south out of Rome. When he was confident that he was not being followed, he put his foot down and headed for Frascati.

Natalie was sitting on a terrace, under a tottering pergola covered in hoary old vines. She leaped to her feet as soon as the little car drove into the courtyard, and rushed forward to fling her arms around Pyon as he clambered out.

"What a welcome, my little angel." Pyon laughed and lifted her off the ground to kiss her.

"Oh, Christy, I didn't know I could be so glad to see someone. I've wanted to be with you so much."

He put her back on her feet. "Just seeing you is all the help I need."

"It must be horrible for you. Not knowing if you'll ever see Laura again."

"I think I will see her soon, but I'll tell you about that later. First, let's go in and see about some food. I don't think I've eaten for a day."

Lucia, the housekeeper, lit up her face with a great smile when she saw Pyon. For years he had come to this simple house when he wanted to be alone for a few days. But since he had bought *Ile Vermont*, he had not been back. Now the old woman was thrilled to see him again.

Of course, she had read about Pyon in all the papers recently, but as far as she was concerned, he was blameless. She was glad to be party to his secret assignation with the beautiful young girl who seemed so innocent and so far away from Pyon's world of money, yachts and powerful people.

In an airy, low-ceilinged dining-room, she served them with a big dish of gnocchi in a thick, garlicky sauce, and a salad of tiny, sweet tomatoes. Between them she placed a bottle of Montefalco, dark red Umbrian wine, and discreetly left the room.

A breeze rustled the vines and the cypress trees outside the open window, and fluttered the faded floral curtains. Small birds chirruped and squabbled on the terrace and the windowsill, and the sun shone on the gently climbing Albani hills.

In this far-away peace, with Natalie, Pyon found that he wanted to tell the truth, wanted to regress to the honest, upright child he had once been.

Natalie listened while he told her about all the emotions he had experienced in the past week. How he had been forced to reassess the priorities by which he lived.

"This television thing I did today was rubbish. But the police wanted me to do it. They wanted the people who have Laura to be told publicly one more time that I won't pay. Of course, they know that I will pay something. I've offered five million already, but I admit that up till now, I've been horse-trading. Now I've come to a decision, and it's you that's shown me that I have the option. If I have to pay fifty million, I will. It'll more or less kill the deal I've spent the last two years of my life planning, and I'll probably never get the chance again, but" – Pyon heaved his big shoulders and a smile spread up one side of his mouth – "what the hell! I'll have my daughter back and I'll still have you. That'll do."

Natalie gazed at him with a smile. "That makes me so happy. The side of you that does business and wants to do deals all the time, that's the part I could never share with you. To make enough money to live, I understand that, but to be making money which you don't need, as a sort of statement, to show how much cleverer, or tougher you are than the next man, that's something I could never be happy about. Of course your daughter is worth losing your deal for. You can live without helicopters and planes and houses everywhere."

"Hey, angel, don't rush me. You'll have to give me time to get used to the idea of poverty. Anyway, I didn't say I'd lose everything, just this one big deal that was important to me. Listen, I'd still try and pull it off if I could, but . . . It's just that I don't mind so much if I don't. I'm glad that makes you happy. It'll make Laura's mother happy too. She's convinced I won't hand over a penny." He glanced sharply at her. "You don't mind that I'm pleased to make her happy as well?"

"Of course not." She smiled and shook her head. "I know that you love me, and underneath all your swagger you're not such a lousy man."

Pyon sighed. "I can think of too many people who would not agree with you and, I'm ashamed to say, not without justification."

Laura and Alphonso, her gaoler, watched her father on television together.

She strained to catch every nuance in his face and his voice, to find some evidence in the features and gestures she knew so intimately that he was not telling the truth.

But she saw none. Her father was telling her captors and the world that he would pay nothing until she was freed.

She knew that was untrue. Gino had told her with complete certainty that Pyon had offered the five million. Perhaps he had now retracted that offer. She could believe that he might do that out of sheer pique at their effrontery in turning him down.

She did not hate her father for the stand he was taking, it was what she had expected, but she had harboured some hope that he might relent. Now, she felt certain he was going to sit it out. And she was frightened.

She glanced at Alphonso, and her heart skipped. He was looking at her with a speculative half-smile and in the dark, kindly eyes, no doubt about it, was real concern.

His smile broadened, and he looked back at the television, where a reporter was wrapping up their latest instalment in the geat kidnap drama.

He chuckled. "The little pricks." And turned his eyes back to her. "Do you think if Gino and Luca gave me the push, your father would give me a job?"

Quite spontaneously, Laura leaned over and tried to put her arms around his huge torso to hug him.

"I'll kill him if he doesn't!" she laughed.

Alphonso was embarrassed by this physical display. With an awkward shrug, like an elephant with an itch on its shoulders, he freed himself from her arms and stood up.

"Hey, don't do that," he said coyly, "I'm not used to girls doing that sort of thing. It's just that I like you, and why should those Gattis think they can keep you here? Who the hell do they think they are? And I'm supposed to guard you, but they never asked me what I thought about it. They're not coming back until tomorrow. I'm going to take you out of here tonight."

"But Alphonso, they'll *kill* you," Laura suddenly thought.

Alphonso chuckled. "Those little pricks couldn't kill a mouse. Anyway, I can go and live somewhere else. Maybe your father can give me a job in America. All the people in Naples, they just think I'm some dumb clod who does whatever Gino tells me. Well, I'm not now." He gave a decisive, satisfied nod. "Come on. There isn't a car here, so we'll have to walk the first few kilometres. We'll go over the hills, so the local boys don't see us."

"Do you think I'd better disguise myself or something?" Laura asked.

He thought about that. "Yeah, sure. You could pretend to be a boy. There's a few old clothes out in the barn." He stopped, doubtfully. "They're dirty, though."

"God, that doesn't matter. If I'm going to get away from here, I don't care if I have to smother myself in pigshit."

Alphonso roared an approving laugh, and they got ready to go.

Over the hills

It was a little after midday. The September sun was high, and still hot, but three thousand feet up in the Gennargentu Mountains, a steady wind took the edge off it.

Alphonso went out of the house first, to make sure that Gino and Luca were not turning up unexpectedly.

In the empty valley, the only things that moved were the coarse broom and the scrubby bushes swaying and jerking as the wind eddied up the hillsides. No shepherd or goatherd ventured up to leave their charges in this no-man's-land.

The track up which Laura had jolted in the back of the jeep eight nights before meandered down to the valley bottom, and snaked back up over a low ridge at the end. Alphonso scanned the ridge with binoculars and, satisfied, beckoned Laura out.

She was dressed in a pair of grimy old flannel trousers that looked as though they had last been used as a mechanic's oil-rag. She had gathered her hair into a ponytail and stuffed it inside the back of a torn and tatty sheepskin coat. She rubbed a bit of dirt on to the smooth skin of her obviously female face. On her feet were an old pair of well-worn gym shoes. She looked more like a late sixties hippy then a Sardinian peasant boy, but she looked nothing like the beautiful, self assured daughter of a billionaire.

Alphonso nodded towards the col that was the easy way out of the valley.

"If the local boys are guarding, they'll be on the other side of that shoulder. We'll have to go straight up the side, over the top and find the road from Fonni to Lanusei. The boys will come up through Fonni, so we'll go the other way."

"You're the boss. I haven't got a clue where we are. I don't know this part of Sardinia at all. How far have we got to walk?"

"Twenty kilometres, not too far, but it's hilly to start with."

"That's okay, I need the exercise."

They started up the hillside directly behind the house. When they reached the cave where the generator was installed, Alphonso slipped in and turned it off. He slashed the fuel line and they watched the diesel gush out and soak into the rocky soil. "We don't want to make them too welcome when they come tomorrow."

Beyond this point, there was no real track to follow. Alphonso led, weaving a zigzag route between patches of thorny bush and outcroppings of rock. The way became steeper, and much of the time they had to resort to scrambling on all fours. Laura's torn trousers were no protection against the sharp rock splinters and small cuts and grazes appeared on her hands and knees.

At the ridge, in spite of the wind, Laura was sweating in her sheepskin jacket. Alphonso offered to carry it for her, but he already had a rucksack full of food and water, and she refused. When, solicitously, he asked if she wanted a rest, she laughed, hoarsely. "No way. The further we get away from that place the better."

Behind them, the desolate, ruined house in which she had been incarcerated was still visible. There were no other signs of any recent habitation, beyond a very faint path between the rocky vehicle track and the courtyard. From this higher point, the valley looked as though it had been made by the wielding of a mighty axe which had cleft a two-mile wedge in the high plateau. In front of them, to the south, the mountains rose to craggy peaks.

"What a God-forsaken dump! I'm not surprised no one found us," Laura said. "Which way now?"

Alphonso pointed to the east, where the hill sloped gently and gave way to a distant, hazy coastal plain.

"The road is about fifteen kilometres down there. There may be some gullies to cross, I don't know, but mostly it's downhill."

"Great. I'm ready."

Four hours later, they scrambled down an embankment, on to a deserted road. It was seven o'clock and dusk. Laura was exhausted. She sat on a grassy levee at the side of the road.

"Shit, I'm knackered!" she said in English.

"*Che?*" Alphonso asked.

In Italian, she said, "Can we stop here for a while? Maybe someone will give us a lift."

"We're still too near. This is part of the territory run by the gang who are helping Gino. People won't know us, and if they hear our accents, they'll talk. We gotta walk, and if anyone stops, we mustn't talk too much."

Laura sighed. "Oh well, I knew I should have taken up jogging when everyone else did. I'm not too fit, that's for sure."

"Hey, you're a strong girl. We've come quite a long way, you know. We'll stop for a bit and eat, but out of sight of the road, and when we get going, we'll still have to get off the road if anything comes."

The night had come down like a thick, black blanket when they started walking again. A few farm vehicles and one or two cars had passed them while they ate and rested. Now there was scarcely any traffic. Alphonso told Laura that they had about twenty more kilometres to walk to Lanusei. This was a small town, he said, where they could find somewhere to sleep, and decide what to do the next day. But after an hour, Laura was exhausted and could barely move one foot in front of the other.

"Alphonso, if a car comes, can we try and get a lift?" Laura begged.

"It's not a good idea. If you're too tired, I'll carry you."

"Fo-fo, you can't!"

"Here," he said, and bent down to pick her up for a piggy-back ride. He hoisted her up without any effort, and gratefully she wrapped her arms around his neck and rested her chin on his massive shoulder.

Within minutes, Alphonso's steady stride had rocked her to sleep.

She woke with a jolt. She found herself lying on the ground with a sharp rock jutting into her side. At first she could see nothing, but she heard a low groaning a few feet away.

"Alphonso?" she asked in panic.

"I'm here."

"What's happened? Are you all right?"

"I don't know. I think I broke my ankle. Argh!" he finished with a grunt of pain.

"Oh my God. How?"

"I caught my foot in a gully at the side of the road and fell, but my foot was stuck. I'm sorry, I dropped you. Are you hurt?"

Laura sat up and moved her arms and legs. "No, just a bit bruised. I think I was still asleep when I hit the ground."

Down in the valley, they were protected from the wind which had got up and now blew high, streaky clouds across a bright young moon. In the pale, sporadic light, Laura could make out the edge of the road, a few feet above, and the hulk beside her that was Alphonso.

She stood up. "How far have we got to go?"

"Not far. Four or five kilometres."

"Can you move at all?"

"No, I've tried."

"I'm afraid I don't think I can carry you. We'll have to get a lift."

"Nothing's passed for the last half an hour. It's after ten."

"Okay. I'll walk. I'll find someone to come out with me to get you."

"Don't do that, not at night. I'll be all right here until morning. Come then, but be sure it's with someone you can trust. Don't go to the police, they've maybe got some arrangement with the local boys in a place like this."

"Are you sure you're going to be all right?"

"Sure. I've got some food. Maybe I'll sleep. I just can't move too much."

Laura clambered back on to the road. "See you in the morning, then, Fo-fo. Be good. *Ciao.*"

Her few hours' sleep had refreshed her, and she strode out. She should cover five kilometres in an hour or so, and a few places might still be open in Lanusei, if it was any kind of a town. She enjoyed being in charge, and in no way was she going to let Alphonso down.

After ten minutes, Laura caught the sound of a truck coming up the road behind her. It sounded like a heavy vehicle, and she had a quick debate with herself. If it was a big truck, the chances were it was covering a distance, and not necessarily driven by a local. The rumble grew nearer, interspersed with loud crashes as the vehicle bounced into the holes that pockmarked the road surface. It sounded too heavy for a farmer's lorry. She decided to chance it.

She stood at the side of the road, and as headlights came into view, she started to wave, frantically indicating that the driver should stop.

The truck slowed at once, in time to pull up level with Laura. A head, topped with a flat black leather hat, poked out of the driver's window.

"*Che passa, ragazzo?*"

It was a massive, high-sided truck, thirty-five tonnes at least. The metal sides were dented all over, and the whole vehicle was covered in fine dust. It appeared to be carrying a full load of rock, maybe from a local quarry.

Laura took a deep breath. She assumed a husky voice, and what she hoped might pass as a Sardinian accent.

"My motorbike's broken down back there. Can you take me to Lanusei?"

"I didn't pass any bike," the driver said suspiciously.

"No, I hid it in the bushes at the side of the road. I don't want it stolen, I just got it for my seventeenth birthday."

This was still bandit country, but evidently the driver found Laura's story plausible and her slight figure in the tatty clothes did not present much of a threat.

"Okay," he said, "I'm only going as far as Lanusei tonight. Hop up."

"*Grazie*," Laura mumbled, and ran round to the other side of the cab, where the driver had opened the door for her.

The truck moved off like a tank, with its headlights sweeping up the lonely road. Laura tucked herself against the passenger door, and hoped that the driver was not too talkative.

But he was one of those people who expect conversation from recipients of lifts.

"Where were you going when you broke down?"

"Just to Lanusei tonight, then down south," she added vaguely.

"Where are you staying, then?"

"I don't know," she mumbled.

He glanced across at her frightened face in the backward glow of the headlights.

"Where are you from?" he asked in a more kindly tone.

"Olbia." Laura wracked her brains to produce a map of Sardinia from her scanty geography of the island. "But I went to Nuoro to visit my uncle."

"That's a long way on a bike," the driver remarked. "It's late to find somewhere to stay. Maybe they have a room at the *pensione* where I stay."

"That would be good."

"You got some money?"

Laura felt abruptly sick. She had forgotten to ask Alphonso if he had any. She was sure he had, but what was she going to do until she got back to him?

"Jesus, no," she gasped. "I left it in the pannier of my bike."

"That was pretty dumb," the trucker grunted. "Still, never mind, I know the people, they're good. Maybe they'll trust you."

They soon arrived in the dimly-lit, empty town. Most of it was shut up. Only a couple of cafés in the main square were still open, with a few desultory last drinkers sitting around. On the far side of town, the driver pulled his truck into a space that had been left by a demolished house, turned the motor off and scrambled down.

"Come on, lad. Let's see if we can find you a bed."

Laura climbed down and followed him into the house beside the truck. She hung back a little, hoping that the lights inside the house would not let her down.

She saw the driver now clearly for the first time. He was a short, oily-skinned man, with cheerful brown eyes. He was greeted warmly by a woman in her sixties, with silver hair gathered in a bun and wearing a bright flowery apron over her plain black frock.

"This lad needs a bed, signora. But his bike's broken down back up the Fonni road, and he's left his money with it."

"Oh, no," the woman said, looking sympathetically at Laura, "I hope no one steals it. He's my only guest tonight," she nodded at the trucker. "I'll trust you to pay me the money when you've got your bike."

"Thank you very much, signora," Laura mumbled.

The landlady gave her an odd look; Laura did not know if it was her accent or her timbre which prompted it. But the woman made no comment, and set about laying a table in the simple parlour in which they stood. She told them that if they washed and came down again in ten minutes, supper would be ready.

Laura was reluctant to take too much grime off her face and slim-fingered hands. She came back down, still wearing the sheepskin coat with the collar turned up. Once again her hostess looked at her speculatively, but said nothing to suggest suspicion.

Laura ate everything that was put in front of her. She acted with what she hoped was the awkward bashfulness of a teenage boy, and avoided uttering more than monosyllabic answers.

Later, she sank between crisp white sheets on a rickety bed in a tiny attic room, and slept without interruption until she was woken by a knock on the door. She remembered just in time to moderate her voice to answer the landlady's instructions to come down to breakfast in five minutes.

She climbed down the narrow stairs, in the same clothes and coating of dirt in which she had arrived.

The grey-haired woman greeted her with a strangely warm smile. She stood over Laura as she sat down to eat. In her hand she held a newspaper. "The driver who brought you here has already gone," she said. "He had to be in Cagliari by lunchtime."

Laura trusted herself only to nod. She quickly stuffed her mouth full of bread and butter, and gulped down a mouthful of thick espresso.

"During the night you were sleep-talking."

Laura froze.

"I think it was in English," the woman went on, "and in a girl's voice." She paused for Laura's reaction.

Laura kept her eyes down as she chewed a large hunk of fresh doughy bread.

"It's all right. I know who you are. I could tell from those blue eyes. I saw them on the television, and here's a photo of you in the paper." She unfolded a copy of a Sardinian daily.

Laura looked up. On the front page was her photo, taken the previous year at a party in Rome. It was a good sharp photo, and a good likeness. One of her friends must have earned a nice little bonus from it. She wondered who.

Laura's eyes shifted from the picture to the smiling face of the grey-haired signora. She gave a resigned shrug, and shook her hair free from the smelly jacket.

"It's lucky you came here, signorina. There are many people in the town who would pass on the information if they recognised you. But my late husband, God bless him, always hated the *banditi*. They killed his father. I won't be afraid of them."

Laura believed her. "Thank you, signora. But I'm going to need some help. The man who was guarding me came with me, but he's broken his ankle, about five kilometres back up the road to Fonni. I must get some help to him. He's very big, and I couldn't lift him on my own."

"If the pigs who took you find him, they'll kill him, you know."

Laura had already realised that the insult to Gino and

Luca's egos would be too great for any lesser retribution.

"I know," she nodded.

"There are not many courageous men who can be trusted in this town, but there is my son, Eduardo. He is not a big man, but he's very clever; he's a lawyer's clerk. I will ask him to help you. You must wait here in the house. If I recognised you, someone else might too. Everyone saw the television. But first, have some more to eat, and go back upstairs and clean up. I'll get you some other clothes."

The old woman bustled out. Laura prayed that she could trust her. She had no other option.

Laura and Eduardo, the lawyer's clerk drove back up the Fonni road to find Alphonso. Laura managed to identify the area where she had left him, and they found him, uncomfortable but cheerful, hidden from the road by a scanty screen of bushes. Eduardo drove them to Lanusei, to their family doctor, who was discreet. The doctor agreed, in the circumstances, to keep Alphonso there for a few days; because he was a compassionate man, because Laura was beautiful and very persuasive, and because he believed the famous Signor Christy Pyon would make it very worth his while.

Like Laura, Eduardo considered it unwise to go to the local police. They set off up the east coast road in the little clerk's ancient Lancia. As they drove they debated their destination. Eduardo wanted to go straight to the police in Sassari. But Laura had other ideas.

Plot and counterplot

Ken Newberry was frankly astonished when his secretary told him that Mrs Elizabeth Pyon was on the telephone for him.

In the early days, he had seen a lot of Liz. It was inevitable when he and Pyon were working so closely together for long hours, sometimes for days on end. More often than not Liz had sided with Ken if she had been around when there was a disagreement. That had been more because she hated to see Pyon bullying him than because she thought there was greater merit in his opinion.

But that was thirty years before, and latterly a year could go by without Newberry seeing Liz. Of course, her living in Ireland and not actually being Pyon's wife any longer meant that she did not come to the few formal functions that Southern Hemisphere held each year.

And yet now she was ringing to talk to him in the midst of Pyon's greatest series of crises.

He took the call at once. "Hello, Elizabeth. How are you? Of course," he went on hurriedly, "you must be very upset by what's going on. Is there any news?"

"Nothing, beyond Christy's latest public pronouncement that he won't part with a penny."

"Until he's seen her alive," Ken added, to show that he was even-handed.

Liz ignored that. "I wondered if you'd be kind enough to come and see me, Ken? I'd like your advice about a few things."

"Of course, Elizabeth. Anything I can do at a time like this."

"Six this evening, at the mews?"

"Right you are."

"Good. See you then."

Ken made sure that nothing held him up for his appointment with Liz. As he walked round to her house, he tried to make something of their short exchange over the phone.

One thing was certain. That she wanted his advice rather than Pyon's suggested that the legendary loyalty to Pyon which she had shown over the last twenty years was faltering. That had to be good, especially if she was looking to him as an ally. But he could only conjecture on the reason for this. Something to do with the kidnap, probably. Maybe even the luscious Natalie, though he thought that might be beneath her dignity.

Ah well, he thought, as he tugged the heavy iron bell pull, I'll soon know.

Newberry was shown up into the drawing-room. Liz's greeting was polite, though not as effusive as his own to her. In the background there was a second woman whom he did not recognise.

Younger, a real hot sexy number, Newberry thought as he took in the long legs and the short dress.

"Ken, this is Maria, Christy's wife. Maria, this Ken Newberry, Christy's oldest colleague."

Maria looked at Ken as though she did not think much of him. But Ken confidently took her hand in his firm, businessman's grasp.

"It's a tragedy we've never met before," he said with an attempt at twinkling gallantry.

Maria did not reply.

Liz offered Newberry a drink, and invited Maria and him to sit.

"Ken," she said, "thanks for coming. Maria and I have been making a few plans, and we thought you might like to help us put some of them into operation."

Newberry nodded and looked as helpful as he could.

"What's the state of play with the Chemco deal?" Liz asked.

"Pretty much as reported by this morning's papers. They can't see it happening now."

"You don't seem very upset about that, Ken." Liz showed no surprise.

"Well," Ken huffed, still not certain of his ground, "you never know with Pyon. He's a terrific fighter. He could produce a few surprises, even with all the problems he's got. After all it's only the bad press he's getting and of course this dreadful kidnap business, that's doing the damage. If that's resolved, our shares may well rise enough to put the deal back into play."

"If Laura's kidnap is 'resolved', as you put it, it won't be as a result of anything Pyon's done. And frankly, Ken, I can't forgive him for that." She gazed at him with steady but tragic eyes. "I'm trying to face the fact that I may never see my daughter again."

"Now, you mustn't give up hope, Elizabeth. It's by no means over yet."

"When it is, I want Christy to lose this deal. I want him to lose everything he's made. I want him absolutely broken."

Ken forced himself not to smile as he listened to this music. "Good God, Elizabeth. What's come over you? I know he hasn't always been the perfect gentleman, but aren't you coming on a bit strong? And after all, to be quite blunt, it's not going to help your position if he does go under."

"I have my own means, and I intend to use the current uncertainty about this deal to add to that. It is normal, isn't it, that those right in the know in a situation like this can do very well out of it? I believe it's called insider dealing, and fairly common practice in this part of the world."

"Yes, certainly. But why do you think I'll help you? After all, I've been Christy's partner for thirty years."

Liz held his eye in hers. "I know you have, Ken, and I know you'd like to help."

There was a silence as this undoubted fact established itself.

Ken gave a guilty, crooked smile, and nodded. "Yeah, you must know the score," he acknowledged, "but where does she come into it?" He jerked his head towards Maria.

Maria gave him a short, cold stare. "You have your reasons to see Pyon destroyed, I have mine."

"I can imagine," agreed Ken. His eyes darted back and forth between the two women, two highly motivated and potent allies. "As it happens, I have a few ideas of my own. I have been thinking about resigning, you know. The wife wants to move out to Gloucestershire. You can get a handsome drum and a few hundred acres there for a million or two, and we fancy taking it a bit easy. You know, bit of shooting, bit of hunting for the wife, pottering about the estate and all that."

"I see," said Liz, considering the implausible picture of Ken as country squire. "And what ideas do you have?"

"If you don't mind, ladies, you did say you'd been making plans. I think I'd rather hear yours first."

"All right," Liz agreed. "First of all, though, I must stress that nothing must happen which might jeopardise Laura's life. It seems to me that if Christy is seen to be going through impossible difficulties, the kidnappers may not wait any longer, and then God knows . . ." For the first time, Ken saw a bleakness in her eyes that explained the earnestness of her wish to hurt Pyon. With an effort, she regained her composure. "Do you understand that?" she asked.

"Yeah, of course."

"The damage done by the recent press coverage makes us feel that's the best weapon to use. But it would be more powerful if it related to the business. In other words, we want to orchestrate a steady campaign of serious, plausible rumours, based on hard facts where possible, to make it easier for the press. They'll do their bit without being asked because that's their job."

"Yes indeed," Newberry said, "they can be very helpful. And, er, what is Maria's part in this?"

Maria still looked at him with the slight distaste she had shown when he first came in, but she now acknowledged that he was going to be an important ally.

"I have used other contacts, from Italy and America," she said, "to tempt Pyon into dangerous waters in the movie business."

"Ah," Newberry nodded, "that was you, was it?"

"Yes, it was me, but I had to use Julian to help. The business will fail, I'm sure," she glanced guiltily at Liz, "but Julian need not blame himself. The problems with this deal will emerge slowly over the next few months. We must be sure that the press have all the details little by little. It will do Pyon's reputation terrible harm at this moment."

Liz nodded her agreement. "Yes, and there are a number of other aspects of Southern Hemisphere and its subsidiaries that are open to question. These must be investigated and aired. For instance, something Laura told me just before she went to Italy. Perhaps you know something about it. There is a Brazilian chemical company, Agrichimica Spa, I think, that's been responsible for ripping down hundreds of thousands of acres of rain forest in the Amazon basin. Is that true?"

At first, Newberry was automatically defensive. "Only indirectly," he said, "but, yes, that could be laid at Southern's door." He warmed to the idea. "That's very controversial, these days, with everyone going green. I can get all the details we gave our PR people. Of course, they were instructed to play the whole thing down, but you have to give them facts first so's they know what to lie about."

"Right, so there's that. That's not going to set the world alight, but if we can come up with a few other similar things, they'll have a cumulative effect. Any ideas, Ken?"

Newberry sat back on the soft, beige sofa and looked at the ceiling. After a few moments, he jerked his head forward. "Yes. There's big trouble brewing in Transvaal. We've got some asbestos mines there, employing five thousand men. They are threatening an all-out strike over conditions as well as pay. We can't begin to meet their demands, but the government there is putting heavy pressure on us to settle. The last thing they want at the moment is a long, messy strike. The lid's been kept on it, and the Western press haven't really sussed the significance of it yet. But if they do, they could go to town on repressive, inhuman practices and all that. As a matter of fact, it is serious. We've got a big investment in South Africa. In the end, though, a deal could be thrashed out with the workers, but not if the thing's blown up into an international news item."

Ken paused, and screwed up his face in concentration. "There's something else that could upset a few people. Some nasty stuff that should have been going to the States has found its way to Iraq. It's not our fault, but one of our customers has been messing around with bills of lading, changing destinations in transit. But it could be construed that we were at least compliant. Produce that out of the hat at the right moment, and that could cause a very big stink."

"Does Pyon know about that?"

"Yes, he does, though he says we're innocent of any malpractice, but the documentation he showed me doesn't actually prove that."

"So," Liz said, "with one thing and another, there's quite a bit to go on. Do you happen to know a suitably authoritative journalist we could confide in?"

"I don't know about authoritative, but I've got a contact

329

who can get almost anything printed, provided there's a grain of truth."

"Good. Let's leave that side of things for the moment. There's another aspect of the Chemco deal which I think we can manipulate. You're aware, I presume, that Christy's got some kind of concert party going on Chemco?"

"Of course. I was in on that. Not just a concert party, support too, and not a very happy party at the moment. Do you know who's involved?"

"Yes. Shemilt, Weintraub, Leo Jackson and Adnan al Souf."

Newberry nodded. "Just so long as you already knew. I don't want to be responsible for letting the cats out of the bag."

"If a party can be got together to assist in a deal like this, and make money, there ought to be a way of reversing the process in which they still make money."

"Between them, there's enough muscle to swing the price a lot, of Chemco as well as Southern."

"Christy has mentioned to me that he expected the prices of both to fluctuate quite a bit while his bid is on the table."

Ken agreed. "To begin with, after we launched the bid, there was a steady move up in both of them, then not much change for a while, because no one could second-guess the decisions of the various State banking authorities over al Souf's suitability. That all changed ten days ago, of course. Southern's price is down by nearly 80 per cent. Chemco's softened a bit too, with the predator gone away. But, as I said, this could all change overnight, depending on the news. The fuss over Christy and his, er, girlfriend will die down pretty quick. After that, it's a question of whether or not Laura's released, and how much he's paid, or not paid."

"But," Maria pressed him, "there are things you can do to influence the price, with the help of the concert party?"

"Yes."

"Good. That's what I told Maria," said Liz. "Well, I can tell you that I can count on the help of Leo Jackson, and Adnan al Souf."

Newberry's eyes opened wide. "Can you, indeed? Are you sure?"

"Yes, Ken, I'm sure."

"That's very interesting, because I can deliver Lenny Shemilt. As a matter of fact, there's no harm in my telling you now, he and I have already done well out of the price movements. Different motives from you, of course. I couldn't care less what happens to Pyon. I don't own a single Southern share, just at the moment."

"What are your motives, then?"

Newberry shrugged. "Organising my pension? You could call it pure greed. But you see, I've no loyalty left for Pyon. He's treated me like the office boy for years. I'm not saying I haven't done well, but I could have done just as well on my own, if only he hadn't got all those Paddies on his side, back in the beginning. Still, there it is. Though our ends aren't identical, the means are the same. And you want to make a few bob out of it as well. I think we could be a good team."

Liz gave a pragmatic shrug. "My enemy's enemy is my friend."

Disguised reunion

Eduardo did not attempt to argue with Laura. He drove to Porto Cervo as she instructed him.

"My father is bound to be staying somewhere around here. Obviously, he won't be in the villa, but if you make a few enquiries around the bars, look for a journalist or someone, it's probably common knowledge." She crouched down, out of sight in the passenger seat of the car, and sent Eduardo off with a long shopping list for which she promised reimbursement within a few hours.

The car was parked in a small shady car park, not too busy, on the edge of the town. Eduardo scuttled down the hill, determined to prove his worth to this lovely girl.

He did well. He returned in less than an hour with the name of Pyon's hotel, a long, blonde wig, a plain white dress and an assortment of make-up.

While Eduardo waited outside the car to divert attention, inside it, Laura scrambled into the dress. She applied a heavy layer of make-up where normally she wore barely any. She pinned her own brown tresses on to the top of her head and pulled the blonde wig over them. Looking in the driving mirror, she carefully tucked in stray wisps of brown hair. She nodded to herself with satisfaction, and called Eduardo for a second opinion. As he approached, she poked her head out of the window.

He stopped and gave a big smile. "*Multo bene!*"

Laura pulled a face. "What? Better than the real thing?"

"Of course not. But very different – unrecognisable."

"Good. Let's go and find my father."

When they reached the hotel, Eduardo parked the car at the back by the service doors. He slid out and walked unhurriedly in through the staff entrance.

Five minutes later, he reappeared with a grin on his face.

"Okay," he said when he reached her, "you owe me another two hundred thousand lire. Your father has the suite on the fourth floor. There's supposed to be a guard on the door to keep the press away, but he'll be distracted for about twenty minutes." He climbed back into the car and handed her a piece of paper with a crude plan on it.

They drove round to the front of the hotel and Eduardo pulled up outside the main entrance.

"Good luck," he smiled. "I'll be waiting just down the drive if you have any problems."

Laura put on her dark glasses, leaned over and gave Eduardo a quick kiss on his cheek before she got out.

Eduardo pulled the car door shut behind her, and she walked up the steps with long, relaxed strides into a huge, plant-filled lobby. The second glances she attracted from the doorman and guests going in and out were not caused by recognition.

332

She looked around casually until she saw the lifts, and walked over to take one up to the fourth floor.

The only other occupant of the lift was an awestruck messenger-boy. He carried on up after she had disembarked. Alone on the landing, she consulted the plan, and headed down a long, quiet corridor to her father's suite.

She knocked on the door.

Her heart was pounding. She was longing to see him, and determined to give him a piece of her mind.

Would he be there? Eduardo's informant in the staff room had not been able to say. It was midday. He could be anywhere, but Laura had been too impatient to check it out first.

There was no reply. She knocked again, louder.

She heard sounds of movement in the room, and then the familiar growl. "Who is it?"

"I've got news of Laura," she said in a husky Italian accent.

"Who are you?"

"Can I come in?"

"For God's sake, I'm not talking to any journalists. The management should have intercepted you, and I'm calling them now to remove you."

"I'm not a journalist. I know the Gattis. Open the door, and then get me chucked out if you want to."

The door opened abruptly, and there was the familiar bear-like figure. Pyon's black brows were clustered in a tangled knot above his angry blue eyes in a way Laura knew well. She smiled.

He glared at her with annoyance, tempered by his appreciation of a good-looking woman.

"Who the hell are you?"

"I told you, I've got news of Laura. Do you want to hear it?"

Pyon glanced up and down the corridor to satisfy himself this was not an ambush arranged by zealous news hounds.

"Okay. Come in and you'd better be for real."

He ushered her in and closed the door. "There's supposed to be a bloody guard on that door. By Christ, that oily manager of this place is going to get one of my brogues up his bum. Right, what d'you know?"

He had left Laura standing in the middle of the room while he resumed his place on the leather swivel chair and looked out of the window.

"Before I tell you what I know," Laura still spoke in a plausible Italian voice, "are you going to offer more than the five million you've already offered?" Laura turned away a little, so that he could not see her full face.

"Okay, so you're from the Gattis. You're mad to come here. I don't want anyone to know about their connection any more than they do. Are you negotiating for them?"

"*Si.*"

Pyon considered the unlikeliness of small, arrogant men like the Gattis entrusting a mission like this to a woman, rather than to the man, Gino, who had come the first time. On the other hand, it was not an entirely stupid idea.

"How do I know you're genuine?"

"Laura gave me a message for you. She said she likes to remember you sitting on a stone block in the stables, smoking a cigar. And she's sorry she didn't obey you."

He nodded. "Okay, you can tell your people that I don't want to piss about any more. I'll pay $50 million. That's my final price, and there is one vital condition. They must issue a statement that they have released my daughter for an undisclosed amount. That should suit them as well as it suits me. Will they agree to that?"

"You are willing to pay fifty million?" The girl's voice sounded oddly hoarse and excited to Pyon. Maybe he had gone higher than he needed to.

"That's what I said." He stood and walked round to face her.

She was smiling at him, and there were tears making runnels through the thick foundation on her cheeks.

"You won't have to," Laura said in her own voice with a breathless laugh. "I got out for free!" She pulled the wig from her head and flung it across the room. She leaped up and threw her arms around his shoulders and plastered his craggy face with kisses and make-up.

"Jesus, Mary and Joseph! Laura!" he gasped, and burst

out laughing with the joy of having her safe in his arms. "You canny little bitch! Did you think your old dad wasn't going to cough up for you? Mind you, I had me fingers crossed you'd get out on your own." He lifted her up to give her an almighty squeeze, then deposited her back on the floor and held her away from him to look at her properly.

"By Christ, it's hard to tell what sort of shape you're in under that lot. Are you well?"

Laura could not speak for a moment. She could only laugh and brush the tears from her cheeks as she shook her happy head. Pyon gazed at her with overwhelming fondness and thought that it would have been worth fifty million to get her back.

"Let's have a drink, for God's sake. I never knew of anything so worth a celebration." He walked across the room and took a bottle of '71 Krug from the fridge. He opened the bottle with gusto and poured them both frothy glassfuls.

"I cannot tell you how happy I am to see you. You're a little star, and you've saved me fifty million. Of course you must have the customary ten per cent of the saving, less my expenses in coming here to attempt to negotiate you out," he added with a laugh.

"So this champagne's on me?"

"That's right."

Laura swigged back her glass and collapsed on to an uncomfortable sofa.

Pyon remained standing, looking down at her. "You haven't told me how you are. Did they look after you?"

"Oh, I was perfectly comfortable. I ate well. As a matter of fact, I cooked dinner last night after I'd watched you on television, announcing to the world that you weren't going to pay a halfpenny for my release. I was a bit depressed about that – you were very convincing, and the lovely fellow who was guarding me felt sorry for me. By the way, I guessed that you must know who had me."

"Sure; the comical little fellas! But they had me by the short and curlies."

"They were certainly pretty careless. They were relying entirely on this chap, Alphonso's loyalty. It obviously never occurred to them that he might get pissed off with them telling him what to do." Laura turned serious. "Look, we're going to have to do something about Alphonso. He broke his ankle while we were escaping and he's holed up in a doctor's house in Lanusei."

"Where the hell's that?"

"Near where I was being held. Halfway down the east coast. The two little shits who are working for the Gattis will try to kill him if they find him. I promised you'd give him a job when we got away."

"Fine. Sounds a useful sort of a fella, though I don't suppose his last employers will give him much of a reference," Pyon laughed.

"And there's Eduardo to look after as well."

"Who's Eduardo?" Pyon asked.

"He's been marvellous. His mother helped me, and he drove me here – I'll tell you all about it – but we must give him some kind of reward."

"Sure, whatever you say. I just want you to promise me one thing, that you'll tell no one, not even your mother, ever, that I was prepared to pay. If it ever got out, you'd be living under a threat for the rest of your life, d'you understand?"

Laura nodded. "Okay, I promise. At least *I'll* always know what value you put on me."

"Nor must anyone know that it was Maria's family who did it; that could be very dangerous. I don't want anyone to draw a connection with the Gattis. And you must promise me you'll never go near Maria again."

"Or Gianni and Caterina?"

Pyon sighed. "We'll have to play that one very carefully. Now will you give me your solemn word?"

"I will," Laura nodded.

"Good girl. Right, I'll go and run you a bath. You can take your drink in there and get cleaned up. Then we'd better decide how we're going to tell the world about your escape. It's the last episode of the series, so you'll want it to go with a bang."

The Sassari police agreed. It was best to get Laura out of Sardinia before they made the announcement.

Pyon's plane was waiting for them at Olbia four hours later, fuelled up and ready to go.

Laura phoned Liz from the Cessna, about twenty minutes before it was due to touch down at Cork.

Mrs Pyon was not there, she was told. She had gone to London two days before.

"What the hell's she doing in London? She promised she would stay in Clonegall if she didn't come out to Sardinia, and Julian talked her out of that. He thought she'd get even more upset. What'll we do? You don't want to go to London now, do you?"

Laura shook her head. "No way. I'd like a few days before I have to face more cameras. Could you send the plane on to London to pick up Mum?"

"Sure. I'll do that. But you ring her there first to tell her that you're safe and home."

A high-risk campaign

Shortly after Ken Newberry left Maria and Liz Pyon, Leo Jackson arrived at the house in the mews.

When Jackson had seen the two women before lunch, he had held back from making any commitments, or from revealing too much. He wanted to be sure that they were serious.

He had no trouble casting Maria in the role of saboteur, but it was very unlike Liz. Before he got involved in what was a high-risk campaign against Pyon, he had to be certain that Liz was really committed, not just reacting out of frustrated, angry maternal instincts. After all, he personally did not have anything in particular against Christy Pyon; on the other hand he had always been a fervent admirer of his first wife. As far as the deal was concerned, he could make money playing it either way.

"I must be clear about one thing, Liz," he opened the conversation, "there is still a perfectly good chance that Laura will be returned, probably as a result of Pyon's negotiations and his agreement to pay a very large sum of money. I don't want to get involved in helping you – and admittedly, myself – to a healthy profit at Pyon's expense, and then find that you've changed your mind."

"Leo, you've known me a long time. Do you really think I would have approached you if I wasn't absolutely sure? First, I am certain that Pyon won't pay. Second, this whole incident must be a direct result of the horrific personal publicity he had just received; and third, that publicity was justly deserved. He's cheated on me and on Maria for years. I have been utterly loyal to him throughout, but enough's enough. I hope I never see the man again. And I'd like to see him ruined. Maria has not been subjected to as much provocation, but she's equally keen. Neither of us is entirely financially dependent on Pyon now, but as there is a chance to benefit ourselves while doing him down, then we will." Jackson tried to ask a question but Liz raised her left hand a few inches. "No, let me assure you there is absolutely no question of my mind changing."

Leo saw the quiet anger burning in her eyes and believed her. He did not speak at once. He stood, and walked to the middle of the room and gazed at a Rossetti painting of Mary Magdalene which hung above the empty fireplace.

He turned to Maria. "And what are your motives, if, as Liz says, you've had less provocation?"

"I have been just as insulted as her. My husband has had a great public affair with a young black girl. At least he left Liz for a civilised woman."

"Maybe she didn't think so at the time."

"Now, Leo," Liz warned, "stop causing trouble. Of course Maria and I have had our differences, but now, you can be quite sure, we are united."

"All right, ladies, I'm with you. I'll have to consider the best way of handling it. It'll take me a day or two to work out the right approach, but as you probably know, Pyon was receiving a lot of support from others besides me."

Liz nodded. "We do know. Adnan will help, I'm certain. He and I have a very good relationship, and I don't think he really approves of Christy much. Also, with the co-operation of Ken Newberry, Lenny Shemilt will take our side. As far as I can tell, he and Newberry have been having a separate little party of their own."

Leo's head jerked up. "What? The bastards, I might have guessed. I've never trusted either of them further than I could piss. But I always thought Ken knew which side his bread was buttered. Now I know, that explains a few strange hiccups in the share price movement over the last ten days." He turned his eyeballs upwards and shook his head with self-blame. "I knew Pyon's team was too big. As far as al Souf's concerned, whatever he thinks of you or Pyon, he'll only help if he benefits, and he was very anxious to get his hands on Chemco's various banking interests. Best of luck in persuading him, but don't tell him what you plan until you've got him on your side."

Liz took this in. "I don't think I'm being naive when I say that you're being too cynical about him. Anyway, if he joins in with us, he could make a perfectly satisfactory sum of money out of it."

"The way to be sure," said Leo thoughtfully, "would be to leak a bit of filth, so that the State regulators have got something on him to justify refusal of a banking licence."

"I don't know any filth, and I really don't want to get involved in that kind of thing," Liz said with distaste.

"Well, you know, eggs and omelettes and all that. I can probably sort something out. Don't worry about it," Leo said lightly. "In the meantime, we have one scam in place which we can turn on its head. We've arranged for a large group of Chemco's gay guinea-pigs to file a joint suit against them for side-effects caused by their AIDS vaccine. The basis of the claims is pretty specious, but it will take a long time to disprove. There's also the risk of a class action from all the other guinea pigs, and there are thousands of them. The idea was to pull that out of the bag when SHR's price had picked up, and bring Chemco's back within striking distance. For a few more bucks, these blokes – if you can call them blokes – will be quite happy to reveal that the whole thing was a scam set up by Southern, and bang goes Southern's price again. There'll be a real roller-coaster, and whoever knows when to get on and off will make a lot of money."

Pyon's wives listened with quiet appreciation. When Jackson had finished, Liz told him about the other plans they had discussed with Newberry, and the disasters in store at the APC studios.

Jackson was impressed. "Well, I should say we've got him, but the timing of each element is going to be critical. There's no doubt the one thing that could really kill the deal, if nothing else does, is Adnan's pulling out of his commitment to buy the banks. Without that, there's no way anyone will believe Pyon's junk bond issue will work, and he'll never be able to find another taker in time. If you *can* deliver Adnan, Liz, I can guarantee you'll achieve what you want. Poor old Pyon, I feel sorry for him already."

"Poor old Pyon, indeed," Liz agreed.

A great party

When Leo Jackson had left, Liz and Maria congratulated themselves on their strategy thus far. Liz managed to suppress the sense of guilt that rumbled uncomfortably within her, but she still despised herself for joining forces with a woman who had been the source of so much unhappiness in her own life, fifteen years before.

But the alliance was sealed now, and there was an undeniable thrill in hatching a plot that would make recompense for so much of the thoughtless treatment she had received at Pyon's hands.

After half an hour and a couple more drinks, they arranged to meet the following morning, and Maria went back to the Dorchester. Liz remained seated on one of the deep sofas in the drawing-room of the house which she had never been able to consider her own. She contemplated what she had set in motion. She was ashamed of the vehemence of her feelings against Pyon. It was an entirely new emotion for her. But she was not uncomfortable with it. It provided an antidote to her overwhelming anguish over Laura.

The discreet trill of a telephone sounded on a table beside the sofa. Before the second ring, Liz answered it in a flat, controlled monotone. "Hello."

"Mum!" It was a young female voice.

Liz could not speak.

She must be hallucinating, she thought. It can't be!

"Mum? Is that you?"

"What . . .? Who is that?"

"It's Laura. Who do you think it is? How many daughters have you got?"

"But it can't be! When . . . where . . . how? I haven't heard anything."

"Mum, I'm home. In Clonegall. I got away. The police are going to announce it tomorrow. I asked Dad to bring me straight here, because he thought that's where you were."

"Your father brought you back? Thank God. Did he pay the ransom?"

"No. He didn't have to. I escaped."

The doubts that had all at once flooded through her ebbed as swiftly.

"Oh my little Laura, thank God you're safe." She wept with a relief that seemed to melt all the muscles in her body. "I thought," she snuffled between sobs, "I was never going to see you again. I'd almost given up hope. I never imagined you could escape. It . . . it's wonderful, wonderful." She took a deep breath. "I must get back and see you, at once. Oh, how can I get back now?"

"Dad's sent the plane to Heathrow. It can bring you back first thing in the morning. They'll be ready to leave at seven o'clock."

"I don't know if I can wait that long."

"Oh, Mum, I wish I could see you now too, but it's only a few hours."

"I won't sleep a wink. Oh," Liz sighed ecstatically, "I can't believe I'm hearing your voice again; I'm so, so happy."

Later Liz telephoned Maria at the Dorchester.

"Laura has escaped from the kidnappers! Pyon has taken her to Ireland, I'm going to fly there."

"What about our meeting?" Maria asked, not responding to Liz's excitement.

"Don't worry, it's only postponed. Pyon didn't part with a penny for his daughter."

"The bastard!" Maria was sympathetic now.

"Quite," Liz agreed. "I'll contact you as soon as I can."

Pyon was with Laura, waiting for Liz at Dublin Airport.

Liz could not meet his eyes.

He saw her aversion, and understood. He watched as she hugged her daughter and wept with joy. Quietly he walked from the private lounge, and out to the car which waited to take him to his plane.

After a while, Liz stood back and put her hands on Laura's shoulders to drink in the sight of her daughter's sparkling eyes and gentle grin. She shook her head with a smile.

"You look amazing. Typical! I'd expected some emaciated waif with rings under her eyes. How on earth did you escape?"

Laura laughed. "It's a long story. Let's go home. I'm going to drive you back. I'll tell you on the way."

Laura drove her mother's Volvo estate car through the confusion of the Dublin rush-hour, out past Dun Laoghaire and down the coast road with the sun shining sharply on the sides of the Wicklows in the west.

She told her mother most of the story, but, as she had promised her father, she did not tell her the names of the kidnappers.

Nor did she mention the first conversation she had had with Pyon, after her escape, when she had worn the blonde wig and the coating of make-up. That was something he wanted kept strictly between the two of them, and she had given him her word.

At Clonegall the whole house was out to greet Liz and Laura, and all the farm and stud staff. No work was done that day. The Guinness flowed, and a fiddler and a piper from Kilkenny – Pyon's idea – filled the air with jigs and, incidentally, tear-jerking ballads of republican heroes. It was a great party, and slowly most of the village and friends from several miles around filled the halls and rooms of the great house. They all came to tell Liz that they had prayed for Laura's deliverance, and how wonderful it was that the Almighty had answered their prayers.

Tom Brophy sought out Liz and said, "It's a terrible shame Mr Christy couldn't stay. Wouldn't he ever have enjoyed a crack as good as this."

But Liz could not bring herself to answer. She had grown to love these people, so warm and genuine in their affection. They admired her, too, she knew that, but it was Pyon they loved and looked up to. It was because Laura was Pyon's daughter, and, in part, a daughter of their own wild hillsides that they were feasting and making merry at her return.

While the party was still in full swing, Julian rang up from California to speak to Laura.

She took the call in the empty library, and shut the door on the sounds of the party.

She heard Julian's incredulous voice. "Laura? Is that really you?"

"Yes, of course. How are you, J?"

"Christ! The news just came over. Someone might have told me before. I couldn't believe it."

"We've been trying on and off all day to get you, but no one knew where you were. I didn't just want to leave a message saying, 'Hello, I'm back.' "

"No, no, you were right. They said you escaped. Is that true?"

"Yeah."

"So Dad didn't have to cough up?"

"Nope. He's pretty chuffed about that."

"I bet he is."

"So, how's it going out there? Mum told me you did the deal, and you're in charge of the studios. Sounds amazing; how do you like it?"

"Well, I'm not on my own, and it isn't going to be easy. There are a few problems to sort out. There seems to be some confusion over the rights we own, and de la Tour – who we thought was going to buy the TV station – is backing away. As a matter of fact, it's hell. I just want to get on with production plans, and make a few pictures. I'm afraid I really need Dad here to sort things out."

"Dad's got problems of his own, by the sound of it. He didn't say much about it to me, but I think his great takeover is up the spout."

"Sure," agreed Julian, without emotion, "that's what all the papers say, and of course they're questioning the wisdom of his buying APC. There have been some nasty innuendos. Still, I'm glad we've done it."

"Would you like me to come over? I don't see how I could help, but you shouldn't come here if you've got all these problems."

"Okay. That'd be great. Just having someone I can trust to talk to."

"Okay. I'll come in a while. Bye for now, J."

Special assignment

The month that followed saw the English winter ushered in by a succession of angry hurricanes. Violent winds lashed the land with biting rain. In the country, beeches and oaks, roofs, garden sheds and greenhouses were whipped up and scattered like toys around a nursery. In London, awnings were ripped from shop-fronts and bowled along the streets while the parks were turned into graveyards for their own stricken plane trees.

The papers and the television news were filled with forlorn stories. Reporters and cameramen vied with one another for shots and tales of disaster, destruction and, occasionally, death caused by forces of nature for which no one, not even a politician, could be blamed.

In the protective warmth of his paper's news-room, where no breeze disturbed the cigarette smoke rising from a hundred ashtrays, Harry Hackwood had other, human-inspired disasters to occupy him – a cornucopia of deceit, double-cross and greed that had been passed to him, and regularly replenished by the quiet, faceless voice on the other end of a telephone line.

He was listening to the voice now.

"Harry, you're doing a good job. I've got a little more for you, and then, quite soon, a nice big one. This time, though, we're going to meet. Just you and me. No one else must know that you're seeing anyone, not your editor or your boss, no one. All right?"

"Of course. When?"

"Good boy. Nice and eager. Go downstairs and wait outside the main entrance. Don't do anything. A black cab with his flag down will stop and pick you up."

"What's all that about?"

"It's not that I don't trust you, Harry, but do as I say."

The cab pulled up almost as soon as Harry was on the pavement outside. He climbed in.

" 'Ello, Mr 'Ackwood," the cabby said with insincere cockney deference, and they rattled off.

Harry was excited about meeting his informant. Nigel Judge, his boss, had caught him on the way out, but he had controlled his excitement. For he too wanted no one to get a line on his source.

The cab headed west along the Victoria Embankment, buffeted by the wind which still hurtled up the trough of the river. They passed under Waterloo Bridge before abruptly peeling off to the right, and taking the street which ran along the underside of the Savoy Hotel – a dead end as far as Harry could remember. But a few hundred yards on, where the street appeared to terminate, the cab dived into a tunnel under a building, and stopped. In front of them was another taxi.

" 'Op out 'ere, Mr 'Ackwood, and into the one in front," the cabby instructed.

Harry did as he was told. When he climbed into the second cab, he received only a sullen nod from the driver, who immediately put his motor into gear, and swung round a sharp left-hand bend in the tunnel. Harry glanced back to where the taxi he had left behind remained stationary, blocking the mouth of the tunnel.

They quickly re-emerged into the daylight, and took a few narrow bends – right, right and left – until they emerged into the Strand. The taxi clattered down the busy street and pulled into the concourse in front of Charing Cross station. The rear door opposite Harry opened and, clutching a briefcase, Ken Newberry climbed in.

"Morning, Harry."

Harry looked at him, and shook his head with a smile of amazement.

"Why the hell didn't I realise it was you? I've considered and rejected you a dozen times."

"I've got a reputation for loyalty to our friend, Harry – a very valuable reputation. That's why I couldn't take no risks being seen with you. But it's okay, we're safe from the blokes that followed you."

"No one followed me."

"Yes they did. I saw them. But they'll take a while to back out of Savoy Place, with a cab broken down in the tunnel, and another one with a very bolshy driver stuck up their tail. Your boss doesn't like to give away the glory, and he's got a helluva nose, they tell me."

"You may be right," Harry said, impressed.

"I am, Harry. Anyway, we can drive around in perfect privacy now. But we don't want to be anywhere where the traffic's bunged up. Someone who knows us might get a gander inside the cab. So we'll take a spin down the motorway, all right?"

They were driving up the Mall now, towards Buckingham Palace. As they swept round the golden statue towards Constitution Hill, they found themselves behind a contingent of Household Cavalry returning to their barracks in Knightsbridge. The taxi pulled past. An officer, trotting on his black horse on the flank of the double column, glanced round.

"Oops," Harry gasped, and dived on to the floor of the taxi. "Hugo Haddon-Havers! I was at school with him."

Newberry shook his head in wonderment. "The old school connections – marvellous! It must sometimes come in handy in your job."

"Not always. Julian Pyon wasn't pleased to see me."

346

"Well, he wouldn't be, would he, not after what you did to his dad."

As the taxi merged into the melee of traffic on Hyde Park Corner, Harry clambered breathlessly back on to his seat.

"Better watch out, there might be a few more chums of yours nipping in and out of Harrods."

"The Knightsbridge Souk? God no, only foreigners and nouveau-riche like you go there these days."

"That's because we're the only one's who can afford to, Harry," Ken smiled.

"Maybe. Anyway, what have you got for me?"

"Let's just go over what we've got so far. Laura escapes. Bloody nuisance, really, because suddenly all the pressure's taken off Pyon. And the business with Natalie has been overshadowed by the kidnap; it's already gone stale. Of course, I'm glad Laura got out, but I wish she'd waited a few more weeks. Southern's price recovers a bit, then a bit more. Chemco lifts fifty cents and then, whoops, twenty poofters start suing for headaches and blindness from Chemco's AIDS wonderdrug. Chemco falls back sharply; Southern rises. Then a nasty little piece – well-documented, mind you – appears in your rag. Saddam Hussein of Iraq is filling his arsenals with some very unpleasant substances, made in Switzerland by, guess who? Stuff should have gone to the States, of course, but very careless, or, maybe someone in our subsidiary knew. Maybe someone on Southern's main board knew. Of course, no one's quite sure if it's true, but what the hell!"

"Is it true?" Harry asked.

"Who knows, Harry? It could be. Where were we, now? Ah, yes. Then you produce a very nice piece – 'The Rape of the Rain Forests'. Pyon is shown not only to be stripping assets from other capitalists, but having a go at Mother Nature herself. Dear old Mother Nature, flavour of the month these days. Everyone's up in arms, including a lot of hypocrites at Chemco, and Southern takes a tumble, again. Then, just when it's showing signs of reviving for the second time, what do we get but threats of strikes in our highly profitable asbestos mine. That was a good plan to give all the legwork on that story to your Southern Africa correspondent – much more authentic than a piece on your page.

"By now, our price has been up and down like a yo-yo on the piss, and people are getting a bit cheesed off. Pyon is a very tarnished-looking golden boy. Where there's muck, there's brass, people are saying, but the muck's obscuring the brass. Pension funds are chickening out. They know the stock's at a 50 per cent discount to assets, but, just in case, they'd better pull out."

"Not just institutions pulling out," Harry said. "There have been some heavyweight players jumping on and off, as far as I can tell."

"Well, you may be right, Harry. There's probably a few people taking advantage, but that's normal."

"Many? Besides yourself, Ken?" Harry asked.

Newberry smiled. "Goodness knows, Harry. I certainly don't."

"Yeah, of course not. Well, what's next?"

Newberry did not reply immediately. They were heading along the Great West Road, swinging round the Cherry Blossom roundabout. Newberry nodded at a recently erected, gleaming office block. A vast billboard, full of clever design ideas, invited prospective tenants to apply for some of the 350,000 square feet of office space.

"They've done well, those boys. I remember when they were fresh out of Harrow, and all they had was a few pairs of brightly coloured braces, and a load of front."

Harry was not interested. "Get on with it, Ken."

"Well, some of this isn't particularly exclusive, or at least, it won't be tomorrow. I take it you know about the Actors' Production Company Inc.?"

Harry nodded. "Of course."

"Pyon should never have got into that deal, but he thought Doug de la Tour was after it. He was being sold a dummy, but he bought it. Unusual for our Christy, but he was already under a different sort of pressure. You've met his son Julian; you say you were at school with him?"

"Yes, though I didn't know him well."

Newberry turned his thin lips into a sympathetic grimace. "Bit of a wanker, eh?"

"In some ways, but not without ability, and a following."

"There's loads of tossers with a bit of a following. What

348

I mean is, Julian's out of his depth in Los Angeles. They'll run rings round him there, pull his plonker until they can tie knots in it and tuck it up his arse."

"He might quite like that," Harry remarked.

"Yeah, but will it make money? No way. He doesn't have a clue, and his old man's too busy to help him out. Tomorrow, the Australian Broadcasting Authority are going to announce that Pyon is an unsuitable person to control a TV station, and tell him he's got to unload it, or close." Ken delivered the sensational news with a quiet smile. He was gratified by Harry's reaction, and went on. "But what's happened to Doug de la Tour who wanted it so badly, I hear you ask? Well, Doug's had his card marked long before. He's keeping mum and sitting on his hands. That channel was the big let-out for Pyon in the APC deal. Now it's hardly worth a ferret's fart. As I say, this will be common knowledge tomorrow, but what won't be is the other bit of bother young Julian has discovered at APC. Unfortunately, between his checking out the title to all those wonderful old movies that they made in the forties and fifties, and signing the deal, all the rights got sold. And, I'm very sad to say, they weren't on the final bill of sale, and nobody noticed. Pyon would have done, of course, but he wasn't there. Julian had power of attorney to sign, and our New York lawyers didn't bother to look, apparently. So what've we got for $30 million and $80 million worth of debt?" He looked the question at Harry, who lifted his shoulders. "A pig in a poke. A parcel of land in a tricky part of LA. Worth a bit, of course, all of $50 million."

"Oh dear," said Harry. "Poor old Julian."

"Never mind Julian. It wasn't his money, was it? Poor old holders of Southern Hemisphere shares."

Newberry opened the briefcase that had lain on the seat beside him since he had climbed in at Charing Cross. "Now. There are a few documents you're going to need to back the story up. Here's the original schedule of assets, and here's the bill of sale; copies, naturally, but totally kosher. Let me show you the relevant sections. They're not very obvious."

Harry noted the salient parts. "How have I come by these?"

"Come on, Harry. You'll think of something. Probably someone inside APC."

Harry nodded, folded up the papers, and tucked them into an inside pocket of his tweed jacket. "Thank you, Ken. I can get a bit of mileage from these. This time, can I ask you an additional favour? When your price drops again, as I presume it's intended to, should I buy a few shares?"

"That's a very intelligent question. And the answer is no."

"Shall I buy Chemco, then?"

"That's entirely up to you, Harry. I wouldn't like you to lose anything, not after all the help you've given us."

"Are you going to give me a hint as to who 'Us' is?"

"I don't think so," Newberry said lightly, shaking his head. "It's not very interesting."

Delivering

Elizabeth Pyon wallowed in the joy of having her daughter returned to her. She and Laura spent hours alone together, walking, riding and just sitting in the quiet peace of the great Irish house. Their enforced separation had strengthened the bonds between them, and they talked with more intimacy than they had ever done before.

But Laura could not tell her the one thing she most wanted to. For, though it had not been spoken, she sensed her mother's new hostility towards her father. She wanted desperately to tell how much Pyon had been prepared to sacrifice for her return, and several times, she almost did; but her promise to her father drew her up. She hoped that, in time, Liz would forgive and they could all pretend, as they used to, that they were still a happy family.

But Laura could never stay in one place for long and her mother was not surprised when she announced that she was going to Los Angeles to see Julian. It was, after all, only fair. Liz drove Laura to Dublin Airport to see her off.

The next day, she went back to the airport to meet Adnan al Souf who arrived in his own 727.

The staff at Clonegall did not find his visit remarkable. He had been several times before, and he was a famous buyer of bloodstock. But this time it was not horses that Liz wished to discuss.

The first night, after dinner when she was sure they were not being overheard, they sat opposite one another in the intimacy of her small drawing-room.

"Adnan," she began to speak huskily, "we've known each other quite a long time. I feel I can trust you as much as anyone I know. Am I right to feel that?"

The Egyptian searched her face with his sharp, black eyes. "There is something a little conspiratorial in your tone which puzzles me, Liz. I don't really see you in the role of plotter. I am guessing that this has something to do with your husband." As he spoke he stood up and walked across the small gap that separated them, and lowered himself beside her on the sofa. One of his long legs, encased in the finest worsted wool, touched hers and he placed his arm along the back of the sofa behind her. She wriggled, but did not move away.

"You're right," she said, "I do want to talk to you about Christy."

"I guessed that you were not pleased with him while Laura was missing. But you may have misjudged him. He was under the most intense pressure from all fronts; he still is, as a matter of fact."

"I don't think I've misjudged him. He announced that he would pay nothing, and he paid nothing. It's a miracle that Laura escaped."

"Still, you must admit that it's unlikely they'll bother to kidnap her again," al Souf said with reasonableness.

Liz had admitted this to herself, but it did not in her eyes mitigate Pyon's sin. "Tell me about the pressure that Christy's under," she asked.

Adnan shifted his arm a little towards her, and began to finger a few stray, still lustrous brown tresses. "The institutions that supported him are pulling out. Tenbury-Hamilton at Anglo-American has told me that he thinks it unlikely they can now underwrite his bond issue. There has been what looks like a well-orchestrated smear campaign against him in the press. He has few friends powerful enough to help him now."

"Are you one of them?"

"Yes."

"The most powerful?"

"Certainly," al Souf said without Anglo-Saxon modesty.

"If you carry on supporting him, will he pull the deal off?"

"I'm not sure. My interest, as I expect you know, is in the Agricultural Bank of Texas and its many subsidiaries. But negotiations to acquire approval are turning out to be very slow, and very expensive. It's almost reaching the stage where the prize will not be worth the fight."

Liz turned her head to look at him directly. Her eyes did not waver. "So you could contemplate pulling out?" she asked.

"I have considered it."

"Adnan, I would very much like you to do something for me."

Al Souf shrugged. "You know that I would do practically anything for a woman as beautiful as you, especially if she might grow to like me a little more."

"Don't underestimate the feelings I already have for you, Adnan. You've been a great comfort to me over the last few years. I often wish that circumstances allowed us to take our relationship a little further, but," she sighed, "somehow, I seem to have stayed married to Christy, even though he went years ago. Now I've decided all that must stop. His behaviour over the kidnap, on top of the affair with the Mauritian girl, has tipped the balance too far against him. I want nothing more to do with him."

"So, you might be free . . . to follow your instincts."

Liz looked at him with yielding grey eyes. "I think I might, soon."

Al Souf shifted his hips. "And what was it you wanted me to do?"

"As if you hadn't guessed," Liz laughed.

He leaned his head down. She smelled the mix of wine on his breath, his subtle cologne, and his strange, Arab scent. His lips touched hers, gently, without aggression or possessiveness, and he pulled away.

"You are a delicate creature, aren't you? But I won't damage you, I promise. And I'll do what you ask."

He lowered his head once more, and this time, their mouths locked in a long, deep kiss, from which Liz had no inclination to turn away.

Maeve

A small, sad group of people congregated around a bedside in the wet, wind-ravaged hills of west Herefordshire. In the big, old sandstone house where she had given birth to her son, Maeve Pyon was dying. The brave old limbs and organs which had supported her loyally for so long had done enough.

Maeve lay on a mahogany bedstead. Between its high, finely carved ends she had gritted her teeth forty years ago and allowed the attentions of little Jack Pyon. On each side of the bed sat one of her grandchildren: Julian, solemn-faced, aware of the significance of her inevitable passing; Laura, weeping freely, and holding tight to the old woman's hand.

Christy Pyon paced back and forth across the wide room, unable to stay seated. His heavy footfalls clumped a death march on the board floor through the thin Turkish rug that covered it. From time to time, he would approach the bed, and lean over to smile encouragement at the small frail face on the pillows. Then he would walk to the window, and watch the wind whip the grassland and shake the the great trees in the sloping woodlands like a terrier might a rat.

He was ashamed of the impatience he felt, but he could not help cursing his mother's choice of a moment to die.

When he came to glance at her, she saw that and forgave him with a feeble, loving smile in her faded blue eyes. She knew that the energy in his big body seethed inside him, looking for an outlet.

His father, she thought to herself, had been a big man, but placid. He still was, and kind and thoughtful. It was too sad that no one else in the world knew, besides her.

She turned her head feebly towards each of her grandchildren.

"Julian, Laura," she whispered, "I want to talk to your father on his own."

They understood. They left the room, and Maeve whispered her last words in an almost incomprehensible mumble.

Pyon strained to hear; remained still as a tombstone as he listened, then watched her close her eyes and die.

He did not move for ten minutes more. A few tears rolled down the side of his nose and plopped on to the white sheet to form a haphazard pattern of small, damp rings.

He leaned down and kissed the pale, dry forehead. When he straightened himself, he dried his eyes, and tidied the sheets around her shoulders. He stood and looked at her for a few moments longer, then left the room to tell his children that their grandmother had died.

The monks allowed Maeve Pyon's body to be laid in the abbey graveyard. The abbey church was full of mourners, all respectful, many truly sad.

"She was a remarkable woman", "A fine example", "A good, devout Catholic", "A first-class farmer" the mourners told her son, with a dozen other superlatives. And he nodded his agreement, and thought of the frightened young girl, with a baby – with *him* – inside her, arriving, terrified, from the Fishguard ferry.

At the house, there was a wake.

"My mother was Irish, so we'll send her off the Irish way," Pyon had announced.

The Irish relations, and all the staff from Clonegall had come across on the ferry in a dilapidated coach. Their Catholic acceptance of death, and their love of a party quickly overcame the Anglo-Saxon reticence of the other guests, and there was a real wake; with laughter, and tears, music and too much to drink.

Pyon oversaw the event with dignified goodwill. He had a word for everyone and accepted their condolences, awkward, clichéd and inarticulate as they were. Tom Brophy took Pyon's hand in both of his, and Pyon knew that the tears in the old Irishman's eyes were not just the result of too much stout. A lot of people had loved Maeve Pyon.

The most conspicuous absentee, made even more so by the richness and colossal size of the wreath she had sent, was Elizabeth Pyon.

When all the guests had finally gone, and only Pyon, Julian and Laura remained, Pyon asked his daughter, "Why didn't your mother come?"

"She loved Granny, as much as any of us, but," Laura faltered, "she said she couldn't bear to see you."

Pyon sighed. "I thought so. But for Christ's sake, she should have come – not for me, for Maeve. I realise she's a bit sore about what's happened recently, but she shouldn't have let that interfere with paying her respects to the old lady."

"That's what I said." Julian shrugged. "After all, it's not as though you've only recently started behaving like a shit. I'd have thought she was used to it by now."

"As you pointed out so clearly when we were in Los Angeles, she has every right to feel, shall we say, a little put out, but she still should have come. Anyway, let's not argue. I'll try and make it up with her. In the meantime, there are a few legalities to be dealt with over your grandmother's death. The will is being read at the solicitors in Hereford tomorrow. The three of us must be there, then I'm afraid I'm going back to London. There's real carnage going on. It was touch and go who'd go first, my mother or my business."

"Are things really that serious?" Julian asked in alarm.

"No, not that serious, but I'm fighting against what you might call financial terrorists. I don't know who they are, or where they're coming from, and I never know when they're going to strike. I know you need some help out in LA, but I can't come just at the moment, Julian. I'll ask Ken Newberry to go over and help. He'll hold your hand until I get there."

"I don't want my hand held by anyone, especially not that greasy little tyke."

"My goodness, Julian, such snobbery from a man of your liberal principles," Pyon said quietly. "Ken may be a greasy little tyke, but he knows how to sort out the kind of mess there is at APC. He knows how to motivate a lawyer. So just co-operate, or we'll get ourselves into a real mess. In the meantime, don't panic. We can start suing Johnny Capra for misrepresentation, and get him indicted for criminal fraud. There should be some healthy damages to claim."

"For God's sake! Didn't I tell you, the lawyers have already said we have no chance."

"They often say that at the beginning of a case, to cover themselves if they lose it for you. Ken will tell you what to do, okay?"

Maeve had never told Pyon how she intended to make her will. In the event, it was unsurprising. Bar a few small bequests to friends and relations, she left everything to Julian and Laura, though their father was to have the right of abode in the house as long as he lived.

Afterwards they had a quiet lunch in a restaurant by the old Wye bridge, looking down at the river, newly swollen with a flux of rain off the Welsh mountains.

Julian gazed sourly at the muddy swirl.

"How the hell did Grandmother imagine Laura and I were going to sort out who was to have what?"

Julian and Laura had flown back together from Los Angeles the day before Maeve died. Laura had been staying with him, trying to encourage him to be positive about his problems there. Two weeks together had taken its toll of their goodwill towards each other.

"She probably thought you'd enjoy arguing about it," Pyon said in answer to Julian's question. "What are you complaining about? Or does your aversion to inherited wealth make you feel uncomfortable about accepting it?"

"Yes, as a matter of fact it does, but since she has left the farm to us, it might as well be dealt with fairly. After all, I've got a good use for some capital."

"Spreading the gospel according to Saint Julian?" Laura smirked. "Don't worry, J, if you don't want to be a farmer, I think I might give it a try. Everything organic, heavy horses and no tractors. Loads of natural woodland, no shooting or hunting."

"That'll make you popular round here. But I'm not going to underwrite your green experiments."

"Fine. We'll have it all valued, and I'll buy out your half."

"What with?" Julian asked disparagingly.

Pyon cast a warning glance at Laura.

"I'll talk the bank into lending me the money."

Pyon laughed. "I can't see you getting up at six to do the milking, or taking your calves to market."

"You'll see. I'll start tomorrow."

After lunch, Hanks drove Julian and his father to Heathrow Airport, Julian to fly to Los Angeles, and Pyon to New York. On the way, Julian was alarmed by his father's moroseness.

"Will you miss Maeve?" he asked.

"Sure I will. She was a very strong and principled woman. I hope I've half the dignity and integrity she had when my time comes, but I fear I won't."

"Are you upset about her, or about the state of your own affairs?"

"Let's just say that thinking of her points up a few of my own shortcomings."

"My God, things must be bad. I don't think I've ever heard you admit to shortcomings before."

"That's not so. I've always acknowledged my own weaknesses, as well as my strengths. That's a lesson you should learn, though I don't suppose you will. Find out your own weaknesses before anyone else does, so that you're prepared when they take advantage of them."

"It strikes me you've been caught a bit unprepared by whoever's attacking you now."

"Yes," Pyon sighed, "that hadn't escaped me. But now, don't let's be too gloomy. I've been in far deeper holes than this. Don't worry about APC, we'll sort it out. Just carry on arranging your productions and leave the nitty-gritty to Ken. The first set of proposals you sent looked like the right sort of thing. I was impressed."

"I did take on board some of your views," Julian conceded.

"Good lad. I'll not let you down."

Julian could find no response to such uncharacteristic submission on his father's part and he spent most of the journey in worried silence.

A lot of people want to see me go down

During the weeks that followed Maeve Pyon's death, her son waded through the quicksand of financial chaos in which he had found himself. At times, he felt that he had sunk even deeper.

In London, Adnan al Souf announced without warning Pyon that he was withdrawing his offer to buy the Chemco banks. He stated that he did not think the cost of the hearings, or Southern Hemisphere Resources' chances of pulling off the deal merited his further interest. When Pyon tried to ring him, al Souf was permanently unavailable.

A London newspaper broke the story of the missing film titles at the APC studios and, once more, Pyon was castigated for his foolhardiness in going ahead with that deal at such a sensitive time. His fiscal judgement was questioned by almost every leading commentator.

Nevertheless, it was hard for them to ignore the fact that after each new nadir had been touched, the price of Southern's shares bounced swiftly back. Not as high as they had stood just before the Mauritius story was published, but, on occasions, within striking distance.

Pyon, still reclusive, instructed Bob MacFarlane, his principal PR adviser, to release bullish statements from time to time, announcing the appearance of another taker for the banks, or the commencement of proceedings against Johnny Capra. He began to feel that, against heavy odds and the persistent doubts of the market watchers, he had pulled it off.

A month to the day after Maeve Pyon was buried, her son felt like joining her. The sensation did not last long, but it was the first time in his life he had experienced it.

It was a little after six-thirty on a sharp autumn morning in New York.

A telephone rang beside Pyon's bed in the Pierre. It was a man's voice, a quiet deferential Wasp voice; a reporter on the *New York Post*.

Pyon cursed, and began to replace the receiver, but before it reached the cradle, he stayed his hand. He might as well hear whatever the gloomy tidings were now as later.

There was a rumour, the reporter said, that Chemco were going to announce that day that they had uncovered a conspiracy.

The hair that liberally coated Pyon's naked body prickled up from his skin. Even between the words, delivered in a studiedly calm monotone, Pyon wondered which conspiracy.

When it came, it was bad.

The group of homosexuals who were suing Chemco because of the side-effects of the AIDS vaccine they were testing had admitted that their claim was false. They had been put up to it, and they were withdrawing their suit.

Did Southern Hemisphere Resources have any connection with the original fraud, the reporter wanted to know.

Just in time, Pyon avoided delivering the customary "no comment", which usually meant yes.

Instead, he drew in his breath sharply, and went for controlled bluster.

"Why in God's name are you ringing me at this time of the morning with this bullshit? It's not even worthy of a rag like yours. If Chemco do make this announcement, I, for one, will be well pleased. I've had great hopes for the AIDS vaccine, that's why I've been trying to buy the corporation for the last six months."

"The prospects for that don't look too good now, do they, sir? The suit has been depressing Chemco's price very substantially the last few weeks. We expect a rise of two or three dollars after the announcement. In fact it's already moving up in London, just on the rumours. And if people make a connection between Southern and these gays' phoney claims, well, your price is going to fall through the bottom. Do you have any comment to make on that, Mr Pyon?"

"No, I don't."

"So you've no comment?"

"I didn't say that, damn you. I said I wouldn't comment on the prospects for our share price as it relates to some wild rumour you've been sold. As to a hike in Chemco's price, we can handle that. We've been moving up steadily for the last few days, and that's in spite of an orchestrated smear campaign, which I may say has been ably supported by you fellas. Now get back to your NYSE screen if you want to see what's really going to happen."

Pyon barked out the words with a confidence he did not feel, put the phone down and sank back on the bed. "Jesus shit!" he groaned. "The bastards have finally stuffed me."

For a while, he lay quite still and gazed up at the elaborate plaster-work in the ceiling cornices of his hotel bedroom. He thought of his dead mother, his father, and Natalie.

He reached out for the telephone, and dialled Tenbury-Hamilton's office in London. After a significant delay, he was put through.

"Hello, Christy." The banker's voice was unruffled. "Weathering the storms?"

"What d'you think?"

"I should think you might be reaching for the life belts, by now."

Pyon had assumed before he rang that Anglo-American had decided to withdraw their services. Tenbury-Hamilton knew he knew, and felt not a twinge of embarrassment at what he was doing to Pyon, clad as the banker was in a hide as thick as an elephant's beneath his chalk-stripe suiting.

"No heroic loyalty from the gallant Brit, then?"

"My dear chap, no one pays me to be heroic, or gallant, come to that. I'm afraid your *Titanic* has hit the iceberg, and we're not in the lifeboat or salvage business."

"I certainly shan't be paying you for anything, ever again, Mr Tenbury-Hamilton."

"I'm very sorry to hear that, Mr Pyon, but obviously we will have to render our account for services to date."

"I'll bet you will." Pyon crashed the phone down before

he gave the banker the satisfaction of hearing him lose control.

For a few moments he continued to stare unseeing at the walls of the room, then, with an effort and a quick exhortation to the Almighty to help him, he reached for the telephone once more and dialled the number of the apartment he had taken for Natalie in Paris.

"'Allo," she answered, breathless.

"Hello, my angel. How are you?"

"Fine. I just got back from my painting lesson, and two of the other girls are coming to lunch. The phone was ringing as I came through the door."

She sounded happy, Pyon thought, what right had he to bring her down with his problems?

But he had no one else to tell, no one else – besides, maybe, Laura – who cared enough. And he could not bring himself to ask his daughter for her support.

"Natalie?" Even as he asked, Pyon despised his weakness. "Would you come to New York for a few days?" He had never wanted anyone's help like this before. "Things aren't too good."

She heard the unfamiliar apprehension in his voice. "Christy, what's the matter?" Her voice was gentle, concerned for him. Just the sound of it strengthened him.

"There's a lot of people want to see me go down. At the moment, they're winning. But I'm not giving in."

"I'll come," she said without hesitation. At last, it seemed he really needed her.

The Pyon expert

Such had been Harry Hackwood's success with the Christy Pyon story that he was now by-lining his own pieces in the news pages of his paper.

He was devoting his whole time to Pyon – his private life and his business life – and there had been plenty to keep him going since his scoop in Mauritius.

The bid for Chemco and the subsequent peaks and troughs of Southern's share price had anyway been a major preoccupation of the financial pages and the satirical magazines, but Harry Hackwood was known to be on the inside track. Now he could make a story out of someone's refusal to speak to him. Persuading Jeremy Fielder to meet him for lunch in the Savoy had been easy.

Harry had identified Fielder as one of the merchant bankers in the deal closest to Pyon. He was anxious to find out who, besides Newberry, was digging knives into Pyon's back.

Jeremy Fielder's manner as he greeted Harry Hackwood was cautious.

Harry attempted to put him at his ease. "Very good of you to see me when the pressure's on. Champagne?"

"Yes, thanks."

In the bar which overlooked the river and the narrow street by which Harry had been driven to his rendezvous with Newberry, the two self-important young men sat drinking a bottle of champagne that cost half the weekly wage of a nurse.

"Have you spoken to Pyon today?" Harry asked.

"I speak to him every day. That's normal in my job."

"What exactly do you do for a client in a bid like this?"

"What any merchant banker does for a client."

"That's what I'm asking, in general terms."

"It depends on the client. In Christy Pyon's case, he knows exactly what he wants to do. One doesn't try to dissuade him or even advise him much, one just does one's best to help and do what he asks."

"In what way?"

"Obviously, letting him have up-to-date information on prices and who's buying or selling, where we can tell; what the arbitrageurs are doing in New York. Preparing statements, generally holding his hand, providing a sympathetic ear and offering support."

"Of his price?"

"Don't be silly. That's illegal."

Harry gave him a quick, keen glance, and a smile. "But your bank have bought several large blocks of Southern."

Fielder shrugged. "Of course, we're entitled to make an

investment. We bought when the price was low because we were confident of a substantial rise."

"Still confident?" Harry asked lightly.

A millisecond's hesitation. "Sure."

"What's the latest position?"

"You must have heard Chemco's announcement."

Harry nodded. "And the latest prices; Chemco up at nearly $8. Southern at $1.25. How can you possibly be confident? Obviously you wouldn't have had anything to do with it, but do you suppose Pyon can deflect the rumours that he instigated the San Francisco claims?"

Fielder glared at him. "He'll sue any paper that prints so much as the faintest implication that he was involved."

"That could keep him busy. I know for a fact that the *Eye* are running an unequivocal piece."

Fielder paled. Harry spotted the drops of sweat forming beneath the line of his glistening black curls.

"Frankly, we'll leave it to them to test the water," Harry went on, to Fielder's relief; the *Eye* had cried wolf on Pyon too often to be taken seriously. Harry drained his glass and stood. "Let's go in and eat."

Over lunch, Fielder remained evasive. He maintained that Southern's price would recover, and that there was still support for Pyon's bid.

"A lot of the Americans privately want him to succeed," he said with apparent confidence. "They know as well as he does what a clapped out management they've got. There is still huge overmanning in the heavier plants. The whole corporation is ripe for unbundling."

"Sure," said Harry, "but the existing management have admitted this. They've come up with proposals to do more or less what Pyon said he would, and I believe they will, so do most others. And there's a very strong rumour that they're having talks with other parties about selling all the Saving & Loans banks. From most perspectives, Southern's bid is absolutely buried, and Pyon with it."

"You've never met him, have you?" Fielder said.

Harry shook his head. "Seen him at close quarters, though," he grinned.

"Why are you so proud of ruining a man, dragging his

private life through the shit, effectively destroying a perfectly good business?"

"I thought you said that Southern would rise again?"

"It will, in spite of the activities of muckrakers like you."

"Listen, I only find the stories. If the public reacts to them negatively, that's not my fault. It's my job to find out the truth and write about it."

"The truth? It's obvious that someone's been feeding you a bunch of specious gossip. Clever gossip that's hard to disprove. But that Iraq story was pure bullshit. When the dust's settled you'll find yourself with your editor in the high court. When Pyon finds out who's been feeding you all that crap, God help them."

Harry smiled placidly, and decided it was time to draw their luncheon to a close. Fielder's performance had satisfied him on one point, at least. Whatever other strokes he was responsible for in the Southern/Chemco fracas, stabbing Christy Pyon in the back was not one of them.

As a parting shot, he said lightly, "I was hoping you might have told me yourself that Anglo-American have withdrawn their services in the issuing of Pyon's junk bonds."

Fielder stared at him in angry amazement. "How the fuck did you get that?" He put his hand up. "No, don't tell me. You wouldn't tell me the truth anyway."

Harry shrugged. "I see your loyalties still lie with your erstwhile client, rather than your employer."

New York

Natalie came to New York to stay with Christy Pyon. He did not care now what the press said or what anyone else thought about his relationship with her.

Throughout the very public drama of Laura's kidnap he had managed to maintain his long-held practice of avoiding public appearances. But his was a familiar face now and he had been caught a few times in New York by door-stepping photographers.

Now he realised there was no longer anything to be gained by perpetuating an aura of mystique when most of the world's financial press was baying for his blood.

Pyon and Natalie lay in bed, wrapped in each others' arms. They had spent the night making love with a tenderness and an intensity which alarmed them both. Despite the energy he had spent, Pyon was invigorated and ready to face the world and his long-heralded demise with his old fortitude.

"Do you mind being seen in public with a pariah?" he asked Natalie. "People are beginning to think that I'm hiding. If I'm to stand any chance of saving my business from being eaten alive, I'll have to come out and show my face."

"I'm glad to be seen with you anywhere by anyone." She gave a gurgle of laughter. "There's not much of us anyway that hasn't already been seen by the whole world. Perhaps they won't even recognise us with our clothes on."

Pyon smiled. Natalie had no regrets for what had happened, she had told him. It was good and normal to make love with the man you loved. She did not give a damn for the judgements the world chose to make.

"But Christy, does it matter about business now? I told you, I don't care about your money; you know I mean that. Why not forget about it all?"

Pyon gazed at her with eyes that wanted to agree, but could not. "Oh, angel, bear with me. It's the way I am. I've been crucified, and I can't just let them get away with it."

"Who? Who's crucified you?"

"A lot of people. People I've trusted, for the most part. People who have done well by me. I'll tell you, I'll tell the world when I'm certain. Meanwhile, I've got to prepare myself to eat humble pie, and I want to make a meal of it. Tonight I'm making my first formal public appearance in fifteen years, to tell a room full of hacks what they already know, what they've been saying for weeks."

Natalie understood what that meant to him. She took his hand. "Poor old Christy. It must be like thinking for months that you're going to have a baby, and then losing it at the last minute."

"Maybe, I wouldn't know. A business is something like a child, though, you're right. It's something you conceive, give birth to, and nurture carefully in its young days. It's that, as much, – no, more than the money that makes me not want to lose all the businesses I've given birth to."

"But your real children, and the children I can have with you, they're more important."

Pyon smiled at her. "I know, but who the hell would want me for a father?" He leaned over her to kiss her wide brown lips.

Pyon kissed Natalie again, a few hours later, before he walked on to the stage of the press room at the World Trade Centre.

The moment he appeared, there was a cacophony of shouted questions and whirring, clicking cameras.

Pyon stood in the middle of the podium, with a cluster of microphones but no lectern in front of him. His large shoulders filled his elegantly cut, dark blue suit. His thick black hair was swept off his broad forehead. He stood upright with an easy nonchalance and his vivid blue eyes swept the gathering with a friendly smile, like a singer greeting his fans from the stage of a Las Vegas auditorium. After a few moments he raised both his hands and the crowd became silent.

"Thank you all for coming," Pyon's deep voice boomed gently through loudspeakers. "As you know, I don't make a habit of public appearances. Well," he gave a chuckle, "not voluntarily." The room burst into laughter and applause.

"I'm breaking with tradition this time to give you fellas the chance to hear it from the horse's mouth, instead of relying on rumours from third parties. You ought to know how unreliable third parties can be, especially over a deal like Southern Hemisphere's bid for Chemco."

He stopped and seemed to look at everyone in the room. The only sounds were the rustle of notebooks and sporadic camera clicks. "Southern Hemisphere Resources is now formally withdrawing its bid for the Chemco Corporation."

There was a release of tension in the room, and a growing murmur. Pyon stood quite still and waited for the noise to die down. When it had, he continued to speak, but with a perceptibly harder edge to his voice.

"There it is; not a rumour this time. But there have been too many, and in the end it is they – in other words, you – who have made our bid impossible. I'm not going to go over our justification for bidding; you've all heard it, and analysed it many times. A lot of other investors in Chemco agree with my proposals, and indeed, Chemco's board, in an effort to sustain their credibility, have adopted most of the ideas which I put forward. Adopting ideas, and having the skill or real inclination to put them into practice are two different things. I hope you will all watch this with as much attention as you have our own attempts to take on the corporation and put it back into some sort of order. Whether or not by talking down our bid you've done a service to the shareholders of Chemco and American industry in general will, I know, become obvious in time.

"Now, I'm not here with a harvest of sour grapes. Of course, I'm deeply disappointed with the failure of our bid, but I think you are all well aware that it failed not through any shortcomings in the nature of it, but through sabotage; a consistent planting of the seeds of rumour, which you people were happy enough to assist in germinating. Some of these rumours have been impressive in their" – he paused to find the word – "in their inventiveness; real flights of fancy. Unfortunately a few people got carried away, or taken for a ride, and I will find it necessary to put the record straight. Then, a few heads will roll." Pyon surveyed the sea of heads below him, as if seeking to identify which came into that category.

Then with a broad smile, and reverting to his original tone, he said, "Well, there it is, ladies and gentlemen. Thank you once again for your attention."

He started to walk off the stage to a pandemonium of questions. One caught his ear. "Mr Pyon, with Southern's price where it is, it's very open to predation itself. Are you in a position to fight off an attack?"

Pyon walked back to the microphone and the clamour ceased. "Vultures only prey on dead meat. I can promise you, we're not dead, or dying. Southern is in very good shape, and so am I." He nodded, and walked once more to the wings of the stage. This time he did not look back.

Al Souf's sense of honour

Victory was not sweet for Elizabeth Pyon.

She saw Pyon on the television, announcing the failure of his bid for Chemco. Apart from his appeal to Laura's kidnappers, it was the first time he had appeared on it since he had left her for Maria. She studied his photograph on the front page of *The Times*, and she marvelled at his resilience.

It was clear from the commentaries that he had made a great impression on these impressionable people, many of whom had never before seen him at first hand. There was an air of guilt in the reports, and some sanctimonious soul-searching about the role of the press in these circumstances.

Liz wanted to confess her own guilt, but no confessor was to hand. Laura was quite unaware of her part in bringing about the collapse of Pyon's bid. Julian, she thought, suspected, but was ambivalent in his attitude towards his father.

Liz never wanted to see Maria again, or Ken Newberry. She felt sullied by her co-operation with them. And the biliousness she felt was made worse by the profit she had made. By buying and selling at the moments Ken told her, in and out of Southern and Chemco, through the Bahamian lawyer he had recommended, she had made a profit of around £2 million. She had even tipped off her father a few times.

She felt less guilt about her use of Adnan al Souf. She had discovered subsequently, at one of her councils of war with Maria, Jackson, Shemilt and Newberry, that Ken had told al Souf the day before he went to Clonegall that the

San Francisco gays were withdrawing their suit, and that
SHR – or at least their representatives – were likely to be
identified as the instigators of the fraudulent claims.

But to Liz's pleasure, and as an indication of al Souf's sense
of honour, two days after he had announced his intention
not to pursue Chemco's banks, the best colt that Liz had
bred the previous year was returned to Clonegall. It was
the animal that Christy had bought from the stud early in
the summer, at a fair market price and in his own name,
and passed straight on to al Souf. Liz immediately returned
Pyon's money, with a request that he sign the Weatherby's
documents reverting ownership to her. She just had time to
submit the colt to the October yearling sales in Newmarket,
where he was likely to be the star attraction.

The newspapers telephoned continuously, tabloids and broad-
sheets. They all wanted to talk to someone, anyone who could
provide a personal angle on Pyon's hugely public debacle.

But she would speak to none of them. Each morning as
she left the house to walk down by the river, she expected to
find journalists and cameramen lurking among the beeches,
ready to pounce, and exacerbate her guilt.

But they weren't there. The main thrust had been put into
trying to find Pyon for his own reaction. But none of them
knew about Paris, and the elegant, fifth-storey apartment
he had found for Natalie on the left bank of the Seine by
Les Invalides, or the simple old farmhouse near Frascati.

Who put the knife in?

Pyon retreated like a snail into its shell. He saw no one
but Natalie. He leaned on her, used her energy to recharge
his own, and her commonsense and wisdom to find his
equilibrium.

They had been in Italy for two weeks. A fresh autumn wind
blew off the small hills around Frascati. Pyon and Natalie

369

sat comfortably after dinner in the small sitting-room of the farmhouse. On the walls hung a few old photographs of the family who had occupied the house for two centuries, and some biblical paintings of heartrending vividness. Pyon sat in an ancient squashy armchair with a glass of Black Bush at his elbow. Natalie was on his lap, nestling in his other shoulder, running her fingers through his black hair.

"I can feel you getting restless," she said softly. "I think you're ready to go back and find out who betrayed you."

"Do you want me to?"

"I don't want you to go anywhere. I love having you all to myself. But I know you want to, and you won't be happy until you do." She smiled at him. "I don't expect a bear to become a mouse in just a few weeks."

"Hey, you never said you wanted me to become a mouse."

She squeezed his thigh, and his genitals, through his loose cotton trousers. "You're right. I don't want a mouse."

"Thank God for that. But, you know, when I go back to London or New York, there'll be a lot of unpleasantness. I think you've seen enough of that."

"I don't want to come. I'm happy to stay here or in Paris, as long as it doesn't take too long."

Pyon shrugged. "It'll take as long as it takes. But I must find out who put the knife in. It had to be a team, and most of them close to me. I'm not going to like what I find. God knows, I've told you, I'm not blameless. I was pulling strokes; you have to, but only against the opposition, not people I thought were on my side. All of the fellas who agreed to help with the deal deserted me, bar one, and he was the least likely hero – an old Jewish wheeler-dealer called Weintraub. He deserves a prize for his loyalty, and b'Jaysus, he shall have it. When I've made sure that all the culprits have had their just deserts, I won't give up until the price of my shares is at least where it was before it tumbled. Then, I'm all yours."

"Do you really mean that, Christy?"

He nodded. "If you'd asked me that a few weeks ago, I couldn't have said that – well, not without lying. But now, I don't care. I want to sort things out for Julian and Laura, and try to build a few bridges between myself and Gianni and Caterina. And then, well, we'll live on the *Ile Vermont*, come to Paris now and again, race a few horses, and spend a bit of time in Ireland."

"With your first wife?"

"No, angel. No need to be jealous. She won't even speak to me. She's convinced I wasn't going to pay anything for Laura, and she won't forgive me. If she's lost that much trust in me, I blame myself."

"From what you say about her, she doesn't seem like someone you would want as an enemy. But what about Maria?"

Pyon eased Natalie off his lap and stood up. He made a face as if a nasty smell had entered the room.

"Maria." He blew a phut of breath out of the side of his mouth. "I'm not a particularly uncharitable man, but Maria was a terrible mistake that I tried to live with. She made it impossible. I'm not a saint."

Pyon paused and gave Natalie a wink and a smile. "Well, I used not to be, but I never deserved her venom. She was one of the factors in this recent fiasco. I suspected it from the moment she tried to get her hooks into Julian. I didn't realise her connection with Johnny Capra and the Actors' Bloody Production Company until we discovered the whole thing was a pathetic bit of fraud. Of course, I should have spotted it, but those lovely snaps of us appeared at the critical moment, and I left Julian and a couple of dozy lawyers to handle it. As a matter of fact, it won't be too difficult to put all that right. They've not had all the money from me yet, and our undertaking on their old debt is full of holes. But, of course, when I realised that I'd been taken for a ride over APC, it made sense of all the other muck that was flying around at the time."

"You mean Maria persuaded Julian to get involved, just to spite you?"

Pyon nodded.

"And Julian agreed?"

"Sure. Look, it was my fault that Julian wasn't too well disposed towards me, and anyway, I'm certain that Maria didn't tell him the whole truth. He genuinely saw it as a way for him to get his ideas across in Hollywood, and he didn't care whether or not I was going to make any money out of it. And I'll admit I was motivated by a desire to arouse his affection for me. He didn't know about the film titles being excluded from the bill of sale, or that Doug de la Tour had been encouraged to make a bit of a play for APC just when they were trying to bring me to the boil." Pyon gave a short laugh. "I fell for that like a nun at a gipsy horse sale."

Pyon wandered around the room in silence for a few moments. He stopped and stared at a particularly gruesome picture of Christ being lashed on the Via Dolorosa.

"I don't know whether she was working with the rest of the back-stabbers, but you can be sure, she'll not be happy with the consequences of her actions."

In the interests of furthering Hackwood's career

Pyon slipped back into London unnoticed next evening.

He asked Hanks to stop in Park Street and check the mews for doorsteppers. There was one, Hanks reported, dozing in a small car fifty yards from the house.

Pyon climbed out of the Mercedes and walked into the mews. He was wrapped in a long Burberry with the collar turned up. He approached the car and tapped on the driver's window. A young, blond man opened his eyes with a start, shook his head and blinked a couple of times before winding down the window.

"Hello?" he said warily.

"Are you waiting for me?" Pyon asked.

The reporter's eyes widened with astonishment. "Blimey," he stammered, "are you Christy Pyon?"

Pyon gave a loud laugh. "No. I'm Margaret Thatcher and it's your lucky day."

He saw a hand reach surreptitiously for the radio-phone on the car's console.

"Don't be such a tit," Pyon admonished lightly. "Leave that alone, and come into my house for a moment."

The young man climbed out of the car as if in a trance. Pyon had to shut the car door for him, before leading him across the mews and letting them both in through his neo-medieval front entrance.

There was no sign of life in the house. Pyon had told Hanks not to warn anyone of his return. He switched on the lights and without speaking to the reporter, ushered him up to the first-floor drawing-room.

"Drink?"

The blond man nodded. Pyon poured them both a generous measure of Black Bush.

"Now, young fella. You'll forgive me for saying that you don't give the impression of being a senior reporter. So, who do you answer to?"

"Nigel Judge."

"Ah. That's your rag, is it – the market leaders in tripe dressed as steak, especially where I'm concerned. And who were you supposed to report to when you saw me?"

"To Nigel, but I was going to get Harry Hackwood first. He asked me as a favour, and he's been very good to me."

"Mr Hackwood, eh? He's not been very good to me, but, perhaps in the interests of furthering his career, he may change his perspective. What d'you think?"

"I don't know, Mr Pyon."

"No," Pyon agreed, "but I think I do. He's ambitious. He'll want to be on whichever horse will take him furthest. So, give me his number. I'll call him myself. What's your name, by the way."

"Peter Jones."

"Okay, let's have the number."

Pyon passed him a gold ball-point and a notepad. He picked up the telephone from a table by a sofa and dialled the number.

After three rings a machine answered.

"I'm sorry that I'm out. If you need to contact me urgently, I'm at Eleven Park Walk." A Chelsea telephone number followed.

Pyon dialled the number.

"Eleven Park Walk. Good evening." A polite Italian.

"Harry Hackwood, please," Pyon said.

"One moment, sir."

After half a minute, an out-of-breath voice muttered, "Hackwood."

"I hope I'm not interrupting a good dinner, Mr Hackwood."

There was a moment's silence, then ill-disguised excitement in the voice that answered. "Not at all. I've just finished a plate of excellent *carpaccio*. How can I help you, Mr Pyon?"

"Glad to hear you're on the ball, Mr Hackwood. My car will pick you up in fifteen minutes."

Harry returned to his table, where he was entertaining the heir to an old Whig earldom and two eager young women. With some reluctance, he announced that he would have to leave in a few minutes without coffee and Armagnac. He declined to say why.

His heart pounded as he fought back the urge to tell them about his telephone conversation, or to call a photographer, until, with a surge of relief, he saw one of the *padrones* of the restaurant weave through the busy room to tell him that a car awaited him outside.

Hanks opened the back door of the dark Mercedes. "Evenin', Mr Hackwood."

"Evening." Harry nodded affably at the chauffeur whom he had several times tried to pump for information.

Hanks closed the door, climbed in himself, and drove off with a whoosh through the crisp night air.

"Where are we going?" Harry asked.

"Not far, sir."

Hanks swung the car around a few corners, and back across the Fulham Road. A minute later he pulled up outside a large stucco-fronted house in Tregunter Road.

The chauffeur leaped out, and opened the door for Harry. "Mr Pyon's waiting for you in there." He nodded at the house, from whose windows a few lights showed through leafless wisteria bines.

Harry walked up the short path to the front door, bursting with excitement.

He rang a doorbell, and Pyon opened the door himself. "Good evening to you, Mr Hackwood."

Harry took the large hand that was extended towards him and submitted his own to a warm grip.

"And to you, Mr Pyon," he said, betraying none of the thrill he felt.

Pyon showed Harry into a library at the back of the house. He pulled a bottle of Krug from a bucket and filled two glasses beside it.

"A drink," said Pyon, "to celebrate the peace."

"Thanks. What peace?"

"The cessation of hostilities between you and me, Harry."

"Have hostilities ceased?"

"If you value your career, and I'm sure you do, then they have. You'll have to decide whether or not to believe me when I say that if I wished to crucify you and your paper over a couple of the stories you published, I could do it in a matter of days. I think, though, from now on, you're on my side."

"I'm on the side of truth and justice, Mr Pyon, like any serious journalist," Harry said with only a hint of a smile.

Pyon uttered a burst of loud laughter. "Of course you are, Harry. But however diligently you check your sources, truth can be a very elusive quarry. You can find yourself writing dangerous fiction. I like to do a bit of story-telling myself, you know. I made up a story about a shipload of nasty chemicals heading off to Iraq, and just to impress my listener, I backed it up with some convincing paperwork. You'll note, I said listener, for there was only one."

While Pyon was speaking, Harry was taking a series of rapid sips from his glass. Now he stopped, and looked at the Irishman, and tried not to flinch before the piercing blue eyes. He looked for a chink in the other man's countenance, through which a bluff might be visible. But he saw none.

Pyon went on, "You know who I'm talking about." It was not a question. "Not very loyal of him, was it?"

"If he believed it, maybe he thought he was doing the right thing," Harry replied. He still had no way of telling if Pyon was merely fishing.

"Come, now. Would you call him an honourable fella, who'd want to do the right thing?" Pyon asked.

That did not narrow the field much, Harry thought. He smiled. "No, but he was probably only protecting his own back by leaking the story to me."

Pyon did not show his glee at Harry's slip. Only one of those he suspected could have been potentially implicated if the story had been true.

"That's where you're wrong. Ken was much too far away from the alleged incident for it to affect him. He leaked my little morsel of disinformation out of malice and greed, don't you think?"

Harry hesitated, tried for a moment to challenge the force that radiated from Pyon's eyes, and was beaten.

"Yeah." He heaved his stout torso in defeat, and turned away. "But as a source of information, his credentials were impeccable."

"And will he stand up in court, d'you suppose, and say, 'Sorry, it's all my fault. I fed Harry Hackwood this stuff to manipulate the share price of the company of which I was a shareholder and director'? He won't, will he? He'll deny ever having seen or spoken to you. I'll bet you've not revealed your source to anyone – have you? – so it's a bit late to start doing that now. And were you ever seen with him? I doubt it."

"Only by a couple of cab-drivers."

"His intimacy with cabbies goes right back to his early days. If you could ever find them, you couldn't get them to admit to anything. So, you're on your own. I can provide incontrovertible documentary evidence that that story was a complete and malicious fabrication. I could possibly convince a court that it was as a result of that story that my bid for Chemco failed. That could run into a few bobs' worth of damages to Southern Hemisphere, and you'd end up with more than just a slap on the wrist."

"I don't think you'd be awarded any damages. There were too many other contributory factors in the failure of your bid."

"Sure, and most of them perpetrated by you, with help from my old colleague."

"The Mauritius story was indisputable."

Pyon waved that aside. "That didn't do much harm. And

who gave you the lead for that? It's okay, don't bother to tell me; I know."

"All right, Mr Pyon. But you told me we were drinking to celebrate the peace, which I presume means that you don't intend to sue me or my paper. What are your terms?"

"Good lad. Right on the button. I won't sue you, if you now co-operate with me. I've not taken it personally, what you've done to me. If you hadn't been chosen, someone else would have been. You were doing your job, and you did it very well. So I'd now like to make use of your talents. If you were me, what would you be wanting to achieve now?"

Harry considered this. "I'd want to recover all the ground lost in my shareprice, I'd want to bring to book the parties behind the failure, and I'd want to divorce my second wife. Not necessarily in that order."

"Very well summarised, Harry, but the order doesn't matter. They'll all be done."

Pyon poured the remaining contents of the champagne bottle into their glasses. "Would you open another bottle for us? Over on the sideboard there."

Harry did as he was asked.

"Now tell me, Harry. Why did you say I would want to divorce my wife?"

"I imagine you want to spend more time with the lovely Miss Felix."

"True enough, but why else?"

"I assumed she was involved in your purchase of APC, which hasn't turned out to be such a great deal, has it?"

"We'll see about that. But how did you know she was involved?"

"When I was being advised about various stories considered to be detrimental to the well-being of Southern Hemisphere, I got the impression that there were several people involved but, not surprisingly, Newberry wasn't saying who. So I did a bit of digging. I discovered that Maria has known Johnny Capra for years. He was a friend of her father." He hesitated at the sharpness of Pyon's reaction. "You obviously didn't know."

"No, I did not," Pyon hissed. "And I think he was more than just an old acquaintance, which would explain why I didn't. Shows what happens if you take your eye off the ball for too long. I did subsequently realise what was going on. Who else have you discovered is involved?"

"No one else so far. I can tell you that your faithful gofer, Jeremy Fielder, and his bosses are not."

"How do you know?"

"Just from gauging reactions."

"Hmm. That's not too conclusive, but we'll assume you're right for the moment. I'll tell you what I want you to do for me, to ensure your immunity from any legal action I might take. I want you to help me establish precisely who the guilty parties are, and provide watertight evidence. Then, you help me expose them. At the same time, I want you to use any influence you have, and I know for a fact that you have two very influential friends on the better class of Sunday paper, to arrange an in-depth interview in which I can put my side of this whole chain of events."

"I see," said Harry. "That shouldn't be too hard. Obviously tracking down the folks who shat on you is a worthwhile journalistic exercise in its own right. But I have the feeling that you really were involved in the American gays' bogus suit."

"I knew about it, and I did not try to stop it, but there is absolutely no way I can be positively linked to it. You can take my word for it, Harry, I've been doing these kinds of deals for a very long time, and I know the risks and how to avoid them. There's no one to prove I'm not clean as a whistle."

Pyon looked deep into Harry's eyes, and placed a hand on his shoulder. "There it is, Harry. I have conditionally forgiven you for what you've already done, and I am providing you with the opportunity to write an even bigger story. I'll give you all the help I can. Obviously no one, but no one, must know of our relationship. To that end, I am going to take you to court over your original articles about Natalie and me. I won't win, indeed, in the interests of thrift, I'll probably drop the case after a week or two, and I doubt that anyone will think much the less of either of us. But they'll know we're not friends. Okay?"

Harry smiled and nodded. That would keep his competitors off the scent, more than anything.

"You'll have to use whatever guile you can to get the other interview fixed up," Pyon said.

"I've a better idea. Jeremy Fielder's still on your side. He knows one of the two as well as I do. And he gives him a lot of information. That particular fellow would do you justice, if only to keep Jeremy sweet. And I'll give him a few leads without him knowing. Then the revelations that will ultimately attribute the blame won't be seen to have come only from me."

"Good lad, Harry. You're thinkin' well. Tomorrow, I'm going to call a short press conference, with a chance for a few photographs, so I'd better get my beauty sleep. Before you go, I'll give you three names for starters. Leo Jackson, Lenny Shemilt, and Adnan al Souf. Now, get going. I'm sorry if you missed the chance of a leg-over tonight, but we'll not be meeting like this again. If I want to see you, it'll be in Paris." He held out his hand. "So, goodbye, and I'll see you in court."

"Good night, Mr Pyon. And thank you."

Los Angeles

Three days later Pyon flew to Los Angeles. He had invited Johnny Capra to meet him at the offices in APC's studio lot to discuss the completion of SHR's payment for the beleaguered corporation.

He had insisted that the first meeting should be between just the two of them. Now he sat in a large swivel desk chair, gazing out on to a village of disused sets, with his back to the door. He heard Capra arrive, and swivelled round. He swung his feet up on to the desk and greeted Capra with a nod at a small vacant chair.

The office door was still open. Pyon swung his feet back to the floor, stood up and walked across to close it.

"I think we'd better keep this meeting as private as possible," he said from behind the American's shoulder.

Capra shrugged. "The terms of our deal are public knowledge," he said with a Californian lack of lip movement. "You only paid 10 per cent, and the balance is overdue. If you don't pay it, we'll sue you. It's not too complicated."

"We'll pay, but there are one or two minor changes to make to our agreement."

"Look, man, it's too late for all that shit."

Pyon walked in front of him, leaned down and put his face six inches from the other's. "Listen to me, you inept little toerag, I'll tell you what's going to happen; you'll listen, and then you'll do exactly as you're told."

He straightened himself and picked up a folder from the desk. Slowly he withdrew a sheaf of photographs from it.

First he showed Capra a picture of a man, taken with a very long lens, outside an hotel in Santa Monica.

Capra started, but quickly controlled himself. "What's so great about a shot of a narcotics dealer that everyone in the country knows?"

"Nothing, on its own. He's been convicted and given fifteen years in jail. They had a clear case against him, but they couldn't quite home in on the financial personnel of his operation, remember?"

"Listen, man, stop pissing me. This ain't got nothing to do with our deal."

"Our deal was about you needing a lot of money in a hurry. The police hauled away fifty million dollars' worth of coke from that bust, remember. So someone must have lost a pile of money." Pyon pulled a second photograph from the folder. "I wonder if it might have been the fella yer man is chatting to in this rather good photograph."

Capra blanched as he gazed at the shot of himself, obviously in serious discussion with the cocaine dealer.

"But," he blustered, "that don't mean a thing. So, I knew the guy, but there was nothing to connect me with his activities."

"Except, maybe, this shot, and a few others."

"Yeah, sure," Capra jeered, recovering, "then why the hell didn't the narcs use them to indict me?"

"Because they haven't seen them. These aren't police shots."

Capra did not move a muscle.

"The fella who took them is a bit of an opportunist, but he's a sensible, patient man. Why sell something like this once, when he could have two bites at the cherry? He'd been waiting for the right buyer. He'd heard a bit of gossip about the difficulties in our negotiations, and reckoned he'd identified one. He was right. I've paid him very well, and I understand that he's prepared to do business with you now. But before I tell you who he is, we're going to straighten up our little deal."

"You some kind of cheap, motherfucking blackmailer, are you?" Capra sneered.

"I'm not, as it happens. All I want is what you and I agreed I was buying, before you slipped a bunch of doctored contracts across my dozy ex-lawyers, who, I understand, are still taking a few instructions from yourself. You'll have something else for them to get their teeth into if you don't do as you're told. I'm not sure, though, that they're the right men to defend a fella on a major narcotics charge."

Pyon steered *Speranza* out through the bottleneck mouth of the Marina del Rey. Behind him, the morning sun was a dirty orange orb above the coastal sprawl of Los Angeles. Pyon looked forward across the Pacific and welcomed the first flutterings of the offshore breezes on the side of his face. With a smile, he turned to Julian, beside him in the wheelhouse.

"By Christ, I'm glad to get away from that dump for a bit. Could you go below and see if they've stowed a few Coors for us?"

Julian ducked down the companionway to reappear a minute later with half a dozen cans of the delicious light Colorado beer. He and his father each pulled the ring off a can. The flax-coloured liquid washed the smog from their throats and put some colour into Julian's careworn cheeks.

"Well, J, I think we've cracked it."

"Yes, I'm amazed we've done it so quickly."

"We were lucky. Johnny's been investing heavily in other areas he knows even less about than the movie business. He's caught a cold – more than that, you could call it fiscal pneumonia. He's desperate for the money."

"But he could have rescinded our deal, because we'd only paid 10 per cent of the price we agreed."

"Sure, but you should have seen the look on his face. He hadn't time to find another buyer."

"Can he still pull out now?"

"Not now he's seen our money. On Monday all those rights will be ours. And, thanks to the strange provincialness of West Coast Americans, those titles have never been properly exploited in Europe. We'll appoint new distributors in London, and squeeze a few deals out of the new satellite stations; they're going to be ravenous for product."

"But what about our production budgets? Can we raise the extra twenty million we need for my projects?"

"At this moment I'm not certain. The board at Southern have in the past been happy enough to jump up and down on my decisions like a good little team of rubber stamps. But at this somewhat critical period, I must be seen to be a listening chairman. Of course, I own the majority of shares now. I bought another 10 per cent at just over $1.50 a month ago."

"Personally? But even that must have cost you fifteen million."

"Sure, but I could see a healthy profit coming from my own holdings in Chemco. I'd bought at $5 and sold at $8, nearly twenty million shares." Pyon heaved his shoulders with a one-sided smile. "Lucky they didn't go the wrong way."

"Lucky? I don't suppose luck came into it."

"Believe me, it shouldn't have done, but it did."

Speranza rumbled out into the Pacific, and headed southwest for Santa Catalina Island. Pyon called the master up to the helm, and he and Julian went aft to sit out on the broad teak deck. They had worked – or rather, Pyon had buzzed and chivvied like an inexhaustible dynamo while Julian watched – for the last week.

It was Pyon's policy when dealing with a problem to come in and devote every available minute to it until it was solved. He allowed no one to rest, and few could match his energy. But now that the matter of APC's catalogue of premium classic movies had been dealt with, he wanted to tackle another more personal problem.

Pyon and Julian settled themselves into old-fashioned wooden deckchairs, and gazed back with satisfaction at the receding skyline under its grimy brown haze.

They opened two more cans of Coors.

"A day or two of this won't do me any harm," declared Pyon, "but there is something you and I have to clear up, don't you think?"

Julian glanced at him, trying to disguise the guilt which he had felt since the beginning of this Hollywood deal.

"Buying APC hasn't turned out to be such a bad deal," he offered by way of pre-emptive defence.

"Balls. It's still a rotten deal. We're stuck with the Aussie TV station. That's got to stop broadcasting on 31 December, and what are we left with? A studio complex, no licence and no staff. It doesn't take much imagination to realise that anyone who wants to buy it is going to wait a month or so before they put in a bid."

"But surely, if they buy it now, they're guaranteed the licence."

"Sure, that's worth a bit, but they'd do better to get their own licence and buy the hardware cheap. Look, we may do a deal on it, but it won't be much of a deal. The Actors' Production Company is a terrible shitty business. It hasn't been run as a genuine corporation for ten years. You realise we should have backed out of it this week, and cut our losses. But, if I've a fault, I'm inclined to be bloody-minded, and I'd like to show these parties that I can make the thing come right. I suppose the truth is, I don't want to admit that I've been tucked up. Anyway, if we're a bit lucky, and handle what lousy assets there are with a bit of imagination, we'll win. Besides, once I've made a commitment. I like to stand by it. And I made the commitment to you. What I want to know is, just how rotten a deal did you think it was when you brought me into it?"

"It seemed to me," Julian answered slowly, "that while

there were a few obvious shortcomings, it was a relatively cheap way of getting to the centre of American movie-making."

"Did Maria tell you that the deal stank?"

"Not in as many words. She wasn't sure what my attitude was. After all, when she first came on the scene, I wasn't one of your great supporters. But I admit I've altered my views over the last six months or so."

"My, that's big of you."

"Don't be like that. That's exactly what I've always disliked about you. Why crow at me? I'm your bloody son, whether you like it or not. I've got my ambitions too, you know, less concerned with profits than yours, but I'm not so idealistic that I don't realise their importance in this industry."

"Okay, okay. How much did Maria tell you?"

"Not much. She was relying on my enthusiasm and your vanity to push the deal along. Of course, she completely took me for a ride to begin with. I met her at Enzo Fratinelli's. She told me she was called Filumena di Francesci."

Pyon sat up. "Of course! I remember. Maria was in Annabel's the night you and I were there. I never made the connection with your Filumena. I just guessed she was up to something malicious."

"That's why you wanted to go so suddenly?"

"Sure it was."

Julian laughed. "What a crazy situation. Of course I was furious when I discovered."

"How did you discover?"

"She wanted to meet Mum. I arranged it. They met before I got there and I interrupted them. Maria was talking about punishing you. Mum told me who she really was and chucked her out. She came straight round to my studio to plead, and I . . . well, she talked me round."

Pyon looked at his son for a few moments, and struggled with an indigestible thought. He turned to look back at the sea and the ever-widening wake of the boat.

"She did, did she?" he growled.

"I asked her if it had anything to do with her scheme to chastise you, but she was adamant that she admired me as a film-maker, and reckoned this was a good step for me."

"And you believed her?"

"Well . . . sure. I'm as vain as the next man, I suppose. After all, *Michael and Mustapha* was still getting great notices."

"Have you seen her much since then?"

Julian thought of the hours he had spent alone in bed over the past months, thinking about her succulent brown body, reliving the supreme moments of their love-making. He glanced at his father, but was no longer deceived by the rock-like face.

"I haven't seen her since August," he answered truthfully.

"Hmm," Pyon rumbled. "You'll understand that I can't let it rest. Her little scam with you was not her only effort. She's not behaved at all gracefully. She'll soon be hearing the fluttering wings of her malicious little chickens coming home to roost."

Channel 21

From Los Angeles, Pyon flew to Sydney. The deal with Johnny Capra was thoroughly sewn up. Pyon had left nothing to chance or the incompetence of other people. He was in the right frame of mind to deal face to face with a man as notoriously hard as Doug de la Tour.

It was the first time they had met in the flesh. Though they had been rival bidders on several deals over the years, communication had always been by letter or lawyer.

Their first meeting was at de la Tour's sprawling mansion, twenty miles north of Sydney, looking out over the Pitt Water inlet.

De la Tour's invitation on the telephone had been affable. He had implied that two gladiators of their stature should meet on friendly ground. He also implied that in Pyon's current circumstances, they would not be fairly matched, and he could afford to be magnanimous.

"Welcome to Sydney, Mr Pyon." De la Tour held out his hand, and Pyon smiled as he took it. His eyes shone like two sapphires in the deep tan of his unfleshy face.

The Australian was surprised by the alert youthfulness of a fifty-one-year-old who had just been taken to the cleaners by the world's media and stock markets, and lost a very major deal. Instinctively, he raised his guard.

Pyon, by contrast, relaxed. "Call me Pyon. Everyone else does."

"Those little turds in the gutter press have been calling you a few other things."

"I didn't particularly object to one of the sobriquets used by one of your rags, "South Sea Island Super Stud", though it was a little inaccurate, for I only covered the one filly."

"She looked like quite a cracker."

Pyon acknowledged the compliment with a slight nod.

De la Tour opened a bottle of champagne, and filled two glasses.

"Now," he went on, "what business have we to discuss?"

"None. I didn't come to talk business with you. I only want one piece of information. I want to know who suggested to you that you should announce your intention of going after APC when you did."

De la Tour smiled. "After the back-stabbers, are you? I must say, I was surprised, even rather unimpressed that you bought that dummy. Still, I was told you would, and it didn't cost me anything."

"And it won't cost you anything to tell me who it was."

"That's true, but it might cost you."

"Oh no. This is outside any deal-making. You and I are from the same stable. There are moments when you must help your own. You know that. Within the rules of the game, you had a perfect right to wind me over APC, but this was part of a far bigger scheme, as you must be aware."

"You've got to hand it to them," de le Tour said. "They dug up a pile of shit, and fed it to the swine with great skill, I thought. I only wish someone had had the sense to tell me as each instalment was going in. But they didn't. So, what the hell, they'll regret it now."

He paused, and walked across to a panoramic window to watch the afternoon sun glint off the smooth sea.

Pyon did not hurry him.

De la Tour turned back to him. "I doubt that I'm going to surprise you much: Lenny Shemilt and Ken Newberry. I owed Lenny a small favour. So," de La Tour shrugged. "But they should have told me what was going up."

Pyon nodded slowly. "Thank you. You haven't surprised me at all."

De la Tour refilled their glasses, warming to Pyon and his idea of a special relationship between them.

"I must say, Pyon, when you rang after this morning's announcement, I assumed you wanted to try and sell me Channel 21."

"What announcement?" Pyon asked, reluctantly believing that some new disaster had struck his beleaguered company while he had been in the air.

De la Tour laughed. "What? Hadn't you heard? Ah well, you'll hear as soon as you get back to Sydney, so I may as well tell you now. The ABA have announced that they're not granting any more television broadcasting licences for two years."

Pyon showed no reaction. But inside he bubbled; all at once, it was a seller's market in Australian TV stations. "Oh, that," he said. "Yes, of course I'd heard it." He had not heard or seen a news bulletin since getting off the plane. "But you'd already made it clear that you had no intention of buying Channel 21."

"Since this morning, I have every intention."

Pyon opened the palms of his hands in a gesture of regret. "I wish I'd known that, Doug. We're well advanced in discussions with another party."

"What?" De la Tour was furious. "What other party, for Christ's sake? Good God, man, we've been talking to your people for months about it. Why are you talking to anyone else?"

"But your last communication was an unequivocal no. We were told that you'd wait until our licence lapsed at the end of the year, and make us an offer for the studios. Don't your people tell you what's going on in this sort of negotiation?"

"All right, all right, but that was all normal bargaining. Of course we wanted it."

"You should have said so. Never mind, Doug, you'll be able to apply for a new licence in a couple of years."

De la Tour became conciliatory. "Look, don't be such an asshole, Pyon. You haven't completed a deal. So, you can reopen negotiations with me."

Pyon shook his head. "I'm not getting involved in negotiations with you, Doug. You already know everything there is to know about the station. You've seen all the figures, you've had a draft contract of sale. I don't want any more fucking about, or renegotiating. Just write down what you're prepared to pay."

De la Tour thought for a moment, then walked briskly across the large open room to the door. Pyon heard his heels click on the slate floor of the great entrance hall. A minute or so later, his footsteps returned, and he came into the room with a smile on his face, and a large sheet of paper in his hands.

"There you are, Pyon. I think that ought to help you make up your mind. As you'll see, the offer's open for forty-eight hours."

De la Tour handed the piece of paper to Pyon, who folded it without looking at it, and tucked it into an inside breast pocket.

Pyon gave a quick, sideways nod of his head. "Grand. I'll have a look at it and let you know tomorrow."

He picked up his glass and drained it. "Thank you, Doug. I must get back into Sydney. I've another meeting, I'm selling a couple of tin mines out on the Mains. Interested?"

De la Tour laughed. "No thanks. I've done my shopping for today."

"I'll be in touch then. Goodbye for now, Doug."

They shook hands, and Pyon walked without haste from the room. His host saw him to the front door, where a Rolls-Royce waited at the bottom of the steps.

When the limousine had glided down the long drive and was out of sight of de la Tour's house, Pyon pulled the paper the Australian had given him from his pocket. He unfolded it, read it, and a smile spread across his face.

De la Tour must have been a lot more eager than Pyon had realised to get into television. His Hollywood deal now looked like showing a healthy profit.

London – business as usual

Pyon was in an ebullient mood as he walked into Southern Hemisphere's Mayfair offices.

He beamed at the commissionaire, winked at the receptionist, and bounded up the stairs to see Ken Newberry.

Newberry's secretary looked apprehensive as Pyon strode through her outer office, and burst through her boss's door.

"Morning, Ken. How are you?"

Newberry looked at his old partner's healthy, smiling face for signs of aggression. He had heard about the visit to de la Tour, and had little faith in the Australian's discretion. But there was no sign of animosity in Pyon. The blue eyes contained a triumphant gleam, attributable, no doubt, to the deal he had done over Channel 21.

"Morning, Christy. I've got to hand it to you, I never thought you'd sort out the mess at APC. As far as I could see when I went there, we'd bought a real pup."

"We did, but now it's on its way to being a halfway decent investment. We'll need to divert another twenty million or so into it for next year's productions, but I've no doubt you'll be supporting me in the board?"

"Well, yes. I mean, I think you've shown that it wasn't such a bad move. The Stock Exchanges are impressed. We're back at nearly four dollars."

"Yes, I've seen. Are you going to engage in another bout of profit-taking on your Southern shares?"

"Of course not, Pyon. I bought at the bottom because, like you, I had faith in our recovery."

"And the price reflected less than half the asset value. But I wonder if there'll be any more sudden revelations to send us back down again."

Newberry could not meet Pyon's piercing eyes. He shuffled around with some papers on his desk. "I doubt it now. You know, I think all that mud-slinging was part of an orchestrated campaign while the Chemco bid was still on the cards."

"You didn't at the time. We discussed it, if you recall, on several occasions. You thought it was just bad luck. However, I think now you're right. I'm banging out a couple of writs today that might eventually shed a bit of light on a few shady traitors who've been lurking in the wings."

Newberry stood up and walked around his desk to divert attention from his sudden pallor. "Writs? What sort of writs? D'you think that's a good idea? I mean, you don't want to stir muddy waters."

"Of course I don't. I'm suing the paper that published those photos of me and Natalie in Mauritius."

"But what can you sue them for?"

"Invasion of privacy, that sort of thing."

"But you don't stand a chance of winning in this country. You might have got somewhere with that in France, but not here."

"We'll see. I'm also suing *Private Eye* over the piece they ran on the chemicals to Iraq."

"Here, that's not a very good idea, is it? And anyway, Hackwood's paper ran it first."

"Sure, but the *Eye* had a lot more detail."

"But they can defend themselves. From what you told me, they were right."

"Ah, well, since I spoke to you about it, I've found out I was wrong. We're absolutely in the clear, and I can prove it. That'll go a long way to clearing our name, and with luck it should point a finger in the direction of whoever leaked, and God help the bastard when I find him."

Newberry did not reply immediately. Forcing himself to sound calm and circumspect, he said, "I hope you do. That story did more damage than any other."

"I don't know. It's hard to say. There was a sort of cumulative effect. It was a splendidly conceived campaign, and it worked. Still, I've learned my lesson for next time." Pyon was silent for a moment, then, with a change of tone, he said, "Right, Ken, there's a lot to catch up with. Can you get me up to date with everything that's been going on? It's back to business as usual now."

Pyon's manner gave Newberry a moment's confidence. He had a reprieve, time to work out a strategy and check that his tracks were well-covered. But fear still churned his stomach like a cement mixer with no 'off' switch.

Harry Hackwood was trying to look worried. His editor had called him in to tell him about Pyon's writ.

"I don't understand," he stammered. "He hasn't got a case at all, has he?"

"No," the editor said, "he's going for invasion of privacy and misrepresentation. I don't think he's expecting to win. He's just trying to make us look as nasty as he can. Our best bet is to be seen to be even-handed. That story you ran about his daughter setting herself up as an organic farmer in Wales or wherever it is was good. It reflected well on the Pyon family generally. We'll want more of that sort of thing. We'll try and run any positive pieces we can, news or social. A nice profile of the Mauritian girlfriend would be good, and something about your old school chum, Julian."

"Hardly a school chum, but I'll see what I can find. You think that'll make Pyon go away?"

"Yes. I'll ring him, and talk to him head-on, tell him what we propose. That usually works."

"But why bother if he won't win?"

"First, the readers don't really approve of kicking a man when he's down; in fact he's almost in the position of underdog, and a natural for a bit of sympathy. Second, I don't want to have to pay hundreds of thousands in barristers' fees, or have the Press Council breathing down my neck."

"All right. I'll look for some nice things to say. That'll make a change. Any excuse to talk to the lovely Laura or, come to that, the lovely Natalie."

"Good lad, Harry. You carry on, and I'll talk to the Paddy. By the way, I've also heard that he's suing *Private Eye* for the Iraq story. We ran that too, so we may have to expect another writ."

"*Private Eye* gave much more detail. Our piece was

deliberately obfuscating, if you remember, because we didn't have enough hard, documentary evidence."

"We'll see. Let's look after him now, and maybe he'll let us off. Now obfusc off and get on with it."

Green matters

Harry Hackwood next saw Laura Pyon at a press conference called by her father. She was sitting beside Pyon on a dais at the end of the room in the Press Centre.

"Morning, ladies and gentlemen. As you can see, I've developed a bit of a taste for making public announcements. I've decided that the more you see me, the less you'll rely on guesswork, and maybe you won't write quite so much balls."

The journalists laughed. Pyon was positive copy now. He had taken his medicine like a man.

"There's just two announcements, and both backed up with press packs which contain something with which you are all fairly unfamiliar, namely, facts. First, we have reached a mutually pleasing, and amicable deal with the workforce in our mines in Transvaal. The terms have the backing of the ANC, with whom, incidentally, we have been talking for several years, for we are as aware as anybody of the essential commercial need for social justice in South Africa. As with most negotiations, the unions were asking for more than they wanted. We knew that, and naturally responded with a lower offer. Eventually we ended up somewhere between the two opening positions. This is how bargaining works all over the world, and it's how it has always worked. Some of you chose to present our stance as unjust and racist, whereas we have one of the best records for industrial relations in the South African mining industry. In your press pack are statements from the two leading negotiators for the unions and a representative of the ANC. Please check their authenticity, and tell your readers. On a fiscal note, the increased wages are partially linked to increased productivity, so our profitability will not be greatly affected."

Pyon paused and looked around to add gravitas to his statement. Some of the journalists began to ask questions, but he held up his hand. "I'm not answering questions today. You have all the details you need in this." He held up a press kit. "I'd much rather you confirmed its contents with third parties.

"Now, my second announcement involves a bit of rank nepotism, except that, in this case, the nepotism is only incidental. As some of you know, Agrichimica of Brazil is a subsidiary of ours. You will also know, because some of you have written about it, that Agrichimica has been involved in a certain amount of forest clearance in the Amazon basin. When the story first became public, I was not fully aware of the truth or extent of this clearance. Since then, indeed, since shortly before then, I had been prompted by my own daughter to look into it. She had recently returned from a fact-finding mission in Brazil, and had identified a company of ours as one of the culprits in deforestation. She was right, though I must correct the wild guesses as to the extent of it. It had been going on, but only a few thousand acres were involved."

There was a buzz of approbation from Pyon's audience.

"A few thousand acres is a few thousand acres too much, I know. I'm not trying to disclaim responsibility for what has been done. It is only recently that the scientists have made us aware of the ecological significance of these tropical rain-forests. And like all macro-climatic effects, they are not obvious to people on the ground. I can announce that we have now ceased all such activity. To ensure that there is no repetition of this, or any other damaging activity by any of our companies, subsidiaries, or joint ventures throughout the world, Southern Hemisphere Resources is appointing its own ecological ombudsman. And this is where the nepotism comes in. That officer will be my daughter, Laura Pyon.

"But before you allow your natural cynicism to lead you to the conclusion that this is all a whitewash and a sop to an increasingly green public, I should tell you that my daughter is entirely her own woman. She has never done what I've asked her, and she's not going to start now. She is passionate about the issues involved, and has already made her own commitment to environmentally friendly farming practices in this country. There is no question but that she will be very thorough, and unstinting in her criticism of any shortcomings she finds in our own companies. I have appointed Laura precisely because she has nothing to lose by carrying out her duties thoroughly. But I'm going to leave her here to answer your questions for herself, and convince you that this initiative which we are taking is genuine and, incidentally, unique among any comparable world-class corporation. Ladies and gentlemen, Miss Laura Pyon."

Laura stood up, to a background of murmuring and shuffling feet, as the journalists prepared to make their judgement of her, while Pyon slipped quietly from the stage.

The reaction to Laura's short speech, and to her answers to the barrage of questions, was all that she could have hoped for. The job had been her idea and she knew what she was talking about. She announced that she was appointing two environmental scientists of international repute as her consultants, and that she personally would deal with every single matter that was brought to her attention.

The journalists were ready to be impressed by this, but what provided a real story for them was the fact that she was a self-confident, very goodlooking woman who had been incarcerated with a half-billion-dollar price tag on her liberty.

Harry Hackwood, jostling among the others of his profession, smiled to himself, and shook his head with admiration. It was a master-stroke of Pyon's to make this appointment. He slightly resented that Pyon had not given him a preview of the announcement, but he also understood that for it to work, it could not have been presented to a single paper.

Even so, having met Laura face to face when he had interviewed her about her farm, he felt he had the edge over most of his competitors when it came to the aspect of Laura that would most fascinate the tabloid readers – her private life.

Laura was with her mother in the brightly decorated new kitchen of the house that Maeve had left to her and Julian.

As soon as she had signed a contract with her brother to buy out his interest in the farm, the house and its contents, she had made energetic plans to transform the ancient manor.

But this early enthusiasm had not yet penetrated beyond the kitchen. Her energy had been diverted by the farm, and the work her father had asked her to do before announcing her appointment with Southern Hemisphere. She had worked hard, and kept at bay the depressing fact that she had none of the love life which might have fascinated the readers of Harry Hackwood's paper. But she was less concerned about this than her mother.

"Laura, darling," Liz was saying, "are you sure you should have agreed to do this job for your father? You seem to be terribly busy here already. You'll have no time left to enjoy yourself."

"What do you mean? I'm loving every minute of it. I had no idea real work could be such a turn-on. Do you know, I learn something new every day. The men on the farm have been amazing. Fortunately, they're used to taking orders from a woman, which seems to go against the grain of the average Herefordian – they're horrendous chauvinists, most of these Anglo-Welsh. Of course, they think my decision to go organic is potty, especially as it will take so long for me to be recognised by the Soil Association. But I know I'm right."

"I must say I never imagined you becoming a farmer. What are you going to do when you get married?"

"If I get married. That looks a distant prospect at the moment. Most of the men I've come across recently are such wankers, and I don't just mean the ones round here. Anyway, I've got plenty of time for all that."

"Well, don't leave it too long."

Laura gave her mother an affectionate smile. "Do stop fussing. You'll have some grandchildren sooner or later. Maybe Dad had a point; I remember him once saying to me that women have three consecutive overriding aims; marriage, children and grandchildren. Only I seem to be abnormal."

Liz sighed. "Your father is a rotten psychologist. He only deals in types, not people."

"I don't want to have another row with you about him. He's been very kind to me, and good company when I've seen him. You've got to admire his resilience; I mean, he's had to put up with some real vilification, and I don't think he gave in. Now he seems to have got all the press and the media on his side. I must say when he agreed to make me environmental officer for the company, I thought he might be laughed out of the room, but they loved it, and that was before I gave my brilliant speech. I know you must have been very hurt by a lot of what's happened, but try not to be so bitter. You put up with it for years, after all, and do you feel any happier now that you won't have anything to do with him?"

"Of course I don't, but there was a limit to how much I could give, and I reached it, that's all. His influence still pervades my life. He's been good about not coming to Clonegall, though I know he'd like to. He thinks about his mother's relations and the people there. He arranged to pay for a new house for old Tom Brophy and his brother. They didn't even have hot water in their old cottage."

"It's nice to have someone like him around to talk to. Of course, I've got Alphonso. He's been the most terrific hit with the locals. They can't understand him, or he they, but somehow they communicate. I only hope the people who kidnapped me don't come here to track him down. Thank God, they'd stick out like a sore thumb if they did."

"Don't you feel a little vulnerable too?"

"Not really. They were real wallies. I don't think they'd even find their way here. And curiously, there's a certain amount of protection in living in an isolated place like this. You get to hear of strangers in the area very soon. Anyway, they probably think Dad's too tight-fisted to make it worthwhile."

Liz looked at her daughter with tears in her eyes. "Don't I know it," she said, but Laura, keeping her promise to her father, could say nothing to correct her misjudgement, although she was longing to.

All she could say was, "Be fair. It's a hell of a good deterrent. It's Alphonso I'm worried about, but as I say, we'd see them coming a mile off."

"What's Alphonso doing for you?"

"A bit of everything, really. Carpentry, driving. He's rather good with horses too, for some extraordinary reason. I've bought a couple just to hack around on, and he loves doing them. He wants me to buy a carriage of some sort. He once drove hearses up and down to the graveyards in Naples."

"We've a very nice open landau in the stable in Clonegall, you know. Nobody uses it there."

"Maybe, thanks, but I'm going to be a bit busy for such peaceful pursuits."

Liz looked out to where the hills waved their crests of leafless trees. In her early days with Pyon she used to visit his mother often and see this view. How little had changed, except that now there was another strong woman in charge.

"It's certainly a good place to be peaceful, but I hope you won't get lonely."

"God, no. I'm in London quite a lot anyway, especially with this new job, and loads of people come and stay here. In fact, there's a nice journalist who should be arriving any time now. I sent Alphonso down to Hereford station about an hour ago."

"But surely he's coming to interview you, or something?"

"Yes, about my ecological activities, but that doesn't mean to say he isn't fun to see. He did that story about my plans for the farm a few weeks ago. It was a great help. Dozens of people have been in touch with offers of this and that."

"But that was Harry Hackwood! You let him do a piece, after all the trouble he's caused us!"

"You can hardly hold him responsible for Dad's misdeeds. Anyway, I told Dad before Harry wrote the piece. He just laughed and said he couldn't do much harm, and maybe he was trying to make up for what he had done."

"He'd be pretty rare among the press vultures if that were the case. I don't understand how you can tolerate him. After all, if he hadn't published that awful story of Christy on the beach, you would never have been kidnapped."

"Well, no harm finally came of that." She shrugged her shoulders. "I'm all right."

"Laura, I went through hell while you were missing. It's not something you can just shrug off."

"All right, I'm sorry, Mum. You needn't forgive Harry Hackwood if you don't want to. So you'd better keep out of the way when he comes."

At that moment they heard the front door being opened. "That must be him now," Laura said, and stood up to welcome her new, ardent supporter.

Harry Hackwood produced a glowing piece about Laura for the Sunday newspaper which was sister to his own. He covered two aspects of his subject; Laura as a new type of environmental watchdog, and Laura as daughter of Christy Pyon, the once enigmatic tycoon, now perceived by press and public alike to be as charismatic as any TV personality.

Pyon's revenge

A week later, on the Sunday morning, Harry flew to Paris. He had with him a copy of a Sunday broadsheet.

After Pyon and Harry first met, Pyon had briefed Jeremy Fielder. Fielder planted the seeds of a story with his old contact on the Sunday paper, and Harry watered the seeds until a great blossom of a puff had been produced. It covered the two centre pages of the paper Harry had with him.

Harry had fed information to his fellow-journalist while expressing serious concern that this new information was going to do his own defence no good at all – especially if Pyon were to sue on the Iraq story, or what had originally been published about his involvement in the homosexuals' suit against Chemco.

It worked well. The journalist felt a passing disloyalty to his old friend Harry. But there it was, a truth had to be uncovered, and if Harry went down for libelling Pyon, that was too bad.

The piece was unequivocally on Pyon's side. It conceded

that Pyon had made mistakes, but underlined how he had made great efforts to put right any serious shortcomings of the companies under his control. The writer accepted that Pyon had very possibly not known about some of the less acceptable practices that were going on.

That there had been a concerted campaign to discredit Pyon, and thereby Southern Hemisphere, was indisputable, the article contended, and that had certainly cost Southern the loss of Chemco. Pyon was lauded for behaving without sour grapes, and, incidentally, for having made a very healthy profit on his Chemco shareholding. Pyon was practising what he preached. He had claimed that Chemco needed unbundling to make more efficient use of its component parts, and he was now engaged in a major unbundling operation at Southern Hemisphere. Channel 21 had been succesfully sold to the de la Tour organisation – no mention was made that Pyon had been adjudged unsuitable to operate it – and various mining interests around the world were being sold off to local owners. Southern Hemisphere's price was climbing steadily back up and that showed that underlying confidence in Pyon's abilities was re-asserting itself.

The article touched only briefly on Pyon's private life. Divorce and remarriage were not unusual throughout society, it suggested, and there was no reason why it should be more reprehensible in a public figure such as Pyon than in anyone else. Reference was made to Pyon's close relationship to his children, and his continuing good relations with his first and second wives.

As Pyon reached this part of the article, he gave a grunt of ironic laughter. He was sitting beside Harry in the car which had collected him from Charles de Gaulle Airport.

"How did he dream that up?" Pyon asked.

"I suggested it," answered Harry.

"I'm not sure that was wise. My first wife won't speak to me, and I have no intention of talking to my second wife."

"No," Harry agreed, "I'm not surprised. I can't prove it yet, but I have a strong suspicion that she threw in her lot with Newberry and Shemilt, and Leo Jackson."

"Have you established if that was the full extent of the team?"

"I'm afraid there was at least one other. I made some enquiries with your staff at Audley Mews, by way of routine, and the maid there told me that, on two occasions in September, just after Laura had been kidnapped, Maria, Jackson, Shemilt and Newberry met at your house."

Pyon's face drained of blood. Quietly he asked, "And who hosted the meeting?"

Harry wriggled with discomfort. "I'm afraid it was Liz."

Pyon stared straight ahead down the autoroute into Paris. He did not speak for a moment. "Oh shit! Oh fuck!" he whispered angrily to himself. He sighed with a deep groan. "I suppose I can't blame her. You know she was convinced I wouldn't have paid for Laura's release, and Laura escaping somehow confirmed that for her. It must have been the final straw. God, I wish you'd not told me."

"I'm sorry. I had to."

"Of course you did. It's going to make it harder for me to deal with it, though. I can't possibly bring Liz into any denunciations."

"She struck me as being a very sound and balanced person," Harry remarked.

"She is. A fine woman. But when did you meet her?"

"She was staying in Herefordshire when I interviewed Laura for that piece last week."

"Was she? And how did they seem to be getting along?"

Harry shrugged. "As far as I could tell, like a mother and daughter with a fairly close relationship."

"Mothers and daughters have relationships that it's hard for us to understand. Jealousy and rivalry can figure, even between the closest. Natalie has had a bad time with her mother. There's no doubt that her father has been a little damaged politically in Mauritius, but he's apparently taken it in his stride. Her mother is adamant, though: it's Pyon or Mum, not both." Pyon sighed. "You'll find Natalie quite easy, but I'm not going to prepare you in any way. Take her as you find her, and write your genuine impressions."

"I'm naturally predisposed towards her. With a little help from you, she made me the hottest hack in London."

Pyon laughed. "By the way, you'd better not offer whatever you write until a week or two after your paper has published the little apology we're to agree on."

"Sure, but it might be better to offer it to *Hello*, rather than my own paper. I could be by-lined with an AKA. They'll take it, especially with shots by Bruno."

"Good. That's much better. Now, when you get back I want you to wrap up this conspiracy. Sufficient for me to confront Ken with it. I'll get all the hard proof I need from him then."

"I should have a fairly full dossier on it by the end of next week. The only thing I've got no way of checking is what shares they bought and sold."

"I can get some of that. I know the routes they'd have used. I'll have to avoid implicating poor Liz, and I'll have to offer Ken some kind of immunity. But God help the others, especially Maria."

Two weeks later, Pyon was in a position to issue a statement about the rumoured campaign that had been conducted against Southern Hemisphere. It was a calculated risk. There were already rumblings about an inquiry by the Department of Trade and Industry into illegal share-dealings, in which Pyon could be implicated. Of course, because Southern had lost its fight for Chemco, there were no other parties goaded by spite to press for such an inquiry, but Pyon's announcement, apart from setting the record straight and chastising his erstwhile partners for their disloyalty, was designed to pre-empt any definite moves on the part of the DTI.

The media were ready for the story, picked it up and ran hard with it for Pyon's side. But what most caught the imagination of the tabloids was the involvement of Pyon's wife, Maria.

Under the headlines, "HELL HATH NO FURY" and "THE BACK-STABBERS", Maria was publicly castigated for the gross abuse of her relationship with Pyon. She was universally portrayed as a vicious and vindictive bitch. And

Pyon's announcement that he would be starting divorce proceedings against her, as well as suing her for damages, was heartily supported. "Give him the children," cried the women's pages about Caterina and Gianni.

No hint was given of the involvement of Ken Newberry, Adnan al Souf or Elizabeth Pyon.

Jackson and Shemilt did not fight back. They were as anxious as Pyon to avoid an inquiry. They could live with a bit of public disdain, but not with a few years in Ford open prison.

Reconciliation

Christy Pyon went to see Natalie Felix's parents, on his own, in their little bungalow in Quatre Bornes. Mrs Felix was alone. She had not met Pyon before, and was reluctant to invite him in.

He understood. His entry into her daughter's life had completely disrupted her own. He personified all her current fears and anxieties.

Pyon placed himself in Mrs Felix's hands.

"Mrs Felix, I've come here in complete humility. I know what my relationship with Natalie has done to you, and to your relationship with her. I know how much it has hurt her. Natalie's happiness matters very much to me. Can we talk about it?"

Behind the compelling blue eyes, Mrs Felix saw sincerity and contrition. The big man stood in front of her small house in a posture of helpless supplication.

"Come in, Mr Pyon," she said.

Natalie waited on *Ile Vermont*. Every time she heard a boat in the lagoon, she jumped to her feet to see if it was the launch from Pyon's mainland jetty. But she had to wait several hours.

When eventually she saw that it was indeed Pyon being

swept across the shallow blue-green water in his Riva, she could see at once from his demeanour that the news was good.

She ran down the steep stone path to the island landing stage, and flung her arms around him as soon as the launch pulled up and he stepped from it.

"I can see," she said, "you left her happy."

Pyon kissed her warm lips and smiled. "Less malcontent, anyway," he said. "She won't be sure until I've carried out my promises, and even then she has reservations."

"At least you've seen her, and she's accepted you," Natalie said happily as they started climbing up the steps to the house. "What did you promise her?"

"I promised her that I'd marry you, so I suppose I'd better."

Natalie stopped still, and turned to him with doubt in her eyes. "But you've always said you didn't want to marry, that we didn't need it. I accepted that. I didn't mind. I don't want you to be forced into it."

Pyon laughed. "I know I've not done too well as a husband so far, but I think I can safely say that my fickle youth is over. I want to marry you, you silly girl. And soon I'll be able to; as soon as I've divorced Maria."

Natalie turned and carried on walking. Her shoulders dropped with depression. "That's going to be so awful. I wish it didn't have to happen. Those poor children."

"There it is, angel. I made the mistakes, I'll have to unravel them, however unpleasant a task it will be. You mustn't get involved. Stay here for a few months. Don't come to Europe until it's all over. Then I'll come and get you. We can't be married in the church, but your mother wants your local priest to give us a little blessing. You deserve more than that, but I'm afraid I don't."

Natalie was a few paces in front of him now, crossing the lawn of springy turf to the steps of the verandah.

"Angel, turn round a moment. I've been very presumptuous. I've not even asked you if you want to marry me."

She turned. She looked at the great bear of a man, who was so strong and so soft to her, and the sudden doubt in his eyes.

"Christy, you're such a fool sometimes. Haven't I told you, lots of times, I'll live with you in whatever way you want. But it would be nice for our children if we were married."

Honour

Maria hated the wet winter winds that eddied around the high cliffs of the Amalfi coast. She scowled as she walked the few yards from her car up to the grandiose portico of her brother Sergio's modern *palazzo*.

Her mood matched the weather, and her brothers were only going to make her feel worse.

They were waiting for her, ranged around a heavy oak table, with Sergio occupying a throne-like chair at the head.

"Sit down, Maria," her eldest brother ordered brusquely.

She sat at the opposite end of the long table, and looked at each of her brothers in turn. They, too, were evidently in an ugly mood.

Several newspapers, Italian and English, were spread out in front of them.

Franco, the youngest and angriest, stabbed a small sharp hand at one in front of him.

"Look at this shit! Eh? What have you done? Your great plan to ruin Pyon! We told you it was crazy."

"You didn't do so bloody well yourselves, did you?" Maria shouted back at him. "Your pathetic attempt to take his daughter achieved nothing, other than making you look complete fools to our friends in Sardegna."

"That wasn't our fault. Gino and Luca should never have trusted that great oaf Alphonso. I'm sure Pyon was going to up his offer."

"But this time," Franco hissed, "it's not his money we want." He drew a nicotine-stained forefinger across his throat. "He has tried to make our family a laughing-stock. No one can do that and live."

"For God's sake," Maria screamed, "you can't kill him! He has been punished. He's lost his great deal, he's been made to look a failure throughout the world. His reputation is destroyed."

"What are you talking about, Maria?" Luigi, her middle brother, asked. "Somehow he's turned the deal in California to his advantage, the price of his shares is rising, the press are giving him a great write-up, and worst of all, they blame you for his problems. It's a disaster. He hasn't been punished at all. We have no choice. To retrieve our family's honour, he has to die."

Maria stared round at their motionless dark eyes.

Of course, it was part of her family's culture that people who crossed them should be punished, but that was a generation ago, not now. They were rich, respected business people, not drug-smuggling hoods.

But she knew that, this time, they were adamant. She had had her chance, and failed.

She listened in a horrified daze, nodding her head in resignation as Sergio went on.

"You will allow him to see the children when he asks, which he will for sure. Don't make it too easy, though, and make it in Naples."

"You can't involve Gianni and Caterina," she wailed.

"They will not be harmed. They'll be right away before anything happens. Despite their father, they are part of our family."

"You mustn't deceive me"

In London, an illicit log fire burned in the grate of the drawing-room in Elizabeth Pyon's mews house. Liz and Laura were warm both with its glow and the intimacy there was between them now. Laura had cooked their dinner, and they had eaten, just the two of them, in Liz's comfortable, rustic kitchen. They had drunk a bottle each of Burgundy, and now nursed large balloons of Armagnac in their hands.

"Will you come to Ireland at Christmas?" Liz asked.

Laura nodded. "Is J coming?"

"Yes. He sounds a lot better now than a month ago. He's still got problems, he says, but they're much more manageable and at last he's getting on with making a film."

"Won't we be a happy little family, then? Except, no Dad, I suppose?"

"Laura, you know how I feel about that. I can't forgive him. I've told you why. Running off with Maria, the other affairs, even the little Mauritian girl I suppose I could have overlooked, but not the way he behaved over your awful kidnapping."

"It really is that, isn't it? If it hadn't been for that, you might still have maintained the relationship you had with him, perhaps even become closer again after Maria had finally overstepped the mark. As it is, you've probably driven him closer to Natalie. Even Dad needs a shoulder to lean on now and again."

"Oh, I know," Liz said. "He's leaned on mine often enough. He's not entirely made of solid granite, I agree."

The warmth of the fire, the wine and the brandy were making Laura's promise to her father look absurd. In the light of her mother's misjudgement of his motives and attitudes, he might be prepared to accept her lack of trust, but she, on his behalf, could not.

"Mum, would it have made such a difference if he had coughed up something for me? He couldn't have afforded the ridiculous amount they were asking for, and they weren't expecting it, but supposing he had negotiated, and paid to get me back, would you have forgiven him?"

"Of course I would, darling, but that's entirely hypothetical."

Laura shook her head slowly, and gazed at her mother so that she could see she was telling the truth. "It isn't hypothetical at all. He did offer $50 million. Fifty bloody million, which would have effectively broken him at that time, I'm sure of it." Laura turned her gaze to the fire for a moment, then back to her mother with a light laugh. "It's nice to know you're worth that much to someone. Luckily, I had already got away. But you've got to believe it, he'd already made the offer. That's why he gave me the money I bought Julian out with, five million – 10 per cent of his savings."

Liz gazed at her. She wanted to believe, and guilt welled up within her. Her hands began to shake.

"For God's sake, Laura, you mustn't deceive me about this. You must promise me you're not lying to cover up for him."

"I swear, on everything that's precious to me, that I am telling the truth." She leaned forward on the sofa where she sat opposite her mother, and told her every detail of her escape, her incognito meeting with Pyon, and the undertaking he had given her before she pulled off the blonde wig.

At the end of Laura's telling, Liz believed her, utterly.

"May God forgive me for doubting him," she whispered to herself, then, to Laura, "I must see him, right away. I must tell him myself that I know. Why, oh why didn't he tell me? Why did he make you promise not to?"

"You must know why, Mum."

"Yes, I think I do. I suppose he thought that you'd always be at risk if it ever came out; and he'd hate to be seen to have changed his mind when he'd made such a public stand against paying for you. By his curious code, he'd consider he was buying my affection if he let me know."

She stood up, with a brightness in her eyes. "Come on, let's see if we can track down the old bastard. We could even see if he'll come to Ireland for Christmas. He'd love to, I'm sure, don't you think?"

"Don't you think I should make the call?" Laura asked. "You'll find it difficult if Natalie answers. When I've got him on the line, I'll pass it over to you."

Liz nodded.

It took them an hour to establish where Pyon was, and to extract a telephone number for him from his reluctant secretary, whom they had woken from a deep sleep.

"It's rather bizarre," Liz remarked, "dialling a London

number to speak to someone in the middle of the Indian Ocean."

"That's just the sort of ploy Dad enjoys, though. It must cost him a fortune. Anyway, it's ringing now." Laura held her breath, and prayed that he was there.

" 'Ello?" A sleepy French voice.

"Is Christy Pyon there?" Laura asked.

The voice became more alert. "Who is this?"

"This is Laura Pyon, his daughter."

There was a moment's silence.

"I am Natalie Felix. I'm afraid your father is not here. He left on the eight o'clock flight to Paris."

Laura felt hugely let down, but excited that at least he was nearer to them now.

"Is he going to stay in Paris?" she asked.

Natalie hesitated. "No, I don't think so."

"Do you know where he's going?"

"Yes, I do, but I can't tell you. He asks that I tell no one."

"But that wouldn't have included me."

"I don't know, he did not say so."

"Natalie, though we haven't met, I feel I know you a little. And I think you'll believe me when I tell you it's vital that I speak to him." She paused. "And my mother is very anxious to talk to him."

Even across thousands of miles, she could hear Natalie sigh before saying, "I realise that's important, and I don't want to come between him and his family. If you know your father, you will be able to imagine what he might be doing, when it is nearly Christmas."

Laura smiled. "Thank you, Natalie. I respect your wish to keep any promise you made him. We'll find him. Goodbye, and *Joyeux Noël*," she added.

She put the phone down.

"Well?" Liz asked impatiently, "what did she tell you?"

"He's gone to see Gianni and Caterina, I'm sure of it. So he'll be somewhere in Italy."

"But where?" Liz cried. "For God's sake I think the girl might have been more helpful."

"She was keeping a promise," Laura said, "I understand

that. And it shouldn't be too hard to find him, but I think we'd better leave it till morning, don't you?"

Her mother agreed reluctantly, but she went to her bedroom feeling as if a blanket of black cloud had lifted from her life

Nemesis

It was Natalie's suggestion that Pyon should go to Italy to see Caterina and Gianni before Christmas; not just to give them a few lavish presents, but to give them the security and stability they would need to get through the months after Christmas, as their parents' marriage was exposed and pulled apart in the divorce courts and the newspapers.

When Pyon landed at Naples, he was met by his Italian lawyer.

"Have you arranged it?" Pyon asked him.

"Si, Signor Pyon. Their uncle will bring them to the hotel, and wait there for two hours to take them back to Amalfi."

"Two hours? Good God, who does Maria think she is?"

"Believe me, signor, it took some negotiations. I had to explain it would go very badly against Mrs Pyon if she forcibly stopped them seeing you when no order had been made."

"Okay, I'm sure you did your best."

The lawyer drove Pyon to the Excelsior, one of Naples' grander hotels, which looked south over the ancient turrets of the harbour walls.

In the *salon* of his suite, Pyon waited for his two younger children. The sea in the Gulf of Naples was grey, flecked with white as it was whipped by an angry wind.

The clouds hung low above the bay and blanked out Vesuvius to the south-east. The view reflected Pyon's own gloom. He was angry and depressed that he had had to resort to sordid negotiations to see his own children.

Less than a year ago, he had spent a happy week with them over the New Year. Maria was already then becoming tetchy about his long absences, but she had been glad when he returned to Amalfi and took Caterina and Gianni off her hands.

It had been a year of terrible contrasts. He had experienced some of the best moments of his life, and some of the worst. He had already succeeded in putting right much of the damage that had been done to Southern Hemisphere Resources, even though he was left with an acute sense of failure over Chemco. But clearing up the wreckage of his private life was a much harder task. He could not rebuild relationships, or sever old commitments with a few well-presented press conferences.

He had no compunction about ridding himself of Maria, apart from the upset that would cause the children, but he was more affected than he would admit to himself about Liz.

But, at the end of it, there was the prospect of a less frenetic existence, with a less cumbersome business to run, and life with Natalie.

The children arrived, bursting with enthusiasm to see him. Despite a steady and vitriolic family propaganda campaign run by their mother, their uncles and their grandmother, their faith in Pyon was unshaken. Pyon had always been honest and consistent with them, he made them laugh, and understood them.

They burst into the room. Pyon caught sight of Luigi lurking outside the door for a moment before slipping away.

He hugged them both, teased them and laughed with them. He handed Gianni the remote controls for a sophisticated electronic dune buggy that stood menacingly by the large French windows of the room. He gave Caterina a box from which she eagerly pulled a dress from the Chelsea shop that had been most talked about by her friends at the Ascot convent. None of the girls her age in Amalfi would have anything like it, and she was just old enough to find that very important.

As they thanked him, he said, "Never mind about that.

What are we going to do to slip past your uncle Luigi? He thinks he's taking you home in a couple of hours. I know," Pyon announced to them, "we'll sneak down the staff stairs, and out the back. We can go and see *Batman* at the cinema, then have a bit of supper somewhere together. What d'you think?"

"Yeah, great!" they shouted.

Pyon poked his head out into the corridor. There was no one there. He beckoned his children to follow him. They came out and closed the door behind them, then ran behind him, on tiptoe like him, to a staff door.

In his suite, the telephone began to bleat quietly. Pyon heard it, made a face to himself, and carried on.

They ran down several flights of stone stairs. When they reached the bottom, Pyon held his hand up to stop them before peering round to see if the way was clear. A maid scuttled past without taking any notice of them, and they slipped through a staff lobby, out into the back courtyard of the hotel.

"I think we've given him the slip," Pyon winked at them.

There was a large open gate at the back of the yard. Following Pyon's nonchalant example, they all strolled out through it into the back street and up towards the Via Santa Lucia. Just as they were about to turn out of the side street, two cars shrieked up behind them. Four men sprang out of each car.

The children were grabbed by two of them, and Pyon was pounced on by three others. A fourth drove a fist six inches into his solar plexus. His body jack-knifed under the impact. He fell to the ground and his head smashed against the kerb. He rolled over on to his front, with his chin resting on the edge of the narrow pavement, unconscious.

Pyon came to with his face pressed against the stinking rear seat of a car. He felt on the point of vomiting, and his head throbbed viciously. Slowly his mind began to focus.

The car was travelling in short bursts of speed, and jerking halts. They must still be in the city. There was someone, one of his attackers, he guessed, pressed beside him on the seat. He could hear three Italian voices – the man beside him and two in the front. He did not look up or give any indication that he was conscious.

"Why did you get such a lousy vehicle?"

"It's the only one I could start. I'm out of practice, for God's sake; I haven't stolen a car for years," another voice growled.

"We've let you get too soft. This is a terrible old banger. I don't know if it'll even get us out of Naples."

"It won't if you go on driving like that, you bloody maniac." A third voice – Gino, the man he had met on the launch off Porto Cervo. "What's the hurry? The big bastard's out cold. I thought he was going to burst his brains open on the kerb. For God's sake, slow down. We don't want to end up arguing with cops about the price of a speeding ticket."

Pyon did not move. In his long career he had caused a lot of anger in a lot of hard men, but he had never been subjected to physical abuse. Now he tried to think himself into this new set of rules. Or need he? There had never been a position out of which he had not been able to negotiate his way. His best plan was to keep still, and learn what he could from the exchanges going on between his abductors.

The voice that he recognised seemed to be coming from the passenger seat, and to belong to the boss of this operation. He gathered that they were driving to somewhere out of Naples to change to another car and dump the one they were in.

When the leader of the three next spoke, even Pyon's overwhelming optimism could not stop his heart from jerking violently in his chest.

"Luigi wants him killed."

"But if we kill him, we won't get any money for him."

"You'll get your wages, just the same. Luigi doesn't give a shit about the money. The Gattis don't need to do this kind of thing for money. He didn't care about the money when we took the girl, except he had to pay off the Sardinians."

"Are Sergio and Franco in on this too?" asked the man beside Pyon.

"Mind your own business. You don't need to know."

"They're all bloody mad," growled the driver. "What's the

point of killing this guy? Maria's a bitch, everyone knows that. You'd have to be a saint to stay married to her, or a martyr."

The car was running more smoothly now, on an open road, Pyon judged. He hoped that they would not reach the change-over place too soon, before he had recovered enough to make some attempt at getting away from them. He realised that there was no scope for negotiation here. The Gattis took their family honour very seriously indeed. At least, though, the children would be unharmed, and on their way back home by now.

Twenty minutes later they slowed down, and turned off the made-up road. The car bounced down a track for five minutes, and the leader swore.

"Shit! Where the fuck is Mario with the van?"

"When did you tell him to get here?"

"He was supposed to leave as soon as he saw us get Pyon. He should have been three or four minutes in front of us."

"Well, what shall I do?"

"Just drive into that old barn. No one will find the car for days out here."

"What about a forester? We should get rid of it, burn it."

"Yeah, sure," Gino snarled, "they're going to take a lot longer to notice a bloody raging fire than an old banger in a tumbled-down barn."

"Okay," the driver conceded.

The noise of the car became a roar as they drove into the building.

"Is he still out?"

Pyon relaxed completely, and felt himself being nudged with a sharp elbow.

"Yeah. He's not going anywhere."

"Okay. Let's get out and wait. Luca, you hang around in case he wakes up. As soon as we see the van, heave him out."

The car doors opened with rusty squeals, then slammed shut.

Pyon judged that one of the windows was down. He could

hear the three men move away a little, and the sound of one of them urinating against a board wall.

With as little movement as possible he brought his left hand up from the floor of the car where it lay and fished in his breast pocket. They had not taken anything. He found a pen and cheque-book.

He slid them out, down on to the floor. Without moving his head from where it rested on the seat, he could see enough to pull out one cheque. He placed it on the book, and holding it down with the heel of his hand, he managed to scrawl just one word.

He folded it, brought it up, and passed it under his body. With his other hand, he tucked it between the bench and the back of the seat.

Carefully, he picked up his pen and cheque book, and slid them back into his pocket.

None of the men said anything that indicated they had seen him. He continued to lie still and breathe deeply to get as much air as he could into his lungs.

An angry shout greeted the arrival of the van.

The car door by Pyon's head opened and someone reached in to drag him out. He did not resist. He let himself be flopped out into a heap on the bare earth floor of the barn.

"For God's sake. He can't still be out. Are you sure he's not dead?"

"I bloody hope not, not yet, not here. Luigi said not to risk killing him until we were up in the mountains."

"Well let's chuck some water at him and wake him up."

"Okay."

Footsteps made their way to the end of the barn. Pyon heard a bucket drop into a vat. The steps returned, someone rolled him on to his back, and a deluge of cold water drenched his head. He managed to stop himself from spluttering and opening his eyes. One of the men grabbed him by his Givenchy tie and pulled him into a sitting position.

A fleshy palm smacked into Pyon's cheek with a sharp sting. He opened his eyes with a blink, and looked blank for a moment. Then, in English, he said, "What's going on? Who are you?"

Over the shoulder of the man who had struck him, he saw the face of the negotiator on the launch. He registered recognition.

"What's all this?" he asked in Italian.

"Hello, my friend. Got a bit of a headache? Sorry."

"What the hell are you doing? You're the people who got Laura. What do you want now? Money, again?"

"I'm afraid not, my friend."

"Well, what?" Pyon blustered.

"You'll see. Now, we must continue our journey in that truck." He pointed at a big plain white Ducato van.

Pyon was heaved to his feet by two men, one small and rodent-like, the other big and dumb-looking.

Besides them, there was Gino, who did not present much of a physical threat, and the driver of the van who was walking towards them now.

They were in a clearing in a well-established broad-leaf wood. The track which led into it, and to the dilapidated timber structure where the car was, showed little evidence of use. And yet, they could not be much more than twenty miles out of Naples.

A thin mist swirled through the trees, and obscured their upper branches. Pyon allowed himself to be frog-marched towards the van. The driver ran ahead and opened the back doors.

Pyon was lifted off his feet and chucked like a sack of grain on to the corrugated metal floor of the vehicle. The two men climbed in and the door was banged shut behind them, but not locked.

Pyon dragged himself across the floor of the van, and propped his back up against the side. His two custodians perched on the wheel arches. There was no partition between the cab and the carrying section, and Pyon watched Gino and the driver clamber in. The motor was started and they lurched off up the track.

Pyon tried to work out where they might be going. He guessed, though he could not be at all certain, that these woods were on the lower eastern slopes of Vesuvius. They were going to the mountains. That could mean any one of several ranges, but whichever, they would have to drive ten or fifteen miles across the plain. That would be his best time to escape. Once in the empty winter hills, he would have no chance of getting away from four men.

The van moved out on to a surfaced road, swung to the right and gathered speed with a roaring of the diesel motor. The men in the back moved up towards the cab, so they could talk with their colleagues. Pyon studied the internal opening mechanism of the two rear doors. As far as he could tell, it would be a simple matter of pulling up a large black lever. He prepared himself to be ready for the moment, and prayed that the van would stop, or slow down enough to allow him to leave without damaging himself too much.

The grey light was dying now. It must have been late afternoon. The road they were on seemed to be fairly free of traffic, and they were keeping up a good speed. Every so often, his captors would glance round at Pyon, and, satisfied, turn back to their friends.

Pyon was wearing only a light suit and a silk shirt. He shivered with cold and fear, neither of which were familiar sensations to him, but he forced himself to stay calm.

When the moment came he was ready.

From the lights that glowed ahead through the mist, he judged they were approaching a village that straddled the road. Dangling high above the thoroughfare was a set of traffic lights, showing red. Pyon did not wait for them to stop, or the men to turn round. He lunged at the big handle of the rear door. It moved easily when he heaved it up, and the left-hand door swung open. There was a large truck, slowing down behind them, but he had to take the chance. He leaped, and rolled to his left as soon as he hit the ground. The twelve right-hand wheels of the truck rolled by, four inches from him.

He lay for a moment, recognising a vicious pain in his shoulder. But he forced himself to his feet and limped on to the pavement outside a small café. He glanced towards the van, in time to see it shudder to a halt with the lorry right behind it.

Pyon ran up the road in the opposite direction, looking

wildly for an escape route. But there were no gaps in the shops and houses at this central part of the village. He glanced back over his shoulders to see three men pursuing him, about a hundred yards behind, and gaining ground.

The traffic flow was not heavy. The far side of the road seemed less built up. Pyon judged the speed of the vehicles coming in each direction, and made a dash across. As he reached the other side safely, he put his foot into a small, uncovered drain. The momentum of his dash carried the rest of his body on to the pavement. With a sharp crack, his ankle broke.

Pyon fell to the ground, limp with pain, and his throbbing shoulder struck the paving-stones.

He had not moved when they caught up with him. They lifted him upright, talking as if he were a drunken friend. Through a haze, Pyon saw the white van crawling back up the road towards them. He did not resist – he could not – as they once again lifted him into the back.

This time, they bound his wrists and ankles. He could not stop a yell of pain as they tugged the cord tight. They propped him against the side of the van with his legs tucked up under him. He was in acute pain now, suddenly freezing cold, weak, and beaten.

As the van moved off, a row developed between the four Italians. Pyon realised that he had had his chance, and lost it.

All the power and wealth he had wielded could do nothing for him now. He was no more than a large, bruised and painful body wrapped in the dishevelled remains of a once expensive suit.

He made no attempt to move again. He accepted the pain, came to terms with it. As the van rumbled on, he accepted that this was the tumbrel that was to take him to his execution. And he prayed, for Natalie, for Liz, for all his children, for the memory of his mother, and for his old, humble father; and he asked God for his forgiveness.

The funeral was held, like Maeve's, at the Abbey church outside Hereford.

Christy Pyon's mortal remains – a bruised and battered corpse – were to lie beside his mother's.

The body had been found two days after Pyon's lawyer had notified the Naples' police that he was missing. A hunter had stumbled across the bulky body in the dark blue, well-cut suit. It was swinging from a branch of a short mountain oak, with a rope around its neck. The tree was halfway up the western slope of Monte Avella, less than thirty miles from Naples.

It was hailed as a gross tragedy, a callous murder, and presented as a sensational mystery.

The mystery lasted three days.

The day that Pyon's body arrived back in England, the stolen car in which he had been abducted from the streets of Naples was found; the microscopic search of the vehicle had swiftly yielded a small, folded piece of paper. A Bank of England cheque in the name of Christy Pyon, and on the back, scrawled in what experts were prepared to state was his left hand, the word "GATTIS".

The Gatti family lawyers were still arguing with the police about bail. Heavy diplomatic pressures had released Pyon's corpse as soon as forensic tests had been completed.

The cathedral choir, borrowed for the occasion, sang the Mozart Requiem. A congregation, gathered from every continent of the world, listened in mute dejection.

Seeing Pyon's coffin, purple draped among a sea of old-fashioned lilies, was like seeing the remains of a great fighting bull being dragged from the ring.

In the front row, in black uncompromised by any dash of colour, stood three beautiful, tearful women.

Elizabeth, his first wife; Laura, his daughter; and Natalie Felix.

Behind them, blinking back tears, were Julian Pyon and Lord Barnstaple.

Laura and Julian read the lessons.

Lord Barnstaple gave the address.

"We're here to say our last goodbye to an extraordinary man. Many of us knew him, or thought we knew him, well. I knew Christy for thirty years. I was his father-in-law, officially for the first fifteen of those, and unofficially for the rest of his life. But I can only claim to have known a few of the many facets of his character. God will be Christy's judge, none of us, but let's consider what there is to go into each side of the balance.

"Christy, or Pyon, as we all knew him, was impetuous, aggressive, thoughtless and a bully; he was also kind, impulsively generous, enormously stimulating. He could ignore you, or he could listen intently to every word you said. He could make you feel loved, or damned. He was a Catholic, no doubt of that, and God was the only person to whom he was prepared to answer, but he would not correct me for calling him somewhat dilatory in his practice.

"He was a father who tried, often successfully, to make time for his children in his frenetic life. They may not always have felt he understood them, nor they him, but at base he did. He knew their strengths and their weaknesses, as he knew his own, and he told them so.

"He was a husband, but he was a rotten husband. Don't gasp at this outrageous slander as he lies before us in his coffin unable to defend himself. He knew it himself and he would have wanted the truth spoken of him now. If I may use such an expression in the house of the Lord, he hated what he always called 'bullshit'.

"But he loved his first wife, my daughter Liz, and stayed loyal to her in his heart. I hope she will forgive me for saying it, but I know it to be so. He admired and treasured her loyalty throughout a life of spectacular ups and downs, and misdemeanours."

"He was above all, it has to be said, an incorrigible wheeler-dealer, a businessman, if you like. But the many of you that I see here who have been on the receiving end of a bargaining session with Pyon know that ultimately he was a player. He loved the game of business, and he was very good at it. To understand that it was the playing, more than the prize, that interested Pyon is to begin to understand the man.

"Beyond the real facets of Pyon's character, there were, of course, those that he sometimes chose to assume and project, and those with which the media chose to endow him. In simple terms, those of you who knew Pyon would probably not recognise him from descriptions that have been published or broadcast. That is the price that is paid for being a source of public fascination, envy or, indeed, adulation. Pyon wouldn't want me to say that he had suffered from the press; he would put it that he had simply played them wrong, that he had made misjudgements. Maybe he was right, but it's sad that what the public were offered as Christy Pyon bore such little resemblance to the real man."

Lord Barnstaple turned towards the coffin, and inclined his head. "I hope, Christy, that you won't find too much fault in what I'm saying, and I'm only sorry that, for once, you can't answer back. I shall miss you. God bless you."

The old viscount stepped from the lectern, bowed stiffly from the waist at the tabernacle on the high altar, turned and walked through a deep silence back to his seat.

At the end of Mass, before the mourners filed from the church out to the graveyard, Laura addressed them from the steps of the altar.

"After the burial, you're all invited home, where my father was born, to drink his eternal health in the way he would have wished."

A firm from Lyonshall had erected a marquee in record time to accommodate the three hundred people whom Laura had expected at her father's funeral. In the event there were nearer five hundred. The church had been packed to standing point, and the mourners now seemed to come into the tent in a never-ending torrent. At first subdued, but as the vintage champagne, Irish whiskey and Guinness flowed, the crowd became voluble. Nearly every man and woman there would miss Christy Pyon in some way, but there was also something awesome about the passing of such an enormous personality.

The Irish jig players struck up as soon as the marquee was full, and an abandoned party spirit filled the place. There was laughter, and there were tears.

Around the edge sat old men from the local countryside who remembered picking up young Christy from the ground where he had been tossed, and trying to persuade him not to get back on some mad young horse, before watching with alarm as he leaped up and galloped off again.

Once more, the dilapidated coach had crossed the Irish sea from Clonegall, and the staff and grooms from the estate called down God's blessing on Pyon with flowing eyes. And old Tom Brophy could hardly speak.